WHEN SHADOWS BLEED

AMELIA J. RIVERS

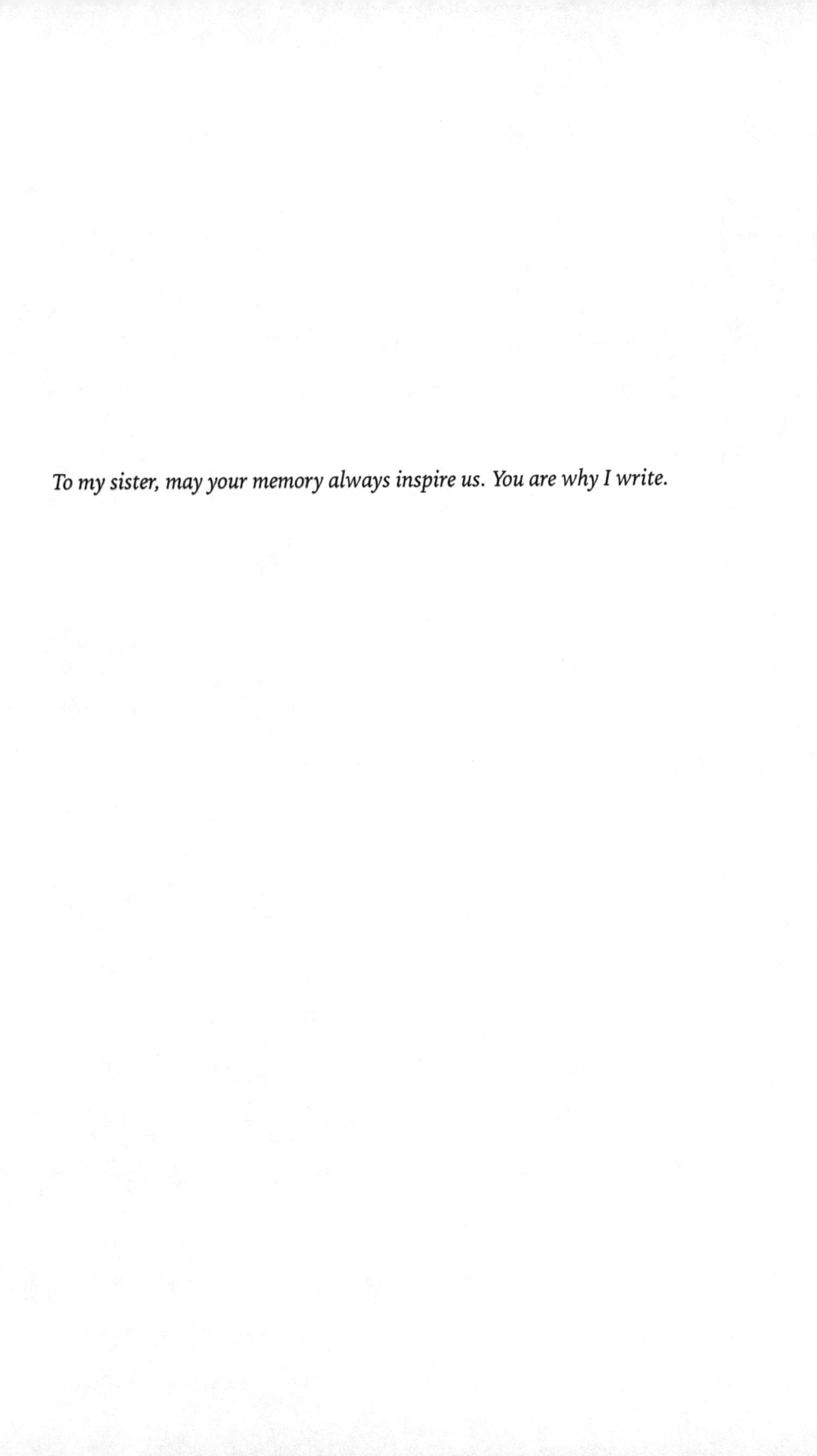

To my sister, may your memory always inspire us. You are why I write.

NOTE: This book has depictions of death, blood, gore, violence, sexual content (consensual), and toxic family relationships

Finders' Handbook

Finders' Law - A Finder is neither judge nor jury. A Finder's role is to retrieve the Soulless. Established I886.

CHAPTER 1

DEATH TINGED THE AIR. It rolled off the Soulless, sweet and repugnant.

The dim lights reflected off the tabletops in a rainbow of colors but left the patrons in pools of shadows. The facade had been renovated from a crumbling brick relic into a dark, cozy neutral ground for customers, some humans and some not. It was the *some not* that brought me in most nights.

My gaze bounced around the haggard faces, most sloshed and their red-rimmed eyes dull with their bad choices. Many of the humans in the bar likely had warrants out on them and didn't know Soulless lurked around them. Most humans thought they were urban legends. Born Vessels, the Soulless were real, users of the death arts, and had target sheets. The Vessels, all born with unearthly powers unrelated to the death arts, simply enjoyed Mason's Bar, a rare neutral spot: the only one in a hundred-mile radius that Finders like me weren't allowed to raid for Soulless. As I licked my lips, my gaze swung back to the door.

As a Finder, I'd been called a bounty hunter, a prostitute, and even a butcher. I didn't seek the lost. I didn't search for assholes. I didn't prey on the weak, and I didn't prey on the broken or misguided. I didn't provide pleasure, but I did get paid.

Those who called me a bounty hunter were most accurate but still wrong. Bounty hunters hunted humans for the police. I preyed on the Soulless, where I wasn't bound by civil laws. I was bound by something more severe— the Finders' Law.

The Finders' Law is harsher and doesn't permit reform or restitution. It is finite and unyielding. Once a Vessel becomes Soulless— a harnesser of the death arts— it is a permanent marker. Just as when a human becomes a Choicer— a human who bargains their soul for unearthly powers to harness the death arts— there are no amends.

My job was not to judge them or listen to their excuses. My job was to bring them to my boss. The Finders' Trust then paid for the Soulless retrieved. They dealt the justice. Some Soulless met death, others faced different repercussions. But that didn't matter. That wasn't my role.

Tonight, though, I sat on my normal stool at Mason's. My body leaned against the bar top. My fingers drummed on the surface as wisps of conversations tickled my ears. The words blurred together into a drone of lust, greed, and hunger.

Tugging my phone from my pocket, I frowned. We'd slipped by eleven already and were closing in on midnight. It was well past her normal time for showing, if she did.

Easing back onto the padded pleather barstool, I cocked my head to the side to catch the trickle of ramblings from a Vessel about ten sheets to the wind.

"It's a big deal!" They pounded their fist on the table, sloshing some of their beer on their grayed hand.

"Brock is a nobody," their Choicer friend drawled while sopping up the mess. The smell of their conversion was fresh. Without knowing the Soulless Companion, it was too hard to tell the Soulless type they were sacrificing others' blood to become. A blood sacrifice was always required for the arts. Some resulted in the victim's death, others didn't. But it didn't matter. A sacrifice was a sacrifice.

"Brock is a somebody," the Vessel pressed. Their green eyes darted around the room.

Brock wasn't one of my targets. With a sigh, I glanced to the door before taking another look around the packed room.

"Keep watching, and she's gonna show," Benny, the bartender, snarled behind me even as he filled up my cola.

I snorted, but my eyes darted to the door again to see if my mom would strut through.

She hadn't been around in a couple of weeks. Not since we came to blows in the parking lot when she wanted a cut of my Finder's earnings. She was a regular at the bar. Like she'd taught me to do, she used the location to get information on her targets. Claudine Petrov had been a Finder before I was born, and in keeping with tradition, she trained me. Four years ago, when I turned eighteen and could legally escape Mom's clutches, I left home.

But tonight felt different. Or I'd called Beetlejuice too many times and a charge sizzled in the air. Once again, I scanned the doorway, the tiny hairs on my neck raised. Without disappointing, she sauntered in. Two men sidled up next to her, a few inches shorter than her, their facial differences lost in the sea of men who constantly swarmed her.

Other than body build, she was my opposite in appearance. Her blonde hair was pulled back in a loose ponytail of curls. Hawkish blue eyes in porcelain skin scanned the room, a pretty smile curled on her pink lips, pulling attention away from the intensity of her predatory gaze. When they locked on me, my body stiffened, and my fingers curled around my glass.

For a moment, it was just us. The only sound I heard was my blood pounding in my ears.

Her chin jutted out and her lips twisted into a smirk.

The night had just taken a turn. One that would likely end up with us both bloody. I hoped I'd remembered to buy more Band-Aids.

"Glass," Benny barked, slicing into my thoughts as he reached his thick white hand out. "You ain't breaking another on her account."

My thumb ran over the white scar on my pointer finger. A gift from her. I pushed my glass across the scarred bar top without taking my eyes from her. A shot of fire burned through my veins. She knew better than to approach the bar top, my normal place. It had nothing to do with me, but Benny, who stood sentinel on the other side of the bar. He never left his domain, and she stayed well out of his arm's length.

She moved to a high-top table, her entourage following dutifully behind. After flicking her hair over her shoulder, she crooked her finger at me, beckoning me toward her and her fucked-up lies.

"What does she want now?" I growled, my hand brushing across the blade at my hip.

"Don't," Tones, the bar owner, warned, appearing beside me. Her scent of tomatoes and fries settled over me like a blanket. She patted a warm hand over mine.

It was good advice, but I didn't have the sense to listen to it.

"It'll just be a minute," I lied, pushing off the chair.

"Dessa," Tones breathed, but didn't stop me. Still, I felt her watching me.

My skin hummed with the Vessels and the Soulless swarming around me as I weaved through the crowded tables, bodies, and chairs. My nose flared and my fingers curled, but I kept my eyes on my mom.

I flinched brushing past a Soulless. Her skin was like ice. My fingers itched for my blade. It'd be easy money. Utilities would be paid for the next month. I hadn't been assigned this Soulless's target sheet, but it had been in the pile my boss John had last night. The cloying, rank smell of death rolled off her, the sweetness turning my stomach and singeing my nerves.

There was no doubt she had participated in the arts recently. Even without her target sheet, I'd get a few bucks for bringing her in.

Around her, a dozen other Vessels and Soulless drank without noticing me.

I cast a glance back at the bar. Haloed in blue light, Tones stood with her lips pressed in a tight line as her green eyes followed me. She didn't allow hunting in her bar, a haven for both Vessels and humans, and I had to honor the neutrality of the place to continue using it for tips. She wouldn't let me back in if I went after the Soulless, warrant or not. And she wouldn't let me around her for breaking her trust.

No Soulless was worth that.

Swallowing down the desire to round them up, I forced my legs forward until I sidled up to my mom's table. Around the table, four high-top chairs butted up against each other.

One of the Soulless men with her said something to me, but it didn't warrant my attention. The musty stench of death lingered around him.

Interesting. I didn't know she fattened and liquored up her Soulless prey before taking them to slaughter in the time after she had started hunting again after I left the apartment.

Her eyes flicked down briefly to her iPhone, a text window open, before her gaze returned to me. Why she chose an occupational hazard was beyond me. iPhones were too easy to track and hack with your face. I kept to the disposable type.

She cocked an eyebrow at me and placed her elbows on the table. Folding her hands together, she rested her chin on them.

"Your hair is hideous." She smiled at me.

The idiots around the table guffawed.

"Did you finally clear up the latest STD?" I asked, anchoring my feet to the floor. The familiarity of the hate was almost a salve from not seeing her for a few weeks. Filling a void. It was an old pattern, one I had lived in for years and hated, but still provided a horrible comfort.

The laughing turned nervous. Without looking at their faces, I knew two were Vessels. The other two were certainly Soulless. Curiosity itched at my eyes, but years of not noticing the people she was with halted any attempts to look at them. She always told me if I saw a face, I could be used as a witness.

My fingers dug into the tabletop, my fingernails piercing the porous surface as I fought the urge to drive my blade into the closest one to my side and haul him in.

I was an idiot. I hadn't listened to Tones and knowingly walked into the lion's den with a stick.

"Funny," she deadpanned. Her eyes gleamed in the pale light. "How's business?"

I sucked on my teeth. The unspoken truth between us, that we both hunted, would get us both killed if either of us ratted the other one out, even if she was with them. Soulless didn't give a shit if someone became collateral. They only cared about survival.

What the fuck was her angle?

"Fab," I said, narrowing my eyes. "What do you want?"

"Ever the well-mannered lady," she chided.

"Want me to teach her manners?" The Vessel to my left leaned forward, puffing his chest out. He didn't smell of death, or the other one's odor was overpowering his scent.

Her eyes cut to him. Something skittered behind them as her smile ticked into a toothy grin.

Shit. Here came another lesson. Another test.

"Sure." She folded her arms over her chest and laughed. "You can try."

Following Mom's Rule Six, not letting one touch me, I yanked his arm behind his back before he could. If I pulled it an inch higher, we'd all get to hear a satisfying snap.

He yipped and bucked into the table, his inhuman wail like a knife to the eardrum.

The tables around us fell silent as I felt their eyes on my back. Shit. I'd fucked up Rule Five. I didn't have my back protected. A downfall of my comfort level in Mason's. Despite that, I knew without a doubt Tones was still watching me.

"Dessa," Mom sighed.

"Mom," I sighed back, releasing his arm.

He sulked back, gripping his arm against his chest.

"I didn't come here to fight," she said.

I laughed. "Sure."

"I just wanted to see you, and you keep changing your number and address."

"Some people would take the hint."

"You didn't send me fifteen percent last month," she said, tilting her head to the side.

Blood pounded in my ears. Red swam in my vision. The greedy bitch...

As I sprang across the table at her, the two Soulless with her clawed at my arms, exposing their augmentations. With the dim lights, it was doubtful the humans noticed.

"You fucking bitch, I owe you shit," I screamed, my fist connecting with her face.

Blood sprang from her nose, splattering on the white paper napkin wrapped around the silverware.

More hands joined in the dance to pull me back, their clawed fingers ripping strips of flesh from my side. I would need to stitch myself up later.

"Enough," Tones' voice shot through the room. The music died and the lights brightened to show everyone's sins.

Like cockroaches, the patrons scrambled to the door.

Mom slid her hand beneath her nose, catching the droplets.

"Look, you fucking little bitch," she growled. "You can cut from my house. You can pretend to be a big girl, but you owe me."

I growled and went to lunge for her again.

Tones' hand rested on my arm, her fingers warm and soft.

Fuck. Tones expected better in her bar.

I pulled back, my hand on my blade. "I owe you shit."

"I trained you," Mom said. "That hasn't changed, even if your address has."

"Earn your own fucking money," I seethed.

"Baby girl, that's what I did. I had you. I raised you. I trained you. I did my part. Now do yours."

"You fucking bitch," I yelled and, seeing and feeling nothing but burning hate, I lunged for her again. My hips banged into the table's edge, but I ignored the pain as I scrambled onto the table.

For a brief moment, Mom's eyes widened and she leaned back. Her lips pinched as she reached for her silverware.

I grabbed for her wrist, but her other hand grabbed a chunk of my blue hair. She yanked my head hard to the right and pulled back her left hand containing the silverware, making me choose my pain.

Once my knee made it on the table, I leveraged it forward and pushed into her, throwing her off balance. We both toppled against the brick wall. She took most of the blow, but her hands clawed into me as she brought her knee up.

She punched my jaw. My eyes watered and white dots popped. The metallic tang of blood pooled in my mouth. I punched her back, her head making a *thud* against the wall. She jabbed something in my side. The bite of metal pierced my skin.

"Dessa, Claudine," Tones growled. "Enough."

We both stopped, our hands covered in both of our blood. The pang of a bruise radiated on my cheek and side, but I smiled seeing the crook in Mom's nose. Her perfect little face wouldn't be so perfect for a few days.

Tones pushed Mom's friends out of her way to grab my arm and wrench me back around the table. I stumbled over the legs of the chair but caught myself on the chair's back.

I grabbed one of the silverware packets and swiped the napkin, dabbing the blood off my teeth. There was no hope for my side without antiseptic and thread. But she didn't fare any better. My smile flatlined. She'd baited me into another fight. I'd happily gone along, again. Acid slid down my throat and pooled in my stomach. Fuck. Would I ever learn? Was this always going to be my life?

I pushed the hair back from my eyes and avoided making eye contact with Tones. I didn't want to see her disapproval.

"If you want money, make it yourself," I finally spat. "I'm done paying your bills. I've been done."

"Baby, you aren't ever done." Mom accepted the hand from one of her cronies. She stood and brushed her clothes, resetting her too-small t-shirt on her flat stomach. "We aren't done."

"Fuck off," I spat.

"Dessa," Tones whispered, pulling my arm along with her.

I cringed but followed her. The patrons had filed out, leaving the too-bright room empty save for our little party.

"Sorry," I mumbled behind Tones.

"You know better than to talk to her," Tones said.

I did.

She wrapped her arm around my shoulder, carefully pulling me into a side hug. I rested against her, letting her warmth seep in even though I didn't deserve her support.

Benny tossed me a towel and a disapproving look.

"I hate her," I growled as I caught the towel. I draped it against my exposed raw flesh.

"Me, too," Benny said with a nod.

Tones sighed as she directed me to my chair, releasing me. She slid water my way.

It was a common topic of discussion. Mom and Tones had a history. One with residual obligations and mixed feelings.

Even if their friendship— if one had ever existed— was over, many of the regulars still came in to see my mom. My first few years of life, she'd been a waitress at Mason's Bar. An unexpected benefit for us was that many of the regular patrons grew to admire my mom and ignore me as an extension. The same avoidance I received as a child got me many tips as an adult, still listening to their conversations. I was no different than the barstool to them. Tones welcomed the business even if she didn't welcome Mom. Mom didn't cause a scene unless I was also in the bar and she was irritated. Avoiding her was a hobby of mine like annoying me was a hobby of hers.

"Dessa," Tones said as she sat beside me and took my hand.

I growled and rolled my head backward before meeting her gaze.

"I want you to make me a promise." Her green eyes bore into me.

I swallowed.

"Leave your mom alone," Tones said. "Don't approach her. Don't talk to her."

I didn't bother lying.

Finders' Handbook

Human - a human has no natural magic. They
can be born to two humans or one human and a
Vessel who does not pass on their magic.

Vessel - A nonhuman that has a nonhuman
ability. They are born with unworldly magic.
All have powers. They have one human parent
and one Vessel parent. A Finder has no right
or authority to retrieve a Vessel who is not
a Soulless.

Soulless - A Vessel who uses the illegal
death arts to gain power, additional body
augmentations, and control over humans or
Vessels. A target sheet is issued for their
capture when identified. Any Soulless,
regardless of target sheet or not, can be
retrieved and brought in. Soulless are not
born but created through the use of the
death arts.

Choicer - A human who bargains their soul to
a Companion for unearthly powers to harness
the death arts. They fall legally into the
same category as a Soulless.

CHAPTER 2

THREE HOURS LATER, I prowled down Maple Avenue. I wore a dark mask that covered my hair and face. My clothes were already perfumed with blood and sweat from a previous fight, blending me into the surroundings.

Decrepit homes with sagging roofs, peeled paint, and boarded windows lined the street. collections of cups, fast-food wrappers, and bottles clumped in the sickly shrubs and curbs.

The lampposts no longer had bulbs, and the only light that pierced the street was from the slim sliver of the waning moon. A rusted door rattled in the thin breeze. It was on nights like this that I wanted night vision. Instead, I slid my night-goggles down, casting the world in a green glow.

My feet silently took me to the corner house, the only one on the street without boards on most of the windows. Ducking down, I shimmied against the house below the windows, fixing my gaze across the street to the next corner lot of Maple Avenue and Bristle Street. Tireless cars dotted a few crumbling houses.

The corner house sported three muscle cars: all pristine, all shiny, all north of seventy grand. The home had two windows with lights burning behind the threadbare curtains. Each car belonged to a different Soulless, each with a target issued on them. Movement caught my attention on the second floor. A curtain fluttered in the unboarded window to the upper right of the door. The lookout. More probably lurked around the vacant homes.

I pulled my phone from my pocket and typed: *Confirmed, 333 Bristle St.*

No response, as expected.

Minutes ticked by. The cold night air clung to my face, numbing my cheeks. Tension hung on the silent street. My eyes skimmed the area, watching for anyone lurking. With another pass, I checked my phone.

Five minutes after the text, tires squealed in the distance, the whine of an engine drawing near Maple Avenue.

Rounding the corner to Bristle, the driver blasted their horn on a rusted-out seventies behemoth while the passenger unleashed rounds of bullets at the vehicles before they sped off into the night. Six forms emerged from the shadows, running into the house.

Shadows moved behind the curtains. Like moths to a flame, they hurried outside to see the damage. There stood ten total hovering around the porch, but hairs stood on my neck. The house wasn't emptied. Before worrying about that, I scanned the group for my target. He stood between other Soulless. He was a short man, around five foot two, and the owner of a rebuilt '69 Camaro RS/SS. According to his target sheet, he'd killed two Vessels and drank their blood. He had no noted physical augmentations, but he was working his way up to them if he was drinking blood.

The house lights extinguished, pulling my attention from my target, and the eleventh and twelfth persons walked out of the house. My breath hitched as I stared at my mom. A man stood beside her, his face blurred to me as I avoided taking in his attributes. My mind reeled in a hundred different ways. What the hell was she doing there? In all my years of her training, I scoped out a target, stalked, pounced, and got the fuck out. We didn't fraternize with them. We didn't infiltrate their den. That shit got you killed.

Despite the dim light, I saw the pink eyes of an unknown banshee Soulless next to her. The specific arts needed for their powers turned their eyes pink along with making their screams lethal. There were at least three with targets. I couldn't be certain from the distance, but more were likely Soulless or Choicers. What the fuck was my mom doing with so many? My nerves sparked and my body tensed, wanting to take them all down. How was she just standing there?

My heart stopped for a beat or two when the one next to her, the one with the blurry face, swung his arm around her shoulder and whispered something in her ear. She laughed, her beautiful chime-like one that turned my stomach over. It usually meant I was going to get punished or someone was going to die.

When her gaze drifted over to the house I stood by, I was certain she'd caught me. Certain I was going to be punished. Her gaze never locked on me and she scanned the entire street. She snapped her fingers at two on the porch. One responded. He was definitely a Soulless with his elongated tongue and white eyes. The other looked human, but that meant nothing. Many of the death arts didn't cause physical augmentations. Or they could be suppressed or hidden around humans. They moved toward the steps. Why were they taking a human's orders?

If it wasn't me who was going to be punished, and he caused her to laugh, he was likely going to die. Poor dumbass. But he chose to hang out with Soulless and their cronies.

The two followed my mom and her… friend… into a silver Porsche Taycan Turbo. Four of the others piled into a black '69 GTO Judge. The last four, including the banshee Soulless and my target, pulled to a stop in front of the white '69 Camaro.

With my phone still in my hand, I texted a number that would be useless by the end of the week.

Me: *Need ride. 333 Bristle St. May be active.*

Unknown: *Roger*

I slipped my phone into the pocket of my cargo pants and gripped my blade.

The Porsche and Judge, only bearing minor damage, pulled away, their engine revs vibrating in the air. The Camaro's back tire, however, was flat, ripped to shreds by the bullets along with a taillight. As I'd paid the hit-and-run driver to do. The two I hadn't confirmed yet as Soulless pulled a spare out and set about replacing the tire.

That left the banshee Soulless and my target, Milford James: murderer, blood drinker, and practitioner of the death arts. A real gem.

For this recovery, I had secured Mom's Rule Three: Know your exits. I had a Driver coming for me. I also had Rule Four covered: Take the surprise.

With two bent over the tire and the other two engaged in a heated debate, my feet silently darted across the street. Being either Vessel or

Soulless, who often had acute hearing, they heard my approach anyway. The two with the tire whirled around, one brandishing the tire iron. They both took a step in front of the two Soulless, blocking my direct path to them. Ah. The muscle.

Death clung to one, decay and mustiness. So, he was Soulless, too. The other didn't smell of death or have any obvious physical signs like eye color, claws, modified flesh or appendages. Shit, a Vessel helping out. He was my first target to neutralize. I couldn't kill him or bring him in without a ton of paperwork and fines. Even if he was helping Soulless.

The Soulless lunged at me first, delaying my plans. His eyes rolled back, and white orbs stared at me before he blinked and his human eyes returned. That meant he'd been born a Vessel.

I ducked before his fist could connect. In the split-second state when he threw the punch and left his abdomen exposed, I sprang forward, driving my blade into his stomach and forcing it as high as it would go. Black blood gushed from the wound, sizzling and bubbling over my gloved hand and blade. With a quick yank, my blade was freed. I kicked his knees, sending him withering to the ground.

The Vessel's eyes bulged, the tire iron motionless in his hand.

"Run," I breathed, a smile tugging on my lips.

Fortunately, he did, leaving the two alive Soulless behind.

The fucking banshee pulled back, sucking in air. She let it rip, the sound blasting past me. The ear plugs I wore did little to stop the assault but spared my ear drums from rupturing. My feet anchored to the ground, braced against the boom.

My eyes swam and my thoughts blurred against the sound. When she drew back to suck in the next blast, I flung my blade at her, hitting her throat. Crimson blood wept from the wound, coloring her hands as she clawed to remove it.

She fell to the ground, her whimpers petering out.

"Milford James," I said.

"Fuck off, bitch," he said, holding a gun out. The muzzle's metal caught in the faint moonlight.

"You have a Level Three target sheet issued on you."

"The fuck I care about that," he said and pulled the trigger. The bullet bit into my arm, tearing flesh. My mind screamed at the pain. I sucked in a short breath.

"So, the hard way," I gritted out as agony shredded at my frazzled resolve.

A whine sliced the air. Shit, my ride was almost there.

"What the fuck?" he spat, his focus pulled momentarily from me by the increasing drone.

I sprang toward him, tackling him to the ground. He pulled the trigger again, tearing at the same side the Soulless at the bar had clawed at.

"Motherfucker," I growled. I pulled my secondary blade from my waist with my uninjured arm.

He thrashed and kicked, trying to buck me off. With one working arm and my side killing me, he was able to unsettle me and toss me to the ground.

He scrambled to right himself, his eyes darting around as a muffled crackle sounded. Despite the pain and my muscles screaming, I grabbed at his flesh with my injured arm, holding him while I jabbed my blade through the back of his neck. His blood joined the black blood already eating through the material of my glove.

"Dessa," a familiar voice said. Duke, my ride.

"Yeah," I groaned. Bile rose up my throat as adrenaline faded. A shudder stole through me, and I blinked at the pain. With three Soulless, maybe I could take tomorrow off for my body to heal. A snort cut from my mouth. There was never time to heal. Besides, I still had another target to collect.

"He almost got you there," Duke said, a laugh in his voice.

"The hell he did." With a wince, I tried to stand up, my side and arm fighting all motion. Fuck, they got my arm good. I'd pay for this for a solid day or two.

"Kit's in the glovebox where it normally is," Duke said, extending his white hand down to help me.

I waved him off, showing my blood-coated gloves.

"You know you could just shoot them, right?" He tossed me a biohazard bag and frowned at the bodies oozing blood on the hard-packed dirt.

"Where's the fun in that?"

"Fun?" He snorted.

My side muscles cramped and my joints wobbled, but I stood up. Nausea washed over me. I stilled until my eyes focused.

"How's Alan?" I asked. Alan, being his fiancé.

"He sends his love," Duke said.

"Counting down to the wedding?"

"And honeymoon. I'm to remind you we still need to do dinner soon. Catch up and all."

I chuckled but my body tightened, sending waves of pain through my nerves.

Duke shot me a toothy grin as he finished laying out plastic in the back seat. Instead of the Porsche he normally drove, tonight he sported a rusted-out Ford Escape. His blond beach waves swept around his head in disarray.

"Will all three fit?" I asked. Grabbing Milford by his feet, I dragged him to the car, ignoring my body's protest. If I wanted money, I had to bring them in. The other two were Soulless and I'd get paid for them, but Milford was my target, and the biggest payout.

"We'll make sure they do," Duke said. "I get a payment for each."

JOHN'S OFFICE buzzed with energy. Some of it human, most of it not. Coffee ringed the bottom of the carafe. The stale, ever-present, metallic tang of blood hung in the air.

I dragged in the three Soulless. Duke refused to ever enter John's, but would still drive if I called, regardless of the time. Besides being one of my only friends, he was my favorite Driver to call.

"You're a fucking mess," John barked from behind his desk. His hulking form dwarfed the sixties-era metal desk with thin silver legs and a bleached yellow laminate top. His computer screen reflected an artificial white glow on his ruddy cheeks, and his unruly dark locks brushed across his face.

"Thanks," I said. The thin stream of air from his rusted desk fan fluttered the tears in my shirt. My side was painted in drying blood over the remnants of the Soulless's claw marks from the start of my evening and the patched-up bullet holes Milford gave me. Both areas would likely be healed before the next night after a shower and some cream from Tones. The shirt, unfortunately, would need the side stitched up.

I pulled out Milford's folded and stained target sheet. Blood, his and the others', was smeared across the edges, but I unfolded and plopped it down on John's desk.

"They're dripping on my floor," he growled and leaned back in his chair. "You best clean that shit up before getting the fuck out."

"Milford." I pointed at the body on top, ignoring John's last comment. "I also have a banshee Soulless and another type Soulless. His eyes went white."

He cocked an eyebrow at me. "You know the fucking rules."

Rolling my eyes, I walked back to the Soulless I'd taken out first. His hands were normal human hands. With the tip of my blade, I moved his face around and opened his mouth. Jackpot. "Since you won't take my word that his eyes went white…"

"White eyes can't be proven once dead," John recited from the *Finders' Handbook*.

I continued, "His only enhancements are enlarged canines."

John grunted. "Got lucky, kid."

"No, he smelled of death. His eyes went white."

John stilled and his eyes tracked up to me. Despite being light in color, they were dark and piercing as he took me in.

Warning bells sounded in my brain. Clearing my throat, I said, "Check and I'm outta here. All three are verified Soulless."

He stared a bit longer, my skin crawling under the scrutiny, but I didn't look away.

"Half on the one you verified in here," he said, scribbling down on a blue checkbook.

"What the fuck?" I yelled, swinging my arm down like a gameshow model. "He's a fucking Soulless."

"You lucked out."

"The hell I did," I said. Like an idiot, I had to push my case with John. Even with my anger, I didn't take a step closer. John stood over seven feet tall, his width in proportion and thick with muscles. He was a rare human Agency owner. Most were Vessels since most humans didn't know or want to believe Soulless existed. Like people with green eyes or red hair, Vessels made up less than five percent of the population, and Soulless were a fraction of that. Unlike red hair or green eyes, Vessels and Soulless didn't necessarily have a tell. Like my family, John was born into the business, and kept it going and the secrets, buried. But being human didn't negate his threat.

"You gonna fuck up," he said. He tore the check from the book and held it out.

Before he could take it back, I snatched it out of his hand. Today he was using checks from a pool company. He cycled through different companies to muddy the paper trail. Cash was a pain to keep safe in the office and on a person. Electronic banking was too easy to track.

"Haven't yet." I held my sigh in. This was a never-ending argument. No matter how many Soulless I brought in, target sheet or not, it wasn't enough to prove I wasn't just lucky.

He met my glare. Silence dragged between us, the clacking of the fan the only sound.

"Any new targets?" I finally asked. My stomach turned at my retreat.

"You still have one out." A smirk twirled his lips up.

"Yep, and you'll get her tomorrow."

"Then ask me tomorrow."

"Fine then." Continuing to argue with John would be stupid. But I still had to push it. "I want a higher level. I'm tired of the Level Threes. I want a Level Two or Level One."

"You ain't got the skill," he said, turning his attention back to the computer and dismissing me.

"Won't know until I get one," I countered.

He didn't respond as I saw myself out.

Finders' Handbook

Target Levels

I - Multiple sacrifices, celebrity or ridiculously rich with high security

2 - B-list celebrity, low-level politician, some notoriety, has influential connections, multiple murders

3 - Murder, blood drinker, violent acts toward humans or Vessels

4 - Helps in ritual, blood drinker

5 - Soulless who acts like bodyguard—more brute than brains

CHAPTER 3

MY SIDE WAS FULLY HEALED by the time I made it to Mason's Bar the next night. Tones' cream had worked again. I sat at my stool, watching the patrons mill in.

A new waitress brought me a beer and slid it in front of me. My eyes followed it, watching the slow trickle of condensation slide down it and pool on the dark wood bar top.

"From an admirer," she said with a wink and took her tray into the throngs of people.

Without a word, Benny reached across and discarded the beer. He slid me a cola and went back to making orders.

"She's new," I said to Benny with my gaze returned to the patrons.

He grunted. His typical answer to anything I said.

Tones slipped out from the kitchen, a fresh basket of fries and ranch in one hand and a side plate with a burger in the other. My stomach rumbled as the fried goodness reached my nose.

"Long night ahead of you," she murmured and slid me the basket containing my free dinner. She pushed her curly silver hair from her face.

Without hesitation, I grabbed three fries and dipped them generously into the ranch. When I put the burger to my lips for a bite, Tones lifted her chin toward my side and said, "Let me see."

I groaned and slumped back in my chair. That was the cost of the free food. She got to mother me and check over the results of my stupidity from the previous night. I hated that a part of me enjoyed her care. It was something my mother had never done. Something I didn't need. And yet…

Around the bite of food, I said, "Your cream worked." But I still lifted my gray T-shirt to show her the smooth beige flesh.

She clucked and ran a gentle finger over the area. A ticklish squeal escaped my lips.

"If you were more careful, you wouldn't need the cream." She helped herself to a few fries minus the ranch.

My mouth dried at the reprimand. Hunting was my life. I accepted the risks like other Finders; it didn't mean those who cared about us did. Life would be easier if I didn't hunt, but I had no other skill. And nothing matched the thrill, either. Instead of responding, I took another bite of the burger.

"Be careful, Dessa," she whispered. She shot me a small, sad smile and patted my hand. After grabbing another fry, she meandered back to the kitchen.

With cola and burger in hand, I moved off the counter and toward the closest high-top table. I kept my back toward the wall, and Benny was the only other person to my right. The dark pool of light hid my features and prowling eyes from others. The table next to me had three people with bent heads, whispering over beers.

My target sheet was for Jennifer Porter, a Level Four Soulless. Unlike a Level Three who had committed murder, a Level Four was only caught drinking blood or organizing a ritual. The sparse file contained a last known address and one accomplice.

"Did you hear about Milford?" one Vessel with short green hair whispered to the two others at her table.

"Did they catch the driver?" the Soulless to her right asked. His trimmed red hair matched the scruff around his jaw. Dark eyes peered out from under thick eyelashes. If he had any augmentations, he kept them hidden.

"Car was ditched and burned." The Vessel shook her head. Her eyes flicked around for any listeners.

"Why the hell did they hit that house? Didn't they know what was going on?" the other Vessel at the table whispered.

Swallowing a sip of cola, I pulled my phone out to stare unseeingly at the screen.

"They messed with Brock's Porsche, you know he'll want blood," the first Vessel said and gave them a knowing look.

"Who cares about Brock or Milford," the Soulless spat. "They fucked with the wrong person."

My mind reeled back to the twelve I'd seen the previous night. First there was Milford, the banshee, and the Soulless and Vessel who fixed the tire, but those three Soulless were permanently dealt with. Brock was another Soulless with a target sheet, but it wasn't mine. Bringing him in would have been lesser pay and I'd have pissed another Finder off. Which was not an option worth pursuing.

That left the three with him: my mom, who was a Finder in the midst of prey, the guy who whispered in her ear, and the two other lookouts with her, one of which was definitely a Soulless. None of them would be "the wrong person" to mess with in the Soulless world. There was a hierarchy, and they weren't high in it. Lookouts were common. They were often newly-converted Soulless still repaying their Companion Soulless back for helping them convert, idiot Vessels, or humans looking to make pacts with the death arts to become Choicers, or Soulless who had one too many bad decisions and were demoted in their group.

Of the six in the house, I didn't know two: my mother's whisperer and Brock's second. But Brock's second would rank lower than Brock in the Soulless world.

But the Soulless lookout took direction from my mom. Which... how the hell had she managed that? Power gained from the death arts brought status. She was a human Practitioner who was also a Finder. How deep had my mom gotten herself? Fuck, was her little visit the other day a way of asking for help? A snort caught in my throat. My mom could be bleeding out, mutilated, or worse, and wouldn't ask me for my help. She'd just want a handout of my money.

I missed bits of their conversation. More talk about repercussions. Easing forward with my phone, I typed nonsense feverishly into the notes app. My eyes darted around the screen as I listened closer to their conversation.

"But he's in town." The first Vessel opened her eyes wide.

"Yeah, well, he's with Claudine now," the Soulless said. A wicked smile cut his face as his eyes shifted to black before returning to human.

Wait. My mother. What. The. Fuck. Who was that man?

"He'll go after them," the Soulless said.

Good luck. The car was destroyed, as was the evidence inside. The only electronic connections were likely burned in the car, and my side of communications had been smashed with a hammer and tossed in a dumpster of a fast-food joint.

"I'd be more concerned about Claudine," the Vessel said and tapped her beer.

The bar unfocused in my view. How did they know anything about my mother? Had she been outed? That didn't make sense. If they realized she was a Finder, she'd be dead, not feared. And the person with her... he had these Soulless in a tither.

What the fuck had my mom done now? And who was she with?

WITH NO TIPS about Jennifer from Mason's Bar, I meandered to another bar about twenty minutes away on foot. Unlike Mason's Bar, it was a joint just for Vessels and Soulless. There was no safety net. The streets petered out to thin strips of weathered blacktop, potholed and crumbling. Little vegetation grew on the graveled sides, bleached from chemicals. The neon sign read "Angel's Bar," spilling a rainbow of artificial light over the cracked sidewalk. Only unlucky humans ventured into it. Built from an abandoned factory, there was nothing but dilapidated businesses surrounding it. You either knew it was there or made an ill-fated wrong turn.

Instead of stalking the building from a distance, which would draw attention from the paranoid Soulless who would hear me anyway, I sidled up next to the building in the back of the parking lot. Most would likely assume I was on a different type of hunt, be it drugs, a trick, or something else illegal in Coving. Just another one of them. Pools of neon light splattered across the parking lot unevenly. The poles toward the back had broken light holders, spilling the light in odd patterns. The music from the bar filtered outside, strumming the air but otherwise unrecognizable. The aroma of grease seeped through the cracks and stirred my once again building hunger.

"Get lost?" a voice called to me from the shadows.

Without my night-vision goggles, I could only make out the outline of the form nearing me. Death clung to him, the odor wafting in the breeze. Guess I wouldn't get ignored.

"Waiting for my girlfriend," I offered.

"In the dark where she can't find you?" the voice taunted back.

A little too perceptive for my liking.

"She picked the spot," I shot back, picking my way carefully toward the light and exit. My spot was compromised, and I didn't need one-on-one time with a Soulless who wasn't my target and in a place they swarmed.

"So you're just gonna leave?"

"What else would I do? I don't need to be pathetic and wait longer for someone not to show up."

"We could get a drink together. Unless your girlfriend would mind."

Go on a date with a Soulless? That would get me inside without much notice, even as a human. Guess it was an ill-fated turn for me.

Swallowing down my nerves, I tucked a strand of my red wig behind my ear. I hadn't worn colored lenses, but I'd lined my brown eyes with blue. A tight long-sleeved T-shirt hid my newest scars before they faded away. It was a recent find at a thrift store along with the faded jeans and Converse I wore. Good enough for a bar, but I could run in them if needed. Which would be likely since I was dumb enough to go on a date with a Soulless.

Tones' warning about being careful flashed through my brain. My stomach dropped. One day, I'd really need to reconsider my life and career and how it led to me on a date with a Soulless.

The Soulless was an inch or two shorter than me with blond hair and blue eyes. Based on his scent, he was a Choicer, a human turned Soulless. No wonder he took pity on me. He likely thought I was looking to become a Choicer, the vilest of Soulless. While most humans chose to live in a fantasy world where Soulless didn't exist, others not only believed, but sought them out. Other creatures like vampires, werewolves, and witches, all real, had similar fan bases.

As a Choicer, he would have hooked up with a Soulless Companion. They are powerful Soulless who help convert Vessels to Soulless and humans to Choicers. Typically, they are sought out for their specific powers from the death arts. Like their own little groupies. Since he was a human turned Choicer, he wouldn't have the natural Vessel powers to enhance whatever death arts he chose. So not only did they sacrifice their soul for this shit, they weren't even as powerful as their idols.

"I'm Mitch," he said, a smile pulling on his lips. He extended his hand out to me.

"Rebecca," I said with a nod.

I hovered back so he couldn't touch me.

He nodded in apparent understanding and let his hand drop to his side.

"How long have you been dating?" he asked as we walked toward the door.

"A couple weeks." I shrugged. "It's new… and I guess over."

He opened the door. The smell of death, fried food, and beer blasted me in the face. My eyes watered and I had to swallow my aversion. This was a horrible idea, and yet I stepped inside behind him. Maybe that life consideration should come sooner.

"You must be hungry," he said into my ear.

My shoulder cringed upwards, but I nodded and forced a smile.

He gestured toward a two-seater against the wall.

I didn't like the spot, as I couldn't watch behind my back. The bar was about three-fourths full. No one paid us attention, probably assuming the Choicer and his human girlfriend were trying to be dark and cool.

If image was my goal, I'd be insulted. Instead, my body heaved, and pinpricks raced along my spine. My fingers curled as my nerves buzzed with the Soulless milling around, their death smell turning my stomach and boiling my blood together.

"You okay?" he asked, stopping short of the bench.

I met his gaze and realized I hadn't moved since we entered. I was not only anything but okay, but an idiot who was going to get herself killed. My behavior was like a neon sign pointing an arrow and saying "doesn't belong." Maybe John was right, and I wasn't ready.

Before I could answer, I noticed a familiar figure across the room. The recognizable blonde hair was braided, and as usual, she wore no makeup. Her shirt was too tight and showed a sliver of her midriff. However, hidden was a tattoo over her heart and ribs. Her hand rested on the arm of a man. I assumed the one from last night, but without taking in his facial features, I couldn't confirm.

Mitch followed my gaze, his body stiffening as if he recognized who they were. Stepping back to me, his fingers wrapped around my wrist and tugged me toward the table. I yanked my hand back, his touch cool and clammy. I reached for my blade but stopped myself.

Fuck. I was making everything worse. My body heaved, but I took breaths through my nose to control my reaction. Instead of tips, I was going to get myself killed like a newbie Finder. Something had me off. Unfocused. Something that always did when she appeared. At least at Mason's, I knew our boundaries. Here… Fuck, I needed to leave.

"What the fuck is wrong? Don't look at them," Mitch hissed, leaning toward me. The musty scent of death clung to his body and I choked as he came closer.

I shook my head and moved to the seat facing my mom.

What was she doing here? Was she pretending to date one? How did Soulless know who she was? My thoughts blurred together, the music a whirl of sound behind them.

Mitch watched me sit down, casting a glance back before sliding in across from me.

"What is going on?" he demanded, pulling my attention toward him. He reached for my hand again, but I slid it against my legs under the table, grabbing my blade.

"He looked familiar," I said.

"No, he doesn't," he warned, his eyes widening. "You forget you saw him."

I met Mitch's gaze. His blue eyes dark with concern turned hard. His likely hopes of getting lucky vaporizing. But he recognized that man.

"Who is he?" My gaze flicked back to my mom. Without looking at his face, I saw the man with her had dark hair and olive-toned skin. His arm was draped over her shoulders.

"Someone you don't mess with," Mitch said. His hand fidgeted on the table, and he sighed. "Maybe…"

He was ready to blow me off, which was fine. He'd picked me up from the shadows.

Again, my eyes traced back to my mom. This time though, her blue eyes were boring in my direction, narrowing as she tried to piece together how she knew me.

Shit.

Her eyes flew open.

Double shit.

She'd make a scene if it meant saving her own ass.

"Hey, Mitch," I said, interrupting whatever he was saying. "I gotta go. I think this is the wrong bar."

Before he could say anything to me, I bolted up. With my hand wrapped around my blade, I barreled toward the door and the patron entering.

Luck somehow found me. My target, Jennifer, fumbled backward into the door frame, her brown hair flying over her face. If my mom didn't out me first, I was going to score my target.

"Wha—?" she muttered. Her eyes jumped to mine, hazy with alcohol.

"There you are, baby!" I flung my arm around her shoulder and spun her back outside.

"Who are you?" she slurred. Her feet stumbled to keep up as I guided her to the parking lot.

There was a commotion behind me. I couldn't be sure if it was Mitch or my mom or both following me out.

I pulled my cellphone out and typed to Duke: *Angel's Bar*

Unknown: *be there in five*

Shit. That would be too late.

Jennifer pushed her hands against my side.

"Shh, baby, it's okay that you're late." I tightened my hand on her shoulder to pull her closer.

"What?" Her eyes tracked greedily over my face.

"For our date," I said. "But that's okay."

"Who?" she started.

Rounding the corner, I pushed her against the wall. Her eyes dilated, taking me in.

"My place or yours?" she stammered. Her fingers on my side curled into the fabric of my T-shirt.

"Mine, but we'll take your car." Even if she was Soulless, her touch sent enticing tingles over my flesh.

She pulled her keys from her pocket. She tilted her head to the side and licked her lips.

If she weren't a Soulless, I'd take her up on the offer. However, I wasn't interested in tasting the death that clung to her. Or being the next source of blood she drank. Soulless were for bringing in money, not dating or one-night stands.

I pulled the keys from her grip.

"Hey," she shouted and reached for my hand.

"Come on, I'm driving since you're drunk." I pulled her arm toward the car. "I need to get you to my place."

"My place" turned out to be John's.

I texted Duke: *NM.*

Unknown: *<thumbs up emoji>*

John might know what my mom was up to, but it was pointless to ask. He wouldn't say anything and would likely take a big percent from my pay for not minding my own shit.

"You brought one in alive?" John asked after he secured her in the backroom.

My gut twisted at the accusation. She was a Soulless, but she'd been nice.

"That's allowed," I countered and tossed her keys on his desk.

"For fuck's sake," John seethed. "I have to dispose of the car?"

I rolled my eyes at him.

"That'll cost you."

Of course it would. He'd piece it out for profit and still charge me.

He scribbled in a red checkbook today. Taking the check, I glowered at the amount. He took twenty percent off for the fucking car.

He tossed me a file.

"What level is it?" I folded my arms over my chest without taking the folder.

Without moving his head, his eyes lifted to glare at me.

"I want a Level One or Two," I said. My heart hammered in my chest at my foolishness. After this evening, maybe John was right. But I'd still managed to bring in the target despite my mom being there. Even distracted by whatever was going on with her and while being at Angel's Bar.

"You ain't ready," he growled under his breath. Something passed behind his eyes. If he was capable, I'd say remorse or fear, but as that wasn't an emotion he could feel, I figured it was a new version of annoyance.

I just stared at him. If I backed down now, I'd never get one.

He sighed and leaned back in his chair. My toes curled, but I refused to show any change in my demeanor.

"Kid," he started, but pursed his lips. He shook his head, warring with himself on something.

The door opened behind me. My body tingled at the smell of sandalwood and fire. Fuck. Why did he have to show up now?

"Dessa the Destroyer," Oliver's silky voice sounded behind me.

My body tightened and I swallowed. Heat built within me, but I schooled my face.

"Fuck, can't any of you not make a mess?" John roared. He stood, toppling his chair backward.

"He's extra gooey," Oliver said and grunted as he hauled his Soulless to the back cells.

I waited until he'd cleared the doorway to finally look at him. Oliver was assigned the Level Fives. They were usually the big ones used more as bodyguards and meat-shields. They often had the grossest augmentations, including pus pockets.

Blue slime trailed down Oliver's white button-down shirt. His dark hair was styled back into long waves. A five o'clock shadow darkened his chin. The Soulless he dragged oozed matching blue goo across the floor.

Oliver had grown up in a similar world as mine, but his mother, Tones, kept him in school, kept him fed on her dime, and tried to shield him from the realities of our lives. She hadn't been happy when he chose to be a Finder versus going to college, but a gift is a gift, unless it's a curse, too. Especially a gift that paid well but usually meant a short life expectancy. Soulless didn't need to organize to hunt Finders; they simply killed anyone they thought was one. Then likely used the blood in their next ritual. Oliver's gifts—strength, speed, and luck—had spared him many times, even if it was muscling down the grossest of creatures.

I turned back to find John staring at me, his eyes fierce and dark.

"You don't want a higher level," he said, his fingers pressing into his desk until they turned white from the pressure.

"Yes, I do," I countered.

John swore and his gaze bounced to the wall behind me. "Fuck it," he growled. He threw his body back in his chair and pulled his middle drawer open. He pulled out a slim file.

I licked my lips as my eyes followed the folder he slid across the desk.

"I warn you," John said. "You can back out now."

"Back out from what?" Oliver called behind me.

My nerves skittered and I bit my lip to stop it.

"Level Two," John said.

My fingers trembled as my heart rate ticked up. Finally, a Level Two.

"About time," Oliver murmured. Now he stood behind me, his presence a shift in the air.

I closed my eyes and willed myself to focus. He was just another Finder. Just Tones' oldest son. And… Oh fuck. Focus.

Pulling the folder off the table, I flipped open the cover. The sheet was sparse, but the picture staring back at me was more than a million words.

My mom's face.

"What?" I stuttered.

"Claudine Petrov," Oliver read over my shoulder. His breath tickled my ear.

I yanked the folder away and shot him a glare.

Oliver's face was a few inches from mine, his hazel eyes fixed on me in concern. My stomach knotted and I turned back to John, hoping my face didn't flush.

"Is this a joke?" I roared. Were they in on some elaborate prank? My mom showed up at Soulless spots to tease me and then John gave me her target sheet? Were they trying to mess with me? John and Mom were almost friends.

John snarled. "Wish it was."

My heart stilled, and my focus blurred. John didn't lie about Soulless targets. My fingers curled around the target sheet. Images of the past few days flashed in my mind. Oh fuck. Fuck.

"You ain't ready," John growled and thrusted his hand back out. "Told ya you weren't."

I stepped back and pressed the folder to my chest. My heart thudded against my hands.

"You can't do that," Oliver said, turning his anger to John. "It's her mom."

"There's no rule on that," John spat, his lip curling.

"Who the fuck cares?" Oliver yelled. "It's not right."

John's eyes slowly tracked to Oliver.

Oliver stiffened next to me. He licked his lips but didn't look away.

"Are you serious?" I murmured. My mom was at Milford's party. She was at Angel's, a Soulless bar. But she was a Finder. She had to have been stalking them… hunting them to bring them in… right?

John nodded. His unblinking eyes watched me. "Just issued."

"How is that possible?" Oliver asked. "She's a bitch… but she's Claudine."

"But…" I choked out. It wasn't possible. It didn't make sense. She taught me everything I knew. She was a Finder. She was a human…

"She's a Choicer," John said.

OTHER WORLDLY MAGIC EXCERPT

Demons and half demons roam the earth. They are not Soulless. Demons typically do not associate with Soulless. They see them as inferior. Demons can harness the same powers as the death arts but without the sacrifices. They tend to be solitary or stick to a common small group. They do not associate with other demons outside of their kin.

CHAPTER 4

"DESSA, you can't fucking be serious!" Oliver yelled behind me as I exited John's office.

What the fuck?

My eyes focused on nothing, blurring paved roads and sidewalks as I automatically walked the path away from John's. In my current mindset, I knew better than to go home. Anyone could follow me, and then I'd have to move again. Instead, I found my way to the river.

Sloshing waves tore angrily at the shore. My feet anchored on the cement step, and I leaned into the cold metal railing. The sensation bit through my shirt and stung my skin. The bite of cold March wind whipped at my face, a remnant of winter that was still fighting for ground. At the odd hour, the waterfront was empty. If anyone lingered, they kept to the shadows and didn't smell of Soulless.

Most Soulless hung out with their own kind. Around the world, Soulless clumped together, usually in larger cities. Coving, the large city I lived in, sat southwest of Lake Michigan. It was easier for them to hide, easier to blend in. But they were everywhere.

My father was a Vessel, according to my mom. He didn't pass any magic on, so I was a human. But then, she and I were Finders who hunted the Soulless, according to her, too. Now her sheet said Choicer. Fuck. The bitch. I ran my fingers through my short blue hair.

The target sheet sat heavy in my pocket. The sheaf of paper holding so many broken truths. Known information listed on her sheet:

Type: CHOICER

Level: TWO (2)

Reason: Arts used by Companion for transformation. Companion's true name unknown and not local.

Previous occupation: a Finder.

The target sheet gave me nothing. I already knew her last known address, knew she was a Finder, knew the places she frequented… Fuck. She'd never been to Angel's Bar before. She'd always warned me against going. She hadn't been around Mason's as much recently, either. And I had no idea who the guy was she was clinging to, other than now I knew he was her Companion, the Soulless who converted her to a Choicer. His association was the reason she was a Level Two. Just fucking great.

A whimper trembled in my throat. Could I have done something? Could I have stopped her? Our years together played in my brain. The pride she'd shown when I was six and found my first Soulless. My heart had swelled at that smile she'd given me. Now it panged and my stomach dipped. She'd taken me with her to John's, and for the first time I was allowed to cross the threshold. He didn't smile then either, but he'd patted my shoulder and gave me a check.

We spent the next twelve years training, honing, and taking down Soulless. Granted, I did the taking down while she critiqued, but she'd had my back. Even if it meant putting a knife in it so I'd learn to never turn my back on my prey. The first and main rule she taught me was to never believe a Soulless. And now… now she was a fucking Choicer.

"Dessa, you can't go after your mom," Oliver growled behind me.

"Go away." My eyes shuttered and my fingers tightened around the railing.

"Dessa—"

"Oliver," I yelled cutting him off. Heat clawed at my face in contrast to the air. "John gave me the target sheet. She's mine to bring in. And I'm going to do it." The words sounded more solid and sure than I felt. She was my mom. She trained me. She knew everything about me... Fuck. No. I'd been out of her place for years. She didn't know how I'd changed. I'd continued to bring in targets even without her watchful eye picking apart my tactics. I... I was still her daughter. Still tied to her. Fuck.

"Dessa, Claudine is your mom. There're so many things wrong with this." He came to stand beside me, his hands in his hoody pockets. His eyes followed the river's current as he licked his lips.

I didn't need his big brother shit. I may have spent time with his family in my youth, but I didn't need his protecting then or now. Needing people only got both of you hurt.

"You saying I can't bring her in?" I countered.

He sighed and closed his eyes. "No, Dessa, I'm not. You're Dessa the Destroyer. You have a perfect recovery record."

My mouth dried. "But?"

"She's hanging out with shitty Soulless."

"Which Choicer isn't?" I asked, my voice catching, and I had to swallow a lump. She gave a part of her soul to someone. Willingly. To a Soulless.

He shook his head, his hazel eyes tracking to me. I looked away before we locked gazes.

"Dessa, there are whispers about her," Oliver said.

"I've heard some." I guess the conversation I overheard was just the tipping point.

"She's hooked up with a Soulless, one that's feared."

"How do you know this?"

Oliver sighed again. "Do you know about the hit-and-run on three powerful Soulless?"

Fuck.

He cut his eyes to me and growled, likely realizing I was behind it.

"How do you know about that?" I asked instead of answering.

"Every Soulless does. It's what almost all Soulless are talking about. Even openly at the bar. I don't know who her Companion is by name, but after the hit, there have been talks, more than whispers. He moved in from the coast."

"She's a Choicer and hooked up with a major Soulless as a Companion. Someone making a power move in Coving. Fuck."

"Give the target to someone else," he whispered. He stepped closer, his shoulder brushing mine. I jerked back from the contact.

"Fuck you," I spat, pushing off the rail. "She's my mother. I'll bring the bitch in."

"She's not your responsibility." He closed his eyes.

"The fuck she isn't!"

"You're too blinded to her." His Adam's apple bobbed as he swallowed.

"What does that mean?"

"She can rile you up just by appearing in the bar. Dessa, this is a bad idea." He leaned his elbows against the railing and dropped his head into his palms. "She knows you too well."

"Well, I know her too," I lied.

Before he could continue the conversation, I turned and headed to a pizza joint. I needed food if I was going to figure this out. Then to find Soulless for answers.

MY APARTMENT WAS a contrast to the gloom and darkness of my work world. The small space was painted a bright white, the furniture various shades of tan, floral, and stripes. In all honesty, the place came painted white and most of my furniture was found discarded on the sidewalk, but I'd been selective in my home décor treasures.

The blank walls held no personal mementos, family pictures, or fun souvenirs. I didn't have knickknacks or collections. My room reflected my life, empty and devoid of personal afflictions. Even my furniture reflected someone else's taste.

I had no delusions that my apartment was safe. I hunted the Soulless for a living; I knew what lurked around corners, could slip through a locked door, and what little could be done to stop it.

I liked to tell myself I didn't have things so I had nothing to steal, but in truth, if I didn't have belongings, I never had to worry about coming home. I had no plants to water, pets to feed, or personal effects to collect if I needed to skip town. Or if I was killed. My life, like most Finders, would probably be short if I stayed one, but then what else would I be? This was the life I knew.

I kept a few twenties tucked under a broken part of the faded Formica countertop, but otherwise I was hand to mouth. I kept a bank account to cash checks and pay for rent and utilities since they were squeamish about cash payments—something about it being shady. It provided a credit score to a fictitious name and made online purchases easier.

After sliding my takeout pizza into the oven, I settled on my one barstool. I had salvaged it from a neighbor moving. A slit ran along the seam, but most of the stuffing was still inside.

All food I didn't make myself I put in the oven. Heat killed most things, and made many poisons change color or omit a different odor. Mom's Rule Two—Don't eat or drink anything anyone gave you—kept me paranoid but safe, even though I always trusted food from Tones.

While the pizza double baked, I focused on my mom. I'd seen her at Mason's but also Angel's Bar. The problem was, she also saw me. If I'd had her target sheet last night before going into the bar... What the fuck was I talking about? I had no clue she was there.

Normally I scoped out a target and hauled them in within forty-eight hours of being assigned the target. A rare few took longer if they were paranoid or didn't socialize often. Most Soulless hung out with other Soulless.

My phone buzzed in my pocket, pulling me from my thoughts.

Hardly anyone but Duke ever texted me unless they were responding to a text I sent.

It vibrated again. If possible, angrier sounding than before.

I tugged it out of my cargo pants and noticed two texts on the screen.

Unknown: *We're in Coving. Food?*

Unknown: *NM. You're probably eating pizza if you brought in a target or frozen garbage if you didn't.*

Me: *Judgmental much?*

Unknown: *Drinks?*

Me: *By "we" does that mean A is with you?*

I purposely abbreviated the name in case it wasn't who I thought it was.

Unknown: *Alan says hi.*

Me: *<smiley face emoji> hi*

Unknown: *does that mean drinks?*

I sighed and rolled my head back. I needed to focus on my mom. The timer on the oven dinged. I retrieved the extra-crispy pizza from the oven. My apartment held no answers. I needed Soulless.

Me: *Can't tonight.*

Unknown: *Another night. Another Soulless. Or two. Drinks soon then.*

THE FIRST TWO Soulless I found were lizard type, or as I called them, tonguers. Their tongues were extra-long and usable like an extra appendage. They also had pocks on the tongue that could emit a poison.

The couple crept in the shadows, following a human couple on a path that ran along the river's front. Trees lined the path but provided pocket alcoves for day picnickers to have privacy and a view of the river. Early in March, the insects remained dormant, and the only sound was the slosh of the river. Although the human couple kept to the lighted path, no others were out that late, or technically early. The sun would rise in a couple of hours.

Along a bend in the path, I intercepted the tonguers. Both were fixated on the humans but heard me coming anyway. They whipped around, tongues slithering in the air. With my knife out, I sliced at the nearest one. Pus and blood bubbled from his muscle. The tonguer unleashed a wail, the sound shattering the cool night.

Instead of trying to be martyrs, the humans gave surprised yelps and darted away from the horrific sound.

The injured tonguer retreated a step, blood dripping with it. The other tonguer tilted her head at me, her eyes turning to slits.

"What are you?" she asked, sniffing at me.

Many cheesy movie lines spun in my head, but instead, I said, "Looking for information."

She snorted.

"I can haul your asses in tonight, get coin for you, or we can have a nice convo." I wanted option one, but I needed option two. They weren't my targets.

"You're outnumbered and outpowered."

Right about then I craved Oliver's restraint, to hold my tongue and action. But I didn't have it. She opened her mouth to say something else, but before she could speak, I kicked out, taking her knee.

She yelled and her tongue lashed out, an uncontrolled poison club. In her daze, I punched her temple. She collapsed to the ground, her eyes glossy, a trickle of blood weeping from her mouth.

The first injured tonguer let out a guttural cry and some profanity.

"She's not dead yet," I spat and dodged his wild left hook. On my return up, I got a blow to his liver area.

With a groan, he grabbed his stomach and stumbled until he took a knee.

"There was a hit two nights ago," I said.

"So?" he hissed.

"They hit the wrong person," I echoed from the conversation I heard earlier.

A laugh escaped his lips. He placed his hands down.

Before he could stand up, I kicked his side, sending him back down.

His cough rattled, spraying foamy acid onto my T-shirt. Great. Acid holes weren't fixable. As he turned to glare at me, his eyes narrowed on my face.

The other tonguer groaned and her eyes blinked.

Shit.

I put my knee on the small of her back and moved my blade to her neck. "Talk," I said to the one trying to get his footing.

"What do you want to know?" he growled.

"Who is Claudine with?" I asked.

His face scrunched and his head pulled back.

"Claudine?" he parroted.

"Yep."

"I don't know her."

For some strange reason, I believed him. Then why did the others know about her?

"Whose house was hit?"

"I don't know a name," he said before a cough jolted his frame.

"What do you know about him?"

He laughed, a choppy, coughy laugh.

"What?" I barked.

"You want death?"

"You gonna kill me if you tell me?"

"Keep asking about him and he'll find you," he said.

"Where is he now, then?" I asked. Wherever he was, my mom was likely near him.

"Warehouse District," the tonguer I sat on gritted out.

"You're awake?" I leaned over to meet her gaze.

Her hate-filled eyes glared at me.

"Idiot," the liver-punched tonguer said.

"Her funeral," the other one said.

Either way, it was the start of real information.

———

THE NEXT NIGHT I drank my cola at Mason's, watching the patrons come and go. If I asked for information at Mason's Bar, she'd find out.

Mason's was for listening and learning, not interacting. We were regulars. She was an eyepiece, and I was as lackluster and unchanging as the barstools. I drank like the patrons, kept to myself, and never showed interest.

For the first time ever, I followed some patrons out of the bar. The red-haired Soulless that had been there previously and talked about my mom and the hit with the other patrons had two new Soulless accompanying him, a banshee and an ogre Soulless. An ogre was exceptionally large and strong. Typically, Oliver hunted them.

The wind had picked up, chilling my skin. Fortunately, I wore a flannel over a long T-shirt. They turned off onto Main Street. A few miles down the road it, opened up to a more human section of town with more restaurants for patrons, bright lights, and the illusion of safety. Humans lived around Mason's, but they usually had records or wanted privacy.

Instead of going to the downtown, they hung a right and headed toward the park. The large greenspace housed acres of hills, planted forests in perfect rows, game fields, and an amphitheater. The three made their way to the concert in place.

After several hours of watching them, they were skunk drunk and my nerves were frayed from the music and number of Soulless around me.

The Soulless from the first night was all over the ogre Soulless. As they ground into each other with the music, an idea came to mind. I picked up the tepid beer I'd purchased hours before to fit in. When the next song started up, I bumped into the banshee, sloshing my beer down his shirt. His pink eyes flashed with annoyance.

My lips quirked up into a large grin, mimicking the one Mom used on others. His gaze fell to my mouth, and I slapped a hand against his bicep. An airy laugh escaped me as I stumbled a step. I slurred out, "I'm so sorry. Maybe I can squeeze it back into my cup?"

His predatory eyes raked over my body.

I giggled. Yes, a stupid-ass giggle, and then added, "If you take it off it might be easier."

He started to tug his shirt when the Soulless from the bar slapped him. "Go get her another drink."

"But…" the banshee started.

Swaying, I brushed into him, letting my eyes get large. "You'd get me another beer?"

"Yeah, sure," he mumbled, his hands copping a feel. The fucker. He still left, sauntering over to one of the beer stands.

"You look familiar," the bar Soulless said, his eyes searching me for the reason.

"I got that face." I shrugged and didn't meet his gaze.

"No," he said, shaking his head. "I don't think that's it."

My eyes flicked to the ogre and then back to him.

"Hey, can you get us another round?" He held out a fifty to the ogre.

She looked me over, assessing me from my feet to my face. Satisfied I wasn't a threat of taking her Soulless, she grabbed the fifty and lumbered to the beer stand with the banshee.

"Well?" he demanded.

My smile fell and he swallowed.

I went for the sympathy route.

"Do you know Claudine?" I asked.

His eyes narrowed and he sucked in a breath.

"She goes to Mason's and Angel's Bar."

He folded his arms over his chest.

"I'm worried about her," I said.

"Wait…" Recognition lit his eyes. "You gave her a black eye."

"Our relationship is complicated," I said.

He opened his eyes wide in mockery.

"I haven't seen her in a few days. I'm worried about her."

"Worried? About Claudine?" he snorted.

"I said it's complicated." My eyes went wide in a pout.

"Whatdaya have to exchange?" he said.

Of course.

"I have a few bucks." My hands patted my pockets.

"My friend is hard up." He lifted his chin toward the banshee in line.

Oh hell no. I'd find the information another way.

My head was already shaking no before I found my words. "No, no, no."

He chuckled.

"Dance with him next song, and I'll tell you where she goes most nights."

Fuck. One dance shouldn't kill me. Hopefully. I'd have to scrub my arms extra hard tonight in the shower.

"Deal." I nodded and blew a breath out. I didn't trust Soulless, they lie by nature, but I could always haul him in if he didn't tell me.

They returned carrying two beers each.

"Thanks," I said. "Want to dance?"

The bar Soulless coughed over a laugh and quickly sipped his beer to hide the noise.

"Dance?" the banshee repeated, his head flinching back.

"Yeah?" I asked, cocking an eyebrow.

Having the beers meant he could only touch me with one hand. My drunken act helped me reduce our contact as I stumbled around the grass. Much of my beer sloshed on the ground, but he didn't notice as his eyes stayed glued to my body.

When the song wrapped up, the bar Soulless leaned over. Shockingly, he held up his end of the bargain and whispered, "Warehouse District, Decker Shipments. Usually midnight to two."

"The fuck," the banshee yelled, the slight tremor in his voice rattling my ears. His beer splashed across my shirt as he shoved the bar Soulless back. "She's with me."

"Dumbass," the bar Soulless roared and shoved him back.

His date, the ogre, turned her gaze to me. She reached for me, but I jumped back. She got a chunk of my flannel and ripped it off.

"Have them both," I said. Chucking my beer in her face, I tore off for the park's edge.

My phone buzzed. The ogre's feet pounded behind me. My eyes darted around the thinning swarms of people. My phone buzzed again and then again. Fumbling with my pocket, I tugged it out to see a call coming in. Although the number wouldn't work at the end of the week, I recognized the digits.

"Kinda busy," I grunted into the phone and weaved between the cars. Her crunching footsteps dragged and grew more distant as my stride ate ground.

"I know," Duke chuckled. "Looks like you pissed an ogre off."

My head snapped back. In my distraction, my knee connected with the side of a car. Biting my tongue, I rolled to the side and darted between the bumpers and front ends of two cars. Gravel bit at my knees. Looking over my shoulder, I saw the ogre was several rows behind me, her body racked with heavy breaths.

"Where the fuck are you?" In my spot, my breaths came in short pants and the cold of the ground seeped into my pants. A few plastic cups rattled next to me.

"About a hundred and twenty degrees to your left," Duke said, but his voice also sounded outside of the phone.

While scooching around the cars to a different side than what the ogre saw, I looked behind me and saw three familiar faces. Fuck, I didn't want them to get caught in my shit.

"Don't come closer." I found my footing and ducked below the car windows as I gained distance from the ogre. Granted, she was walking at this point and out of breath.

"Oh, sweets," Duke cooed. "That is so nice you care about our well-being."

I snorted. Damn it, I hated that he was right. Softness only got people killed.

He ended his side of the conversation. The phone beeped in my ear before falling silent.

"Have time for drinks now?" Duke stood two cars over. A toothy grin dominated his face. Next to him, and holding his hand, was Alan.

Black hair framed his reddish-brown face, and dark brown eyes gleamed with amusement. Alan smiled, his small and sweet.

The third familiar face belonged to Oliver. His hazel eyes watched me and he folded his arms over his chest.

"What are you doing here?" I asked lamely. Obviously, they were here for the concert, but I wasn't expecting to see anyone.

"I think she needs food," Alan said, ignoring my dumb question. He held his hand out for me to join them.

My gaze jumped to Oliver's for some reason. His lip tipped into a smirk.

"Or are you going to lug her in?" Alan asked. His eyes flicked to the ogre who was now joined by the banshee and red-haired Soulless.

I could bring in the three. It'd be a huge score. But John would note it wasn't my mom. Even if they were part of my search for her. He'd likely only give me half the price.

"She's actually considering it," Alan scoffed.

"Of course she is," Oliver added. "She's Dessa the Destroyer, always on the job."

I flipped him off. I didn't want to hear his truths.

He laughed, the rich sound warming me. I frowned instead of joining in.

"I know Patricia isn't her target." Oliver nodded at the ogre. "She's one of mine."

My eyes lit up. "You bring her in, and I'll haul the other two in."

The three frowned at me in unison. I reared back. "What?"

Duke shook his head. "There'll always be Soulless. Let's eat."

"Maybe this is why John only gives you Level Fives," I directed at Oliver as I fell in pace with them.

His smile dimmed and his eyes lowered to the ground. He shrugged. "She's just enjoying a concert with her boyfriend. There'll be another night."

"And more death arts," I muttered.

"How's the hunt for your target?" Duke asked.

"Great. I have solid leads."

Oliver stilled, his body going rigid.

My eyes cut to him, my lip curling.

"What's wrong?" Alan asked.

"Give us a minute." Oliver grabbed my elbow and whirled me around into an outcrop of trees with buds just starting to show. His fingers were warm and gentle, and a jolt shot through my arm from his touch.

I tugged my arm away and rubbed the spot. His touch should mean nothing.

He faced me with his back to Duke and Alan and the world. What an idiot for not taking precautions. My gaze jumped to the patrons moseying to their cars, seemingly oblivious to us.

"Dessa," he breathed. My eyes flicked to his. Emotion, dark and raw, reflected back.

I licked my lips and my breath hitched. His gaze moved to my lips for a moment and darkened. He blinked and his eyes shuttered all emotion before returning to mine. He was wearing his Finder face, the face he also used when we were kids and wanted to tell me what to do.

"What?" I said, my voice huskier than normal.

He leaned closer. My breath caught in my throat. He swallowed. Silence lingered.

"Oliver?" I croaked.

He shook his head and eased back. "Dessa, you don't have to go after her."

"After who? Patricia? Don't worry, I won't take your target."

"Your mom," he growled, and his eyes flashed.

My heart fell and disappointment settled in my veins. He always had to play big brother.

Other Worldly Magic Excerpt

Shadows are remnants of magic that take on sentient form.

CHAPTER 5

I FOUND my way back to Tones. Back to my base. In a few short hours, I'd go to the location the Soulless had given me. For some reason, hollowness settled in my heart. My whole life. the bitch had raised me to honor the Finders' Law, to purge the world of the Soulless, and she'd gone around and joined them. What. The. Fuck.

Neon lights greeted me. The cold, artificial light like a beacon. The familiar smell of fries, beer, and the unmistakable hint of death clung to the air. As I neared the counter, Leo, one of Oliver's brothers, slumped over a book. Catching a glance of equations, I grimaced. He'd be an accountant, or banker, or someone who worked with money and math.

Tones appeared through the archway to the kitchen. Her gray locks frizzed in the warm air. Behind her, Matteo whined about something. He was the youngest brother, ready to graduate in the spring.

"No," Tones droned, her eyes sharp with annoyance.

"But Mom," he whined.

"Matteo, knock it off," Leo growled, his fingers twisting through his dark locks like Oliver.

"Bite me."

I snorted a laugh. Three sets of eyes turned to me.

"Dessa!" Matteo cheered. With arms spread wide, he started a dance run my way.

"I'm taking Tones' side."

He frowned at me, halting his dash toward me.

Tones shot me a curious look, her eyes darting over my face. To block her scrutiny, I lifted my cola to my face.

Leo smiled at me, only the right side curling up. His brown eyes shone in amusement.

"Shouldn't you be out Fin…" Matteo caught himself. "Doing your job?"

Tones, Leo, and I all rolled our eyes. We never spoke the word "Finder" in the bar. It was like screaming "fire" in a movie theater.

"Oliver's not here," Leo said, his eyes focusing back on the squiggly stuff on his page.

"Good," I said even though my stomach hardened. Besides, he'd only give me shit about tonight, anyway. The night would hold its own challenges without his opinions sprinkled in.

"Oh come on, Dessa," Matteo cooed. He skirted around Tones, making sure to stay out of her swat range. "You don't even know what my side is."

Without looking at him, I sighed. I was going to find out, though, if I wanted to or not.

"Remember when Oliver wanted to join you… in your business?" Matteo said. He sat on the barstool next to me, resting his elbow on the bartop and settling his head on his hand. With reddish-brown hair, he was the only one to resemble Tones when she was younger. All the others took after their dad.

My gaze flicked to Tones. Her lips pressed into a tight line.

"I kicked his ass."

Leo chuckled. Tones tried to fight it, but her lip tugged up.

"What?" Matteo asked, looking to the others for backup.

Placing my cola down, I turned to face him. When his brown eyes met mine, I said, "He wanted to be a hero. It's tough work. Most of us die early and painfully. I still don't think he should be one."

"But..." Matteo's brows furrowed, and he cautioned a glance to his mom.

She cocked an eyebrow back. "See."

"But you've done it for years. Even as a kid."

I shrugged. My gaze fell to the ground. He wasn't wrong, but I had had my mom when I was a kid. She made sure I stayed paranoid and watchful. She didn't care if I was in the shower, sleeping, or reading on the sofa. Any place could be an impromptu attack. Soulless were always Soulless. I always needed to be ready. The scars had long since healed over, but I knew every place my mom had used my body as a pincushion for her knife. Each one a reminder to be cautious and alert.

"She's not normal," Leo offered with a sigh. Dramatically, he flipped the page, the harsh whooshing sound stilling our conversation. "Mom said no. Dessa said no. I said no."

"Dude, you're the one studying at a bar," Matteo shot. "Like your opinion matters."

"Why do you want to be one?" I asked, interrupting their spat.

"'Cause you do good work. You bring in all the unredeemable ones." A large, naïve smile curled his lips.

"None of them are redeemable."

Tones sucked air between her teeth, and her head shook.

I didn't want this argument again. She believed everyone deserved a second chance. I believed in the Finders' Law—I wasn't judge or jury. I simply retrieved those with target sheets after the use of the death arts was confirmed. The other part of the Agency handled the rest.

"Matteo," Leo groaned. "No one supports your dumbass choice."

"What did Oliver say?" I asked.

Matteo's smile fell.

"Mhm," I mocked.

"What do you care what he thinks?" Matteo asked pointing a

finger in my face. "All you ever do is tell him off, ignore him, or stare with goo-goo eyes at him when he's not watching."

Fire clawed at my cheeks. Instead of responding, taking the bait, I sucked in a breath. For the record, I did not stare at Oliver with goo-goo eyes. That crush was long dead.

"He's not wrong," Benny offered, sliding me a fresh cola.

My eyes shot to him. "Now you talk?"

He shrugged, his frown less pronounced.

"Like you have room to talk," Matteo laughed.

"For fuck's sake, shut it," Leo growled.

Benny folded his arms over his chest and threw him a look daring him to continue.

Warning bells sounded in my mind. If I were Matteo, I'd be making distance for the door.

Instead, only for a moment he hesitated, but stupidity won out. "It's like the looks you shoot Claudine!"

The world stopped. There was no noise. No lights. Nothing. Just stunned silence. Then everything came racing back to life. Benny half launched across the bar top toward Matteo. Leo slammed his book shut before grabbing Matteo's collar and pulling him away from Benny's reach.

My eyes caught Tones'. Love and annoyance burned brightly behind them.

"They're yours." I lifted my cola in mock salute.

"And you'll always have a place with them."

MOM'S RULES

Rule Four: Take the Surprise

CHAPTER 6

ONE VISIT TO THE BAR, five Soulless, two destroyed T-shirts, one pizza, one fight with Oliver, and a dozen new scars on my arms and sides later, I had a location and time for Mom.

The Warehouse District was across town next to Lake Michigan. It spanned several miles, a grid of boxed, nondescript buildings in fading tans and off-white metal siding. Each housed a square-letter name in red or the occasional blue to spice things up. Unfortunately, they weren't in alphabetical order, but a quick Google search got me to the location, including an aerial map with red pins showing me exactly where it was.

A mix of humans, Vessels, and Soulless strolled around the docks. Most businesses ran twenty-four seven, importing and exporting legal and illegal goods. An internet search on Decker Shipments got me an early aughts basic website with clashing colors. More searching yielded that they stored stuff for others. So basically, a front.

No one patrolled the building on the exterior. The time ticked by, the people changing but not the volume. At a quarter to one, a familiar GTO Judge rolled up. Two occupants exited and headed to the building. Mom's blonde hair was tied back in a ponytail. Despite the chill, she wore her typical too-small T-shirt, skinny jeans, and Converse.

The lone lightbulb by the entrance did little to provide determent. The corners of the building also sported lights, but the large box of a building was left mostly in shadows. Keeping to the dark pockets, I crept up to the building. No one was inside standing guard. Mom and her Companion weren't visible. I tested the door, but it was locked. With nimble fingers, I picked the lock and moved inside.

Nothing sounded. No hurried footsteps, no breaths, no sirens. My eyes took in the systems on the walls. Nothing blinked. They weren't afraid of people breaking in. Likely because they were Soulless and would deal with it in their way.

I wrapped my fingers around my pommel, my mom's rules reciting in my head, especially Three, Four, Five and Seven.

Rule Three: Know your exits. The door behind me would be easy enough to push open. I saw three exterior doors. I could see one to the left, but a wall sat to my right. Those exits were to other rooms.

Rule Four: Take the surprise. Well, I hoped I had the surprise, but she was my mom. For all I knew I was on video, and she was eating popcorn watching me.

Rule Five: Never turn your back or drop eye contact. She'd trained me to be paranoid. Rule Five ran through my blood.

Rule Seven: Always carry a weapon. I had my trusted blade, two extras, and a handgun I'd swiped from a Soulless.

The warehouse seemed more vacant than anything. The area I stood in was empty except for a reception desk. To the left was an open space a legitimate company would likely use as a show space. Walls to the left, right, and straight ahead boxed in the room. The walls on the side each had three doors, and the wall to the front had one door. Death, sweet and cloying, clung to the space, turning my stomach. My nose flared as I took whiffs from the handles. Tingles raced down my spine at the different smells, all belonging to Soulless.

The middle door on the left had the most recent hint of death and my mom's floral perfume.

Blade in hand, I cracked the door open. Again, nothing sounded, and nothing popped out. Taking slow, steady breaths, I crept into the room. Lines of shelving ran vertically with the length of the room. Nondescript white banker boxes cluttered the shelves. It looked like an evidence room more than a warehouse.

A new smell tickled my nose. Unlike the prominent smell of death, the metallic tang of fresh blood wafted around me. What the fuck was she doing?

A scream sliced the air, long and fluid-filled. Silence descended, enveloping the darkness. My mouth dried and my fingers tightened around my blade. It wasn't her scream. Acid burned down my throat. Was she sacrificing someone? Was she doing it willingly?

Biting my tongue, I pulled my thoughts back to the present.

Keeping my back to the door, I cased the room. There was only one other door besides an emergency exit with a neon sign buzzing over-head. The push bar mechanism was clearly labeled "emergency use only." Well, at least it would be an easy escape when I nabbed her. I didn't want to try to drag her back through the building. Once I had her, I'd have Duke pick us up. The text was already written, waiting to be sent.

She wasn't in the main room, so that left the door. I could bust into the room, but her Companion was with her. He was powerful enough to turn her to a Choicer, and many Soulless allegedly revered or feared him. Without knowing what exactly lay beyond the door, I was better off waiting for her to come out.

My plan was to wait behind the shelving. Once they started to exit, I'd put a bullet in her Companion's head. Not knowing if it would kill him or not—most, but not all, Soulless are permanently allergic to bullets—I had another blade ready. Whether it killed him or not, hopefully it'd delay him enough for me to get my mom out of the building.

Events started as planned, until everything fell apart.

After about forty minutes, the door swung open. The pungent

smell of death and death arts twirled out, coating my tongue and watering my eyes. Mom's blue eyes flashed in the dim light from the auxiliary ceiling lights. A wicked smiled curled her lips. Blood smears raked around her shirt in fingernail patterns. Droplets dotted her arm. It could have been hers or someone else's. Behind her, her Companion slinked out. His dark hair was meticulous, and his button-down light-blue shirt was splattered in red and black blood. Blood covered his face as if he'd eaten raw prey like a lion. His hands and arms were coated up to his rolled-up sleeves.

Without thought, I lifted my gun and put two in his forehead. His head flung back, smacking into the closing metal door. He stumbled a step backward before sliding down the door with a blood trail showing his descent.

"You fucking bitch," Mom sneered, her gaze pinning me.

A lump bobbed in my throat, and I couldn't swallow past it. My body numbed as my brain screamed a million thoughts. My mom had sacrificed someone. The evidence decorated her. She used the death arts. She'd broken every moral rule she'd given me. There was no denying she was a Choicer. She teamed up with Soulless. She sacrificed a life.

"I'm going to kill you," she seethed and stepped toward me.

I blinked and gasped, freeing my air and thoughts. "Claudine Petrov—"

"Don't you fucking dare!"

"You became a Choicer," I started.

She laughed, slapping her hand to her chest.

Startled by her display, I hesitated. One mistake in a list of many.

She lunged at me. I went to block, but she raked her fingers across my cheek, drawing blood.

I kneed her, connecting with her abdomen at the same time she punched my lower ribs. I blinked as pain rocketed up my side.

My blade was still in hand, but she pressed against the arm, stopping my attack.

Instead of fighting for the blade, I dug the other one out of my waist and pushed it into her stomach. She gasped, her eyes widening.

For good measure, I yanked it back out and slammed it back in again until her rib bone stopped my progress.

Her hand fell to her side. Bloody fingers pushed at the wound, trying to stop it.

I grabbed my zip ties to bind her. Another big mistake. I should have just gone for her throat.

She wrapped her hand around my wrist. Her scalding blood burned through my flesh.

I screamed as heat sizzled my nerves. I tried to push her hand off, but she pressed harder, sending jarring pain through my body. My knees buckled. I fell to the ground, the cement biting at my joints.

"You think you got me?" she sneered. "You dumb little bitch."

I was a dumb bitch. I'd thought I could go after her.

She gritted her teeth and shifted her side to reduce the pressure on the wound I inflicted. "You owe me."

"No," I groaned, the word barely recognizable.

With her free hand, she pulled the blade from mine.

"Yes," she countered, a bloody smile on her face. She thrust my blade into my stomach. "You owe me your fucking blood, you bitch. What I got at Mason's wasn't enough."

I arched forward, gasping for air but unable to find any. The lack of oxygen burned my lungs. White lights popped in front of my eyes. The world grew to a loud silence around me, her words nothing in the void.

My body trembled. My heart thudded in my throat, pushing more and more blood toward the wound as it fought to keep everything going but pushed me closer to death.

"Blood?" I choked out.

"You're always at that dump. Easy target," she said, and twisted my blade. "Piss you off and you go dumb. But I didn't get enough blood."

She took my blood during our fight?

A rancid smell snaked through the room, of burnt blood and flesh, followed by a single cough. Mom flicked her eyes momentarily to her

Companion. When he twitched and pushed up, numbness overtook my body.

He wasn't allergic to bullets.

His face blurred before me as he neared, but dark shadows swirled on his cheeks. The blood on his arms gone, likely absorbed in the magic he used with the bullets.

They exchanged words, my ears and brain unable to process as my body succumbed to the chaos.

My eyes blinked, the dark world welcoming. But then they opened again. My mom and her Companion had carried me into the room they'd left moments before. The closet was out of a horror movie. The cement had long grooves dug into it. The remnants of blood darkened the curves.

An altar sat on a small platform. The cement block also had designs carved into it. A lifeless Soulless or Vessel lay on the slab. The smells were too much to tell the difference. The body was contorted into an unnatural fetal position, the fingers gnarled and the flesh gray.

Her Companion shoved the body off, exposing the chest with hunks of flesh missing. My stomach turned and fear speared my heart.

She was going to sacrifice me.

It took both of them to lift me onto the slab, my legs and arms thrashing of their own accord. The numbness in my brain bled away, leaving violent and overwhelming panic.

"Hold her," Mom yelled, her words finally audible above the buzz in my mind.

"Keep the blood on the altar," he grunted, pressing my wrists down.

With strength that wasn't mine, I bucked against the table. My foot connected with my mom's face. Blood burst from her nose, spraying my pants and the table. In the motion back, I dug my nails into his fleshy hands.

Instead of loosening his hold, he pressed tighter. My wrist snapped under his pressure, the searing pain coursing through me. I thrashed against it, but couldn't get purpose.

"You little bitch," Mom said, coming to stand beside me.

So many thoughts bubbled in my brain, but my voice failed me.

She laughed in response.

"Do you have the stuff?" he asked, his focus on Mom.

"I wasn't expecting her so soon," Mom said, glaring at me. "But then I guess she was always ruining plans."

Bitch.

"We need her alive," he said.

"We'll keep her as long as possible." Mom moved away from me to a metal table off to the side.

What. The. Fuck.

I willed my body to move, to do something, but it was broken and empty, a prison for me to watch them through.

She returned with my blade in her hand.

"Now, this will hurt, a lot," she said with a cheery smile. "We enjoy your screams, so please have at it."

She sliced down my side, the searing pain dulled by all the other pain consuming my body.

"Oh, I've been hoping for your screams," Mom said with a pout.

I grunted, unable to create words.

She stabbed my blade into my gut, twisting it twice.

My vision tunneled and petered out. Only agonizing pain remained.

Finders' Handbook

Shadowtalker - A person who can speak with shadows. Some Vessels are born with the ability. The only other way to obtain it is illegally through the death arts. It is a rare ability.

CHAPTER 7

DEATH WAS PEACEFUL. Resurrection was a painful bitch.

And it smelled of debt and blood.

A thousand voices sounded around me, stealing my thoughts. Sensation stole across my body. Pinpricks stabbed into my muscles, making them contort until everything shattered around me. Everything stopped in an instant. Sound. Feeling. Breath.

I blinked, but nothing came into focus. Only stale darkness surrounded me, numbing my mind and singeing my nerves. The aftermath of a fight gone wrong.

I willed my limbs to move, to resist oblivion, but my muscles didn't contract. Instead, I floated alone in an abyss, independent of my body.

The silence was deafening, like being locked in a closet overnight, waiting for my mom to return or a Soulless to break in.

A scream rolled on my tongue, but nothing sounded. It pooled in my stomach before bubbling up and clogging up my throat, the sharp acid scorching my tongue, triggering my body to fight.

"Dessa, breathe," the air commanded. Liquid sensation oozed down my throat, challenging me, demanding me to respond.

I grasped on to survival, the will to escape overwhelming. The primal urge burned through the fog and limbo, forcing my body to violently shudder and gasp.

The breath was like swallowing smoke. Searing tendrils clawed down my throat. My lungs burned. I coughed to release the poison and bring in life. Life that wasn't mine.

"That's my girl," the air trumpeted. But the voice wasn't my mom's or Tones'. It was something else. Something from my dreams. My nightmares.

Then the world hissed around me. It wasn't a flash forward scene like in the movies. It was an awareness first of sound. The slither of movement, the rustle of murmured voices.

Then smell. Mustiness and bleach dampened the air, burning my nose.

Touch was next, like icy fingers snaked around my flesh. I was lying on smooth cement. The cold, hard surface seeped through my clothes and chilled my skin.

Tingles overwhelmed my flesh, forcing my body to shiver and cringe, my muscles and tendons scrunching together in a painful grasp on life.

"Dessa." My name sounded like a breath in the air, the voice still eerily familiar and yet unknown. Phantom hands smoothed across my face, startling me.

The moist word tickled my ears, causing me to draw my shoulders up to my ears to protect them.

I blinked again, and although the area was still pitch-black, the shadows swam in long slender strands and then rippled into squat, round bulges. Individual presences slithered against each other, scrambling around, merging and separating again.

"Dessa," they hissed, unique from the earlier voice.

The shadows could talk to me.

I wasn't a Shadowtalker; at least, I hadn't been. If you weren't born one, it was a horrific process with death arts to become one. I'd wanted it for my job hunting Soulless but had relied on my other senses and night-vision goggles. It was an easy obstacle to circumvent. Unlike death.

I blinked to clear my mind, to remember.

Something felt off. Wrong. A flash of a memory sliced my thoughts and I saw my mother's serene face, her flaxen hair, and sharp blue eyes.

Her sweet smile had contorted, and her eyes dulled.

I gasped and tried to push myself up. My mother was a Choicer.

I was supposed to be hunting her.

And I'd found her.

I'd followed her rules, too.

I pushed myself up to a sitting position with my legs still pronged in front of me. The sudden rush of movement should have made me dizzy, but everything was clear. Pristine. I could still see the shadows moving, their dark dance reminding me I didn't belong here.

The room had no windows, but a small door was tucked in the corner. Glass fragments from the shattered lightbulb littered the floor like discarded confetti, crunched and smashed, but I could still see. I rubbed my eyes, but I still saw the room as if it were day.

But if I was in the room, where was my mother?

The tang of aged blood hung in the air. Looking down, I found the source. Thick blood pooled on the floor in deep channels, but there wasn't a body. Nor footprints to show she'd escaped.

My hands rested on the cement slab, catching in the slicked grooves. Smears of blood dotted the channels carved into the surface, designed to draw blood away from a sacrifice. My perch was a blood altar.

My body… had been the sacrifice?

I swallowed and ran a finger over the pad of my thumb, feeling my pulse. Blood coursed through my veins and pounded in my ears, reminding me I was alive. It couldn't be my blood. I couldn't have been the sacrifice…

"Dessa," the shadows whispered again.

My neck hairs raised, and my muscles tightened.

I instinctively reached for the hilt of my silver blade on my hip. My stomach curled and I cursed, realizing it was empty. My fingers tightened into fists.

"Dessa," they whispered again.

I swallowed. I didn't want to acknowledge I could hear them.

That I'd crossed an impossible line.

Necromancy was the art of the Soulless. One used to control and contort. One needed to talk to the shadows. One I refused to use.

I licked my lips and swung my feet over the slab. I nearly toppled over from a searing pain in my abdomen that shot up my side and clenched my heart. Doubling over, I grasped my stomach, and my hand hit the handle of my missing blade.

It was odd, the blade was right there. How'd I miss it? Yet, it wasn't where it was supposed to be. I grasped the handle and tugged to free it. My body lurched from the motion and my hands dampened.

I steadied myself and finally looked down.

Jutting out of my stomach was my silver blade, the hand holding it covered in fresh blood oozing from the wound.

My blood. My eyes darted back to the floor, to the pool of blood from the altar I sat on. Acid curled in my stomach.

"What the blazes?" My voice echoed in the cement walls.

"Welcome back, Dessa," the shadows hissed.

My eyes darted up in surprise, but it was too late.

The glowing black orbs locked on mine and the shadows bobbled in front of me.

"He saved you, Dessa."

"He?" my voice cracked.

Then the night came rushing back crystal clear. I had found my mother, but she hadn't been alone. Her Companion had been a master of the death arts. They'd... they'd drained me of blood.

My blood was all over the floor.

Pain twisted in my gut, forcing me to gasp and clutch my stomach. I remembered her attack. They'd kept me alive as long as possible to get the cleanest blood.

Then...

She'd killed me.

She'd sacrificed me using the death arts.

I'd followed every rule my mother had taught me in life. I'd obeyed the Finders' Law.

All had failed me.

But something intervened. Something that used the forbidden death arts to bring me back.

There was no way my mother had helped me… Tones didn't work with the death arts. Or anyone I associated with.

A familiar voice tickled my thoughts. A satisfied chuckle reverberated down my spine. Who—or what—had brought me back?

The shadows' chattering scratched at my ears, pulling my attention back. Their agitated dance bordered on paranoid.

"What?" I finally spat at them.

"You owe him. He'll expect payment."

"Him?" My voice echoed in the room.

"Your father."

DESSA'S RULES OF SURVIVAL

ONLY OWN WHAT YOU CAN CARRY

CHAPTER 8

THE ROOM'S door hadn't been locked and the shadows didn't try to stop me from leaving. But why would they? Shadows lurked everywhere, always watching, always talking. We're just usually fortunate enough not to be able to hear them.

Unfortunately, I could hear them now, and their presence was a weight on my shoulders. I covered my ears to muffle their garbled whispers. Their unrelenting chatter tortured my scrambled mind. I had enough of my own thoughts to make my ears bleed. Not only had my mom sacrificed me, but my father had... what? Somehow resurrected me?

The warehouse was empty as I pushed out of the emergency exit I'd planned to carry my mom through.

There were few people out as I stumbled home. Probably for the best, as my shirt and any visible skin were stained in drying blood.

My apartment was as I'd left it. I worked in the dark, in the shadows. The irony was not lost on me that they now could talk to me. However, I hadn't *lived* in the shadows.

I flipped the light switch on, flooding the room with light and killing the shadows. But not my thoughts. Deafening silence descended on the room. I rubbed my ears and shook my head to gather my wits.

As I entered each room, I switched the lights on before entering or looking in. Traversing the five hundred square feet in less than a minute, all the lights were on.

The absurdity and cruelty of the situation bubbled within me. With nothing else to flip, my body trembled as I slumped against the wall. Tears rimmed my eyes, threatening to spill over. But they wouldn't stop if I let them fall. I blinked them back, choking a shrill laugh.

My mother had gone against all the Finders' Laws and become a Choicer. As a human Practitioner, she had limited powers to conjure magic with spells, but that hadn't been enough for her. She was scrambling for power among the Soulless. But why? Yes, she coveted money, but never spent it. Soulless sacrificed to gain more power. It wasn't a full transfer, but when they sacrificed a Vessel, the Vessel's powers bolstered the Soulless. Some Soulless could defy death, such as Isaiah had done with the bullets. Some could bend people to their will. What could a human Finder want with Soulless powers? She chose to practice the death arts to get more power.

She killed me.

My mother killed me. No, she sacrificed me.

My father... interfered. She'd killed me. Of that, I was sure. But he brought me back to my broken body, created a debt, and expected me to pay him back. He'd be disappointed. Fuck, I didn't even know who he was. Or how'd he known... Or why...

Acid pooled in my mouth and reality clutched my stomach. Running to the bathroom, I hurled into my porcelain throne, my thoughts settling as my body emptied itself.

I sat trembling with my head over the bowl for longer than necessary, my elbows propped on the cold plastic rim, holding my head in my hands. I blinked and let my gaze unfocus. A swirl of my blue hair fell across my face, reminding me I needed to touch up my brown roots. I pushed it aside with my bloodied hand, smearing blood across my cheek.

When nothing more came up, I stood and wiped my mouth with the hem of my shirt.

Fuck. With my brain too crowded to think, my body went on autopilot as if I'd been in a fight with a Soulless and needed to assess injuries.

My shirt was soaked through and still slightly damp. I tossed it in the tub to rinse out. The knife hole was low enough that I could sew it together without affecting the fit. No sense in wasting a shirt.

The shirt would be easy to fix, but my body was another story. Blood covered my arms, face, and neck, drying into dark, flaky clumps.

I finally looked down to my torso. Whatever death art used to bring me back had healed the wound. The small line faded with each minute. On a whim, I picked up my trimmers and sliced across my finger. Blood blossomed and I cursed. The bite of the blade smarted, and I sucked on my finger.

My blood, still normal red, tasted like my blood. I wasn't a blood drinker, but I'd cut myself enough times to know what I tasted like. I didn't notice an odd aftertaste or a different color. So, whatever he did to bring me back had regenerated my own blood. That both comforted and concerned me. If I hadn't seen my blood on the floor, or my knife in my stomach, or remembered the pain in too-vivid detail, I would have thought I dreamed it. I was standing in my bathroom as if nothing unusual had happened.

I stared at myself. I was supposed to be dead. But my blood still darkened my blade along with my skin and also pumped inside me. I could talk to the shadows. I had night vision. What else could I do, and why?

Why?

Why had he saved me? He wasn't a benevolent being. I didn't know him, at least not to my knowledge. Had I made a bargain? I searched my mind. No one but her and her Companion, who clearly helped kill me, were in the room. I'd followed the rules.

I flipped my wrists over, looking for the golden scroll to mark an agreement with a Soulless, but my wrists were clear except for my known scars. I paused and looked around the room. It wasn't an illusion, was it?

I sighed, closed my eyes, and flipped the light switch off.

The noise was deafening. The angry clatter fought to be heard. Dozens of whispers scolded me and berated me for shunning them and locking them out. But they were shadows. They'd reappear at every turn.

I turned so I wasn't facing the mirror. I hated the mirror in the dark, and I wasn't sure how much worse it'd be with night vision. Most fear the reflection in the mirror. What is trapped there, wanting to escape? What lurks behind us that we're ignorant of and purposely avoiding? The mirror reflects back more than our image.

Instead, I faced the painted brick wall and braced myself for the shadows.

They swirled before me in an angry dance. The billowy forms shifted and contorted into exaggerated human forms before merging back together only to separate again.

"Where am I?" I asked steadily, making sure my voice didn't crack.

"You don't know? Did she hit your head?"

I forced myself not to roll my eyes. The gesture turned into a long, blank stare.

"Am I really at my apartment?" I worked to stop my teeth from clenching.

"Where else would you find such ugly towels?"

My glance flicked to the yellow towels with dancing ducks embroidered on them. They'd been free and they were still fluffy, a perfect combination.

I ran a hand through my hair and grimaced when it got caught in dried blood.

I was home. I was brought back. I wouldn't call it being reborn. Though there was blood and likely screaming and cursing my father, I wasn't anew or branded, yet. I'd have to figure out his game while figuring out what to do about my mom. I still had her target sheet.

My stomach clenched at that thought. The growing pains of hunger fought with my anxiety from dying and both came out as foam in the toilet.

I wiped my mouth again and flipped on the light switch. My thoughts spun without purchase. I needed a distraction so I could think about answers to my questions. I also needed to shower and rethink my life, and I didn't need the shadows' opinions to do so.

I stood under the scalding hot water until a tinge of lukewarm snaked through the water and then hurriedly shampooed, conditioned, and body scrubbed.

My rosy skin tingled as I wrapped the duck towel around my body. I didn't worry about the smidges of blood still left in my crevices. I wore blood as a contractor wears dust. It's part of the job. I tucked my hair behind my ears and grabbed a T-shirt and shorts from the laundry basket that I kept in the bathroom. Why bother trekking around to get dressed?

Maybe I needed pizza. I licked my lips and walked to the kitchen. The Formica countertops were chipped and had decades of stains older than me, but with it came charm. I slid the trim from the side lining the stove. Tucked underneath in long, flat sheets should be several twenties.

However, in place of my twenties was a business card. I knew the owner before reading it. The scarlet red card had familiar gold writing scrawled across it.

It was my mother's.

The bitch.

She killed me. Cleaned me out. And left her fucking business card tucked under my counter.

Out of morbid curiosity I grabbed a butter knife and flicked the card out of the counter hidey-hole. I didn't trust her and followed Rule Six: Don't let them touch you. She could've laced it with anything.

Written in the upper corner: "You shouldn't have intervened."

I clamped my teeth down and my jaw throbbed. Who the fuck was it meant for? John or my dad? Either way, how the fuck would they know where I lived? Why did he care?

Next to the message was a loopy unconnected heart. That was the part that finally broke me. Next thing I knew I was on the floor, sobbing into my hands. My eyes bulged and burned from dehydration, and my vision blurred. My face throbbed from crying.

My life was a joke. I was a joke. I was a failed Finder. I had no other skills. I hadn't been to school since I was expelled for exposing my principal as a Soulless. My mom had taken that as a sign that I had the gift. The gift. Bullshit.

I could flush out the Soulless. I didn't know most others couldn't, and Mom had called it a gift. I went around exposing all I saw like we were playing *I-spy*. I'd been paying our bills since I was six.

I hadn't lost a target yet.

Until my mom.

Yep, my mom had taught me all my skills and used me to feed us.

And then, she went and became a Choicer.

The card fluttered to the ground and I stared at it. She'd made me and then killed me. I screamed into my hands and banged my head back on the counter. What was left? I'd failed.

I FAILED.

I bellowed into the room. My voice cracked from crying but was still guttural.

My neighbor threw something against the wall and yelled indiscernible words at me. I assumed he wanted me to shut up. He could go to hell. Everyone could go to hell.

I was a joke.

I stared at the card for a long time until the red morphed and deformed before me into a bloodied vision of past targets. I was alive again. I had a chance again.

I'd make that bitch pay for raising me to believe all my truths and then becoming the lie.

I'd make her pay for killing me and letting me rise again.

Ha. Who was I kidding? She'd kill me again.

CHAPTER 9

I SLUMPED in my usual spot and nodded toward Benny. His cold glare pierced through my skull.

I rubbed a hand over my forehead. The bass of the music vibrated through my shoes and into my bones. I felt the violent throb pulse through, and I savored the sensation. It blocked out the sound of my own blood pumping, reminding me of my mom.

"You're a mess," Tones' voice chided.

I shrugged. I wouldn't argue. She was right.

Despite not looking up, I still felt the disapproving sneer. The insistent toe tapping wore through the music and I ground my teeth as the tip-tap echoed in my ears, reminding me of my heartbeat. She wanted me to answer her unspoken question. Tell her my secrets.

"It's early for you," Tones said and brushed against me as she slid into the chair. "Very early."

Although I didn't look up, I got a full view of her curvy body. Her purple velvet dress was slit to mid-thigh, and she wore sheer tights over her fleshy legs.

"Dessa," Tones said, her voice finally the soft whisper that made me want to curl against her and cry. Many times, after training with my mom had turned bloody, Tones would feed and hug me.

I scratched my head and blinked to force the tears back.

Her arm snaked around my shoulders, her warmth heavy and

comforting on me as she drew me in. The smell of expensive perfume and fries wafted up, enveloping me in an aura of old comforts and long-lost security.

"Dessa, baby, what's going on?" Her words muffled in my hair as she held me close.

I sniffled but my mouth refused to open.

Tones' hands curved around my jaw and lifted my face up. I kept my eyes cast down, but she hummed and made a clicking sound.

Involuntarily, I lifted my gaze to meet hers. Tones' warm green eyes searched my face, confused and scared by what she saw reflected back. The deep lines around her eyes crinkled and for a moment she looked her age. Her silver hair never aged her, but when she looked at me like I was a volatile toddler, her decades darkened her face.

"Dessa, were you dead?"

Tones had powers I didn't understand. She wasn't a Vessel. She didn't have the smell or aura. She was a Practitioner, a human who could wield magic with spells, like my mom but more powerful. We weren't related, but she'd often watched me back in the days I was in school and before my mother made most of her money exploiting my abilities. She kept me fed and hydrated while we used her bar.

As a child I sat there, twirling a straw in a Shirley Temple while Mom worked. A three-year-old at a bar didn't entice the clientele Tones had wanted. Tones wanted adult predators after adult predators. She said all patrons wanted something from the others. Sometimes they aligned and both parties' needs were met. Often, one took more than the other. In the end, most just lost parts of themselves in the transactions but always sought to recoup their losses the next go round.

Tones didn't care what the people sought if it was adult based; she didn't know the details of their wants and therefore the legality of it, and it kept business running through her bar.

"Dessa," Tones' voice cut through my foggy thoughts.

"Tones," I sighed and fell into her caressing hands.

"Who killed you?" Her voice barely a whisper.

I didn't ask how she knew. I accepted that she did. She was Tones.

"Dessa." Her voice grew agitated.

"My target," I choked.

Her eyes searched mine, trying to catch a lie. "You've never lost one before."

"I know."

"It had to be someone who knew you," she said. Her voice tapered off, leaving me room to answer.

I shrugged and sniffed. It wasn't a proud moment.

"Who… who brought you back?" She smoothed a hand over my head.

My eyes fell to the ground. My mom killing me made enough sense to me, Choicer or not. But I didn't understand why my father would intervene, much less bring me back.

"Well," an annoyingly delightful familiar voice rang out. "If it isn't Dessa the Destroyer in the flesh. Nice to see that you're alive."

I rolled my eyes and growled, tightening my muscles as I pulled away from Tones. I didn't need his "I told you so's" and I didn't need him telling me to give back the target sheet. Even if he was right that I wasn't ready for my mom, I didn't want to hear it again. Not right after she'd killed me.

Tones removed her hands from my face and whipped around to smack the source of the taunt: Oliver.

"Hey!" he roared and rubbed his hand over the bright red spot on his handsome face. Of course I noticed he hadn't shaved his dark, scruffy beard that matched his tousled dark locks.

"Apologize."

He huffed and glared at her, his thick brows furrowed over his hazel eyes. His straight nose flared out. Through clenched teeth he said, "I'm sorry Dessa."

"Whatever," I said. He wasn't. It was his version of "I told you so." This was the same old song and dance we'd played since we were kids. Tones didn't want kids in the bar. She would take me from the bar and shuffle me off to a tucked-back office to wait for my mom. Her kids often played back there, too, when she worked.

Oliver was the oldest, the closest in age to me, and didn't like that his mom had taken an interest in me and babied me while he had to watch his younger brothers. He saw me as the annoying little sister who needed protecting. Not wanting a big brother, I did everything I could to annoy him.

"Should I apologize for getting your target, too?" Dark eyes finally glared at me in challenge. His lips were pressed into a flat line.

What the fuck?

"You got my target?" I asked measuredly, refusing to look at his hazel eyes. There was no way John gave it to him. It was unheard of to give a target to another Finder because it brought too much notice when multiple people were looking for the same one. At least, that's what John claimed. I never had a target remain open long enough for another to snatch it. And my mom was way above his pay grade and ability. Oliver had to be lying.

"You died," he said matter-of-factly, and his jaw twitched.

My stomach twisted.

"How do you know that?" his mother and I asked simultaneously.

"John said so."

Tones stared between us, calculating our reactions. She pointed at me and I gulped. "Who was your target?"

I shook my head. I didn't want to admit it. I didn't want to admit I failed at it. I didn't want to admit she was even a target. That she had bested me, again, when it really counted. I'd tell Tones after I caught her. After I figured out what my dad wanted. After Tones couldn't try to stop me.

"Oliver?" she said.

Oliver looked at me, and then his mom. I was shocked to see the decision warring on his face. I'd thought he'd have sold me out right away. Gotten in another free "told you so."

"What is wrong with you two? You always tell me your targets." When neither Oliver nor I spoke, she went for the guilt. "You use my bar to get information, and you won't even tell me? Am I in danger? Will this come here?"

I groaned and waved my hand toward Oliver, giving him permission to share.

"Claudine," he whispered, and I felt his eyes watching me.

Heat crept up my cheeks, and I was thankful for the dimly lit bar.

"What?" Tones barked. Her eyes flared, and her gaze searched around the bar in an unfocused attempt to understand what he said.

"She's a Choicer," I croaked. The word acid on my tongue.

Tones' eyes narrowed at me, and she shook her head slightly.

"She's not," Tones muttered.

She gave my mom too much credit. My mom was a greedy bitch. She'd finally crossed the line to get more power. Even if it went against what she taught me.

Oliver cleared his throat and flinched looking at me. "Mom, she's the target. She's listed as a Choicer."

"They're wrong."

I gave Oliver a pleading look. Her loyalty to my mom was fogging her reasoning.

I barely noticed the door opening, but I did notice Tones stiffen and her gaze fixate at the front.

I followed her gaze and my mouth dried. My vision blurred. My mom had entered the establishment. I clenched my fist around my hilt and stood.

"That bitch," I growled.

"No." Tones moved in front of me and flicked her hands behind her back. "Hide."

I wasn't going to hide. I was going to finish this. I'd pay that bitch back for killing me, for being a Choicer.

Oliver wrapped a hand around my arm and tugged me toward him. His action caught me off guard, and I stumbled into him.

My mind momentarily stalled, focusing on his hand on my arm and my body pressed hard against him. Tingles raced along my nerves. He wrapped his other hand around my cheek, and in one quick movement his lips were on mine.

My eyes shot open, and I probably yipped from surprise. It wasn't my best move, but I was living a tween dream of mine, and maybe a modern-day dream of mine, too. Heat curled in me as his hand on my arm shifted to my back, pressing me into him.

His soft lips moved on my own, and he whispered against my lips, "Play along."

I stood frozen, my brain and heart warring with each other. I wanted to kiss him back, live a moment I thought about too often as a teen, but it felt like a practical joke. There was no way he'd voluntarily kiss me. Hell, he even said play along. He probably hated it. It was a farce. I didn't want to fake kiss him.

Tones shifted, and my gaze flickered to her. Oliver's large frame blocked me completely from seeing my mother, and I realized then why he was kissing me. He didn't want her to see me. He was fucking trying to protect me. I didn't care if she saw me. I'd kill her here and now and drag in her body all the same. Even if I could never step foot in the bar again.

I heard a hiss from the shadows but then Oliver licked my lips. That got my attention. My lips... involuntarily... moved against his. My brain flashed *no* as my heart picked up pace. His eyes were hooded, and his calloused hand tenderly caressed my face. The soft kiss heated as his hand fisted in my hair by my ear. He was a damn good actor. I almost believed he wanted to kiss me.

"Where the fuck is that bitch?" Mom's voice rang out over the music.

Oliver's hand guided to my waist to walk me backward. Instead, I pushed him back, breaking the kiss. His eyes, hazy, flicked up to meet my gaze. "Dessa, don't," he breathed.

"What the fuck you want?" I yelled back.

The patron's heads bounced to stare at me.

Tones' gaze flicked to me, her eyes large with fear.

"You're fucking mine," Mom yelled. Her face was screwed up in hatred, her mouth open and baring her teeth.

Everyone's eyes turned back to her.

"Your fucking sacrifice didn't work," I screamed. I thudded a hand on my chest. "Still my blood."

A look of shock washed over the patrons.

"You tried to steal my blood and life!" I yelled.

"I got it!" she yelled back. "It is mine!"

"Not anymore."

"I should have cut you to pieces!"

"Your mistake," I snarled.

She laughed. Dark shadows swam across her face.

"If that fucker hadn't intervened." Her face contorted, the shadows rippled, and her eyes flashed.

My breath caught in my chest. What the fuck type of Choicer was she?

"He doesn't give a shit about you," she spat as she pushed through people stalled to gawk.

I knew that, but curiosity is a fucker. "Then why'd he stop you?"

"Stop me? Dumb fuck. He waited until we were done."

Her lips twisted into a gnarled smile. She was lying. I wasn't sure about what, exactly, but it didn't matter. I didn't trust her, anyway.

I heard a hiss again, and a familiar scratchy voice said, "Run, Dessa."

"Go," Tones whispered in a panic, standing between Mom and me.

Before I could move, Mom used some sort of magic and leaped onto a table. The people there fell back, their bodies graying.

"What the fuck," I breathed.

"Go!" Tones screamed, shoving me toward Oliver.

"No," I yelled and darted at my mom. Fuck her. I couldn't let her get away with becoming a Choicer, trying to kill me, and then invading Mason's Bar.

Mom jumped to the next table and the next one after that, narrowing our distance.

I hopped onto a chair and then the table, like a normal person.

Mom met me on the next table. Her fingers lashed out for me, gray swirls shooting from her fingers.

I kicked at her knee. She lurched forward, catching her balance, but her gray cloudy stuff dissipated.

"I'm going to kill you with my bare hands," she gritted out. "I'll tear you limb from limb."

Kicking at her again, I grabbed my blade. She anticipated the attack, as I expected she would, and juked to the side. I slashed my knife across her stomach. Her blood sprang from the wound before resealing in moments.

With inhuman speed, her fingers wrapped around my neck. They squeezed at my throat, her nails digging into my flesh. Blood oozed from the gashes. Silvery yellow stars popped in front of my eyes before gray mist clouded her out. My lungs burned, and my blood singed my veins.

"I won't stop until you're dead," Mom gritted out. Despite all her magic, her breath still smelled like her. Still smelled of peppermint and chocolate. Not death and decay as a Choicer should. "He won't be able to bring you back again."

My knees buckled as I gasped for air.

"Enough!" Tones roared. The lightbulbs shattered, colored glass flying everywhere.

Mom flinched but didn't release her hold.

"Claudine!" Tones roared.

Mom screamed. Her grip loosened and she clasped her heart.

"You aren't strong enough to kill me, witch," Mom gasped. She fell to her knees.

"No, but I can stop you," Tones grunted, her hands in a gnarled pose. "Run, Dessa."

Mom's blue eyes, filled with hatred and pain, flicked to me. She gasped for breath, each one causing her to flinch. "I'll drain your blood. When you don't have Tones to protect you."

Oliver's strong arms threaded under my arms and hoisted me up. The light changed and I realized we were in the hall. He continued to carry me until he pushed against something, and the cold air surrounded us, and the lone parking lot light shone down on us in coppery neon.

He set me down and withdrew his hands from my body. I was instantly cold. His raspy breath cut the quiet night in sharp bursts.

He ran a hand in his dark hair as his eyes darted around. He turned and walked a few paces away, turned to look back at me, and then took a few steps toward me with his hands out and his gaze on my lips. He stopped again, turned away, and muttered, "Shit."

He ran a hand over his mouth and looked back at me. His heated gaze caressed me and then he blinked. His eyes shuttered, becoming unreadable. He slowed his pacing and took a large breath. His body calmed and his demeanor changed back to cold and aloof. His Finder pose.

"What the hell?" I yelled.

His head jerked back in surprise, and then he frowned. "I had to get you out of there."

"We coulda just brought her in!"

"How?" he seethed. Oliver stepped closer and extended his hands again. He caught himself and folded them across his broad chest.

"I don't care," I whispered loudly. "She killed me!"

Tears welled behind my eyes and I cursed. I blinked to keep them at bay, but based on the way his face softened, he'd noticed them anyway.

He stepped forward again, reaching for me, but didn't pull back this time. He yanked my arms and pulled me to his chest. When he wrapped his arms around me, I unproudly snuggled against his warm, hard chest. I'd take a few moments of stolen solace from him. His mother was protecting us. Mine killed me. And then tried again.

"Dessa, it's not safe for you."

I bristled. I could take care of myself. I didn't need a big brother.

"Don't do that," he said into my hair. "I'm not denying your skill. She'll keep coming at you."

I put my hands on his chest to push away from him.

"She already killed you once." His voice cracked with emotion and I involuntarily looked up. His face twisted in anger, but he quickly masked it with his stoic expression when he caught me watching him. "You need to get out of town. Stay out of her sight."

I closed my eyes. He wasn't wrong. I wasn't safe. My apartment was always vacant and ready for my departure. She already had my hidden cash. I could swing by any ATM machine, withdraw the cash I had, and never see this town again.

I had nothing left here. I was free. I could start a new life. Otherwise, what? If I couldn't bring her in, I'd have to watch my back forever, waiting for her next attack. She'd be unrelenting. She'd target everyone to draw me out. Everyone I knew would be in danger. But if I left, she'd win, in a way. She'd have scared me off. Bested me. Even though my father brought me back. It'd been in vain. I made no deal with him. I owed him nothing. They could duke out the reasons why he did it.

Would she track me through my targets, though? It'd be easy for her to locate me that way since she knew the Finder system. I'd only ever known being a Finder, the shadows, the hunt. Could I make it out there without hunting? All the questions I wondered before came swirling back. This was my chance for a fresh slate, and not to indefinitely be Dessa, Claudine's daughter. I could carve my own path. A quiet path without blood. If one could even exist.

My life had followed the path my mom paved all the way to my death. She'd exploited me since I was six and I hadn't had a choice. Now I did. I could make life what I wanted. Have choices. Whatever that may be. I'd miss Tones, Oliver, Duke, and Alan, but they were much safer with me gone. I only brought death and pain.

I smiled up at him, and he returned it.

"You're right." I swallowed.

"I'll let Duke and Alan know. If you need anything…" His voice caught, and he shook his head. He reached a hand into his jacket pocket and produced a phone. It was a classic burner.

I nodded, and not knowing what to say, I muttered, "Have a nice life."

His smile dropped and he looked down at the parking lot pavement.

Before he lifted his eyes, I melded into the shadows and walked away. My heart in my throat, tears stinging my eyes, and his phone clutched in my hands.

DESSA'S RULES OF SURVIVAL

RELY ON NO ONE

CHAPTER 10

SHADOWS SWARMED around me as I navigated the narrow lanes between the tables. A tray of drinks perched on my hand above my shoulder. After boarding a bus three weeks ago and traveling nine hundred miles away, I'd hopped off the bus when warm air greeted me instead of the sting of the lingering winter. The air was brined with salt and going any farther east would have put me in the ocean. Now I worked at The Red Fox, a tavern two blocks down from my apartment. My hair was ombred red and my eyes tinted blue with contacts.

Setting the tray down, I doled out the beverages, not taking in the human faces around me. Manchester, a city on the coast, had Soulless —all cities did—but I purposely settled in an almost all-human section to avoid the draw of the hunt. Avoid the constant need to round them up and haul them to an Agency. Avoid exposing my location. And hopefully stay out of sight of my mom or dad.

"Dessa," the shadow blob called to me.

I ignored them.

"Dessa," the shadows sounded again.

"What would you like to order?" I asked, plastering a smile on my face. A chunk of red hair slipped in front of my eyes and I tucked it back. The group over-ordered food and didn't look like the doggy-bag type. Looked like free dinner for me tonight.

As I took their orders, my neck hairs raised, and my fingers furled into fists. A Soulless had come in. Forcing my attention to stay on the group, I itched to turn around and see what was there.

My nose flared as I darted back to the kitchen to scope the room.

"Dessa," the shadows hissed.

"What?" I breathed.

"Place the order," the shadows moaned beside me as I rounded the counter.

Shit. I veered off to the server stand. My fingers nimbly entered the information as I scanned the dining room. The place hadn't been remodeled since the eighties or seventies. Red indoor-outdoor carpet lined the room. Thick oak tables with ornate chairs crowded together to fit as many people as possible. Grease and beer filled the air, but a hint of briny seafood undercut it.

Around the room, regulars sat drinking beer and soft drinks, and eating overcooked, unflavored food. My eyes fell to the corner where a slender woman with straight blonde hair and sunglasses on sat staring at me. Real smooth, sunglasses in a dimly lit bar.

When I finished entering the order, I sauntered toward her table.

"Don't," the shadows hissed.

"Who is she?" I whispered, keeping my gaze set on her table.

They tittered.

"Not helpful," I gritted out.

Had Mom caught me? Was she sending scouts? None of it seemed like her. She'd rather publicly embarrass me herself.

"Need something?" I asked, siding up to the table. Only an old faint whiff of death clung to her. She was a Level Three at best.

Her eyebrows arched over her glasses, and her lips ticked up in a smirk.

"Nope," she said sweetly. "I'm already being served."

"Who sent you?"

"Sent me?"

"How much is she paying you?"

"She?" she questioned, her face scrunching in confusion.

Oh fuck. If it wasn't my mom, who was it?

My neck hairs raised, and I whipped around. Nothing was out of the ordinary. No one new had entered, but my adrenaline coursed in my veins for the hunt. The Soulless behind me wasn't the threat setting me off. She was a decoy.

"Looking for someone?" the Soulless murmured.

"Who's here?" I asked turning to face her.

"Just you and me and a bunch of humans *now*, sweetheart," she drawled.

The shadows stirred around my feet, their hisses frantic and a blur.

The Soulless lifted her chin to get a look, her brow furrowed. She lifted her reptilian eyes over her glasses to glower at me. She tsked.

"Problem?" I asked.

"Not for me," she said.

"Maggie," a cook's voice boomed behind me. Maggie being my known name at the bar.

Fuck. I had an order up.

I turned on my heels and went to the counter.

"It's gone now," the shadows blabbered.

"What was there?" I asked. My gaze flickered back to the now-empty table where the Soulless had sat.

They hissed a shriek.

"Should I be worried?" I asked.

"Yes," they agreed in unison.

On my way home, I took a detour through the small town, the feeling of being watched trailing me. I stopped at the library for new books and grabbed a six-pack of cola from the corner store to go with my doggy-bag leftovers. My nerves had settled, and I asked the shadows, "Is it safe to go home?"

"For now," they answered.

I pushed the door open to my one-bedroom apartment.

My apartment was a repeat of the last, but I'd painted it a faint yellow instead of the white to bring some cheer to it. The furniture was new street finds. My laundry basket housed in the bathroom had my work clothes—polo shirts for the sports bar and jeans. Besides my work polos, I had two T-shirts. They didn't have holes or bloodstains. I was living large.

I tossed the leftovers on a paper plate and slid it into the microwave to nuke. My eyes slid past the corner drawer. The only thing inside of it was a drained phone.

I'd stared at the phone Oliver gave me many nights, wanting to reach out to the one number that he had pre-programmed into the phone. I wanted to hear his voice. Continue the fantasy I'd enjoyed. But that's what it was, a fantasy. He'd played a big brother part, protected me, and sent me away.

Many nights I'd hoped he'd call just to check in on me. But I guess it slipped his mind, or I wasn't important enough to follow up on. Any possibility stung, and I ended up tossing the phone in a kitchen drawer. I'd wanted to toss it in the garbage, but I couldn't find the time or energy to do so.

When I texted Duke to let him know what happened, a message kicked back saying the number was invalid.

I let it charge while the food started to pop in the microwave, the grease making a mess as it heated up. The screen lit up, but as usual, no notifications. Frustrated at myself for giving into the silly hope, I tossed the phone and charger back in the drawer.

Cool night air brushed past me as I exited The Red Fox. The hoodie I wore was enough to keep me warm. The shadows swirled around my feet, weaving around the streetlamp's glow. Unlike where I had lived previously, the streets had a plentitude of working lighting. The shadows hovered in the eaves and edging.

"Your hair needs a touch-up," a shadow jeered.

My hand fell to the top of my head. My dark roots had started to show through. I swung around and headed for the corner store a block on the other side of the tavern. My nerves skittered and my muscles tightened.

A few others strolled down the sidewalks. Too late for throngs of people, couples scurried home in hopes of whatever and others appeared haggard, like they'd finished their shifts. My gaze bounced around and I strained to listen, but nothing stood out.

The warm light of the store spilled out the windows and cast away the shadows from the corner.

I hesitated. "Am I being followed?" I whispered. My breath hung in my throat, and I licked my lips in anticipation.

The shadows bulged together, snaking around one another, before one replied, "Yes."

"Human or Soulless?" My fingers squeezed together. Something in me wanted a Soulless. To feel the hunt again. The surge of adrenaline and the release of tension. I snorted at myself. I was being a fool. Life was simple. Death didn't lurk on my door each day. My life was what I wanted.

They tittered to each other.

"They're gone now," the shadows said in agreement.

"Human or Soulless?" I gritted out again.

"Human," one finally responded.

I let out a disappointed breath.

Inside the store, I grabbed pepper spray and a new hair color—amethyst. I understood human laws, but killing a human was worse than a Vessel. Killing a Vessel was a big no-no, but it usually meant fines at most. Killing a human meant going to court unless you pled guilty.

With my new pepper spray in hand, and hair dye and a package of licorice in a sack, I exited the store. A pungent wave of death rolled on the air. The dank and musty odor watered my eyes. Adrenaline coursed through my veins and my muscles ached for the hunt. My gaze flickered around. The Soulless wasn't nearby. I sniffed the air, taking in the direction. My pulse ticked up.

"Don't," the shadows hissed at me a few feet away.

My feet carried me across the street and down the perpendicular road. The smell intensified. The street was lined with dark and locked-up businesses waiting for the morning to lure customers in. Despite everything closed up, working streetlamps dotted the streets, bathing the empty passage in artificial light.

"Dessa," the shadows hissed at me.

"Shh," I shushed back.

As I neared, the smell mixed with the metallic tang of blood. My hand automatically grabbed my blade.

Rounding the corner, I saw two Soulless together. The smell intensified, overwhelming my senses. They huddled together, appearing more as lovers than immediate threats. There weren't any Agencies within two miles of my apartment. I'd found a small one tucked into a crumbling brick building by a salvage yard five miles from my apartment. Old habits and all. In case something happened, I'd wanted to be prepared. Agencies don't broadcast what they do. They usually deploy no signage, but they are almost always in a brick building and a have specific repugnant odor they try to mask with chemicals that are repulsive to Soulless. Then reality hit. I'd have to carry them the distance since I didn't know a local Driver. I could possibly hot-wire a car and hope to not get caught...

"Dessa," the shadows hissed.

I ignored them.

Vehicles lined the streets. The older models were easier to hijack.

"Dessa, if you take them in, she'll know," the shadows said.

I stilled, my mouth drying. A phantom pain stabbed through my abdomen. Fuck. She trained me to be a Finder. Profited from it. And was still using it to control me.

MOM'S RULES

Rule Five: Never turn your back or drop eye contact

CHAPTER 11

ONE WEEK and four days later, the knock came at my door.

I'd gotten back from my shift and was kicked back on the sofa with a cola, new library book, and pillow. My intention was to read my new novel until I fell asleep. However, the knocker continued to knock despite my attempts to ignore them. The shadows were quiet and didn't stir. It was disconcerting since they never shut up, but I'd grown accustomed to their squeaky hisses and endless chatter. I didn't like their quiet.

The polite knock turned into a loud, vibrating knock. I checked the date on my new phone. It shouldn't be the landlord; rent wasn't due yet and I'd paid this month already. It could be a neighbor, but I didn't have music on, and I didn't have sugar to lend. Who had found me?

On the eighth knock that sounded like it dented my door, I finally stood up and walked to the bedroom. It was time for Mom's Rule Seven. I grabbed my pistol, a new purchase, and headed back into the room. My trusty silver blade was still strapped to me, but I didn't want to get close enough to the door to use it.

The pounding stopped and I strained to hear the person on the other side when my new phone rang, startling me. I stared at the number and didn't recognize it. I let it go to voicemail.

A single knock resonated through the apartment and then my phone rang again.

I looked to the few corners where the shadows were. They were still eerily quiet.

"Well?" I whispered to them.

A strained whisper came back, "Your father."

Well fuck. I stared at the door. I swallowed. He was being polite by not just intruding. I doubted the door was a real obstacle for him.

I holstered my gun and walked to the door. I hesitated and, sucking in a big breath to force bravado, I opened the door.

I looked into a mirror of my eyes. They were the same dark brown. Involuntarily, I searched the rest of his face and I found my pointed nose, high cheekbones, beige complexion, and smirking grin. His dark brown hair was neatly trimmed but fell past his ears in product-induced waves that looked natural. He was stocky, whereas I took after Mom's muscular physique. He was the older version of me, or I was the younger version of him.

Without a doubt, I was staring at my father. I didn't feel a biological urge to hug him, or a draw to be near him. Instead, I felt a deep brewing rage that made me want to throttle him and bash the smile from his face. It was a similar feeling I had around my mother and the Soulless.

My mother had told me about him, or more precisely, had warned me about him. Despite everything she'd done, had lied about, staring at this man I had no doubts her warnings were accurate. I wondered for the briefest moment if she'd been preparing me for this encounter. That hunting the hundreds of the Soulless over my lifetime had been in preparation for this one moment. But that would imply she cared and had been trying to protect me. I let the moment pass, but not my training.

His eyes met mine and the hairs on my neck rose, tickling my nerves. He was powerful, but I couldn't sense the normal instinct to bring him down as I did with the Soulless. He didn't have the smell of rancid blood that builds up or the sickly-sweet smell of a fresh kill. He smelled… like nothing.

I wiped my face of emotion. Even the forced ones, like a polite smile when a stranger is at your door. I'd never learned this tactic with my mother, which is probably why she was able to kill me. Instead, I let confusion pinch my face, as if I hadn't realized who he was and saw only a stranger. According to my mom, he thrived on others' emotions like many Soulless do, even those who did not use the death arts. I knew he was so much worse than the Soulless I hunted. He was real. He brought me back. He was my father. And he'd found me. He was probably who I had sensed the day the Soulless visited me.

His smirk turned into a broad toothy smile that didn't reach his brown eyes, but the cockiness did. It was an illusion; the smile of friendship and caring. I learned to read it and knew it meant danger from so many targets.

"Hey, kiddo," he said breezily and walked past me as if I'd invited him in. But I had opened the door.

I crossed my arms over my chest and stared at him.

He stopped past the entryway and surveyed the room. His eyes scanned the blank walls, the sparse furniture, and the novel lying open face down on the coffee table.

"Nice place," he lied.

"Thanks." No use in not playing along. It'd just move this along.

"Not as much blood as your last place."

I stiffened and hoped he hadn't noticed. I rubbed a hand over my eye like I was bored and tired, but it was to school my face. He'd been to my other place, and I had never known him.

"What do you want?" I asked measuredly. I wanted to ask why he brought me back, but I didn't want to imply in any way I owed him something.

His gaze shifted back to me. His eyes narrowed and scanned my face. It was the same expression I used in the mirror when I looked for traces of blood I missed.

"Straight to the point, huh?"

"Sure."

He studied me again, his ingenuine smile growing into a real one. I held my breath not to react. It was magnetizing. I wanted to smile with him, be a part of the moment. Bathe in the enjoyment. It was a trap. I didn't give any emotion back but maintained a cool and indifferent expression.

"You're just like her."

Anger rolled through me and burned my eyes. I bit my cheeks to stop from retorting. I didn't clench my fists. It's something us Finders looked for to see if we've elicited a response. Instead, I curled my toes into tight painful balls.

"Who?" I choked out, sounding almost normal.

He chuckled. It was a delightful sound that made me cringe and want to shower.

"You hungry?" he asked.

I wanted to say no. I wanted him to leave, but I didn't want to lie. That was as bad as showing emotion to a target. I took in a breath and steeled my nerves. I'd treat him like a target. I wouldn't be shocked if there was a target on him, but he didn't smell of blood, have any body enhancements, and he hadn't done anything other than be creepy. Although I knew he was the one who brought me back, I didn't have proof and he didn't smell of the arts. I didn't know if it was because it was his magic that brought me back or something else. I'd watch him, figure out his angle, learn his moves and patterns, and then, instead of bringing him into an Agent without proof he was Soulless, I'd avoid him.

I shrugged noncommittally. I willed my stomach not to rumble.

"I am," he said as if I'd asked him. "Dinner's on me."

He gestured toward the door, the serene smile still lighting his face.

"Why?"

His expression didn't change, but his demeanor did. His face darkened and I saw something skitter across it. My stomach tightened and I swallowed hard.

"You want to keep this farce up? Or are we going to have a meal?" His tone was hard and dangerous.

The sentences sounded like questions, but they were warnings. If I wanted to survive, I needed to play along.

I again shrugged and lifted my mouth in an "eh" gesture. "I have Hot Pockets," I said. "Safer than eating out."

He smirked. "Just like Claudine."

I fought the urge to flip him off.

"Do you know why your mom killed you?" my father asked as he sat on the picnic table bench outside my apartment.

Straight to it, huh?

"Guess she didn't like being hunted," I drawled, setting my Hot Pocket down in front of me as I slid onto the cracked wooden seat. One benefit of my lifestyle was not enough furniture for a guest to sit down.

"Hm," he mumbled and stared around the small greenspace butting up next to the parking lot. There were two antiquated picnic tables, worn and bleached from time and the elements. A small rickety playset sat between the two apartment buildings. Beyond was a back alley and railroad tracks.

I didn't elaborate and the silence weighed heavily. He knew why. He wanted me to ask. He wanted the power of the knowledge. The thing was, I cared why she killed me. I really did. But in the end, she tried to kill me, and he was using it as leverage, and he wasn't trustworthy.

"What do you know about your mom?" he finally asked. The words sounded so innocent, so benign. Like he asked if I wanted water or tea.

"She's a Choicer," I said. It was clearly on her target sheet.

"No," he said matter-of-factly and even shook his head slightly.

My father was the second person to say that. I ignored it. It didn't change that she was a Soulless, and his lie about her not being a Choicer wasn't enough for me to argue.

I stared at him.

He looked up and met my gaze. I didn't like that I shared his features.

"How long have you known that I exist?" I asked and took a sip of my cola. I'd assumed at a young age it'd been a short-term fling.

He smirked. Oh, I hated that smirk already. "Since you were conceived."

"Ah," I said. So, a deadbeat. Shocking.

"Your mother didn't want me around."

"Okay." I didn't care. They'd both lied about the past, and nothing was going to change. He wasn't a part of my past and I didn't want him in my future.

"When we got married—"

"What?" I sputtered, interrupting him. My surroundings blurred around me.

"Your mom and I were married."

My mouth fell open and I just stared at him.

He didn't offer any more information.

"She never said you were married," I said, realizing too late I'd shown that I'd cared.

He shrugged, and said, "It doesn't change that we were."

"Hard to believe you two didn't make it work." Even if they were married, it didn't change much. It just made him more of a deadbeat. It was a tidbit, though, I could file for later with Mom.

"You're so much like her," he said disappointedly.

"You've already said that." I didn't let the annoyance tint my words.

"Don't you care about what happened? Don't you have questions for me?"

Even if I did, I wouldn't trust his answers.

"Do you care that your mother killed you?" he asked when I remained silent, arching an eyebrow.

I choked on my can of cola. I wiped my mouth and put my can

down. I mimicked his expression and noticed his jaw twitch. "You want to put it out there? Fine. What is it you want to tell me?"

"Definitely rude like her."

"Yep. You caught me. And like her, I'm going to get up and leave. Either ask or tell me what it is you came all the way out here to tell me. You didn't feel it necessary to visit for the first twenty years of my life. Now you find it necessary to bring me back from the dead and visit. You have an agenda. Tell me what it is so we can move on."

"Your mother is a Soulless."

"Noted, ergo why I hunted her."

He narrowed his eyes but continued. "She's in the wrong guild."

I rolled my eyes. The marriage thing was jarring, if I believed him. But it didn't change much, and Mom hanging out with the wrong people was nothing new. "Tell her. She doesn't give a shit about me."

"I don't care about your mother."

"Then why are you here telling me this?"

He rolled his lips through his teeth and glared at me.

I glared back.

"I do care about her acquaintance."

Now he had my attention and likely my answer. He hadn't intervened until her Companion showed up.

He paused and gave me an expectant look like I was going to interrupt. I smiled sweetly at him and rolled my hand in the common sign to continue.

He sighed loudly, and I'm pretty sure hid a smile with a lick of his lips. "He's an issue and I want him exterminated."

"Come again," I said. Exterminated was a harsh word. Even for a Finder. I didn't have the resources or the knowledge for that route. I didn't even know who her Companion was. And if he was with her and a death arts master, he was way out of my league.

"I want him terminated."

I snorted a laugh. "I don't see how that involves me. You seem more than capable. You brought me back, so I'm sure you can."

He waved away my words. "Resurrections are easy enough. I can't get close enough to destroy him completely."

My eyes enlarged. "And I can?"

"They'll sense me long before I can get close enough and interfere."

His dark eyes bored into me but somehow his lips maintained a smile.

"Besides, you're her kid. You can get close to her. She underestimates you."

Underestimated me? "She killed me."

"Yes, and you're back—"

"How is that possible?" I interjected, resting my elbows on the table and leaning forward with faux interest.

"Do you always interrupt?"

I shrugged.

"Your body is simply a container."

"That's reassuring." I wanted to ask about my soul, but I couldn't form the words on my tongue. I didn't think I'd like the answer from my Vessel father about the death arts he used. And that I couldn't smell on him.

Instead, I asked, "So I'm indebted to you? For a favor I didn't ask for? I know because I don't have the scrolls." I used the horrific air quotes when I said indebted and then lifted my wrists to show there weren't any markings.

He stared at me, searching my face and eyes for something that he didn't find. He grimaced and shook his head. He looked back at me, grinning serenely, the beautiful "everything is wonderful and I'm in danger" smile. My senses flared and the hairs on my neck stood up.

"You're not *indebted*. I'm asking a favor of someone who owes me a favor. You can say no."

Sure I could.

"What is it you're exactly asking for in this extermination?"

"I need blood from her acquaintance."

"So, nothing too difficult to get?" I deadpanned. My mother had killed me, and he wanted the blood of the person she was working with. Enough so he brought me back from the dead to get it. A person

I hadn't met, didn't know existed until recently, and my father feared. Just lovely. It'd be like trying to get a lock of hair from a fish.

"I'm glad you see it that way."

"Why?"

"What?" he said and frowned.

"Why do you want it?"

"Do you really want to know?"

"No," I said and thought at the same time.

"Then we have a deal?"

"No, I don't promise the impossible."

"It's not impossible for you. She wants to kill you again," he said with another charming grin.

It wasn't possible to hate him more than I did then, but I also guessed he'd prove me wrong in the future.

I stood up, pushing my chair in.

He reached for my hand, but I yanked it back before he could touch it.

His eyes raised to mine. They were dark and something slithered behind them. I wanted to swallow, but I stood ramrod straight as I stared into his black Vessel eyes.

"You have two weeks to decide," he said.

I stuck my tongue in my cheek to not retort and nodded my head in understanding.

"Don't bother hiding again. She can't find you now—you're welcome—but I can."

Good to know, I thought as I walked away without responding. Once again, my father was protecting me from my mother, but this time he was clear about what he wanted.

OTHER WORLDLY MAGIC EXCERPT

Veiners — Veiners are neither human nor Vessel. They can slip between dimensions. They have the ability to take others with them. They rarely stay long on our plane. Offspring of Veiners with humans often live in our plane.

CHAPTER 12

AFTER THREE DAYS, I finally dug Oliver's phone from my kitchen drawer. I ran a thumb over the screen and the only thing that stopped me from calling Oliver that moment was the phone was dead. I'd kept it charged for weeks despite how much I hated it. A part of me still wanted that phone call. Still wanted the line.

I popped a Hot Pocket into the microwave and grabbed a cola while the phone blinked on. As I leaned against the counter, watching the seconds pass on my dinner, I noticed the phone icon had a notification. I was disappointed in myself when I felt excitement and hope stir in my stomach.

I didn't recognize the number. That didn't mean much—most of us went through burner phones like potato chips. I clicked on the voicemail and tried to read the transcription. The gobbledygook meant nothing to me, and I braced myself to hear the voice of either a telemarketer or a voice from home.

Disappointment punched me in the gut when it wasn't Oliver's voice on the other end. It took me a few seconds to recognize the voice, and my blood pressure hitched up.

"Hey, Dessa. This is Duke. Alan and I just got back from our honeymoon. We missed ya at the wedding. Heard some interesting stuff about ya. Let's catch up." Duke's baritone voice sounded chipper as usual, and I could picture him running a hand through his sandy blond hair.

A text from Duke wasn't unusual; a call was odd, but one to a phone from Oliver was terrifying.

I called Oliver's number first, the one he programmed into it. I didn't put much thought into why. It rang and I was sent to voicemail. I didn't leave one. He'd see the number he gave me and he'd make a decision to either call back or not.

I steadied myself and stared at Duke's number. I glanced toward the shadows and watched. They shifted around, avoiding my glance.

"Do you know why he called?"

They skittered around and said, "Call him."

"That didn't answer my question."

"They need you."

"Need me?" My voice went unnaturally high. Duke and Alan never needed me. The two had more than enough power, and besides, they had Virginia, a Glock that shot silver bullets. They'd stolen it from a more powerful being.

"Call him."

I stared at my phone, imagining it self-combusting in my hand. Did I want to know what was going on? I'd get dragged into it. There was no way I wouldn't help them once they requested it. I looked to the shadows. They didn't lie. Sarcasm, sure. Lies, no. Nothing would stop my involvement now.

I clicked the number and listened as it rang.

<hr>

BITING MY LIP, I wiped my palms on my jeans and rocked in my seat. It'd been two days since I talked to Duke, and I was still confused. Duke had been cheerful on the call, but it felt forced. He wouldn't give me details over the phone, but instead said they'd meet me.

Tingles raced down my spine and I jiggled my feet as I searched the street. I wondered if I wanted something to happen, to rattle things up. I had liked the calm, enjoyed my quiet nights, but it all felt like foreplay. Like I was living someone's life and kept bracing for them to barge into the door and demand their life back.

I was more prepared this time, as I figured I'd be moving again after meeting them. If I never saw my apartment again, the landlord would find some Hot Pockets in the freezer, cola in the fridge, and chips and plasticware in the cupboard. I wouldn't need my work shirts, so I'd double dipped for practicality and wore both my t-shirts and tied my flannel around my waist. After returning all my books to the library, I was packed and ready to go.

The high-pitched whine and gear shifting of Duke's Porsche sliced through my thoughts. It was supposed to be a quiet ride, but Duke had modified it. I looked up as his car came to a halt in front of the sub shop. Alan got out first, a scowl in place, along with his trimmed and styled black hair coiffed, and dress shirt and pants without lint or wrinkles. He strolled around the car, his hands exaggerating a strangling motion as he yelled profanities at the driver. The only new thing was the gold band wrapped around his reddish-brown left ring finger.

Duke opened the driver's side door, a large toothy grin in place as his disheveled sandy curls ruffled in the breeze. His green eyes stared in amusement at Alan's rant. He wore a faded thermal shirt, flannel, and old jeans. His white left hand was also adorned with a matching gold band.

He said something and chuckled, but Alan's face pinched in anger and he kicked a tire. Duke's mood shifted abruptly and he stood straight up and pointed a warning finger at Alan. Alan mocked his stance and pulled his leg back to kick it again.

"Don't you dare, or I'll get Virginia!" Duke bellowed, drawing the attention of many people.

"Hey," I shouted to draw their attention and stop the brewing assault.

Neither noticed.

Neither were Vessels, but I knew Alan could talk to shadows and more, and Duke controlled things I didn't want to know about.

I looked to the shadows and said, "Can you get Alan's attention?"

I knew better than to command the shadows. They were like toddlers and were fickle and temperamental.

They swirled around and darted through the street, wrapping around Alan's ankle. Though they were weightless, his attention shifted immediately to them, and then to me.

His scowl broke and his lips tilted up. Duke flinched in surprise as if it were a trick and followed his gaze.

"Dessa!" he shouted and darted to me, picking me up and swinging me around.

Alan jogged over and hugged me when Duke put me down.

"So, congratulations are in order?" I said and looked between them.

Duke swung his arm around Alan, and Alan returned the gesture, both smiling and nodding, the earlier confrontation forgotten.

"Sorry I missed it," I said and frowned, seeing their expressions shift.

"No, we're sorry. We didn't know about..." Duke's voice trailed off.

"How are you holding up?" Alan asked.

I shrugged and looked away.

"Oh, sweets," Duke said and pulled me to them in a group hug.

Emotion welled behind my eyes, and I sniffed and blinked to push it back. It wasn't the time. I cleared my throat and, slightly hoarse, asked, "So, why are you two here?"

They didn't share a look, they didn't have to, but they both shuddered slightly and went stiff.

"What?" I asked. What could possibly have them so upset? I'd already died.

"Not here," Alan said and moved back toward the car.

"What's going on?" I asked.

Duke looked between Alan and the car and me.

"We need to go someplace safe," he said and tugged me toward the car.

"No place is safe," I protested, not liking their sudden change and avoidance.

"One place is. We can't stay long, but it'll be enough."

He tugged on my arm again, but I didn't budge.

"Dessa, we gotta go," he said and tried again to tug me forward while scanning the streets.

"Then go," I snapped.

He sighed. "By 'we' I mean you, too. Let's go."

I shivered and felt the telltale sign of danger as my skin crawled and heat raced up my spine. I reached for my knife and heard the shadows. They hissed in warning, telling me to leave.

I didn't bother to look over my shoulder at what was stalking us and jumped into the car. I buried my head in my lap and cringed when Duke cursed. The car lurched to the right, like we'd been hit by a truck, but we didn't spin out of control. Instead, there was a tunnel sound and a pop.

"It's okay now, sweets," Duke said. His voice calm and serene.

I looked up and gasped at the sight. I didn't know what it was, but lights shimmered and danced around us, going on into oblivion, but I didn't notice land or objects around us. We were in a void of sort.

"Where are we?" I whispered.

"Don't worry about that," Duke said and turned in his seat to fully see me.

Alan rolled his eyes but nodded. "We won't stay long."

I stared between them and the lights.

"We didn't know you left town," Duke said and looked to Alan, who nodded.

"Sorry," I started.

"Nope, nope, none of that," Duke said and patted my knee. "We understand. Your mom's a bitch."

I snorted in agreement.

"Do you know how you're alive?" Alan asked while watching my response.

"Uh," I stalled.

"It's okay," Duke said. "The workings of the magic are intricate and boring. What are your plans?"

"My plans?" Did they know about my father's request?

"Are you going to live and die as a barmaid on sabbatical, or are you going to be Dessa again?" Duke flicked his gaze to Alan's.

"What do you mean?"

"Dessa, come on. Playing chicken isn't your thing," Duke chided.

"Duke," Alan warned.

"Sorry, sorry. I know," he said, raising his hands up in a placating manner and turned his gaze to Alan. "This isn't how we roleplayed it."

Alan's face turned crimson at Duke's admission. I wanted to be mad that they'd planned an intervention, but I was more moved someone cared enough to try.

"Anyway," Alan gritted out. "Dessa, we're concerned."

"Why? I'm fine."

"Fine?"

"Yeah, I have an apartment, job, books, food. What else do I need?" My stomach curdled. Who was I trying to convince? Them or me?

They stared between each other.

"As far as I know, my mom can't find me. You guys now know how to reach me. I'm good," I said and added a large smile to seal the deal. I just left out my dad wanted me to get my mom's Companion's blood and he was the reason my mom couldn't find me.

"She's smiling." Alan pointed at my face.

"Yeah, it's a little freaky." Duke grimaced.

"A little?" Alan countered.

"Hey, I'm right here!"

"This isn't going well," Duke said and shook his head. "Let's start over."

Duke's phone chirped with a text, and I remembered my own phone.

"So, how'd you get my number from Oliver?"

They both froze and stared into space. I wasn't sure either was breathing.

"Hey, what?" I asked fear clawing at my throat.

They looked at each other unblinking. Oliver. What was wrong with Oliver? Cold pierced my stomach and dots danced in front of my eyes. He'd claimed he had a target. One that was out of his league and John would never really give him. One who I ran from so he and everyone else would be safe. And he had Tones. Mom wouldn't cross her.

I stuttered, "Is he—is he okay?"

Duke licked his lips and nodded slowly. "He's okay now."

"Now?"

Alan looked up and met my gaze. His black eyes rimmed in red, and the emotion caused him to blink repeatedly.

"What happened?" I screamed.

"Your mom," Duke started. His bravado fell and he slumped against the front seat, eyes closed and pain contorting his face. "He tried to bring her in. He doesn't have the blinders you do to her. Your mom didn't want to get caught. She baited him. She's gotten stronger. She tried to… to…"

"She tried to kill Oliver, too," Alan finished for Duke.

"But he's okay?" I asked, hope bubbling up and gargling my words.

"He is… but…"

"But what?"

"Sweets, she hurt Oliver bad. Tones…" Duke swallowed hard. A shaky breath rattled him, and he shook as tears streamed down his face.

"What about Tones?" I asked Alan.

"Tones saved Oliver, but no one could save her."

The blood drained from my face. I stared, not seeing anything. Not feeling anything. The blood pounding in my ears deafened me.

"My mom… she…"

"Killed Tones," Alan finished for me.

Finders' Handbook

Driver - A person Finders call for a ride to an Agency. Agents have lists available to Finders. Drivers receive either a set fee or percentage of a target. Terms are negotiated between Driver and Finder. If an Agent sets up the arrangement, they receive a percentage of the Driver's fees.

CHAPTER 13

MY LIFE STOOD STILL, even if nothing else did.

At some point Duke turned around and drove us out of the light show. I thought they asked me questions, but I heard nothing other than Tones' voice rattling around in my head. Years of her reprimands, praise, and encouragement.

It was my fault she was dead. I failed to bring my mother in, and then ran when given the chance.

I hadn't checked in, either. I'd waited for Oliver to call me. Thought my leaving would be enough to satisfy her. In the end, he'd been injured, and his mother killed. And no one brought her back.

"Hey," a voice shouted. "Dessa, hey!"

I finally looked up and realized Alan was shaking me. We were stopped, the sun was shining, and we were in a cute neighborhood with postage-stamp houses, detached garages, and trimmed lawns.

"Let's go inside." Alan looked at a white house with blue trim and then back at me.

Despite a full-body numbness, I undid my seatbelt and exited the car. I blinked to block the sun but didn't bother raising a hand to shade my eyes.

"Sweets." Duke waited until I looked at him. "We love you. We want to help."

"Help what?" my voice croaked.

"You. You've been through a lot and shouldn't be alone," he said, opening the front door and waiting for me to enter.

"I'm fine," I lied. They needed to stay away from me. Stay out of her sights.

"Ok then, you'll be fine here." Alan said and spread his arms out to encompass the interior of the house.

Still my feet stayed planted on the washed-cement walkway.

Duke came behind me. Instead of touching me, he leaned to whisper in my ear. "She's not dumb enough to come here."

"But..." my voice cracked.

"If we stay out here, she could get a shot in, but not past our barrier."

With a sigh, I listened to his reasoning. Alan was at least half demon. Duke was half Veiner or something else of old magic. Both were an unimaginable force. Crisp air greeted me as I stepped across the threshold.

I robotically turned around and noted the new furniture, covered walls, and knickknacks and pictures around the room. This was a home. This was their home, based on the pictures. I'd never been there. We'd always met elsewhere. I snorted a laugh, realizing I thought they lived in the car. Something inside me shattered and I clutched my stomach and fell to the floor, gasping laughs, thinking about how wrong I was. Then the other things I was wrong about flickered to my mind, and my laughs turned to body-wrenching sobs.

"There she is," Duke said and plopped down on the floor beside me. He wrapped his massive arms around me and pulled me close. He rocked us gently as he petted my hair and whispered nonsense.

"Here, drink this," Alan instructed and thrust a glass of water in front of my face. I flinched back, causing him to spill some.

"Sorry," I said and went to wipe it with my flannel.

"Stop it." Alan swatted my hand away and got a towel.

"Okay, first drink the water to rehydrate, then shower and change," Duke said.

I looked down at my clothes. I had all my clothes on.

As if reading my mind, Alan said, "Don't worry, shower and I'll run and grab you something from the store."

"No, no, no, no, that's not necessary," I said, brushing him away with my hands. I needed to leave. Even if she couldn't breach their house, I didn't need to bring attention to them.

"Shower and new clothes are definitely necessary," Duke said and pinched his nose.

"Ha, ha."

"No, I'm serious. And say your farewells to the clothes. Did you wash them in the shower with you?"

I shot him a dark look.

"I'm guessing I'm right," Duke said and jumped away from my fist.

"I appreciate the offer, but I can't stay." Heaviness settled on my heart, and each breath was a struggle.

"Look, sweets," Alan said and waited until I looked at him. "Your mom is not going to mess with us."

My head was shaking before he finished. She was a bitch.

"We're not easy targets. She went after Tones because it would hurt you most, and to save her pride. Tones protected Oliver. Tones protected you."

"But you're protecting me."

"Tones publicly stopped your mom from going after you. Then she saved her son from your mom and word is spreading. She killed Tones to send a message to the Soulless. Her name is whirling around like wildfire."

The words all sounded good, and probably correct, but it was a risk.

"If your mom shows up," Duke said. "I'll get us out. I'm faster than her."

That he could.

"Now go shower," Alan said before I could open my mouth.

Despite my protests, I caved. They had a specialty showerhead that had a massager built in. It worked wonders on my back, and I stood under it until the water ran cold. When I turned the water off, someone knocked softly on the bathroom door.

"Clothes," Alan called from the other side.

I wrapped a towel around me and cracked the door open, accepting the clothes. I didn't have enough attachment to my other clothes to fight for them.

I pulled on the jeans, tank top, and long sleeve t-shirt he gave me.

"We're going to make dinner," Alan said and rolled his eyes. "Well, I'm going to make dinner and Duke is going to drink. It'll be an hour or so. Go to the purple room and rest."

"No, I'm good." I yawned.

"Want to try that again?"

I glared at him. He wasn't my brother or parent. He didn't need to baby me.

"Dessa, I'm going to dump on you right here and now."

I flinched and my fists instinctively balled.

"That's what I'm talking about. You're always ready for a fight, and before you protest, I get it. It was how you were raised. But, sweets, I'm hurting, too, by what happened to you and Tones." His voice caught at Tones' name and he swallowed hard. He blinked but his eyes remained glassy. "What I need more than anything is to take care of you. I need to smother you with love to release all the anger and frustration I have before it eats me alive. If I can't take care of you, I'm going to shoot someone."

Duke arched an eyebrow and then nodded in agreement.

Orange lightning charges zipped across Alan's eyes.

"I don't…"

"Nope, not about you right now." Alan shook his head. He pointed to a bedroom, I assumed the purple one, and said, "I need to know where you are and that you are safe and being cared for. That means you take a nap now."

I opened my mouth and then snapped it shut. I darted my gaze to Duke who just shrugged and gestured to the bedroom.

I rolled my eyes but went in there, anyway. I closed the door so they couldn't see me not sleep.

I paced the floor for a while, staring at the silent shadows. I flopped on the bed and stared at the ceiling. My eyes drifted shut and images of Tones came forth. My eyes shot back open, and I jumped up from the bed.

I couldn't let my mother get away with touching Tones. She'd killed me and then Tones. She'd almost killed Oliver, according to Alan and Duke. I'd given up everything I'd known to leave this town and leave her. I'd let myself be a coward for self-preservation, and she'd gone after the one person I loved like a parent. I couldn't let her touch anyone else I loved.

Duke and Alan were great friends, and I would protect them, but Tones had been my conscience when mine was broken. She'd been my soft place to land and the hard kick in the ass. She'd loved me despite my choices and never expected anything from me in return, and my mother ended her life.

I had to avenge Tones. I had to make sure her loss wasn't in vain. I couldn't protect her, but I'd honor her. I'd bring my mother down. I'd seek John and get my assignment reinstated. Take it from Oliver. I'd load up from his arsenal and come at my mother until one of us was dead.

THE NIGHT AIR chapped my face, and I rubbed my hands together, both to keep warm and out of nervous habit. It was just before nine, and John wouldn't be in the shop for at least another thirty minutes.

Sirens wailed in the distance. The wind scuttled some wrappers and bits across the aged cement. Other than a dog barking a few blocks over, nothing stirred around me. I stood in the shadows. Random streetlights dotted the alley. Some had broken bulbs and others cast dim golden circles on the ground, leaving everything else in the pitch-black. The darkness wasn't a concern. I could still see fine, and the shadows continued to tattle on any living creature that ventured close.

So, it was a shock when John stood before me, and the shadows hadn't so much as whispered a peep.

"Traitors," I mumbled and shoved my hands in my pockets. I kicked off the wall and, continuing to angle my face down, I lifted my eyes up to look at him.

"You ain't got business here," he barked and walked past me.

"Like hell I don't." I trailed after him.

"Get the fuck outta here." He unlocked the door to the shop, keeping his back to me.

He pushed the door open and entered, neither inviting me in nor slamming the door on me. I wasn't a threat to him. I was a Finder who had died.

He flipped light switches on as he moved through the office. I entered but leaned against the wall by the door. He booted his computer up, started the coffee pot, and plopped down in his chair with his feet on the desk. His eyes swung to me and he snarled. "I told you to get the fuck out of here."

Pleading wouldn't work with him. He didn't like meek or weak. I couldn't argue with him because he was stronger and arguing with John always led to him becoming violent. Reasoning was out of the window. We dealt with paranormal criminals while pretending none of us existed. Reasoning was for the delusional. So, I had bargaining left. The problem was, I didn't know what I could offer. He was the one who paid me. I didn't have anything to add as collateral and my skills weren't the best he had, as he regularly told me.

I stared too long without speaking and he narrowed his eyes and shifted in his seat, putting his feet on the floor. Not a good sign. I pushed off the wall and sauntered halfway to his desk. His eyebrows inched up with each step I took, and his fists got tighter.

"I want my assignment back."

"You don't have an assignment."

"Has anyone brought her in?"

His jaw ticked and he growled.

I forged ahead. "She's gone after two of us and killed a friend."

"How d'ya know that?"

I maintained my blasé expression while my mind reeled. Was it a secret? Only Duke and Alan had mentioned it, but Duke and Alan had connections everywhere. They weren't in the same circles as John, so something had leaked. I wouldn't give up my source, it'd put them at risk, but I still had the upper hand.

I shrugged and took a step closer.

"She killed you once. You lost it."

I flinched. His crassness wasn't unexpected, but still stung.

"She's too much for you. I'm raising the level."

"I may have died—" I hesitated, my brain trying to stay ahead of the situation and regain the upper ground. "But I came back."

He snorted. "Back don't mean better."

"Oh, I'm better." It was kind of true. I did have night vision and could talk to the shadows. So far it hadn't amounted to much, but in my Finder days it'd have given me a huge upper hand.

"What do you mean?" His eyes flickered over me even though he tried to remain indifferent.

"It means I'm ready for the next level." I sure as hell hoped so.

He laughed. I fought not to roll my eyes, but I lost the battle.

"Listen, Dessa."

Oh shit, he used my first name. That wasn't good.

"You're a nice kid, even with your parents. But you don't got what it takes."

I started to argue but he raised his hand.

"You died. You're done."

"What?"

"You're done. Finished. I don't have any more jobs for you. Enjoy life."

Wait, what? He wasn't only denying my mother's assignment, but he was letting me go?

"You're making a mistake," I said, heading for the door.

"No, but you are if you continue to pursue your mother."

I WALKED AIMLESSLY AFTERWARDS. There were others out. I felt the telltale signs of the Soulless. My skin itched as the hair on my neck rose and my pulse quickened. I didn't bother to stop for them. John had made it clear he wouldn't hire me again. I'd have to find another Agency. I knew of a few, but they paid less. My mom had gone to John since I could remember, and he took me on as a solo teen, likely out of pity or fear of who my mother was.

And now, my mother was the reason he wouldn't hire me.

She was the root of so much, my internal roadblock to peace, the constant predator to my well-being.

But I had knowledge. I knew how the Finders and Agencies worked. I knew how assignments were handed out and where they lurked.

My feet carried me to familiar ground. Neon light spilled out of the bar onto the sidewalk, drowning it in artificial light. The stale stench of fried food and beer lingered in the air. Tones would be so angry. The smell of beer was fine, but it should be paired with freshly fried food.

People moved around inside the bar, seemingly oblivious to the tragedy. I stood in the shadows watching. The cold air clung to my clothes and stung my exposed skin.

I watched as Benny wiped the counter down repeatedly. He cracked a grin at a patron, and I stumbled backward. He'd only ever frowned or stared the entire time I knew him.

My eyes swept the room again, looking for the familiar blonde hair and entourage of fawning men. Not seeing it, I took another sweeping gaze. It felt sacrilegious for her to be there, but that would suit her.

Benny's eyes diverted up and he smiled again. I took a step closer to see who had broken his armor and recognized the handsomely dark features of Oliver. He sat at the bar nursing what looked like a cola. He wore long sleeves, but bandages littered his face. Anger curled in my stomach, and I took a large gulp of air to rein in my visceral reaction.

Disappointed, I walked away. I couldn't stand to see him enjoying his time while his mother was dead and her killer roamed free.

Despite my efforts to put distance between all my reminders and my body, I found myself in the back alley. I stood in the same spot Oliver had slid me a phone and I decided to start a new life. It was the spot I'd turned into a coward, and Tones had paid.

"Tones," I whispered. I felt guilty saying her name, knowing how I'd failed her. "I'm so sorry. This is my fault."

The shadows stirred but I ignored them.

"I'll make her pay."

"At what cost to you?" the shadows hissed at me.

I blinked, watching the swirling shadows. They took on a familiar structure, one I'd known my whole life. The ethereal figure swayed in the corners, the light scorching away the edges.

"Tones," I whispered, unable to stop the word from tumbling over my lips. My heart clenched at the possibility that it was really her.

"You look like hell," the shadow said, Tones' voice a gut punch. The shadow hardened into almost a ghostly form.

"You look so much better," I shot back and instantly regretted it.

The shadow chuckled and the sound warmed me.

"How… how are you here?" I flicked my fingers at her form.

She frowned. "Your mother killed me, but I was able to tether my essence to the shadows. It takes a lot to shape them into something recognizable. They are stubborn creatures. Spirits are much easier."

And yet she'd done it to see me.

"Dessa, my girl, what are you doing here?"

"I don't know. I just found my way to the alley."

"No, I mean back in town."

"I heard about your death." I choked saying death.

"Those boys should have never told you." She tsked, her shadow flashing red, and I stared at the oddity.

"Tones, I was too late. You paid for my sin."

"This isn't your sin! Your mom killed you. Your father..." Her voice grew to a growl.

"What? Brought me back?"

"He didn't bring you back out of love."

"Yeah, I got that. He wants me to..."

"He brought you back to do a suicide mission."

"You know what he wants?"

Tones made a disgusted sound.

"I didn't agree."

"Then why are you here?"

I shrugged and looked away. There was a lynchpin in all of this: my mother. She killed me. She killed Tones. She hurt Oliver. She was why my father brought me back. If I ended her, truly just ended her, I'd have revenge for the three of us and my father would leave me alone.

"Dessa, listen to me."

I turned back to the shadow. Her edges were petering out.

"You are not responsible for your mother."

"But—"

"No! She made her choices. Your job is to protect yourself."

That didn't feel completely right.

"I want you to do me a favor."

I hated favors. They were undesirable tasks you did out of obligation or fear.

"What?"

"Leave this town and never look back."

"Sure..." After I killed my mother.

She shifted, her shadow dissolving more. "Dessa, do one more favor for me."

"What's that?"

"Well, it's a clustered one. Tell Oliver it's not his fault and I love him. I also don't mean for you to leave town after you kill your mother. I mean now."

"I'll let Oliver know," I said, the acid pooling in my stomach to have to face him again.

"Dessa, don't be a fool." Her voice was barely a breath of air as her form completely dissolved.

I stared at the shadows for a long time. I knew she was gone, but watching the shadows, I wondered what they were. They slithered around, forming words and thoughts, providing warnings, but they also feared my father. I wondered if they needed retribution, too.

Finders' Handbook

Agent - A person who issues targets to Finders. They can select targets from the master database. Assignment is at their discretion.

CHAPTER 14

I DREADED SEEING OLIVER AGAIN, being reminded of losing Tones, but he'd returned my call. Unlike me, he'd left a message. Well, he sent me a text when I missed the call.

I stared at it again. He'd sent it the day before from the number he'd programmed into my phone.

Unknown: *Tmrw 9 normal stool*

I'd had the past twenty-four hours to consider everything and had two more hours until the meeting. I'd promised Tones I'd deliver her message, and I would.

From the bar, I'd taken a stroll down the river, letting the water sing to me, the sloshing of dreams being carried away. Rivers cleansed and erased. They stole debris and artifacts into their oddly curated collections. They had no mercy and no remorse. They didn't mind spitting back bad treasure, bloated bodies, evidence, and long-buried secrets. While also hoarding them away from anyone seeking them. The river's song always reminded me that life was ever going, ever changing, and all I had to do was follow it.

I was in my wistful mood, walking in the pool of neon light to block out the shadows' chatter, when I felt the presence. My neck hairs bristled, my muscles tightened, and instinct took hold. My blade was in my fist. I hunkered down and spun on the creature before my footstep hit the pavement.

My quick reflexes did nothing to deter him. The eyes shone pink in the light. A banshee Soulless, but he had more augmentations than they normally do. His claws slashed at my arm, and blood sprung through my shirt. I cursed at ruining my new shirt already. While his arm swung at me again, I drove my blade through his side and dug until it jerked against bone. Then he started wailing.

"For fucks sake, shut up," I grunted and stepped backward, shaking my head.

He sprang on me, tossing me against the railing. His gaping mouth was an abyss of swirling spittle and death. His eye shone on their own accord, darkening at the prospect of my blood. His claws held my arms in place as I strained to get away from his sound. He even drowned out the rush of the river.

I startled at the sight rushing toward me. As the banshee pushed onto the rail, he blocked the light of the streetlamp, thrusting me into its own shadow. The shadows I'd desperately been avoiding swirled around in the darkness and scrambled over my face, darkening the world around me. I blinked as they slithered across, shielding my face and crawling into my ears. Although not a complete earplug, it blocked the sharpness, and I could hear my blood pounding in my ears and the river rushing beneath me, singing my song.

My blade still rested in my hands. My feet, no longer immobile from the sound assault, now scrambled to get footing on the crumbling cement barrier. Digging both into the flat top, I launched forward, shoving my knee into the bulk of the creature. He gasped and loosened his hold as he processed the attack. I used the opportunity to wrench my wrist free and plunge my blade into the cavern where his heart should have been.

He wailed and sputtered and clawed at the handle embedded in his chest. I kicked him in the knee, causing him to stumble forward. With the same motion, I grabbed my blade back and slashed him across the neck, separating his head.

Even without a target sheet, the pink eyes and body augmentations would mark him as a Soulless. It was worth something. But I didn't have an Agency. Because of John's connection to my mom. Fuck them both.

I stood, taking in ragged breaths. I couldn't tell if he was sent for me or had chosen to come for me, seeing an opportunity. John knew I was back, but I doubted he'd tell my mom if he had a target sheet on her. I sighed and kneeled. I rubbed my bloodied hands on his clothes; they were cleaner than mine. I tugged on his shirt, but it was tattered and the gash from my knife was large. I patted through his pockets and found a few bucks, a scarlet business card, and a house key.

I pocketed the money and tossed the key to the river. The river would get a prize today. I let the business card flutter to the ground. The bitch had sent him. I used the banshee's finger to flip the card over.

In her neat, all-capitalized script, it read "I WANT HER ALIVE."

Well, that was interesting. I guess she wanted to be the one who killed me again. I checked his pockets for more information other than the card but found nothing. How had he known I was his target? Or was I just an easy target alone at the river?

But the card meant she knew I was back. Or had she always been looking for me? Fuck. My dad said she couldn't find me because of him, so was this her way to circumvent it? Any way, it meant there wasn't a reason for me not to turn in a Soulless. If I killed enough of the ones she sent for me, it might make it easier to find her, especially if my dad really was blocking her from finding me.

I scanned the street. No one was close, or if they were, they went running when blades came out.

Duke would drive if I called him, but where would he take me? My eyes tracked to the street signs: Ivy Lane and Miller Street. It was a block to another Agency's place. They didn't pay what John did, but I should be able to get a week's worth of groceries for the banshee.

Instead of calling Duke, I carried the Soulless' head in my left hand

and dragged the body with my right for the block. I covered the short distance without hearing sirens, screams, or the hurried sound of someone hiding.

I walked into the small storefront tucked between a tailor and a barber in a brick building painted dark brown decades ago that had started chipping right afterward. Citrus and sage danced on the air. The door was grime-covered and had six locks running the length of it. I tried the handle and pushed the door open.

A pistol at the forehead greeted me.

"What the fuck you doing?" a voice barked.

"Soulless." I lifted my hands, each carrying a piece.

"No shit," the voice shot back and shut the door behind me.

"I don't have a target sheet," I said and dropped the pieces on the floor. "But it tried to kill me and has augmentations."

"Ha, on the carpet?" she groaned.

I wiped my hands on my pants and stuck my hand out to shake. Her petite hand gripped mine back and shook.

I had to look down to meet her eyes. She was rail thin with a thick head of dark curly hair. She wore large circular glasses over her brown eyes. They were about a third of the size of her face. She wore what looked like a velour leisure suit but was form fitting.

"The Impressive Dessa, yes?" she said and walked to her desk.

"You recognize me?" I asked, hand readying for my blade.

She snorted a laugh. "Agents and Finders talk. You know my office. I know your reputation even if I don't know your face. Goal is for Soulless not to know, but you don't leave witnesses."

Fair point. Also why she had six locks, a pistol, and who knew what else. From her smell, she was also a Vessel.

I shrugged.

She plopped down in her chair and put her boots on the desk. "You gonna clean that mess up off my carpet?"

"You gonna pay me?"

She smiled, her pert red lips tweaking up on the right side. "There's no target sheet."

"Soulless," I said and waved backward.

"Vessel if you don't have a target, and a dead one leaving goo all over my floor at that."

"He's a banshee screamer."

"Hence the separated head," she said leaning over her desk. She clasped her hands together and rested her chin on them.

"You want me to take him somewhere else? He has the pink eyes and other body augmentations."

She raised an eyebrow at me and then looked to the banshee screamer and back at me. She shrugged.

"Ok." I lifted my shoulder and turned around.

"He's dead. I can't give you full price," she said to my back. "The Finder Trust prefers them alive."

The Finders' Trust still paid on the dead ones, though. "How much can you give?"

"I have a Finder after this bastard. Has been for two weeks."

I grimaced. "They suck that much?"

She laughed. "Not everyone is Dessa."

I again stared at her. I didn't know what game she was playing, praising me. No one praised me to my face or behind my back.

"Who was he?" I asked, nodding toward the Soulless.

"Benedict Smilit."

The name meant nothing to me, but it gave me a lead toward my mom.

"I can give you fifty percent."

"Eighty," I said.

"Sixty, unless you want to clean up the goo."

I looked back at the body fluids oozing out of it. "Seventy-five."

"Seventy."

That was better than I expected as a new-hire and no target sheet. "Deal."

"You looking for more targets?" I heard the slightest bit of excitement and hope in her voice.

"Depends, what do you got?" I said before thinking it through.

"I have a Level One and two Level Twos," she said, patting three folders.

I blinked and stared ahead, not really processing what she said. A Level One was the highest level. Was this a joke?

"What? Not good enough?" she asked. She crossed her arms and stared at me behind her too-large glasses.

I shrugged to hide my confusion and held out my hand, forcing it steady despite my excitement at the higher levels. It was worth a shot. Whatever their levels were, there'd be money for them and a chance to dig up information on my mom.

"You want all of them?"

"I can have them all?" I asked before I could stop the words.

"Why not? You're Dessa. You're legendary."

Wow, she was really laying it on. I rolled my eyes but grabbed the folders. I'd look at them later when she wasn't watching. Even if they were lower levels, it would be money.

"Payment?" I said and nodded my head toward the banshee.

"Ah yes, we wouldn't want to forget that." She pulled out a ledger from her desk. She scribbled on it and handed it across.

I did a double take at the number above the name Mandy. We'd agreed on seventy percent. With John, the target would have brought in three hundred. The check in my hand was for seven hundred. Was that another lie from Mom? But she wouldn't go there unless he paid the most… Fuck. Was this another area she used me in? Did John give her a cut of my fees?

"What? Not enough?" she barked, leaning against the desk. Her fingers were splayed and pressed into the dark wood, and her head tilted slightly to the side.

I met her gaze.

"Not as much as John pays?" She sneered and rocked back on her shoulders.

"It's fine," I said, not wanting to lose the extra funds. "Thanks for the business." I stepped back, keeping my eyes locked with her, and patted the folders. "I'll see you soon."

THE FAMILIAR KALEIDOSCOPE of neon colors flooded the street in garish designs. I stood back, watching the patrons trickle in and linger. The sound of laughter drifted out. I didn't see my mom, but I did see Benny standing sentinel at his normal spot, a washrag in his fist and a scowl on his face.

The shadows slithered around me, hissing their thoughts, reminding me Tones wanted me to deliver the message and leave.

"You gonna tell him for me, then?" I asked.

I chuckled at their decline.

"Then shut up," I said and walked through the pools of light.

The familiarity of the place was like a punch to the stomach. Music thrummed through the air, the atmosphere thick with smoke, booze, hormones, and desperation.

The regulars didn't bother to glance at me. I'd been gone for two months, but like a roach, I came back. My presence in the bar didn't send a shock wave or create tension. Even after my mom's display. I'd been the dog that slinked off to lick their wounds before returning to the fold.

My usual stool was empty, despite the packed bar. I slid onto the seat and shuddered when I expected Tones to slide up next to me. My chin quivered but I swallowed to control it. I just needed to hold it together to get her message out.

A cola found its way in front of me. I looked up to see Benny scowling at me, but it almost looked forced. His eyes shone with sympathy, and after a quick nod he scooted away to another patron. That was the most emotion I'd ever seen him give except for when he threatened my mom.

I smelled Oliver's woodsy cologne before he sat down. I licked my lips as I stared straight forward.

"Ah, my mute siren." His words were like salve.

I'd longed to hear his voice and cursed myself for the foolishness. I was here to give a message, and then I'd never see him again. I owed him that line of protection. If my mom had wanted him dead, he wouldn't be here. He'd been a warning, and collateral damage with Tones. I just needed to keep distance to keep her focus from him.

"Oliver." I nodded.

"So," we said together.

"You first," I said and turned toward him. I didn't meet his eyes.

"Dessa," he whispered, which caused me to look up at him. Mistake. Big mistake. I got lost in his hazel eyes, the sorrow that made them heavy and the relief that made them bright. It was a dichotomy that meant he'd survived and a loved one didn't. It was the guilt and pleasure battle that wears us down and makes us old.

I wanted to interrupt him, tell him how sorry I was, take the blame, his hatred. I should have believed him when he said he had her target sheet. I owed him some sort of victory. I'd failed at the target, and he'd tried for something he wasn't ready for. Then his mom paid the price. But I couldn't rob him of his right to berate me.

"Don't," he said, shaking his head, his lips pinched in anger.

"Don't what?" I shot back and internally cursed myself for the aggression. I'd already gone off the rails.

"I don't want your pity."

"I'm not giving it," I lied.

"Why'd you come back?"

"Wow, great to see you, too." I pulled my shoulders back in an exaggerated shrug to show how much I really didn't care, but somehow my hand had ended up in Oliver's and my shrug failed. He didn't release my hand but held my fingers in his and stroked his thumb over my knuckles. It felt good, and it shouldn't have.

"I didn't say that," he said and sighed. "Dessa, it's not safe for you."

"It's less safe for you." Again, I regretted my words.

"She actually killed you," he seethed.

"And Tones," I whispered.

He let go of my hand and I missed his warmth, his soft comforting caresses. But I didn't deserve them.

"You're saying that to piss me off," he said and drank my cola.

"Am I?" I asked, but also wondered if I was. I guess I was already trying to create a chasm between us. I'd hurt him so he wouldn't feel bad about hating me, too. Maybe he already did. But if he did or didn't, I had to make sure he did.

"You called me," he finally said and leaned against the bar, resting his elbow on the bar top and putting his head in his palm.

"Yeah, I called after I heard from Duke and Alan. Why didn't you tell me?"

His eyes narrowed and searched my face. Finally, he said, "Why would I?"

Another punch to my gut. "She killed Tones. She tried to kill you." I struggled to keep my voice low.

A cough from Benny when he slammed down two colas made me flinch and lower my voice more.

"So?"

"So!" I yelled.

Benny's eyes cut to me and I felt my face flush. I gulped down my cola and looked back at Oliver. His face was pinched, his eyes dark and assessing, and he held himself away, leaning into the back of the chair.

"I would have helped," I said.

"I know."

I stared disbelieving at him.

"That's why I didn't call. You got a fresh start. I wanted you to take it."

He didn't understand. "She's my mother. My responsibility."

"No, she's a target."

"You could have taken her in for the credit."

He snorted and threw his head back. "That's what you think this is about? Credit?"

"I don't know what it's about. That's what I'm trying to figure out."

"Enough, you two," Benny said. He leaned across the bar, his large frame dwarfing the wooden relic. "Take it outside."

I looked around and noticed way too many people watching us.

I nodded and pulled out a twenty that I'd taken from the banshee.

Oliver placed his hand on mine, staying my motion.

"Keep your money," he said, and not releasing my hand, pulled me back toward the hall. I let him lead me. I could at least let him pretend he was in control.

He slammed into the back door and the cold air bit at my face, and I blinked.

Once we were outside, he let my hand go. I stared at it for a moment. Uncertainty and disappointment snaked through my stomach. My crush was juvenile and distracting and needed to end.

"What is this about?" I yelled, annoyance at myself bubbling up and unbridled by the possible eavesdroppers.

"Dessa, I fucking care if you are okay."

"Tones was worried," I started.

"No, not my mom. Me. I care," he said, pressing his fingertips against his chest.

"Oh," I said, unsure what he meant.

"If I can stop her from hurting you, I will."

Oh, he was doing the stupid big brother protection shit again.

"You don't have to watch out for me."

"Someone has to," he said, throwing his arms in the air, facing away from me.

"Hey! I can take care of myself."

"Says the woman who died."

"Fuck off! I'm here. I got targets, and I have a plan." In my rage, I'd managed to embellish about having a plan and told him I had targets. He was throwing me off by showing compassion. I preferred the mocking Oliver that called me Dessa the Destroyer while I crushed on him from behind a cola in the shadows.

"You have targets?" he asked, whipping around to face me.

I didn't answer. I wasn't going to confirm what he heard all while hoping he forgot.

"Who gave you targets? John?"

Everything was derailing. We were fighting. The one thing I'd hoped to avoid. I cursed and stared up at the stars. Why couldn't I do anything right? I sighed and counted to ten, my breaths ragged as I curled my toes to work the tension out.

I finally met his gaze again, my face void of emotion. Void of argument. I wasn't here to talk about my choices. I was here to talk about Tones.

"Oliver, I didn't come here to talk about me."

"Oh? Did you come to talk about your plan?"

I gritted my teeth and bit my lip to not shoot back a nasty retort.

"No, I came with a message."

"A message? From whom?" he said, putting his hands on his hips and tilting his head. When he did it, it reminded me of Tones when she called out my bullshit.

"Tones," I choked.

"Mom?" he asked, his bravado falling, and his face crumpling with grief.

I felt a punch in my gut again, one I'd caused and couldn't take back. I nodded, bracing myself.

"How… how do you have it?" He didn't say so accusingly or mockingly, but true confusion.

"That's the thing. Since I woke up, I can talk to the shadows."

"You're a Shadowtalker?" His eyes traveled up and down me, looking for something out of place.

"Yep."

He stared at me, and finally said, "Okay, what's the message?"

I licked my lips. I had to blink repeatedly to continue to meet his gaze. Words formed but didn't come out. I needed to finish this so I could move on. Create distance. Forcing a breath out, I let numbness and disassociation relieve the sharp, unrelenting pain stabbing into my heart. "She says she loves you and it's not your fault."

I didn't give him a chance to argue or deny what she said. I left him as I did before, standing in the pool of copper light while I darted into the shadows.

MOM'S RULES

Rule Seven: Always carry a weapon

CHAPTER 15

I DIDN'T SEE Oliver again until two nights later, when I was covered in green blood and carrying a Soulless over my shoulder.

The Soulless was one of my Level Twos. After carefully reading the file for thirty seconds, I looked at the picture, the clothes, the background. Unlike most of mine from John, the Soulless was an affluent up-and-coming politician. He was on the ticket of banning everything in the name of religion while personally committing every sin.

I found his office location and slipped on a blonde wig and my thrift store finds: baggy khaki pants with pleats at the waist, a blue polo shirt, and clunky brown loafers. A baseball cap with a local water delivery company logo was the final touch.

Going in as a food delivery person will get you everyone's attention. They'll come out of the woodwork to smell it and hope they can get some. Come in carrying something heavy and awkward and people will bust ass to open a door without touching it or scurry away so they can't be asked for assistance.

I waited until the headquarters office was close to empty, but not completely. I walked in carrying a watercooler bottle, much easier than carrying a Soulless.

One person stopped me. She was cute, with perfectly curled hair, a tight pencil skirt, cardigan over a white blouse, and stereotypical schoolteacher glasses. Her stiletto heels were the coolest blood red. I hid my smile. She wasn't a Soulless, but she certainly was a predator.

"Can I help you?" she sneered.

"Yes, I have two more in the truck. Can you grab one?"

She lowered her chin while she cocked an eyebrow at me. "We don't have a watercooler system."

"This the headquarters for Peterson?" I asked.

"Seriously?" she drawled and pointed a manicured fingernail at the big banner that read "ELECT PETERSON."

"Then this is your water," I said. "It's paid for. I'll just set it here."

I started to lower it right by the door to create the biggest obstacle possible.

She sighed and tapped her toes. "Fine," she growled. "Put it in the back room."

"Yes, ma'am," I said with a nod and strolled back into the separated office.

Craig Peterson sat at his desk, his hands hidden as his blue eyes followed me.

"Reception said back here," I said and tapped the water jug.

He lifted an eyebrow and smiled at me. The sinister smile made my skin itch. His Level Two status came from his growing fame as a political frontrunner, but the repugnant waft of must, rotten eggs, and mildew meant he practiced some nasty death arts.

"I have two more in the truck," I said while I cased the room. Nodding toward a door that read "EXIT," I asked, "Care if I use that back door?"

His smile ticked up a bit and something skittered behind his eyes as they flashed brightly.

"By all means," he said, and waved a hand toward it.

I quickly exited the facility and darted around to the back. There were cameras in the front, but the back cameras had been removed. I guessed Craig did that on purpose.

I texted Duke's new number: *Peterson Headquarters, 8421 College Ave.*

Unknown: *About time*

An unexpected smile skittered over my lips which quickly fell. While everything was changed, and Tones was gone, life moved on and so much stayed the same. Duke's responses and the thrill of hunting Soulless. Like everything was fine. And yet Tones wouldn't be there to bribe me with fries and fried food to lure the story out of me. The unexpected wave of numbness, sharp pain, and the urge to run and stop altogether robbed me of breath.

Or would I be able to slink to the back and catch a few minutes of her essence?

Fuck, what was I doing? Getting distracted? That'd only help the Soulless and wouldn't bring Tones back.

The door was ajar by the time I made it around. He was waiting beside it, a smile plastered on his face.

"Gonna help?" I asked.

"You must be built under all those clothes, huh? Lifting all those bottles?" he asked, his eyes scorching over my body.

Gross.

"So, Mr. Peterson," I started, allowing the familiarity to ease through me and focus me.

"Call me Craig. All my friends do," he said and winked.

"Thanks, Mr. Peterson." I stepped into his space.

His eyes dilated. He blinked and for a moment his eyes went completely white before returning to normal.

"My assistant is leaving for the night. We could order dinner. Get to know each other. Work for your vote." He winked.

Ew.

"Oh, we don't need dinner for that," I said checking to make sure the other door was still closed. "Is it locked?"

His smile grew and his crotch started to tent. "Uh-huh."

"Great."

I kneed him and he screamed.

I tossed him against the desk and stood over him.

"You like it kinky?" he said and reached for his pants.

"Mr. Craig Peterson, you have a Level Two target issued on you for the practice of the death arts."

"What?" he howled, his eyes going white again.

Apparently, he didn't recognize me, so maybe Mom wasn't sending pictures.

His smile turned to a snarl and fangs jutted from his mouth. A rank, rotten odor escaped his lips. "You fucking little bitch."

I punched him in the nose and gagged as his green blood spewed over my knuckles. There was something about the green blood of the Arctic type that made me squirmy. Blood should be red or black or blue. But the translucent green was just gross.

He crumpled to the ground, holding his face.

"Do you have a red business card?" I leaned over to meet his eyes.

He growled and lunged at me with his teeth.

Since I didn't need to shoot his second heart to subdue him, I bound his hands and legs. I injected him with a sedative.

I scanned his desk, but nothing red stood out. I tugged out the drawers, but again nothing. So, she wasn't sending the cards to everyone.

I lugged him over my shoulder and exited through the rear. A familiar whine popped in the distance. A red Trailblazer swung around the alley with Duke in the driver's seat.

His green eyes narrowed in on me, and instead of a smile, his lips were pressed into a thin line, seeing Craig.

He popped the trunk without getting out. I tossed Craig back there and jumped into the front passenger seat.

"A congressman?" was all he said.

"The cameras don't work in the back."

"Level Two?" Duke asked, his eyes finding mine.

"Yep," I said with a grin. Fuck John. I had the skills to bring in a Level Two.

Duke fist bumped me, and then eased back in his seat.

My smile tapered. "That was too easy," I muttered.

"What?" Duke snorted.

"He was no different than my other Soulless. Sure, more money and sleezy charm, but my others are physically harder."

"But Craig has more power. He's more dangerous."

I grimaced. "Maybe his level was a mistake." If my mom could have arranged a joke assignment, she'd do it to mess with me.

Duke blinked at me, his face stoic and hard. Finally, he shifted the car into gear.

We were silent as he wove through the alley. He slowed to turn left and head in the direction of John's.

"Wait," I said and flinched.

His eyes cut to me and he waited silently.

"I'm going to Mandy's now. It's on Ivy Lane."

Duke's jaw ticked. "What happened to John?"

"I failed at bringing my mom in, so he won't give me any more targets."

Duke rolled his eyes. "Jackass. Won't give you her target back either, huh?"

"No," I murmured.

"And yet, Level Two," he spat, glancing to the rearview mirror.

We road in silence until a smile cracked across Duke's face. I followed his gaze and saw Oliver coming out of the coffee shop with a lidded cup and pastry three buildings down from Mandy's.

Duke honked as he pulled over.

"No, no, no," I yelled. "Why did you do that?"

Duke waved me off.

Oliver peered back at us and smiled seeing Duke.

Fuck.

Duke pulled around to the back sheltered unloading zone. A canopy covered a bricked-up carport.

I jumped out of the car and opened the trunk on a breath. With a yank, I had the Soulless out and on my shoulder. The harsh smell of dew and sage clung to the air, but a thread of decay underlaid it.

"You're kidding me." Oliver's voice cut through me, and I grimaced. I shifted the Soulless on my shoulder and walked on without acknowledging him. I'd given him his message, and now we needed to move on.

"Dessa, is that a target?" he mocked.

"No, it's a date." I couldn't help it; I rolled my eyes, but I smiled too. Damn him.

"Wait, is that…" Oliver's eyes bulged, and he peeked around me to get a look at the Soulless' face.

"Yes, Congressman Peterson."

"But he's a Level Two," Oliver said and stared at me with awe.

"Yep, he'll be a down payment on an apartment."

"John finally gave you a Level Two?" he asked and moved to walk beside me.

"No."

His eyes gazed up to the building, finally realizing where we were. "You're working for Mandy now?"

"You don't want to hear about this."

"Dessa the Destroyer, the most underused Finder gets a Level Two, and you don't think I want to hear about it?"

"What's with the flattery?"

"Oh yeah, I forgot. You believed the bullshit your mom and John fed you. No matter how many times we tell you otherwise."

"What the hell are you talking about?"

"You should have had Level Twos years ago."

"I don't have the finesse for them," I said, quoting John.

"And yet," Oliver said, waving a hand like a game show model at the Soulless.

"Why would John rob from his own pockets, then?" I asked.

"Maybe he was afraid of your mom," Oliver said and swallowed.

"Why would she keep me from bigger targets?"

"Keep you in need," he said.

It was too logical and I didn't like it.

I adjusted the Soulless on my shoulder.

"He'll just get heavier the longer you hold him."

Damn him, once he said it I could feel the weight bearing down on me.

"Or I can hold the door open for you, so you don't have to fumble with it."

"Whatever," I conceded.

Oliver pushed the door open and yipped when a pistol was leveled at his head.

"I don't pay partners," Mandy said, moving aside to let me bring the target in.

"We're not partners," I said and dropped the Soulless on the same carpet, which had been cleaned since my last visit.

"What is with you and carpets? And who's the cutie?" Mandy asked, shutting the door and locking it.

"Do you have a receiving room that doesn't have carpet?" I asked.

She huffed at me and strolled to her desk. She met my eyes and then looked to Oliver who was standing behind me, glaring at Mandy.

"He's a friend," I said awkwardly and stepped closer to her desk.

"That's a shame. If I were you, I'd be way more than friends with him."

I stifled a laugh as I sensed Oliver following me to the desk.

"Unless you like girls?" she asked.

"Either works," I said.

He brushed against me as he stood off to my right, watching Mandy.

"You're her *friend*?" Mandy asked him with an evil smile.

"Sure," he said. His hand rested on my waist, signaling he was ready to fight if need be.

"Do you know how she found a Level Two in three days? Three days! I had that target sheet circulating for a month with no bites and two missing Finders," Mandy said, pulling out the ledger. "This is the second Level Two in a week from her!"

"Second?" I parroted.

"The banshee was a Level Two," Mandy said.

My brain stalled. What the fuck...

She chuckled. "You bring in more Level Twos than anyone." She hopped in her seat, a wicked smile lighting her face. "John's going to be so pissed."

I brought in Level Twos and John hadn't said anything… What the fuck… Unless Mandy was embellishing for my benefit. My gaze bounced to Oliver.

"She's Dessa the Destroyer," Oliver said. His fingers tightened. He gave me a knowing look. He mouthed, "Told you."

I frowned at him. It couldn't be right.

"Oh, I like that! Dessa the Destroyer," Mandy repeated and pumped her fist in the air.

If I'd been bringing them in, then why hadn't John said anything… Ah fuck. The asshole. He'd pocketed all the extra money from them, too. Or, more likely, funneled a portion to my mom. My face flushed and I curled my toes. Either way, they'd both lied for years. And I'd believed them over Oliver and Duke about levels. About everything Finding related. But why wouldn't John lie about fees and levels? He was always deducting my pay for bullshit stuff.

"I can't believe John was stupid enough to let her go," Mandy said, signing the check with a flourish.

"I failed to bring in my last target," I murmured.

"One target? So what? You bring in the most Level Twos, but you can't get them all."

"Yes, I can," I said and met her stare. I'd gotten all my targets assigned to me, and apparently a fucking bunch of Level Twos while being told I wasn't good enough. For years. My stomach twisted, my body heaving as the weight of her words settled on me. But somehow, my mom's target was different. Be it she knew me too well or I was too blind to her.

She smiled at me like she was in on the joke, but her face fell, and she looked to Oliver. "She caught them all?"

We both nodded.

She stared at me, holding the check in limbo until it bent in half and folded over her hand.

"Why did he let you go? The real reason?" she asked, her voice dangerous.

I stared at her, unwilling to divulge the information. The truth no longer felt like the truth.

Oliver stepped slightly in front of me. He snatched the check from Mandy's hand and handed it back to me while maintaining his focus on Mandy.

"I don't know if I can do business with you," Mandy said, her eyes narrowing into slits.

"I'm sure a Level One retrieval will change that," I said and, turning to leave, I pulled Oliver after me.

After walking with him to the bar, I left for my apartment. My mind reeled about Mandy's change in demeanor, the Level Two Soulless I collected, the other Level Twos I'd brought in, and Oliver. My thoughts kept looping back to him. He should hate me. My mother killed his mother. My mom had tried to kill him. If it'd benefit her, she'd try again. Instead, he still wanted to protect me? We had some unresolved issues. And he was a distraction. I was less aware around him, less focused. Just like when I was walking and didn't notice the large figure standing in my path. A figured that screamed at me, drenching me in spit and food chunks as they drew a gun.

Finders' Handbook

Soulless Rights - They have none. By
their choice of the death arts, they
negate all laws surrounding Vessels. It
is a Finder's choice to declare what
they are charged with.

CHAPTER 16

I WAS quick to pull my blade out, but the Soulless was quicker. It pulled off a shot, but luckily the shot was crap and it only grazed my shoulder.

I bit back my curse as I kicked their feet out from beneath them. It screamed again, and backflipped over my attack, landing on all fours. A wicked tongue flicked out; its poisonous, pocked appendage wriggled in freedom from the too-small constraints of its mouth.

Before I could mount an attack, a hole ripped through its arm, spilling blood down its shirt. It whirled around at the new attack and hissed.

I pulled my pistol from my holster and shot it in the head. It howled in an inhuman voice, blathering on as it faded.

I pushed myself up to find my dad standing a few feet away.

"Are you fucking following me?" I spat.

"You should thank me. Your mom is picking up her search for you. But she won't be able to find you… yet."

"I want her to find me," I countered. Then I wouldn't have to track her through the targets and red cards. I could just end this, one way or another.

He chuckled at me.

"No, you don't. Four days left. I can't have you getting killed before you decide," he said.

"I can just tell you no now, then." I stood up and tightened my grip on the blade as I braced myself for his argument. "Let her find me. I want to find her. I don't give a shit about her Companion."

He smiled at me like I was a cute toddler who just learned the word no. "See you in four days, unless you need me sooner."

It took all I had not to shoot him. I probably should have, but he didn't seem like the type that would die, and then I'd have wasted a bullet.

I watched him disappear into the shadows. Tones' words filled my ears. Who did I think I was going after, my mom or her Companion? They'd killed me once. And I wanted them to find me? My father was only using me, and then what? Two dudes were having a pissing contest and I didn't want to be the judge.

My new life was turning into a repeat of my past, but it was life I knew and was comfortable with. I could easily fall back into my routines. Fight with Oliver. Hang out with Duke and Alan. Bring in a Soulless. Bask in my loveless life as I mowed down ramen noodles and sale-priced insta-crap. Hopefully continue to visit Tones in spirit form. Or I could return to Manchester, pick back up with the quiet, boring life there. Neither would be an option until I brought my mom in. And no one around me would be safe. I'd avenge Tones, get rid of my biggest threat, who was sending the Soulless after me, and eliminate my connection to my father's wants. It was a lose-lose situation, but I didn't have a win-win. At least in this scenario, I got to crawl back into my life versus running scared. Even if death was sooner.

Since he was blocking us from finding each other, I needed a different way. Knowing she'd keep sending Soulless for me gave me an idea. I'd make myself an easy target. Pick up my hunting and rattle the Soulless. Then I would get information from the ones she sent for me.

She couldn't pursue me directly, so I should be resting easy. Her sending a Soulless was the best chance I had to survive and get the element of surprise.

I USED my Finder's money to put the first and last month's rent down on an apartment. My new location would reduce the risk to Duke and Alan when Soulless came looking for me. Instead of my typical location, I was a few blocks from Duke and Alan's. I wasn't delusional enough to think I was protected there. Soulless may not be the most organized in going after Finders—we were easier to take out when we approached them—but the neighborhood had better restaurants.

Oliver had called and left me several texts, which I ignored. He needed to let go so he could be safe. Distance from me was for his safety. My world only brought issues.

Unfortunately, his bar was a hive of information and my common stomping ground. Soulless my mom sent would look for me there. He'd have targets to retrieve, too. The bar was profitable, but it covered his family home and younger siblings. Their college tuition was expensive. His targets were easy bumps of funds and provided instant cash.

Once Oliver left, I slipped in. I didn't go to the bar. Unsure what Oliver had shared, I didn't need the distraction of Benny's disapproval or reporting back to Oliver that I came in.

I found a two-chair table in the corner and leaned against the wall. I ordered a beer but let it sit sweating down the table, turning tepid. I pretended to swig from it, but I didn't let it touch my lips, following Rule Two. Even though I trusted Benny, as Tones did, I didn't trust anything that wasn't directly from his hand to mine.

The bar was crammed with people bumping into each other and trying to steal my second chair or sit in it. I had three different people casting glances my way, more than just for the chair. All three were Soulless. It'd be a big score, but Tones always told us to leave them in the bar. It was the neutral ground. We could use it for information, but never take them from the bar. Even if she was gone, I wouldn't disobey her. This bar was still hers in spirit.

My heart rate ticked up as one of the Soulless grabbed a chair closer and closer to me every few minutes. He'd flash a grin my way. As expected, I guessed Mom had spread the cards here, too. When he was two tables away, I slipped a twenty to the waitress for my one beer and walked out, expecting him to follow. All three watched me go but moved their glances to others in the bar.

No one followed me out, but I almost collided with a different one outside Mason's as I exited the bar. Another Soulless next to him laughed.

The one I almost ran into swore at me, but I ignored it. I didn't need their shit as I looked for Mom's Soulless minions.

But they followed. They weren't my assigned targets, but they'd decided to be by tailing me. Looked like I misidentified the Soulless who had Mom's cards.

I could take both out, but I wanted information, too. That was the tricky part, using finesse, especially when facing two. If they were working together, it'd be harder. If they fought each other, it could turn deadly for all of us.

I slowed my pace and ducked into an alley. The shadows swam around me and laced through my legs.

The Soulless entered the alley, sticking to the shadows. I watched them search for me. Although I was shrouded in the shadows, if they were Vessels or Soulless, they should be able to see me.

They crept past me in their search.

I waited to see if it was a trap, for me to let my guard down. They didn't flinch or slow.

When I stepped forward to watch, the shadows drew back to me, snaking around. That's when I realized the shadows were hiding me.

I cracked a grin. For all their chattering, they could be very useful.

I reached for my pistol. There were two of them and I stood better chances with bullets. They wouldn't willingly go with me, and they would use whatever death art enhancements they had to destroy me. A moment's hesitation stopped me, though. If I shot one, I'd naturally go for the second one, too, call it a night, and enjoy a feast of frozen pizza, or real pizza since there were two.

Nope, I needed their information.

I stalked behind them, trying not to scrape my shoes or walk heavily, but their ears twitched and heads tilted back trying to find my trail. Their noses scrunched as they caught a whiff of me. Even if I was invisible in the shadows, they knew someone was there.

Despite the awareness, I still had the element of surprise and lunged forward. In one swoop I sliced across the chest of one and into the other. On my return thrust up, I jabbed the blade backward and brought up my right leg, driving it into the dent between the hips and ribs, causing that one to crumple.

I didn't wait to see if they were down or just stunned. The other one swung at the air and connected with my shoulder. The shadows hissed and swirled toward the Soulless' face, disorienting him and allowing me to regain my balance. I thrust forward with an uppercut and then a knee to the groin.

After zip tying their hands and legs, I brushed the street debris on my hands on their jeans. They were Soulless and could escape from ties, but it delayed and pissed them off.

I dragged them to the shadows and propped them against the wall behind a dumpster with the smashed-up, gooey bits of food and garbage that hadn't made it in the bin. Rats scuttled in the dumpster, the only other living creatures around us. The lightbulbs in the alley's light posts had been long ago broken and the shards smashed into dust, but I didn't want any helpful Samaritan that walked by to think they were saving the world.

Even though I wanted answers, I aimed my gun at them.

I kicked the one on the left and they gurgled. I kicked the other one and it swore. Winner!

"Is the card on you?" I asked.

"Bug off, bitch," he spat.

"It'd be red and have fancy print. Is it on you?"

He snarled in response and tried to adjust himself into a comfortable position.

I kicked him in the calf, unsettling him.

"No," he finally said.

"Did you get one?"

He remained slumped but turned his eyes up to me. The white orbs no longer mimicking human ones.

"Where is she?" Soulless could kill for the fun of it alone. The level of reward could encourage a desperate Soulless to do really stupid things.

He remained still but his eyes shuttered, hiding all emotion.

I took out my blade and rubbed a finger along its edge.

"Where is she?" I repeated and jabbed my blade down into the fleshy part of his leg.

He howled and I grimaced at the noise. At least it wasn't a banshee, but still high-pitched and guttural. Unless he had a pack, the noise would send any other Soulless scurrying away.

The cry, however, stirred the one next to him.

I smiled at the alert one. "I'll cut you all up and leave them," I gestured with a thumb toward the other one, "unscathed as they tell me all I want to know."

"You are a bitch," he spat.

I plunged my blade into his other leg. Blood pooled on the ground, sending the shadows into a frenzy as they swirled around him.

The Soulless roared and panted, and finally asked, "Why do they help you?"

I raised an eyebrow at him and cleaned my blade on his lower pants that were still dry.

"Come again?"

"The shadows." He nodded toward the slithering shapes running along his frame.

"I'm awesome," I said smiling, but I had no idea why they were helping or for how long.

The other Soulless groaned and started to shake its head.

"Oops, time's up," I cheered toward the one I'd used as a pincushion.

"Wait," he croaked.

"Where is she?"

"She's—" He choked and lurched forward as the Soulless next to him plunged their long tongue into his ear canal. The tongue darted back out dripping blood.

"You wanted to be the one to tell me where she is?" I asked while leveling my gun at them and bracing for the attack.

They hissed and sprayed blood from the other Soulless at me.

"I see," I said and blasted a hole into the Soulless.

Fuck, no information from either.

I pulled out my phone and texted: *Two, alley between Forrester St and Lovers' Lane.*

Unknown: *Damn you're fast.*

As I waited, I wondered if Mandy would allow me in after last time, or if she'd just put a bullet in my head.

I owed her the respect of choosing.

A whine and pop sounded, and Duke appeared with the Escape again.

"Same place?" he asked as I hopped in the car.

"Yeah, Mandy's."

His eyes tracked back to the Soulless and then me.

Thoughts spun in my head. Had Duke known all along about my Level Twos? Or, as a Driver, did he not care? He had flat fees.

We rode silently until we reached Mandy's.

"Want me to help?" he asked, unbuckling his seatbelt.

"Naw," I said. Swallowing down my reservations, I added, "Thanks, as always."

"You tip the best," he said with a wink.

I shot him a smile before hopping out and grabbing the Soulless.

Instead of just entering her place, I rapped on the door with my right hand while still holding one of the Soulless. Its blood marred the brown door and I grimaced.

I only allowed one knock. I wouldn't beg.

I waited a few moments, ran my tongue over my teeth, and accepted that I'd have to find a new Finders' Agency. I considered which one when the door opened. Mandy stood there in her black velour body suit and her mass of curls pulled off her face with a headband.

"When did you take to knocking?" she spat and stepped back to let me in.

"I don't have Level Ones to change your mind, and after last night, I wasn't sure I was welcome here."

"When has that stopped you?" she said and sized up the Soulless.

"Did you get a receiving area or is the carpet fine?"

"Ha ha," she said, "just wait." She went into a small door and returned with flattened cardboard. "Here, put them here."

I obliged and pretended not to notice the blood trail the Soulless had already made from the door to the cardboard.

She noticed and sighed. "Next time, call so I can prepare."

I nodded, though I doubted I'd call.

"I decided I don't care why John fired you. You're Dessa the Destroyer and have already brought in four Soulless in a week. Most struggle to bring in two in a month."

I stared at her. Flattery again, but I did notice the comment about John. "So, he wouldn't tell you?"

She pursed her lips and rolled her eyes. "He says I should kick you out and cut the loss."

I stared around the office. "But you ignored that advice."

"Of course I did. His caseloads are going to rocket, and he won't have his closer. Without you to wrap up the difficult ones, he'll drop on the list. I love it," she said with a clap and small jump. "The Trust will be here soon to collect, so this helps my monthly numbers."

A curl of joy twisted in my veins. Fuck John. He stole from me and undersold my abilities for years.

"Where's that cutie you were with?" A dark glint twinkled in her eye.

Despite my best efforts, heat crept up my neck and across my cheeks. I didn't bother with a response. I could deny him and sound wistful or get mad and sound pathetic.

She handed me my check with a smile.

HABITS ARE A BITCH. My habit had me walking back to the bar. I stood a block away, staring at it. It still felt like my refuge, my place I belonged, but I needed to get over it.

I rubbed a hand through my hair and groaned when it stuck in some of the dried-up goo bits. Instead of easing into my stool, gulping down a cola, and ignoring Benny's scowl or Oliver's prying, I opted for a coveted delivery pizza from a local place and a six-pack of cola. Dinner of the champs.

I stepped out of the shower and grabbed the T-shirt and pants from the top of the laundry bin, which I rightly had back after leaving Duke and Alan's. No matter how I protested, Alan would put my clothes in the dresser drawers. He didn't believe it was needless work. I didn't bother to blow-dry my hair but wrapped it in a silk cloth.

My third apartment was much like the others with plain walls; however, Duke and Alan as an unwanted surprise had decorated it for me. My skin itched just looking at the stuff that could gather dust and would be abandoned when I left. I'd need to leave them a key so they could retrieve their treasures. Regardless of my optimism at starting over, I didn't dare to believe I'd get to keep my current life. Something would happen. Most likely involving my mother.

I hung a towel, another gift from Duke and Alan, over the painting on the wall. It had people in it. Even though I'd yet to discover a Vessel who could merge into a painting, I still found it creepy to have painted eyes staring back at me.

The doorbell rang, pulling me from my decorating. I hoped it was my pizza, but I looked to the shadows to make sure it wasn't my dad.

"Is it really pizza?" I asked.

"Yes," they affirmed, but their voices were higher pitched than normal.

I grabbed my blade to be on the safe side. I didn't bother looking through the peephole. They'd see my shadow by the door and get the upper hand.

It was my pizza, but carrying it were Duke and Alan.

"You only got one?" Duke asked.

"It was meant only for me," I said and took the box and slid the pizza into the oven.

"It's already cooked, sweets," Alan said and popped a cola open.

"She's paranoid." Duke grabbed his own cola and plopped down on the sofa. "She thinks it's laced."

I was the proud owner of a matching sofa set. I'd used part of my Level Two money, under heavy pressure from Duke and Alan, and bought furniture instead of curb shopping.

"Why the surprise?" I asked.

"We wanted to see how you are doing," Duke said.

"I'm here and alive." I grabbed my own cola.

They shared a look and then turned their gazes in unison to me. Marriage made people creepy.

"Dessa, sweets, we love you," Alan started.

"Oh, great, is this an intervention?"

They paused and an awkward beat passed.

"On what?" I yelled and threw my hands in the air.

"You were silent in the car. Normally I get a vivid rundown. So, I assume tonight had to do with her because you refuse to talk about her."

"Which her?" I choked.

"Either, actually," Duke said and patted my knee.

"What would you like me to say? I'm the reason Tones was killed and I'm going after the psycho bitch who killed her?" A familiar pain clenched around my heart.

They shared another look. I was going to gouge their eyes out. I forgot how much they did this before marriage.

"You are not responsible for Tones' death," Alan said evenly.

"Like hell I'm not!" The clenching tightened.

A fist pounded on the wall. I'd yelled one too many times for my fancy neighbors. I walked over and punched the wall back, easing some of the tension in my chest. It dented slightly and I decided I'd move the creepy painting there.

"What do you mean you're going after the psycho bitch?"

I stared at them. I didn't want to tell them she'd sent Soulless after me, that I was still hunting her, or my dad was involved in hiding us from each other. They'd flip out. I opted for silence, even if it wouldn't last long.

"Okay." Duke put his feet on the floor and his hands on his knees. He shook his head, which appeared to be more in response to his internal thoughts, and finally snagged my glance with his green eyes. "Okay."

This felt like a trap. I pulled back slightly, flexing my fingers in preparation of something. I'd never battled Duke nor wanted to.

"What do you mean okay?" Alan gritted out, glaring at Duke.

Oh, good cop bad cop, huh? I rolled my eyes.

"I mean okay. She has every right to go after Claudine. The bitch killed her. Oliver mentioned the Soulless that attacked her. If the Soulless are attacking Dessa, it means someone's paying them to. You don't stalk a tiger unless you're gullible, desperate, or have a death wish."

Wait a minute, how did Oliver know that, and why did he share it? Did he share about the Level Twos also? That I'd been duped by John for years?

Alan's eye shifted to me and his expression eased. He asked, "Is it true? Is she sending the Soulless after you?"

I bit my lips to keep my rant from escaping. I was going to slice Oliver open and pull out his organs one by one.

"I take it yes," Alan said, searching my face.

I growled. I hated that they knew me. That was the problem with friends; they knew you too well to let you lie to yourself.

"Why didn't you ask for help?"

I shifted my gaze to Duke, and then shaking my head, went to get the pizza out of the oven.

Duke followed me and wrinkled his nose at the pizza.

"It's crispy now," he said but still plucked a piece.

"Most things can't survive heat." I plopped the pizza down on the bar top, no longer hungry. My hatred of Oliver's betrayal filled me and fed my anger.

"She's more upset than when we arrived," Duke said and used a finger to circle around the air in the direction of my face and then took a bite of the steaming pizza without flinching.

"We're talking about her mom, of course she's mad." Alan pulled a slice of pizza onto a plate.

"Nope, that's not her mad-at-mom face. That one, she has a demented smile while plotting her demise," Duke said. "This is betrayal."

Alan stopped and eyed me up. I snarled at him. It wasn't my finest moment.

"Sweets, what's going on?" Alan stood and walked over to me.

I fisted my hands on my hips and separated my legs to gain space. I mustered my best "leave me the fuck alone" expression I had and stared him down.

"Oh, she's really mad," Alan said without stepping back. To my horror, he reached out and wrapped an arm around my shoulders. "Tell us what we did."

"We?" Duke choked. "We didn't do anything but show up with pizza."

I laughed at that. "My pizza, you jackass."

"Ah, there she is." Duke slid me a plate with a slice on it closer to me. "Eat up."

I took a bite, but it tasted like cardboard.

"Since you've been a barren land of details, Dessa, what is your plan to take down your mom?" Duke asked.

I shook my head.

"We want to help," Duke said.

Alan slid him a wild glance but then rocked his head back and forth and nodded. "We'll help."

"I appreciate it, guys, but it's best if I do it alone."

NOISE – RESIDENT AGREES NOT TO CAUSE OR ALLOW ANY
NOISE OR ACTIVITY ON THE PREMISES WHICH MIGHT DISTURB
THE PEACE AND QUIET OF ANOTHER RESIDENT AND/OR
NEIGHBOR. SAID NOISE AND/OR ACTIVITY SHALL BE A BREACH
OF THIS AGREEMENT.

CHAPTER 17

TO SAY I was baffled when Duke and Alan left me to go after my mom alone was an understatement. I didn't want their help, but they weren't known for giving up. However, they'd shrugged my plans off, eaten pizza, drunk cola, watched a movie, and left.

My suspicions were right, though. I'd gone to bed and woken up to an angry ant march of text messages. Bing. Bing. Bing! Bing, bing, bing!

I slammed my hand on my phone and turned it to vibrate. But the noises didn't stop. Instead of Bings! it was knocking. Heavy knocking and what sounded like cursing.

I pulled my gun out and almost shot a hole through the wall to silence it before reconsidering.

"Who is it?" I asked the shadows.

They tittered but didn't respond.

The pounding continued, and I could hear my neighbors getting up. They weren't loud, but I sensed it. I could just let them deal with it. They'd turn into a bathrobe-wearing militant group complaining about noises after a reasonable hour and drive the person away with their endless chatter and ranting. I turned to go back to bed, but then I realized if it were my dad, he'd just kill them.

"Is it my dad?" I asked as I stormed to the front door.

"Nope," they giggled.

I grimaced at their creepy tittering and yanked open the door, holding my pistol at head level.

"What the fuck is wrong with you?" Oliver screamed at me and pushed me into the apartment.

I stood dumbfounded, still holding my pistol, and staring into an empty doorway.

Someone cleared their throat, and I looked up to see all my floor mates out in the hall. Most with bats, some with a gun, and all with a cellphone, and yes, all wearing some form of bathrobe attire.

"Sorry," I mumbled, turned, and walked back into my apartment. They'd probably assume a lovers' spat. I heard the shadows beneath me and looked down.

"They're calling the cops," they sang mockingly.

"Oh, for fuck's sake." This is what I got for living in a better part of town.

I flung the door open and stepped back out. The few remaining shrank back, startled.

"I'm sorry, really, he's a little drunk and forgot his key." I smiled brightly at them all. I made sure to show a little but not too much teeth and bat my eyes. It was my mom's look, but it worked.

"You sure?" the one holding the phone asked and looked for reassurance from the others around her.

"I haven't seen him before," an older neighbor chimed in. "How many boyfriends do you have?"

I suppressed an eye roll. Tomorrow, I'd be looking for an apartment back in the part of town I was accustomed to.

"I didn't say he was a boyfriend," I smiled cheekily and closed my door.

Once my door was shut, I whirled around to ream Oliver, but he wasn't behind me. He paced the living room, staring unseeingly at the floor, his eyes bouncing around, his hands pressed against his scalp, tugging on his locks. My skin flushed and I licked my lips. I wanted to run my hands through his hair. I shook my head to clear my thoughts. Sleep deprivation was catching up with me.

But I didn't have time for that nonsense. I stalked into the room and blocked his path. He reared back, startled by my sudden presence. His lost expression focused and hardened into anger.

"What the—" he started bellowing again, but I slapped my hand over his mouth. A heated jolt shot through me and I pulled my hand quickly away.

"My neighbors want to call the cops, so quiet the fuck down or leave. On second thought, I didn't invite you in. What are you doing here?" My thoughts were scrambled, and I couldn't focus on my main question.

"What the fuck do you think you're doing?" he said between clenched teeth, his eyes flaring with each syllable.

"I was sleeping, but someone woke me up." I swept my hand toward him.

"You're going after your mom?" He threw his hands out to the side.

How did he know? I ran my thoughts backward. Oh yeah, Duke and Alan. The tattletales.

He took ragged breaths, staring at me. The longer he stared, the more heated I felt and unraveled my brain became. I wanted to grab his face and other body parts and rub against them.

"Dessa, what the fuck are you planning with your mom?" He didn't yell, but his anger rolled off in waves.

His fucking big brother crap. My stomach curdled and the heat in my stomach twisted out.

"Who you gonna report it to?" I spat back.

"What?"

"You told Duke and Alan my mom sent the Soulless after me."

"You thought that was a secret?" He laughed humorlessly.

"What are you talking about?" Stepping back for distance, I went to the kitchen for a beverage to settle my stomach.

He reached into his pocket and pulled out a Ziploc bag that contained a scarlet red card.

"Is she passing these out as favors?" I asked.

"Dessa, you're in trouble."

That was an understatement. She was handing out the invitations to my permanent retirement. I rolled my tongue over my teeth to control my retort.

"Why'd you tell Duke and Alan about the Soulless?" I asked, pulling two cans of cola from the fridge. Damn my manners. Tones had taught me that one.

"They care about you," he said, accepting the cola. "And you'll listen to them."

"What does that mean?"

"Really? You blow me off all the time and won't tell me shit."

"You tattle," I said, pointing a finger at his face.

"Grow up, Dessa," he said with a sigh.

"Oliver, I've taken care of myself for years."

"I know, but Dessa, she already killed you once," he said and tilted his head back against the wall to stare at the ceiling.

"And I'll make sure she doesn't again."

He closed his eyes and snorted. "It's not just your mom, she has an army."

"An army?"

"You know what I mean. Her Companion is powerful. Lots of the Soulless are flocking to him. It's rumored he can make Level Ones look tame."

What the fuck? No wonder Mom was obsessed with him if she was a Soulless.

"Who is her Companion?" I asked. My memory flickered back to the room. A shiver stole through me, but I focused on him. I had to have seen his face, but years of honing only seeing blurry faces with whoever accompanied her won out. All I could remember was his impeccable clothing and dark, tidy hair. Even without my mom's men blinders on, I hadn't recognized his voice.

He shrugged. "I don't know yet. I haven't met him, but I've heard the whispers. You have to be careful."

"I can't stand by and do nothing. She killed me. She killed Tones.

She almost killed you." I blinked back my emotions. I didn't want him to misread my words and think I needed comforting or sympathy.

"You're being foolish. Mom wouldn't want you to avenge her."

I just stared at him. I already knew this. She told me. But Tones was the only real parental figure I'd had. She tried to provide me with a measured innocence growing up in her bar. My mom had not only killed me, but she'd robbed me of the one source of comfort I had.

He let out a long sigh and rubbed his forehead.

"Dessa," Oliver whispered and stepped forward, closing the distance between us. He reached out, grabbing my hands.

My breath caught in my throat as I stared up into his dark eyes and his thumbs rubbed circles over my hands.

"You're stupid enough to do this." His words caused me to flinch. "But you're not alone."

I LIVED with the delusion I'd get my way for a couple more hours. I lay flopped on my sofa, reading a novel, enjoying a drink when the shadows started in again.

I enlarged my eyes to focus on the words and hummed slightly to myself, but their chattering only intensified. They swam around the walls and the floor in a frenzied dance.

"What," I finally barked.

They hissed back in annoyance.

I sighed in defeat. "I'm sorry, what happened, oh wonderful slithering creatures?"

Despite my mockery, they responded, "She's made an attempt."

I stopped breathing, my heart stopped beating, and I stared at the wall for an indeterminate amount of time. Finally, I licked my lips, and forced myself to ask, "Who did she go after?"

They swirled around, all talking at once, creating an insistent drone.

"Talk in unison or only one talk," I said.

"She went after Oliver."

That idiot went after her for me.

I was out of my chair and to the bar in record time. The sun beat down on me and I blocked my eyes with my arms. The building looked foreign in the bright light of day. The brick facade was painted a pale yellow, recently touched-up, I'd guess from Tones. The windows were clean, but the blinds were drawn. I pushed on the door, but it was locked. I didn't bother knocking, and instead darted around the back to the employee entrance.

I picked my way in. Unlike at night, the facility was empty and only the drone of fluorescent lights and appliances filled the space.

I didn't go to the front restaurant area. I veered to the left and ascended the narrow steps that led to the private family area. It wasn't a section I ventured into often. Even with Tones, her kids normally stayed in the back offices. The upstairs was only for sleeping, and I didn't sleep over.

We'd snuck up there a few times as kids, so I knew my way around. Nostalgia still sucker-punched me when I topped the steps. The same avocado-green appliances were in the kitchen, the beige carpeting, patchwork sofa, and a plain cozy vibe dominated the room.

I licked my lips and allowed myself one moment to take it in. Then I darted down the hall to the four bedrooms. The one in the back left corner was the master; the one across was Oliver's. As the oldest, he got his own room. The four other brothers split up the two rooms. None were large, but worked.

I paused in the hall to listen for voices. Finally realizing I was intruding, I glanced to the shadows. They seemed chipper, which I was beginning to realize meant Oliver and I were alone.

Even if he'd been a loud jerk at my apartment, he'd waited for me to open the door, even if not invited in, before entering. His mom had taught us some manners. I knocked on his bedroom door.

Only silence greeted me, but I felt the startled tension through the door. He was purposely being silent.

I knocked again, and called out, "Oliver, you awake?"

"Dessa?" he called back. I heard shuffling on the other side, like he was picking up items and discarding them and shoving things around.

"Yeah, open up."

He cracked the door open. His hair was disheveled, his beard fuller than normal, and his shirt was halfway pulled down with his abs exposed like he'd yanked it on while opening the door.

I may have licked my lips before my eyes darted back up to meet his. That's when I saw it. A massive bruise spread along his jaw and trailed up his cheek. His right arm was bandaged and hung stiffly to his side.

My fingers curled into fists and I pushed the door open harder than planned. He stumbled back, still sluggish with sleep. I caught his arm to help steady him.

His fingers wrapped around my arm and lingered. I swallowed and a flush warmed in me.

"What did she do?" I used my other hand to touch his cheek.

He flinched from the contact, and I retracted my hand, but then moved it back to rub the area that wasn't bruised.

"Dessa, it doesn't matter," he murmured, closing his eyes.

"Bullshit," I spat and crowded his space, standing on my toes to examine the damage.

"It's my fault."

"What?" I leaned back to catch his eyes. Mistake. Now I was focused on his face and not as much on his words. I blinked and pulled my gaze back down to see if there was more damage. I'm going with that. I wasn't really checking him out. That'd be rude and creepy after he'd been attacked.

"I still have her target," he said, not willing to meet my eyes. "She heard I was looking for her. She found me. I didn't even see her coming."

"You what?!" I squeezed his arm way too tight, my nails digging into his flesh until he winced and yelped. Not only had John given it to him, something I thought impossible, but he hadn't taken it back, either. What the fuck was wrong with John? I wasn't enough to mess with? "Why didn't you tell me?"

"I didn't want you going after her alone."

I shoved him, separating our hands. He winced as he stumbled a step.

"Stop thinking I'm weak." His big brother bullshit again.

"It's not that," he said and flinched.

Like hell it wasn't. He wouldn't keep going after her if he wasn't trying to protect me. He didn't think I could stand up to her. Even if he didn't realize it, I had to protect him instead. She was toying with him. She'd almost killed him twice now, but he survived. It was a message for me.

"You know what, Oliver?" I stepped away from him. "I'm a disaster. I'm like a tornado and suck up everything in my path and spit it back out damaged or ruined."

"What are you talking about?"

"She's coming after you because of me."

"No," he interrupted. He held his hand up. "Dessa, she's a bitch but this isn't about you. She went after me because I went after her."

My eyes narrowed. He went after her because of me. It was a circle.

"She didn't finish killing me," he gulped. "As a way to taunt you, piss you off. So you don't know when it is really coming. She wants to fuck with your head."

Fuck it. I needed to stay away from him so he didn't try more heroics. Not just distance. "I'll stop using the bar. Pull her attention away from you." And his from her. Perhaps that was the best way to protect him.

"Whoa," he said, reaching for me, but I stepped back. "That's ridiculous, the bar is the best place for tips. It's a neutral spot."

"I'll find another way." A lot harder and more dangerous way.

"No, you won't," he said and stood taller. "Ever realize why the bar was so good? Why a Finder could get in with the Soulless, and they never recognized you as one?"

"Your mom's magic," I said. My mom had made sure I understood to never speak of Finding or hunting Soulless while there. Tones' magic masked our scent. Our smell was why many Finders struggled to bring in the Soulless—they could detect Finders coming. With our scent masked, the only way we'd be outed was if we messed up. It was the reason I never associated with other Finders and changed my appearance often. Then I couldn't be recognized. "Her magic masks our Finder smell. But we can still tell the Soulless from the Vessels and the Vessels from the humans. Just not smell the Finder on them."

He shrugged and looked away.

"What? What does that shrug mean?" I said mimicking him. My mom may have often lied, but I knew I was right about masking the Finder smell—besides, Tones had confirmed it. "I'm right. I can't smell the Finder on you in there."

"Kind of." He rubbed a hand over his neck, his lips warring with his choice of the next words. "It's supposed to make everyone smell the same—Finder, Vessel, Soulless, and human. I can't detect them there unless you point them out, and I can't really tell a Soulless from a Vessel unless I see their enhancement or have their target sheet with a picture. You have a true gift."

"Stop with the flattery."

"For fuck's sake, Dessa, it's the fucking truth. You can root them out of a mile-high pile of garbage. I can't. Mom didn't want us hunting there because we shouldn't have been able to. Period." He shifted on his feet and scratched his neck. His eyes darted to the side.

Fuck. His flattery was a distraction.

"What aren't you telling me?" My chin lowered and my brows furrowed.

He sighed and licked his lips.

"Tell me."

His eyes flashed, and a smirk skittered across his lips before his face slackened. The fucker. "I will tell you if you promise to not go without me."

My head jerked back. If it had something to do with my mom, I shouldn't let him go with me, we needed distance. But if he still had a lead… maybe I could work around him.

He met my gaze and cocked an eyebrow.

What could he possibly know that I didn't?

"Oliver."

"Dessa. You have to promise."

His smirk reappeared and I growled. Dammit. "Fine."

"There are other neutral spots."

"Yes, Oliver, I know." I rolled my eyes. "This isn't new information. There's one in Detroit and one in Milwaukee. I doubt my mom or her Companion are commuting."

A triumph smiled curled his lips. "You sure those are the only two?"

I stilled. My heart skipped a beat and my eyes darted around. I ran through all the places I knew. Mason's was the only one that I knew was neutral in Coving. A spark of hope ignited in my chest. I stood a chance of finding my mom.

"There're other places like Mason's? In Coving?" Did Mom know? Wait… Did she always know? Of course, the bitch probably did. Was she using one?

He narrowed his eyes. "There aren't other bars. And they aren't as safe."

"Okay, but other places that are neutral?"

He nodded. "There are two others in Coving."

"How do you know? How long have you known?"

His gaze fell to the floor and he swallowed. "Mom was part of a group. She didn't want us to know. She left a note on the paperwork in case I found it. She knew we… you respected her neutral zone but wasn't sure you'd respect others."

Damn. She didn't trust me… but she had a point. I only respected her rules because they were hers.

He swallowed and averted his eyes. His jaw ticked. "I found out after…"

Fuck. I ran a hand through my hair, my stomach twisting. I couldn't undo what my mom did, but I would do my best to stop her. To avenge Tones. "Where are they?"

"We go together, remember?"

I nodded. Once he showed me where they were, I could go back on my own. If it was a neutral zone, there was a chance my dad's magic wouldn't work there. Neither would my mom's. I could access the place she was at without either of them knowing.

He narrowed his eyes and scrutinized my face. Finally, he sighed and shook his head.

"Fine, tomorrow, ten p.m., we'll meet out front. No targets, though."

"It's a date," I said and groaned later at the innuendo.

MOM'S RULES

Rule Three: Know your exits and options

CHAPTER 18

I SHOWED up in my typical gear: T-shirt, flannel, cargo pants. I didn't bring the gun; I wanted to honor my word, but I didn't travel without my blade. Oliver should know that.

Oliver, true to his word, loitered outside of the bar. He wore dark jeans and a dark sweater. He smiled naturally when he saw me and pushed himself off the building.

I stopped a few feet away, unsure about the next steps. This was new territory. Finders didn't work together. I shook my internal head. We weren't Finders tonight. We were just hanging out, at a place with Soulless, and we were Finders. This was going to suck. It'd be against all my training and instinct.

He chuckled at my expression and slipped his hand into mine. A pleasant jolt shot through me. I froze at the contact but covered it by starting to walk even though I didn't know where we were going.

"No need to rush, there's no time limit. It doesn't stop existing at midnight."

"Ha ha," I retorted lamely. I cringed at my awkward side that he brought out of me. The one that I hadn't had to deal with since I didn't go to school or deal with common affairs.

"Hungry?" he asked and gestured toward a taco truck.

"I'm good," I said and of course my stomach rumbled at the delicious aromas wafting our way.

"Really?" He smiled. "What type of date would it be if we didn't eat?"

I closed my eyes and wished away the words I'd said and the situation. I opened them to see Oliver grinning at me. My stomach fluttered. I fought an eye roll and sucked on my teeth. I smiled in return. They had bagged chips and cans of soda. "If you're paying, sure."

"Glad that's settled," he said and pulled me next to him. While holding my hand, he lifted his arm to wrap around my shoulders so my arm crossed my chest while still in his. A flush built on my neck and clawed at my face. My heart kicked up the pace and I licked my lips.

"Really playing this up, huh?" I choked.

He leaned close and whispered, "Only getting started."

My eyes, the traitorous jerks, darted to his face. I didn't lose myself in his eyes or mouth, but I saw red looking at his bruises. They'd faded since yesterday, but greenish blemishes swirled through the pattern and laced his jaw. He'd let his beard grow out a bit, which was delightful in all the wrong ways, but I could see the pattern beneath the stubble. If I didn't know it was there, it'd look like shadows.

"So where are we going?" I said, fidgeting in the line.

He chuckled, the rumble vibrating through me, and I fought my own smile. I hated that he had any effect on me. I knew he was playing the part. We were on a fake date. He liked to tease me, rile me up, and get under my skin. I hated that it worked.

"Just relax," he said and stepped up to order.

Relax, sure. I was a wolf in sheep's clothing, set to scope out my prey's home and find its weakness. If I was right, I could pass through these areas undetected, and if Oliver was right, I'd still be able to detect them. I'd be able to find my mother without her finding me. Without my dad's interference.

I'D EXPECTED A DARK, abandoned factory; likely with strewn bits all over, rodents crawling everywhere, the smell of urine, feces, and blood thick in the area for the death arts. Instead, we walked into a club, Violet Vibes. The strobe lights reflected off the surfaces, creating artificial light but pockets of solitude. You could see everything, but the thick air provided privacy. Instead of human waste, the smell of chilidogs and hamburgers wafted about.

"This is the place?" I mouthed to Oliver over the music.

He smiled and nodded.

I thought he'd tricked me, but once we walked in, my entire body tingled, and my amygdala was overwhelmed. My flight or fight went askew and tried to do both at one time.

"Calm down," Oliver warned. He wrapped his arms around me and pulled me close to him. His breath was hot on my neck and his warmth seeped through my layers.

"They're everywhere," I shrilled and backed up. Blood pounded in my ears, thrumming over the music. My breath came in short pants, my nostrils flaring as my fingers clawed around Oliver's torso. I searched for an exit, but in my frenzy, I couldn't see anything, really, or get my bearings as everything became a blur.

I was a shark in a pool of blood. I wanted to attack everything.

"You're drawing attention," he said and pulled me back by him.

"They know it's me," I said and turned to bury my face in his shirt. His warmth centered me and swirled heat within me.

"No, I think they think you're tweaking," he said, rubbing a hand over my hair.

"What?" I said and smacked his chest.

I caught a glimpse of a person walking by. My brain clicked recognition, but I couldn't place him. His eyes widened as he searched my face, trying to figure out how he knew me. I ran a hand over the blade in my cargo pocket.

Oliver whirled me around and backed me up to a wall. His large frame consumed me. My senses went from flight or fight to turned on.

He pressed against me, bringing my attention solely to him. His eyes darkened, and his gaze fell to my lips.

"Oliver?" I croaked. Heat curled in my stomach; my lips parted in anticipation.

He blinked repeatedly and then shook his head. "It's okay. He's a guy from the bar, and you almost popped him."

"He was staring at me like I was prey."

"Odd term, but he was trying to figure out how he knew you and how he could get to know you better."

I rolled my eyes at his lame flattery.

"Take a deep breath," he said, his eyes focusing on me.

"You're right." I pushed him back from me and sucked in the fresh air that swirled between us. I needed to focus on my business.

"I know." He wrapped an arm around my shoulder, reclosing our distance and guiding me toward a bar.

A few tables away I saw Jameson Ray, a Level Four target from six years ago. Fucking figured he'd be in a neutral spot. He'd been released. The Trust had either stripped him of his resources or fined him, but either way, they released him after rehab. However, no matter how much I sniffed, only the smell of Vessel rolled off of him. His eyes shuttered to black as he laughed. Well damn. Only Vessels could shutter their eyes black. Once they went Soulless, they turned white.

Oliver frowned at me, his eyes flicking over my face before following my line of sight. Dark eyes returned to me. I offered a smile. He shook his head, a smile fighting on his lips.

He took my hand, and as a jolt shot through me, I let him lead me but continued my perusal of those around us. My entire being hummed with their essence. I had to fight instinct to not draw my blade and end all the Soulless. I'd be set for years with the fees.

The oddest thing happened, though. Other than the flirty looks or checking out my frumpy form, they didn't pay attention to me like at Mason's. The sheep didn't know the wolf was in their midst. I wasn't even wearing sheep's clothing.

I ran a hand over my face. "They really can't tell. She has cards out and they can't tell."

Oliver's eyes searched the ceiling. He squinted and shook his head. "She didn't give a picture. I doubt she has one. You look nothing like her. They're likely looking for your odor and they can't smell it here."

He grabbed our drinks and steered me to a bar-top table tucked by a wall and a pillar, a completely wretched spot if you wanted to watch the stage, but perfect for cover.

"Vessels and Soulless smell differently from the arts," I started.

Oliver cocked an eyebrow at me.

"They do," I insisted for the millionth time. "Humans have their own scent. But Finders don't use the death arts. We can be human or Vessel. Outside of here, I can tell you're a Finder, but not in here. So how do you think we get our smell? It's not like it's an innate thing. It's a career."

"I think once we kill enough Soulless their blood stains us, giving off a warning," Oliver said and sipped his beverage.

"Then I must reek to them."

"I don't know," he said, shaking his head.

"Why?"

"You take them almost always by surprise. They don't realize it's you until too late."

"What about the two that jumped me outside your bar?"

"What?" he breathed.

Oh fuck. I'd gotten too comfortable with Oliver. Abort mission. I put my cola to my lips and pretended to drink.

"What happened in my bar?" he gritted out.

"Nothing," I said and looked around for exits.

"Stop that," he said and placed his hand on mine.

I jumped at the comfort and swung my gaze to him. I made sure it was dark and annoyed.

"Pah-lease, that face won't work on me. Stop avoiding my question and looking for an escape to bolt through. You do this every time."

"Here we go."

"You're doing it again. What the fuck happened in my bar? And don't say nothing."

"Or what?"

He narrowed his eyes at me and the muscle in his jaw tweaked.

"Dessa, my bar is supposed to be safe. What happened?"

I had three options. One, tell him. Two, run. Or three, lie. Problem is, I'm not good at being a coward. I tried it once and ended up back in town. He'd also just follow me because he's a jerk. I also won't lie to friends. Fuck family, you're born to them, but friends, you choose. You owe them more than lying. That left the truth.

"Can I be a part of the conversation in your head?" he asked.

I growled.

"Mature. Tell me what happened."

"It wasn't in your bar. It was *outside* your bar."

He blinked at me, and his jaw ticked again in annoyance.

I sighed. "*Fine.* Two nights ago, I was in the bar."

"When? I didn't see you."

I sighed and pinched the bridge of my nose. "I waited for you to leave."

"I see," he said and tightened his hand. I'd hoped he'd let my hand go in his disgust, but no such luck. "Benny didn't mention anything."

I rubbed my neck, which had just gotten red and itchy, and I looked around the tabletop as if my truth and guilt lay on it somewhere.

"You have a spot at the bar. It's always been yours," he said, sounding hurt.

"I know," I whispered.

"So, what were you doing hiding from me and Benny?"

"I was making myself a target."

"Why?" he sighed.

"The night before, a Soulless had tried to sneak up on me. I found her card. I wanted more information. I thought she sent them, but no one in the bar followed me out. I ran into two outside of it."

"Fuck," he said and rubbed his forehead. "So, your solution, if I heard correctly, was to become bait and draw them out of my bar. You didn't tell me or Benny, who could have provided support."

I snorted. "You wouldn't have approved."

"Doesn't mean I wouldn't help. Dammit, Dessa."

I just stood there. I'd told him the truth. He could do with it as he pleased.

"So, what is your plan moving forward?" he asked through clenched teeth.

I stared at him.

"Are you going to target more people at the bar? You going to come back here and follow people?"

He was turning on his big brother mode, even after she had hurt him again. No. I needed to stop him. I needed to protect him.

"Oliver, I appreciate the dinner, the beverage, and the help scoping this place out. Have a pleasant evening."

I slipped my hand from his and didn't look to see his reaction as I threaded my way out of the club.

AN HOUR and a Soulless attack later, I splashed water on my face, but it didn't help. Blood ran down my cheeks in droplets and dampened my shirt. Globs of it streaked my forehead and fingerprints marred my T-shirt.

I'd managed twenty feet from the club beside an alley before I was jumped. I couldn't shake the overwhelming scent of the club, and my body hadn't calmed down, so he'd taken me by surprise. He buried a silver blade into my shoulder. As I crumpled, I'd let out a cry of panic, but he'd slapped his hand over my face, muffling the sound.

My shoulder killed, but it hadn't deterred me. Part of my training was my mom inflicting damage to see how much I could take. I didn't bite my lip or tongue to control the pain, I'd only damage my face and lose flesh.

As soon as my hands had touched pavement, I pushed backward, letting my skull crack against his nose and face. The breaking of bone serenaded me.

From my knees I hopped to my feet, keeping my balance low. I twisted an arm behind my back and yipped slightly as I tore flesh removing the blade.

He righted himself and leaped at me. His claws raked my face and tore hair from my scalp. I flung his own blade forward and embedded it in his torso. I cut up and stopped when it met bone.

He gurgled and flailed at me. I kicked his legs out and rolled him on his back.

"Are you fucking serious?" Oliver's voice rang out.

I ignored him while I secured the Soulless in the alley, zip tying its legs and hands.

I bent down and dug in his pocket while he squirmed in the final throes of life. I felt the thick cardboard and tugged out the folded and bent scarlet-red business card through the material of his pants. It fluttered to the ground and lay in the Soulless's pool of blood.

Oliver moved to stand behind me.

"She sent it after you? How did it find you?"

Ripping his shirt off, I used it to sop up as much blood as possible and then tucked it into his jacket's sleeve. Not knowing whose blood it was, just his or a mix of ours, I didn't want to leave it to chance. One ritual with my blood was more than enough. I stood without looking back and lugged up the Soulless.

"I don't know, but I will," I said. Either it was following me or got lucky.

I texted: *Violet Vibes Club*

Unknown: *Roger*

Oliver stilled, his face pinched in a frown. He sighed and ran a hand through his hair. "It's Gerard."

I stilled. "Who?"

"A bar regular from when we were kids," Oliver said, his eyes still focused on the mutilated face. "He always followed your mom around like a puppy."

So she sent him. Maybe I should have remembered faces.

"I'll see you later," I said, turning my back on him. There were countless Soulless out there that had known me. I brought most of them in, but my mom was calling in favors. I'd gone into a Soulless's lair, an attack was imminent. At least inside the club they hadn't sensed I was a Finder. If my mom had been there, I'd missed her, but she'd missed me, too. With the Soulless unable to sense me, I'd visit again, but be more careful leaving.

A whine mixed with the music of the club. Duke slowed to a stop by me, driving an old sedan this time.

"Go home, Oliver," I called over my shoulder after I loaded the Soulless. I hopped into the passenger side without looking back at Oliver.

Remembering her request, I called Mandy ahead this time. She didn't answer, but when I arrived, cardboard littered the floor from the doorway to her desk.

She sat smugly behind her desk, her hands spread wide on the surface and her back ramrod straight.

"Is it one of your targets?"

"No," I said and dropped it on the cardboard.

"You're a mess," Mandy said, blinking at me through her large glasses, and then did a double take. "Is your shoulder bleeding? Did it hurt you?"

"Huh." I twisted my face to look over my shoulder. My shirt was torn and almost black from the drying blood but wet around my shoulder from the blood still oozing out. "I guess it was deeper than I thought."

Mandy made a high-pitched squeal and scurried from her desk at me. I moved to a defensive pose, but she ignored me as she darted to the tucked-in closet and pulled out a first aid kit.

She fumbled with the kit, and had the contents strewn around in a half-circle.

"It's fine," I said, waving a hand at her.

She ignored me as she clutched the alcohol wipes like a trophy. "I found them!"

I stared at the little wipe and back at my shoulder. It was like a teaspoon for the ocean.

"I'll take care of it at home," I said and moved to the door.

"What? No, it'll get infected. The bathroom's right through here."

She grabbed the items with one hand and pointed to a second door with the other.

I started to protest, but from the slit in her curtains I saw a form moving toward the building. That must be how she always knew when I was coming. But more disturbing was that the frame reminded me of Oliver. Be it another Soulless or Oliver after me, I didn't want to face either one.

I nodded dully and walked into the room as directed.

"I'll get rid of him," she said and rolled her eyes as she shut the door.

I had more blood on me than I had thought. My own red blood soaked my shirt and mixed with the Soulless' black blood. My hands were a morbid mosaic, and my face was the victim of finger painting with blood.

I scrubbed at my face and hands; the shirt wasn't worth the effort.

I'd cleaned most of it off. My face was still shadowed with the blood, but clean enough to walk home in.

I leaned back and took a deep breath and instantly regretted it as my shoulder screamed in protest. Adrenaline had vanished, and heaps of pain remained.

My shirt clung to me in a damp stickiness, and the creep up of nausea from the extra hormones curled my stomach. At least if I could get home, I could crash in the bathtub until I had the energy to shower and use my kit. I'd stitched my skin up before, but I wasn't sure how I'd manage to do my shoulder. I considered Mandy, but I didn't want to ask my financier for medical help. She could see I was injured, but I didn't want to look helpless in front of her. She might decrease my pay. John would.

I opened the door and jolted back in surprise. I tried to swing the door back shut but Oliver's muscular arm splintered the particle wood.

He'd been standing outside the door, arms folded over his chest, head tilted down, and a surly look on his face that looked murderous.

"You're gonna pay for that," Mandy's voice shot out from behind.

"Good job getting rid of him." I pulled the door back open and ended up holding a large, detached section of it in my hand. I flinched at the pain in my shoulder and dropped the door.

Mandy appeared just behind Oliver, clutching her hands, and standing on her tiptoes to see.

"He can be quite persuasive." She blinked at me behind her glasses.

I cut my eyes to him. He heaved with anger, and his look matched mine.

"Go back up front, Mandy," Oliver gritted out.

"Uh…" She looked to me.

"I'll join you," I said to Mandy.

"In a minute, she will," Oliver said and stepped forward to completely block the doorway.

Mandy nodded, and said with her finger in the air, "I'll cut the check."

"Turn around," he said.

"No."

His eyes flickered up and his anger intensified behind them.

I cursed, realizing a mirror was behind me. He could see how bad it really was.

"Dessa," he whispered.

Oh, I hated when he did that. It made me melt and feel all good. It was the dirtiest trick.

"What?" I groaned.

He pulled off his sweater and held it out. His rumpled t-shirt allowed his abs to peek through, and I averted my eyes. A flush threatened my cheeks. He finally reached out and, taking my hand, put his sweater into my palm and closed my fingers around it. He gently laid my arm back against my side. My body hummed with sensation.

I swallowed but didn't say anything.

He put his finger on my chin and lifted it up, my eyes naturally following to meet his gaze.

"You're not alone."

MOM'S RULES

Rule One: Never bargain with or believe a Soulless

CHAPTER 19

I'D SHOWERED three times since the night before and had let the water run cold each time before stepping out. Oliver had only agreed to leave me alone last night if I let him stitch me up. Since I didn't have the energy to argue, and I wasn't ambidextrous enough to stitch myself, I agreed on his first request. He seemed shocked by it, like he expected a fight, but he held true to his word. He left the room and stood a few paces down in the hall for me to take my shirt off and cover myself with a fluffy black towel in the bathroom.

He was silent the entire time he stitched my shoulder up. His warm fingers featherlight on my shoulder as he threaded my skin back together. Instead of the pain, my mind focused on his touch and longed for it to continue. I cursed my emotional weakness but didn't bother trying to stop myself from enjoying it. Any reaction I had could be brushed off as pain.

Before exiting, he took my bloodied shirt and flannel, forcing me to wear his sweater or go topless. As he exited, he said, "Tomorrow, ten o'clock, meet me at your stool."

His sweater hung on my bathroom doorknob, a reminder of what happened when I let him distract me. Whenever I ran into him, my chances of being hurt escalated. Same as his. I was too busy awkwardly crushing on him while he tried to be my big brother.

I knew he wanted to plan tonight. He could. I had my own plans, and they purposely excluded him. While I ruminated on my plans about my mom and dad, I decided to bring in one of my targets. Mandy may be impressed with my skills, but I didn't want to become a vigilante rebel lone wolf who did what they wanted but still expected a payout by bringing in any Soulless instead of given targets. Once I took my mom in, assuming she didn't kill me first, I'd have nothing left with my father, but I'd still want to eat and have rent money. Normal targets had been my meal ticket.

I ran a hand through my hair and turned toward the river. I had two targets. The Level One was a high-ranking executive at a lucrative firm. They likely had tight security. The Level Two ran a chop shop off Main and likely was paranoid and had security. Something about knowing I'd brought in Level Twos regularly left my stomach knotted. Knowing it made these assigned targets feel heavier. More important. The others felt like a fluke. Like ignorance had been a veil.

I decided on the executive, Harvey. He'd at least believe in the illusion of sanctuary. The ivory tower was a true mind warp, and even the Soulless fell victim to its lure.

I swung by my favorite thrift shop, and for ten bucks walked out fully costumed. The easiest way to be ignored is to be essential but mousy. I strode in wearing my pencil skirt, white blouse, and cardigan, but let my shoes dangle from my finger. The rest of my supplies were tucked in my bag.

As I neared the building, I slipped on the shoes and pulled out my other treasures. I had several files filled with blank paper, a couple pencils, and fake readers. I slipped my blonde wig on, the same one as before, and scurried into the office, taking the quick steps of an underappreciated person who does more work than imaginable, while looking down and avoiding running into people. I squeaked out a few apologies as I came dangerously close to someone and ducked into an elevator.

I kept my eyes shyly averted and fidgeted in my spot while caressing my folders. When it dinged at the level noted on the building's directory for his company, I jumped out and scurried forward. I swung into the restroom and let my breathing calm down.

For an hour, I watched as the numbers dwindled from the shuffling of people going home. I waited for the third wave. The first was the early birds who came in early to leave early, followed by the "I'm paid for eight hours, I only work eight hours" group, and then those who stay too late regularly, which left me with the group who lived at work. I couldn't avoid them, but then, they weren't focused on me. They were either climbing an imaginary ladder, had illusions of grandeur, or didn't know how to say no.

I walked into the office, head bent but eyes scanning. I pretended to read a sheet in the folder and walked to the forest of cubicles. I found one that was messy but looked like the owner had left. I bent over, fiddling with the folders, sorting the papers like I needed to leave them something but had to find it first.

I scanned the floor; most of the cubicle dwellers had left, leaving the wall offices and corner offices. Most of the wall offices were also empty, but the corner ones were lit and hummed with voices.

I slowly walked the perimeter, remaining focused on my list while noting names on the office doors. My Level One target sat leaning back in a chair, a cell phone to his ear while rolling his eyes and shaking his head no. Then a velvety voice came out of him, affirming everything the speaker had said and he had just mocked silently.

With a quick glance over my shoulder, I scanned the area. The neighboring offices were dark. Two down on the left and a few on the right were lit. I had to be quiet.

I slipped into the office, shut the door, and pulled the blinds before his feet hit the floor.

"I'll have to call you back," he barked, his voice harsh.

I turned around, an evil grin tugging at my lips.

"What the fuck do you think you're doing?" he said and stood up.

He was big, about six four, well-built, and wide. He'd fuck me up if he got the chance.

"Do you know who I am?" I strutted forward in the stupid heels. I had to focus to not wobble.

He blinked at me and took in a long lecherous look. My skin crawled under his perusal, but I didn't stop him.

His eyes grew dark, and he smiled at me. "No, but I'm going to find out what makes you scream."

I stalled a beat. Did he mean he wanted to torture me or screw me? Both sounded about the same from him, and I didn't want either.

I had to remember my setting and costume. Batting my eyes, I smiled at him like my mom did to her targets. I leaned across the desk, showing how low cut my top was.

His eyes darted down, and he licked his lips and shifted his stance.

This was a tricky situation. I could stab him and drag him, but it was a long distance and too many witnesses. Security would never go for it. I wanted to get him to his car, willingly.

I smirked at him, made a lewd gesture with my mouth, and said, "Only if you can catch me," and then darted for the door and out of the office.

He followed me out, hesitating and giving me more time, as he scanned the cubicles for witnesses. Then his feet pounded behind me.

I'd mapped the floor while waiting for the others to leave and made it to the executive elevators. They were too good to ride with commoners and needed their own special air to breathe. As he rounded the corner where I stood, his eyes lit up and he sauntered to me like a victor going to take his spoils. The elevator opened and I jumped inside, giving him my best "come hither" look. His eyes flashed with danger and he crowded into the elevator.

I hit the button for the garage. I had to survive thirty seconds with him.

He chuckled at me and stepped closer, enjoying being the prover-bial cat. He ran a finger across my jaw, down my neck, and slowly over my breast. I wanted to vomit or knee him, but I had twenty seconds left.

He backed me up against the brass wall, and our distorted images danced in the mirrored walls like a surreal portrait of our game. When my back hit the wall, he pressed his body against me, rubbing his erection on my stomach. I swallowed to keep the bile down. He took it as a sign of nerves and ground in more while kissing my jaw and taking small bites.

The elevator dinged but he didn't notice.

I put my hands on his chest and pretended to push. He pushed back with his body, pinning me to the wall.

"Unless you want this on video, we should go to your car," I fake panted, trying to pretend I was turned on by his disgusting display.

He blinked at me and turned toward the corners, each holding a black swiveling eye.

He grabbed my hand and hauled me behind him. We reached his Jag and he pushed me up against it, again pressing himself into me. I clawed at his jacket and shirt and tugged at his pants.

"Hurry up," I said. "Get us out of the cameras."

He opened the back seat and shoved me down. He unzipped his pants and reached for my skirt. My knee met his nose, and blood squirted everywhere.

"What the fuck!" he bellowed as he fell forward.

Despite his weight, I rolled him over and punched his face. I straddled him to zip tie him, which unfortunately also turned him on as his bulge rubbed against me.

"Oh, you like it kinky," he purred and reached for my skirt again while trying to grind into me.

I wrapped the accosting hand behind his head and zip tied it to the door handle. After zip tying the other to the passenger seat headrest and his legs together as I folded him in the car, I dug his keys out of his pocket.

"What are you doing, you teasing bitch?" he sneered.

"Paying rent," I said and climbed over the seat, not caring if he got a peek.

As I positioned myself in the seat and started the car, I noticed the scarlet red business card in his cup holder. One side had swirling gold script and the other had perfectly formed upper case letters in fine-point sharpie.

I stared at it until his complaining bled through and I remembered where I was.

"I'll pay you double to let me go," he pleaded. "I got money."

"I don't want your money," I spat. It wasn't uncommon for them to plead or bargain. But taking it would go against Rule One and the Finders' Law.

"I'll do anything, let me go," he begged.

"You're a Level One," I said dryly.

"You're a Finder?" he stuttered, his eyes widening as he took in my reflection in the mirror.

"What did you think this was?" I said and met his gaze in the rearview mirror.

"Hit for hire, or sex worker who takes money—"

I snorted.

"You're a Finder..." His voice tapered off and his gaze landed on the card. "You're the one she wants."

I gritted my teeth.

"What the fuck does she want with you?" he said and laughed humorlessly.

"What do you know about her?" I asked, regretting the words.

"What's it worth to you?"

I DROVE us out of the garage and to the riverfront. I turned the car off and stared out the window. The river snaked below, reflecting threads of moonlight.

Harvey was a Level One. I was assigned to bring him in. He'd be my biggest score ever.

"You let me go, I'll tell you whatever you want to know about her. I know where she spends some of her time. When she'll be at certain meetings."

Sold.

I cursed to myself. Was I really going to do this? I wasn't a Hider. I didn't help the Soulless. I was a Finder. I brought them in to face justice, not avoid it. I was born and raised to be a Finder. We lived by the Finder's Law.

But the law and her rules were my mom's way, her teachings. It was John's promise. They both exploited me. They meant nothing now, and I was about to go against everything I'd been taught.

I tried to feel guilty. I wanted to. I wanted to find a reason to not make this promise. To not go against everything I'd believed in.

I didn't have loyalty to Mandy. I didn't have my mom or John in my life. My Finder promise had led to Tones' death, my death, and two attempts on Oliver's life.

No, it wasn't my promise anymore.

I made a new promise to end my mom. Even if it meant breaking my every vow.

OTHER WORLDLY MAGIC EXCERPT

Tethering is a magical phenomenon certain people can do. Soulless cannot typically tether. Usually, witches and demons can tether. It involves connecting two souls. The caster can feel where the other is at all times. If they disagree with an action, they can pull the tether, stopping the other person.

CHAPTER 20

ARE YOU DEAD, Oliver's text read.

I sighed and turned my phone off. I'd skipped out on Oliver. I sent him a text that I couldn't make it.

I'd let my Level One go. He was the first Soulless I'd ever let go and I needed to wallow in ice cream topped with whipped cream, drowning in root beer.

For the price of untying him and giving him a five-minute head start, I'd learned where my mom frequented, drove to it with him for confirmation and I recognized some faces, and learned about two meetings she had scheduled. I had two chances to get her. I decided I'd use the first one to confirm his information about her locations and the second one to take her out.

After I exited the car and made a restroom stop at a fast-food joint, he was gone. I didn't normally take a Soulless' word. They lied, but I'd taken several candid pictures as he feared, had a copy of the elevator coverage, and a copy of his phone contacts. He could skip town, but he'd have to leave the life he built if he lied.

Considering what he told me, it was a fair price for letting him leave. We both took hits in the deal. With his information, I could finally go after my mom and my dad couldn't intervene to get me to help him.

A knock sounded on my apartment door and I rolled my eyes. I ladled another spoonful of the sugar overload and ignored it.

"Sweets, we know you're in there," Duke's muffled voice carried through the door.

I smiled despite myself, trudged over to the door, and let him and Alan in.

Duke's smile faltered as he scanned me.

"What?" I asked and looked down to see I still wore the skirt and blouse. I reached for my head and patted it, relieved to know I'd taken the wig off.

"Well damn, sweets, you look like you're up to trouble," Duke said.

I waved him off with my spoon, padded back to the kitchen, and pulled out the carton of ice cream and bottle of root beer. I pulled two glasses, which they'd bought, and slid them over to them.

"Help yourself," I said.

"Are we going to talk about this outfit?" Alan asked, scooping ice cream. "I have to say, it looks very nice on you."

"Did you wear heels with it, too?" Duke eyeballed the shoes discarded on the table as he slid onto a stool.

"And here you didn't think you had polished enough skills to go after big targets," Duke said and punched me in the arm.

"What level requires this?" Alan asked.

A growl trilled in my throat. I didn't want to talk about my missed target. Well, not missed. I'd done a catch and release, and though I hadn't felt guilty about it, I hated that I failed to bring him in.

"What happened?" Duke asked.

"Nothing," I mumbled.

"You're eating sweets, which is unlike you. You like salty. You're dressed very lovely, but very unlike your normal lovely style. You have heels on the table. You have a blonde wig crumpled up next to them, and you willingly shared your food."

"The food sharing is the scariest of all this," Alan said, slurping his mixture.

"You guys suck," I laughed.

"It either means her mom or her mom," Duke said.

"What does that mean?"

"You don't get worked up over your dismal love life," Duke said.

"Which wouldn't be dismal if you'd open your eyes," Alan said.

"My eyes are open. You two are already married to each other."

Alan rolled his eyes.

"You don't get worked up over targets because you just catch them. That leaves money and family," Duke continued.

"You've never cared about amassing money. You live hand to mouth," Alan said.

"So, it's family," Duke said triumphantly. "And since you don't know your dad, that leaves your mom."

I gaped at him, unsure how to proceed. Several of his dismissals were what bothered me.

"What? Too harsh?" Duke asked Alan.

"No," Alan said, scrutinizing me. "What is wrong?"

I threw my hands in the air and let out an exasperated sigh.

"Is it your mom?" Alan asked.

I stomped my foot.

"Is it your dad?" Duke joked.

I winced and paced across the living room.

"Wait, is your dad in the picture?" Duke said, standing up.

I didn't know what harm it would be to tell them.

"Your dad is in the picture now?" Duke stood in front of me and gripped my shoulders so I'd have to face him.

"He wants a favor," I whispered.

"Wow, okay." Duke ran a hand through his hair. He tugged me into a hard hug. "We're not offering to help, or to tell you not to do what is stupid."

"Okay," I said rigid in his embrace, not buying it.

"But." He released me enough to stare in my eyes. "I want to know where you'll be so I can retrieve your body."

There it was. The guilt. I brushed him off.

"It's fine, I'm not engaging her today," I said, taking another bite.

"Today?" Alan asked, raising an eyebrow.

"No, today is reconnaissance."

"Hm." Duke looked unconvinced.

"I'll tell you what," Alan said, scooting his chair up and resting his elbows on the table. He steepled his fingers and rested his chin on them.

This was a dangerous situation. Alan wasn't a wild card. He was even-toned, hard to rile, and always 100 percent honest.

I tried not to swallow, but I choked slightly and grabbed my ice cream.

"We're not going with you."

I didn't respond. It was a trap.

"As Duke said, we're not offering to help, or to tell you what to do."

Here it comes. My body tightened and I actually held my breath for whatever reason, like I could will away the fear and anxiety.

"You will tell us where you are going."

"Oh, I will?" I laughed sarcastically.

"Yes," he said and leaned back, "or I'm tethering you to me."

My mouth fell open and I sputtered. Alan rarely showed his powers. He didn't mean binding me with rope. That'd be easy enough to thwart. No, by tethering he meant he was going to bind me magically to him. I wouldn't be able to move without his knowing and approving. If I understood tethering, the recipient and caster had to know each other, share something in common. I was fuzzy on if a chant or spell or whatever had to be done. But Alan would know.

Duke whistled low and shook his head with large eyes.

What a friend. What a way to stand up for me.

"Fine," I gritted out. "I'm headed to the Stakeout."

"The club?" Duke asked skeptically.

"It's a neutral ground," Alan said.

"You know about that?" I asked and swung my gaze back to him.

"Who told you?" he asked and watched me over his cup as he took a sip.

Duke sighed. "Oliver needs to pick a side."

I chuckled. "He has. His own."

Finders' Handbook

Seer - A Vessel who can see into other's minds to varying degrees. Rarely a Soulless but do not necessarily support Finders. Some say they have gold eyes.

CHAPTER 21

THE STAKEOUT, the location Harvey provided, wasn't as vibrant as the last club. Instead, the furniture was neutral colors, the lighting muted, and instead of techno dance music, the music was more bass and encouraged lounging around with beverages.

I licked my lips and slipped onto a barstool. My body tightened, ready to strike, but I'd taken a shot of vodka before coming in to loosen my tension. It wasn't enough to distort my senses. I'd given myself twenty minutes to be here and confirm the information the Soulless had given me.

Despite the short stint, I didn't doubt my mom would recognize me if she looked, but she wouldn't have a need to look. I'd donned another thrift find: skinny jeans, which were an abomination. How could I store stuff in them or hide a gun? I opted for an oversized sweater, well-worn and droopy, but with pockets that allowed me to holster my gun without easily being detected. Since most Vessels were armed, the Stakeout didn't have metal detectors.

To confuse my mom, I'd dyed my hair black. I'd had every color of the rainbow since I was twelve. I never opted for a natural color. Over-sized glasses similar to Mandy's perched on my nose, and I had bright red lipstick on. I was as far from my style but still casual as I could get. I'd also taken Alan's suggestion and used several temporary tattoo stickers, lacing my neck and visible shoulder with swirling designs.

After ordering a beer, I pretended to swig it as I peered around the club. It was active but not packed.

Tingles raced down my spine as a couple walked in. They were both Soulless. Most of the Vessels in the bar were Soulless. I couldn't grab my blade for protection without notice, but I wrapped my fingers around the neck of the bottle, ready to brandish it as a weapon should they recognize me. One was a banshee type, their pink eyes glowing in the room. The other didn't have any obvious modification, but was a Choicer. They were still mostly human and even their smell still hinted at a fresh conversion. They walked past me, unfazed by my presence. I shook my head at their weakness.

I looked at my watch as my skin burned and neck hairs raised in distress. Less than two minutes had passed. I sucked on my teeth and repositioned myself on the stool.

As I pretended to swig my beer, a Vessel meandered over to the bar, leaning against it. She cut her eyes to me. They glistened gold and I held my breath.

She smiled slyly at me, and said, "Here alone?"

I gulped. She was a Seer Vessel and she couldn't detect me. If she did, she had no tell, no defense, no hackles raised. They were rare, and never a Choicer. They were born Vessels. They didn't normally become Soulless, but they would rat out Finders.

"In the bathroom," I choked and put my bottle down.

"Shame." She took her bottle from the bartender. "Maybe next time."

I nodded and watched her walk away. How had she not known I was a Finder? No one was on guard. No one was circling or whis-pering in my direction. Yet, I could tell each type of Vessel as I scanned the room. The ones in the death arts: Soulless and Choicers, and the ones who did not partake in the arts. The bartender was a Choicer but had bound his soul years ago. His human scent was gone, but his smell was not natural for a Vessel.

I ordered another beer while nonchalantly depositing my full one on another table. I sat for about ten minutes before I noticed a flurry of activity by the side area that was sectioned off. The front was open, but frosted plexiglass covered it. The other three walls were closed off.

I couldn't distinguish the figures, but there was rough activity, and the shadows of people twirled in a dark dance. One slammed into the plexiglass cover, sending cracks racing from the center in a spiderweb.

I cut my eyes to the bartender to gauge his reaction. His brow furrowed as he stared at it, but quickly averted his gaze and hyper focused on washing the bar top.

My hand wrapped around the pommel, but I didn't draw my blade. I slid so my feet touched the floor, but I was still on the stool.

I looked to the corners, but the light was too much for the shadows. There was also no way they'd talk to me with so many Soulless around. I gave myself a mental smack for starting to become dependent on them for information.

The blobs moved, and the body smashed against the compromised glass again, shattering it into small bits of death shards. The body lay sprawled over the jagged edges remaining, blood dripping down. I didn't care about the Soulless fading in the glass; my focus was solely on the person who'd thrown him. My mom.

I held back my primal need to dash over and smash her face. My heart stuck in my chest; my breath lodged in my throat. My face pinched in disgust as I watched her. Her long blonde hair was bundled in a braid and laid across her shoulder. Her too-tight T-shirt advertised the bar, and she wore skinny jeans. Blood splattered across her face, and instead of her normally playful smile, she scowled.

The scowl broke my trance, the world whining back into focus around me.

She never scowled. She didn't use the lame saying, "it's easier to catch flies with honey than vinegar," but she said it was easier to deceive with politeness than brashness, or however she phrased it. I just heard her tell a lie.

Someone handed her a towel, and she dabbed her face. Her eyes tracked up, and I shrank back. She didn't make eye contact, but her expression shifted. The familiar vixen smile dominated her face.

She moved to the back of the room, becoming a gray blob through the remaining plexiglass.

As Duke and Alan warned me against doing, I became foolish.

My hunter instinct kicked in, and I walked in the direction of the restroom, skirting the wall. My blade was in my hand, nestled in my sweater. Before my brain caught up, I snaked behind the privacy wall and down the hall to the door and had my hand on the door handle.

The handle turned without my help, and I realized someone was coming out. With an about-face, I darted down the hall, aiming for the shadows.

The dark hallway teemed with them. Different hisses wove together into a distressed warning. I cut into the beckoning light of the social area and dove into the bathroom. Running for the exit would be a blazing sign I didn't belong. A sprint to the bathroom sent a different message.

I locked myself in the stall and squatted with my boots on the toilet seat but crouched below the door's span.

I perched there for longer than necessary. My heart still raced, and my mom's face kept flashing through my mind. She was right there. She was here. She'd killed a Soulless in front of others and they'd done nothing. She wasn't attacked or restrained. It was like she'd thrown the trash out and dusted her hands.

Curiosity killed the cat, but it was my motivating factor when I finally climbed down and surveyed the restroom. I was alone. It's not that the doors were open, and I couldn't see shoes, but my senses were calm. My skin felt relief from the flood of adrenaline to capture.

I walked to the door and looked to the shadows. A few slithered on the marble floor.

"Can I leave?" I whispered, hoping I couldn't be heard outside of the restroom.

They were quiet, rumbling about, before confirming, "It's clear."

After stepping out, I hung close to the wall, making sure no one was watching me and walked back to the bar. Harvey had been right on his tip. I licked my lips. Possibilities reeled through my mind. My body thrummed with the promise of a hunt. But that would be foolish…

"Need food?" the bartender asked.

"Huh?"

He nodded toward the restroom. "Easier with food."

He was correct; food was easier to vomit than foam or watery bile. "Sure, what do you recommend?"

"Burger's good. If you're vegan, we have nachos."

I snorted, and said, "Vegan nachos?"

He smiled and shrugged. "We get a mixed crowd."

Ah, humans probably came too, not knowing what a neutral spot was.

"Burger'd be great."

He nodded and punched some buttons on his pad. "Who ya looking for?"

I raised my eyes to him in question.

"You keep scoping the place."

Shit. I forgot I was with Soulless and Choicers along with Vessels. Born paranoid, hunted by people like me, and constantly on guard. Of course, he'd recognize my behavior.

I shrugged. "New to town."

He furrowed his brows at me. "Huh, I thought you looked familiar."

I licked my lips and willed the color not to creep up my neck and face.

"I got one of those faces," I said.

He leaned over, staring in my eyes, searching for something. I met his stare and allowed my face to slacken.

"Figure it out?" I asked.

"You remind me of someone," he said, shaking his head at the thought.

I didn't look like Mom, but I knew I had quite a few of her mannerisms. My foolishness was on display. I may not look like her daughter, either physically like her or the one she raised, but I thought I could go into her domain and parade around and not be detected.

My phone buzzed in my pocket, startling me from my thoughts. Fortunately, it dinged loudly enough to provide me an escape.

"How long on the burger?" I asked, palming my phone but not looking at it. There were three people who would text me, and they wouldn't be sending encouragement right then.

"Few minutes," he said, relaxing his forearms on the bar and leaning into them for support. He frowned at me. I suspected he was trying to register who I was.

I nonchalantly glanced at my watch as I lifted my bottle. I had two minutes left in my self-appointed window.

I pulled out two twenties and threw them on the bar. "Enjoy the burger, I gotta run." I shook my phone as an excuse.

"Hm," he said noncommittally and eased back.

His eyes skittered over me again and focused back on the plexiglass room. My gaze followed. The Soulless had been removed, and someone was removing the bits, with a new pane waiting. If nothing else, they were resourceful and thorough.

Either I was cursed or blessed, because at that moment I noticed a figure walk through the small pocket of light in the hallway. My mother. My breath caught and I strained to see if anyone was with her. Night vision was handy, but I couldn't see through walls or around corners.

The bartender had moved down the counter and was wiping down glasses. He wasn't affording me his attention. I'd paid my tab. The twenties were gone, and I was dismissed.

Keeping an eye on him, I subconsciously, or maybe consciously, moved to the hallway. I didn't hover, that'd only draw attention, but I did pause, like confirming this was the correct creepy hall, before entering.

My mom stood at the far end by herself talking on her cellphone. I scanned both ways and slipped into the hall, tiptoeing behind her. My footsteps were solid but silent.

She turned slightly, and I froze. I didn't know if she had night vision. She hadn't before becoming a Choicer, but neither had I. Her Companion could have given her anything.

She cursed into the phone and looked to the ceiling. I don't know why, but I took the opportunity and sprung forward. Mistake number one.

I slammed her into the wall, but I took the blow against the wall to reduce the sound. I clamped my hand over her mouth to muffle her scream. Mistake number two. She bit down. Blood trickled down my hand and stabbing pain radiated from my soft palm.

She elbowed my face, but in doing so left her side opened slightly. I dug my blade into her ribs and jerked it up.

Her mouth flew open, and her eyes bulged as she lurched forward.

I was a horrible person. Relief coursed through me as she struggled to breathe, and her body collapsed. Finally, finally I would be free of her wretched ways. I could move on without looking over my shoulder.

I was wrong.

She whirled around, blood damping her T-shirt and smeared across her arms. She grabbed my calf and dug her nails in. She went for meat and tried to rip my leg apart.

I shoved her forward with my hands and kicked at her, but she moved too quickly. She shouldn't have been moving with the blow I gave her. The silver blade should have destroyed her as a Soulless. But the silver bullets hadn't worked on her Companion, either.

She looked up at me, blood staining her lips, and laughed.

That pissed me off.

"Look at you," she snarled, and wiped her mouth of my blood still dotting it. "Did you think I didn't notice you?"

My face burned at the ridicule. I'd been foolish and she caught me. It was worse than dying.

"You are the dumbest bitch I know," she said.

She was fucking right. I swung at her again, but she parried with her arm and kicked at my stomach.

I blocked her kick with a twist of my leg but both our blows missed.

"Thomas told me you were watching," she said, smiling as my face scrunched in confusion. "He's quite loyal. Obviously, you didn't drink what you were given."

The bartender. Figures.

"I taught you well," she said.

"Fucking bullshit," I said and kicked at her despite knowing I wouldn't connect. I'd become a toddler again when faced with my mother and was throwing a temper tantrum.

"Second Rule, don't drink or eat what you've been given."

"What's in the burgers?" I asked and anchored my feet to the floor for the next blow.

She laughed.

Guess I didn't want to know.

"Third Rule?" she asked and wobbled to her feet. Looked like she may be in pain, but I figured it was a ploy. I wouldn't take the bait of an easy hit and give her the advantage.

I couldn't take my eyes off her, but I needed an exit. I hadn't followed Rule Three in the hall. I could tell her all the exits and options of escape in the main room, but I'd failed to do that in the hall in my fury to get her. My lust and greed had blinded me. She knew it, too. She liked toying with her prey.

"Third Rule?"

I lunged for her, taking her slightly by surprise, but not enough to do damage. My blade skimmed her arm.

"That's Rule Four. What's Rule Three?" she demanded.

I squatted low again for another attack. I didn't get the chance. Rule Three came to bite me in the ass.

MOM'S RULES

Rule Two: Don't eat or drink what others give you

CHAPTER 22

HER BLOW LEFT a searing headache and one of my eyes wouldn't focus.

I fucked up Rule Five in my next move. I turned to face the new attacker, her Companion based on his size and body, leaving my back to my mom. The thing is, for years she had my back. I may have done most of the recovery, but she'd put a bullet in someone if needed. Sometimes, in moments of distress, we forget reality. I forgot years of reality, and was again a tween, thinking my mom was everything. She was everything, just everything that'd kill me.

Reality came screaming back when her hand snatched my left shoulder and yanked me back, digging her nails into my flesh and squeezing. I knew that grip. It was the phantom grip I still felt time to time, always making me cringe. It was the one that meant I'd gotten caught snitching food when she'd withheld it as a punishment, or when I'd sneak out or in and she'd been waiting, or when I did some-thing that made me unworthy of being her daughter in her eyes, which was often.

Rule Six came to my defense. Perhaps because I'd failed to follow two of the rules, she thought I'd forget more, but I used her rules against her. Rule Six was simple: Don't let them touch you. Countless hours of her charging me came flooding back, kicking in instinct and calming my nerves. In one swift motion I grabbed her hand with my right and stabbed at her with the blade in my left. I threw her forward, slicing her flesh as she flew. My fresh shoulder wound protested, skin tore and the dampness of blood blossomed against my skin.

Fisting my hand, I nested my nails into my palm to diffuse the insanity of pain in my shoulder. Suffering an injury wasn't an option.

Mom rebounded quickly, as she usually did. Lying face up, her eyes rolled to me and she smiled devilishly, almost with a hint of pride. She flipped to her feet and stood next to a person I once knew. I'd been young when he died, but standing next to my mom was Tones' husband, Oliver's father, Isaac. My brain stuttered. I didn't know how to process the situation.

"But you're dead," I said lamely.

"As were you," he said, his voice velvety, and that's when I realized it wasn't Isaac. He was a close imitation, but his eyes were different, blue instead of hazel like Isaac's and Oliver's. There were other subtle differences, and they became more apparent as I stared at him.

"You're not Isaac."

"No," he said with a chuckle. "He was weak."

I took that to mean this man had been a part of Isaac's untimely death. I had no proof, and I didn't care about that, because thinking he killed Isaac had my blood pulsing with anger instead of fear.

I took in a breath, letting it fill my lungs and exhaled it with all my tension.

Like usual, I couldn't smell or sense my mom, a perpetual pitfall from years of torture. However, Not-Isaac had a definitive smell and presence. My senses tingled and my body heaved with the expectancy of Soulless prey.

Another person joined us, and I hated myself. Stepping behind them was Harvey, my Soulless escapee. He wore an expensive suit and was freshly shaven with his hair slicked back.

He leered at me and sneered while folding his hands triumphantly over his chest as if he'd won a battle. And that's when I realized he had. And I'd been played. I fucked up Rule One and he got to gloat.

"I'm curious, what did you offer for them to bring me in? I found your cards all over."

Mom smiled, her charming innocent smile, and batted her eyelashes.

"You'd be surprised how many people want to maim and eventually kill you," she said sweetly.

"Oh, you're trying to stop them or be the first in line?"

She chuckled. I hated it.

"How'd she trap you?" Mom asked Harvey over her shoulder, tilting her head to the side but keeping her eyes on me.

His pompous stature dissolved. Fear skittered across his eyes before he blinked, and they shuttered into a blank expression.

Mom moved her gaze to me and cocked an eyebrow. "How'd you trap him?"

"What are you talking about? He's still walking."

"Showing you failed Rule One. Have you fallen that much? Or missed me that much?"

I bit my cheek until I tasted blood and glowered at her.

"You don't miss, ever, baby," she said and smiled proudly at me.

When Mom called me baby, it meant I'd made her really proud. It's awful to admit, but I felt warmth course through me and my heart lifted at the idea I'd finally made her proud again. The mind is a fucked-up place. The moment was short, and the descent to reality was brutal, leaving me more brittle and annoyed. She still had an effect on me, even after killing me, sending Soulless after me, and trapping me again.

"That means," she continued, narrowing her eyes and lowering her chin, "you let him go. Your first Level One."

Harvey blanched. His face turned ashen, and his eyes darted around for an exit. Good luck, buddy. I wanted one, too, but was trapped with a wall behind me and two people who had already killed me in front of me. He licked his lips and ran a hand over his jaw and mouth.

His feet shuffled a couple steps backward.

"First *assigned* Level One," I sneered.

She chuckled. "Finally figure it out?"

So she and John had been in on it together. Fucking figured.

"Why would you let him go and disregard Rule One?"

"Who says I follow your rules?" I countered.

"You're still alive, baby. That means you do."

I hated that she was right. I hated that she got to call me out on it. I hated that it felt good that she called me baby again. Lowering my head, I slumped my shoulders but didn't lower my eyes. Rule Five: Don't take your eyes off of them.

Harvey's eyes found me, wide with panic, and he shook his head at me as he stole glances at my mom.

He was afraid of her. That was one of the smartest things he'd done.

"Do you owe him something?" She cocked her head and sent me a sympathetic look.

"No," I spat, falling for the trap.

She smiled. Sucked for him. That closed-mouth smile meant his fate was sealed. He still stood there, not running; like either he had a chance or was tethered.

"What did he offer you, Dessa baby, that would let you forget Rule One, or ignore it?" Her voice sounded calm, but danger hinted in her even tone and steely eyes.

I owed him nothing. I met her gaze and said, "You."

"Ah. If you wanted to see me, you just had to call," she cooed.

Harvey's hard eyes turned white and murderous as he gauged me. I smiled sweetly back at him.

"You've done well," my mother said, her voice full of sincerity, which meant she was lying.

She tilted her head back slightly to Harvey but didn't turn around or face him.

He looked confused and an uneasy smile spread across his face.

Mom smiled at me.

"Did you know she's my daughter?" Her voice sounded funny, like she had real emotions and was sad.

Harvey's eyes bulged as he pivoted between looking at Mom and me.

"Thank you for bringing her to me." She sniffed.

I just breathed as Harvey screamed and life drained from him. His skin slackened on his face, withering away into a gray bark. His muscle and meat contorted beneath the changing flesh, bulging and expanding and then decompressing as if it was warring with itself. His high-pitched screams petered to gargled nonsense.

Not-Isaac stood silently, assessing us. His face blasé and unimpressed by Mom's declaration. Harvey's demise seemed to originate from him, as his eyes glowed and blinked repeatedly as Harvey perished. Even if Harvey was tethered or bound to him, he took a life without blood. What next-level death art bullshit was he pulling? This had to be why they were all clambering to him.

Then his gaze swung to Mom. "We have a meeting. Claudine, finish this or I will."

What he did to Harvey sure as hell looked painful, but it was quick and way better than the bullshit they tried before.

Mom licked her lips.

"Yeah, Mom, why'd you want me here?"

"We need to discuss matters," Mom said, her facade dropping, disappointed Mom making a reappearance.

My stomach tightened and face slackened. I should be used to the swing of emotions. I'd survived them for years, but I was still a helpless ship in her sea of extremes.

"What's to discuss? You killed me."

Not-Isaac sneered at me and clenched his fists. This was the first sign of anything from him, and it was interesting my death made him mad. Or, more likely, my resurrection.

"You hunted me," she countered like we were in a school debate.

"You became a Choicer!" I screamed, my voice echoing off the walls.

Both she and Not-Isaac laughed.

Still chuckling, she said, "Oh baby, no. I was born this way. I was born a Vessel."

"What?" I said, my brain screaming, processing nothing. That couldn't be possible. Tones' and my father's words played in my mind. What had they meant?

To add insult, she said, "Your father was born a Vessel, too, like me. Like you."

"How—how is that possible? I have no powers." I'd know if I was a Vessel.

She laughed again and shook her head.

"Two Vessels can't reproduce, they're like mules," I said, clinging to my crumbling foundation. Grasping for my truths. We were human. I was human. She was a Choicer.

Mom tilted her head, a dark grin spread across her face. "You've always been so gullible."

Only with her.

"I'm human." My voice cracked.

"Do you think a human could hunt as you do? Could sniff out the faintest traces? Heal like you do? You can tell Soulless and Vessels, even in a neutral spot. You couldn't smell Finders there, even when I paraded them in front of you. You're a Vessel, and like every other Vessel, you were born with your own unique powers."

I stared forward. She blurred in my vision, a swirl of blue, yellow, and hate.

I had to focus. To prove her wrong. Prove she was lying.

"You two... you both should have targets as Soulless," I said.

"Who says we don't?" She smiled.

"But John..." My voice trailed off. But John what? She and John were close. "How long has one been out on you?"

"How long since you were conceived?" she asked, her eyes darkening.

I was so disoriented I heard colors. Her mouth moved but I couldn't hear anything, and her words didn't have smell.

"Wait..." My mind reeled backward. The countless people that were a blur of faces. Had they been… Had she gone after Finders? Had I helped?

"Yes?"

"Wait, wait, wait a minute." Reality caught up to me. My thoughts were like dozens of puzzle pieces from different boxes strewn about. Too many, and unrelated, at once. "You're not my real mother."

"No, I am your mother."

"Two Vessels can't…" I said, staring into her blue eyes.

"Doesn't change that he and I birthed you." She smiled smugly.

"But how?" I asked before I could stop the words.

Her smile turned lecherous, and something skittered behind her eyes.

My mouth dried and vomit curled in my stomach, threatening to come up. She'd been Soulless since my conception. The death arts. That was something I didn't want to explore.

NO. She was her. She had to be lying. Fucking with my mind.

I cracked a sarcastic smile. "So, I'm supposed to believe you now?"

"We're not horses, donkeys, and mules, but you are my child. I birthed you. You're of my flesh and blood. And your Vessel father's. You know how the arts work. Life for a life. To conceive takes a few more than one life for a life." She shrugged.

"I wonder if he'd confirm that," I murmured, not realizing I was talking out loud until she gasped. It was like music.

"Who are you talking about?"

I smiled; it'd flashed only a second, but her face contorted in real fear.

"I'm not sure if you're divorced, so should I say husband or ex-husband?"

Color drained from her face and Not-Isaac stepped back, glaring at Mom, communicating something only they could understand.

Mom rebounded, and setting her jaw said, "Even if you hunt your own kind, you're not better than them. You are still one of us. You were born to two Vessels. You are a Vessel. You will be Soulless. It's in your nature. You were created from it. He can't save you from that."

Nothing could save me now. Not if they were telling the truth and

I was born to Soulless parents. Not if I was born of the death arts. I was a creation of them. Twice, my life had existed because of the death arts. How close was I to being a Soulless? Everything I was, was because of the death arts. I knew what I'd done to catch targets, the blood, hunting, pain I inflicted. How close was I to having a target on me?

It sadly fit together too nicely, too cleanly. It made too much sense based on who they were. How I'd grown up. How I could tell all types of Vessels. As Oliver put, I could root out a Soulless in a mile of garbage. She not only honed my physical skills, but likely had helped me develop my enhanced senses, too. I had just thought it was normal.

I didn't have the time or energy or desire to think about it too much. Not with her in front of me. If I died now, it wouldn't matter, anyway.

She hated my father. At least, she had always said she did. But I realized, more than anything, she feared him.

A smile cut across my face, and my eyes narrowed in evil delight.

"No, he can't save me now, but he can bring me back again?" I asked, raising an eyebrow at her suggestively. "Even if you try to sacrifice me again."

Not-Isaac stilled and turned a calculating expression toward me. "It wasn't a sacrifice, but a ritual, but it doesn't matter. Your blood wasn't enough. It was too diluted with your mom's to work correctly to reach him."

Mom rolled her eyes and her jaw ticked. Apparently, she was finally inferior in something. That was a small, delightful victory in the face of a blood bath.

"That's nice." I smiled.

"He can sense us if we get too close. We couldn't use your blood to reach him. But if you're in contact with him…"

Oh, for fuck's sake. I was going to get another favor request.

MOM'S RULES

Rule Six: Don't let them touch you

CHAPTER 23

HE DIDN'T GET a chance to ask his favor. Screams rang from the open area and they both froze.

"He better not be trying to break in," Not-Isaac spat at Mom. Guess he meant my dad. A small curl of joy twisted in my raging stomach that Not-Isaac also seemed to blame my mom for my dad's interruption.

"He can't tell we're here, only guess," she growled back.

So, the neutral spots did block their senses.

"I'll deal with it." His eyes rolled white and his fingers elongated into talon-like claws. A pulse of death arts rolled from him, the rank odor watering my eyes before he left my mom with me. He stormed to the main club area, tendrils of magic snaking around him. What the fuck was he? He truly was above a Level One, but what did that make him?

"Guess he's important here," I said forcing my eyes to stay on my mom.

"Oh, grow up, Dessa," she spat.

There was my loving mom, back and filled with cheer.

"He owns the place. All the Mason brothers owned one." Her lecherous smile returned.

Wha...? What the fuck?

"Didn't know that, did you? The Masons created the neutral spots because he and his brothers are Soulless."

My mouth dried. The Masons? Wait. She was trying to distract me. It was a damn good lie. Or was it? Fuck, she was playing her mental games.

Steeling my face, I didn't drop eye contact. "Well, he seems like a real swell guy. Brother killer and all."

"Isaac was no saint."

Every fiber in my body didn't want to believe her, but she had already planted the seed of doubt. Already had me second guessing. "No one is," I countered.

"Your father's dangerous," she said and stepped forward.

"My mom's a bitch, too." I smiled wide and stepped toward her.

She didn't smell like a Soulless and it was unnerving. I'd been gung-ho to destroy, but faced with her, nature reared up. She was my mother. I couldn't deny she was a horrible mother, but I'd survived, been fed, and she coached my marketable skills. My bar was low.

I still held my blade, her blood drying on it.

She held no visible weapon, but I still felt at the disadvantage.

The screams became ambiance accentuated by loud crashes, gunfire, and glass shattering.

She didn't flinch but instead stepped forward again.

"Your blood was enough," she seethed.

"Nope, don't think so. Not-Isaac said it was because of you," I countered but didn't take a step. Instead, I opted to anchor my feet and steady my frame.

"Not-Isaac?" She chuckled and shook her head. "Isaiah, his brother."

That was a nugget to investigate later if I made it out.

"I found your cards. You wanted me alive. Why?"

"Pumping blood is stronger."

"Mine didn't help Not-Isaac." I needed to use the name. I'd always remember he was creepy, but something about the familiar is more dangerous than the unknown.

"Your father interrupted. He killed you." Her expression matched her words—red-rimmed, glossy eyes and a trembling mouth—but I didn't believe them. It still stung and made me doubt everything. This was her game. I still couldn't win it.

She took the opportunity of my distraction and lunged forward, spearing my stomach with her shoulder blade and knocking me into the wall. She slammed my injured shoulder again into the brick wall, sending pops of light dancing in front of my eyes. My mouth gasped for air.

She smashed my shoulder again and pried my blade from my hand. I clawed at her to keep it, but my body was in overdrive and I couldn't control my faculties.

"I don't enjoy this," she said with a huge smile and laugh. She ran the blade down my neck, slicing a thin path, sending searing pain pulsing through my body. "Those tattoos are so awful."

She plunged my blade into my shoulder. I howled in pain and before I could muster a defense, she pulled it out, wiped my blood off on my sweater, and jabbed it into my other shoulder.

Her face distorted, dark shadows skittered across, and her eyes shuttered to white pupils before shuttering back to her blue eyes. Maybe she wasn't a Choicer. I'd never seen one able to do that. Only Vessels could change their eyes black when they use their natural powers and Soulless to white.

Crap. My dad was right. My mom actually told the truth. She wasn't a Choicer. But that made me... made me... I didn't have time to think about it as she rammed the blade into my stomach and twisted.

I listed forward, unable to stop my motion. My blood ran from me. My vision blurred and blackness ebbed. She'd killed me again. She'd finally won.

Somehow, I heard her curse and then yell.

A bullet blasted through her, tearing at her chest, exposing her tattoo. The swirling pattern seemed to swirl and twist, and blood blossomed on her shirt. She didn't fall back but turned around to face the attacker.

There were voices. So many voices.

I slumped to the ground; the cold linoleum stopped my fall and coated my face in grime. I clasped my arms to my stomach, but I didn't have the muscle power to press against the wounds.

She was distracted, and no matter the pain, I had to get out of there. I willed my feet to push me toward the corner. My head bumped into the wall. I allowed myself one moment to breathe before the agonizing effort to push myself to a sitting position. There were three people besides me in the hall. Two were slashing at my mom. Based on their size, I was sure they were Duke and Alan. Fuck, I was going to get them killed. Why'd they come?

With an electronic whine the power in the club cut out, plunging us into darkness. My night vision kicked in, but oddly, more shadows than normal swarmed around, like rats at a picnic.

They passed over the others and swarmed. I cursed. They'd smelled my blood and had come for the kill.

Instead, they swirled around me, plugging my wounds and applying pressure. Their ethereal presence lifted me up, literally. They hovered around until I braced myself against the wall. I still hurt but stood.

My mom's gaze turned dangerous as she scanned me, and a look of betrayal consumed her when she saw the shadows. That confirmed my fears. She had night vision and could talk to shadows. She had to have done a huge sacrifice to get those powers.

With blinding light, the power kicked back on, sending electronics to reboot with an orchestra of electric squeaks, rumbles, and beeps. The neon lights bathed us in an artificial glow. My blood smeared on the floor and walls. My mom's arms were coated in my blood. I could only guess what a sight I was.

Before Duke and Alan could respond, a fourth person showed up. One that wasn't supposed to be there and one I was suddenly afraid I'd witness the death of.

A cocktail of anger and fear clogged my senses. They didn't listen to me, and she was going to get four kills today.

She must have thought so, too, because she laughed and cracked her neck. "Seems a little unbalanced," she taunted. "Want to call a few more?"

"Claudine Petrov, your target lists five acts of vulgar nature not including the murder of your daughter," Oliver said using his flat Finder tone. What an idiot. He shouldn't be here, and yet he rattled off the Finder's sheet.

"She's right there," she snarled.

"Also to be included later will be the second attempt on her life," Oliver said, ignoring her defense.

"Don't forget Harvey," I added and earned a scowl from my mom.

"Is that Harvey?" Duke asked, pointing at Harvey's deformed remains.

His body was deteriorating rapidly, emanating a rank smell. Vessels usually followed the normal pattern of decomposition, but I guessed Not-Isaac added a touch of something special.

Oliver pulled out a pistol and I gaped. He'd never carried one. He preferred muscling down his prey, but then I considered who he was facing, and it made sense. Her kill rate was high, and this would be the third attempt on his life. And we know what three means.

"Oliver Mason," my mom scolded, and I choked a laugh. It was highly inappropriate to laugh but hearing a mom voice come out of her was like hearing a cat barking. "You know better than to raise a weapon at me. Your mother would not approve."

All of us gasped and stared at her audacity.

"You bitch," Duke barked and raised Virginia.

Before he got a shot off, Oliver unloaded six rounds into her. All hit her. Three passed through her and bounced off the brick wall. The other three I assumed were lodged in her.

She did a Matrix-esque move, swirling her arms, making her body fluid and nimble, but she wasn't in *The Matrix* and Oliver was an excellent shot. His closeness helped, too.

Unlike when I felled her, she crashed to the floor, her body splayed in an unnatural position as her fluids poured from her body.

I made an attempt to walk around her from my corner, but my body gave out without the shadows to carry me. I slammed into the floor hard. Fortunately, my arms took the impact for my head. Unfortunately, that meant my shoulders gushed open again. Pain rocketed through me, stealing my vision, sending ringing to my ears, and making me unable to move. I curled into a fetal position, accepting death. Hell, if she died, too, then it was all worth it. A little fitting, too.

But that's not what happened. Oliver moved to my side, cradling my face. He scooped me up and started to carry me down the hall.

I heard Alan's voice, pitched with concern say, "We need a hospital."

"We have to get out first," Duke said.

To my dismay, Oliver handed me to Duke.

"What are you doing?" Duke yelled.

Oliver reached into his pocket and pulled out zip ties.

"Are you fucking kidding?" Duke barked. "She's not worth the money."

"It's not the money." Oliver reared back like he'd been slapped in the face. "I need to make sure she's dead and can't come back."

"He's right," Alan said, peering around the corner. I assumed the chaos was still going on if no one had bothered to come back to our ruckus.

"Fuck," Duke barked, which was even louder as I lay against his chest. "Hold on, sweets," he whispered and held me with one arm as he did something with his watch.

A familiar whine pierced the air and the room vibrated with a new magic. The ceiling reflected an array of colors as I heard Oliver's screams.

OTHER WORLDLY MAGIC EXCERPT

Silver can kill most magical beings. Some are naturally immune.

CHAPTER 24

DUKE WHIPPED around and my head spun from the motion.

Oliver made another sound and I pushed myself from Duke's arms, oblivious to my pain and life-threatening conditions. The shadows had stopped the worst of it. I clutched my side from the impact of hitting the floor.

My mom was covered in blood: mine, hers, and now Oliver's. Oliver stumbled until he backed up into the wall. His uneven breathing came in pants and he clutched his torso. She'd put my blade through his chest. She'd aimed for his heart, but he was still standing, so I doubted she'd been successful. Success or not, rage rolled through me and I shot forward. Her frame was mangled from mine and Oliver's attacks, but other than looking like she was hit by a train, she moved as if nothing happened.

I had three options. Shoot her in the head, but I doubted that would work. Second, decapitate her. Easier said than done, and even less easy with it being her. Third, run, which I'd planned on doing but now didn't seem possible.

"Now look, baby," Mom said, turning to me with a hand on her hip and the other gesturing to Oliver like a game show. "You didn't follow Rule One and look what happened. All your friends are going to die."

She was right and it pissed me off. I'd worked with a Soulless, hadn't cased out exits, and instead of leaving at my wisely self-appointed time, I'd gone wildly after her.

But she was wrong about something. I knew the source of the growing sound. I just needed to hold her off.

"Dessa," Duke's voice rang in my ears.

"I'm okay," I lied and took a few steps forward. My body protested, my stomach tightening and twisting against the strain.

Duke and Alan wrestled with something, grunting loudly, and then the light over us went out with the sound of shattering glass. Although it was darker, the shadows didn't come.

My mother's gaze drifted over my shoulder. I assumed at Duke and Alan, but I didn't wait. I jammed my right fist over my stomach wound and barreled into her. Someone screamed, likely both of us.

Her gaze darted back to me a moment before I crashed into her. She lifted an arm to brace for my impact, but I threw her against the wall. I didn't have the strength to follow through with my weight and instead crumpled to the ground.

Blood flooded my mouth. My vision swam, the edges darkening.

A thunderous crash with accompanying tremors tore through the wall. Another light went out, and shadows danced around me.

"Come on, Dessa," Duke yelled.

I couldn't move.

Strong arms dug under me and lifted me up. My body rag dolled. I didn't feel pain anymore, but cold shivers trembled down my nerves and I wanted to sleep.

"No, get Oliver," I said.

"Duke has him," Alan said against my ear.

He put me in Duke's car, his palm brushing against my bloodied hand. A hum rang through me, ebbing some of the pain. Before he shut the door, I caught a glimpse of my mother trying to stand up, but the shadows held her back, their dark forms trembling around her, bulging and restrengthening as more came to help.

I couldn't hear her, but I didn't need to, I could read her lips: "You're dead."

I woke up at Duke and Alan's house nestled in the bed I had slept in before. I'd been stripped, cleaned, bandaged, and put to bed. I had the best friends. Not only did they come to rescue me from an ill-advised mission, that they said not to do, they'd saved Oliver, and taken care of us, too.

Flashes of my mom popped in my head. Her words hung as a noose around my neck. She, my dad, and Tones all said the same thing. Had it just been her and my dad, I could have ignored it. I could have assumed it was all lies.

Tones confirming Mom was born a Vessel meant it was the truth. I was born a... Vessel. The impossible. Unless... I didn't know what it meant, though. How many had they sacrificed to conceive me? For them to be Soulless at my birth meant it was the death arts, and brutal. Vessels couldn't naturally reproduce with another Vessel, just humans and Practitioners. What did it mean that I was? A Vessel, sure. What about Soulless?

Why hadn't Tones or Oliver noticed? Could Oliver really not smell us? But had Tones known?

But what about the other Finders? Why hadn't they tried to bring me in? I had killed Soulless when bringing them in. Blood was on my hands. Sure, I hadn't done the death arts, but I was a product of them and killed. Would they now? So many lies rolled through my thoughts. Stacked up, I saw the house of cards. I'd accepted for so long what my mom had told me since first memory. I never stopped to evaluate it. Stopped to run against what I knew about the Soulless world. All my "gifts" were just my Vessel nature.

My gaze flicked to the darkened corners. The shadows shifted, not engaging me.

They'd known.

I was going to be the monster I hunted.

I ran a hand through my hair, a black tendril coming into focus.

Duke's muffled voice carried through the walls. A soft murmur and laughter. They had to have known. I took down the Soulless hunting Duke. They could tell Vessel from human. Did they assume I knew?

I closed my eyes and focused on Tones' face. All my thoughts would only pollute me. Make me a weakness for the others. Maybe I could go back to the bar and see if Tones' spirit was still there. Maybe she could provide me answers since all my answers sucked.

Answer questions about the Masons and either confirm or rebut my mom's claims.

I snuggled in the sheets, trying to piece together the truth until the throb in my shoulders wouldn't ease and my stomach cramped. My thoughts would have to wait. Unable to hold my bladder, I finally sighed, tossed the covers back, and rolled over. My feet sank into plush carpet and I noticed a note on the nightstand.

"REST! THAT MEANS GO BACK TO BED. NOW!!!"

I chuckled and stood up. I instantly regretted it as I crumpled back onto the bed. I felt the pull of skin on my stomach and flinched, touching the spot. The bandage darkened, and I knew I'd ripped it open.

My bladder became more urgent, and I forced myself back onto my feet. Stars popped in front of my eyes. I hunched over and clutched my stomach while I leaned against the wall to the door. With effort, I cracked the door open.

I stopped and panted from the exertion. Beads of sweat rolled down my face and dizziness sent my head spinning.

"Dessa, what are you doing?" Alan's alarmed voice sounded behind me. "You need to rest."

"Pee. I need to pee."

"Oh, of course," he said soothingly and wrapped an arm around my mid-back, avoiding both my stomach and shoulders. "Lean on me, sweets."

I snorted a laugh but leaned on him. His sweater smelled of lavender and lemon. It made me want tea.

"How about some tea?" he asked, seemingly reading my mind.

"That'd be great."

"Soup too?"

My stomach rumbled. My body was ready and willing to do what he wanted.

He chuckled and took small steps toward the bathroom.

"How's Oliver?" I whispered, my heart tightening at the possibility.

"He's in the other room," he said, lifting his chin to the room next to mine.

"Is he…." My voice trembled and cracked.

"Oh sweets, go pee and we'll visit him."

Progress from the bathroom to Oliver's room was agonizingly slow. Alan assisted me to his room despite my attempts to brush him off.

I gritted out, "Why did you come after me? You said you wouldn't help."

"No, we said we weren't offering to help. An offer can be denied." Alan guided my elbow with one hand and my back with his other hand.

I rolled my eyes. "So why did you show up when you did?"

"You didn't answer the text."

"What text?" I asked before my brain remembered the text I ignored. I groaned.

"We texted you, saying if you didn't respond in five minutes we were headed inside."

"I rarely answer texts, and never on a hunt, you know that. And I didn't want to read your scolding."

Alan shrugged. "It worked out."

Going against every fiber, and afraid of encouraging it, I muttered, "Thank you."

"Oh sweets, you're not alone. We love you."

Duke sat in the room with Oliver, fiddling with a fluid bag and checking his forehead temperature.

I hesitated, taking in the scene.

"He's in a coma?" I asked, inching toward the corner of his bed.

"No, but he does have a sedative to help with pain."

"Why does he need fluids?" I asked, staring at the tube lodged in his skin.

"Not everyone heals like you," Duke said.

"I'm still in pain," I huffed defensively.

"I'm sorry, you're right. You're a weak flower who is feeble and despite at least three stab wounds, one being to your gut, you're standing up a day after being attacked. My apologies."

"Jackass," I choked and laughed through the pain. "Wait, a day after?"

My body would normally be mostly mended by now. I licked my lips. Another sign I'd ignored.

"Yes, you were attacked yesterday. Again, one day later your delicate body is standing like a wimp."

I went to punch him, but my shoulder stilled the motion. Yesterday was the day my dad wanted the answer. He must have realized I meant no. Because I had meant it.

I didn't want to see him again, especially knowing he'd told the truth. About him. About Mom. About me. Seeing him with lies was easier to handle. I didn't have the desire or the mental fortitude to focus on it. I had a lifetime, however hopefully short, to fixate on it after we were healed.

Now it was time to focus on Oliver and fixing what my mom had done.

"Has he been awake?" I asked, resting a hand on the bed and staring at Oliver's pale face. Even though he was asleep, his face pinched tight with pain.

"Not much," Duke said and moved by me to wrap an arm around my mid-back. "She missed his heart, though."

I didn't know how to stop her. She'd thwarted an attack that'd take down multiple Soulless. Hollowness settled in my veins.

"I'll go make you soup." Alan rubbed my arm and offered me a smile.

"I can help you get back to bed," Duke said.

"Can I stay here until the soup's ready?"

Duke smiled. "Sure."

He steered me to the chair and helped me down.

I sat, creepily staring at Oliver. I didn't mean to be creepy, but what else do you call it when you watch someone sleeping and you aren't supposed to be in the room?

"Oliver," I whispered. I knew he couldn't hear me, but I had to talk to him. "You shouldn't have followed me. You said you wouldn't help."

"I said you weren't alone," his voice, barely audible.

"Oh my God, Oliver," I breathed and leaned forward. I cursed at a muscle tweak in my side and eased back to loosen the pain. "What were you thinking?"

"Me?" he breathed, squirming in discomfort.

"Shh, don't fidget, you'll hurt yourself." I scooted a bit on the chair so my hand could touch his on the bed.

Oliver's hazel eyes opened. They were hazy from medication, but they still locked on to me. "Dessa, I promised you I'd bring her in."

"You don't owe me."

"Dessa." He flinched, his breath pained.

"Shh, rest."

He blinked. "I know you think I'm weak."

"No, I don't."

His dark eyes cut to me. "You're Dessa the Destroyer. I'm not..." His body tightened.

"Oliver."

His head jerked to the side as he took a labored breath. His fingers curled around mine. "I used to want to be like you. A destroyer."

I stilled. Acid pooled in my stomach and my mouth dried waiting for his next words.

"But I'll never be as good as you. You are the best. I'm the backup, but I'll always have your back. I'll do anything I can to help you. Even when it pisses you off."

Emotion lodged in my throat, stealing my breath. I was a fucking monster and he wanted to protect me. "Oliver…" Words failed me.

"Dessa, you aren't alone. I'll die before I let her touch you again."

She would kill him, and I couldn't stop him from going after her again. I was the monster she created. The one he was trying to protect. Then and there I decided I'd take my mom down, no matter what, even including using my father for help.

DESSA'S RULES OF SURVIVAL

IF IN DOUBT, DESTROY IT

CHAPTER 25

MY FATHER WAITED until that night to show up.

I'd made it to dinner at the table and forced myself into a sitting position on a chair even when Duke shook his head and rolled his eyes. I didn't eat a ton; the food put pressure on my stomach. This was one of the longest recoveries I'd ever needed after an attack. I didn't want to admit it, but it was nice having Duke and Alan close by while my body took its sweet time recuperating.

I didn't pass on the ice cream, or whipped cream and chocolate topping.

"So," Alan said, sitting across from me with his own bowl. "What are we going to do?"

"We?" I asked with a raised eyebrow.

"That's not up for debate," Alan said, pointing his spoon at me.

I didn't want to tell them I didn't have a plan. If it were yesterday, I'd tell my dad I was willing to help him. I'd get Not-Isaac's blood for him, and Mom's head if he asked. I'd worry about all the truths they laid out afterward. But yesterday had passed, as had my window to answer my father.

I spooned in a chunk of ice cream to delay my response, but the knock on the door did more.

My eyes shot to the shadows cowering in the corner. My stomach roiled. Maybe I still had a chance.

"I'll get it," I said and winced, standing up.

"We're not expecting anyone. Sit down," Duke said, making no show to get up.

"I know who it is."

They passed a look and then turned toward me.

"You have another skill we don't know about? X-ray vision?"

"Ha ha," I said and walked to the door. They didn't stop me. I opened and moved to step outside, but before the door was fully open, both Duke and Alan stood behind me like two sentinels.

"Interesting," my dad said with a crooked grin. "How many boyfriends do you have?"

"It'll just be a minute," I said to Duke and Alan.

"Pardon," Duke said, and stuck his hand out. "I'm not acquainted. Please come inside and tell us who you are."

It was a polite request, with no malice in his voice, but it was also clear saying no wasn't an option. Alan even looped his arm into mine and steered me to the sofa.

My dad didn't shake his hand but nodded in response and trailed behind.

Duke stood at the door watching him, and when my dad sat down, he shut the door.

"You must be Dessa's father," Alan said and wrapped an arm around my neck, careful of the wounds. "Damien, is it?"

My father's eyes cut to Alan. Even if my mom raised me, I had his resting bitch face. "It's Nicolai."

Hm. I realized it was the first time I'd heard his name. Not only had my mom been married to him but told me I was the result of a fling, she'd never told me his name and I'd never asked, assuming she'd lie. And I never asked him because I hadn't cared.

"Nicolai, why are we privileged with this visit?" Alan asked.

"How's the boy?" He lifted his chin toward the other room.

"How is it you know what's happening in this house?" Alan asked. His eyes shimmered orange.

"Dessa, have you made a decision?" my dad—I mean Nicolai—asked, ignoring Alan.

"I believe she's already answered you," Duke said, finally sitting on my other side.

Oh man, they were subtle. A chuckle stuck in my throat.

Nicolai's eyes traveled from my shoulders to my stomach and up to the fading tattoos.

I rested a hand on each of their knees.

"Are you ready to accept my help?" Nicolai asked.

"I don't owe you anything," I said measuredly, rubbing my wrist where the tattooed scrolls would be if I owed him. "I didn't ask for the favor of coming back."

Nicolai's mouth pinched up slightly and his gaze moved to the ceiling as he considered my words. He nodded once in acknowledgment, a glint in his eye. "How's the boy doing? You know she uses poison."

Duke sucked in a breath and Alan growled.

Poison. That bitch had probably poisoned both of us.

"What type of poison?" Alan finally asked.

Nicolai chuckled and tilted his head.

"You can help him?" I saw where this conversation was headed and wanted to get there faster.

"Can you get the blood?"

It was then I questioned all the events. He knew too much but I'd made too many mistakes, hadn't had enough information and my mom-blinders had blocked me from more than just her. I didn't think they were working together. I could be wrong, they *had* been married, but their hatred seemed woven into their core. His "help" in protecting me from her meant both that I couldn't find her again and she couldn't kill me again—meaning I needed him to get her and that meant I had to get him the blood he wanted.

I was certain I was missing more pieces. But I was stuck. I'd played into too many hands: my mom's, Harvey's, John's, and my dad's. I'd need to change the rules. Carve out an advantage.

"Weren't you supposed to be here yesterday?"

An approving smile spread across his face.

"Weren't you incapacitated?"

"You didn't show."

"All right, what are your terms?" Nicolai asked, rubbing his hands on his knees.

"Dessa," Alan and Duke warned in unison.

I snorted a laugh. They could warn all they wanted. Without his help, I'd never find her again. She'd make sure I never got into a neutral zone again. I'd always be looking around corners for both of them.

"Help us heal Oliver. I also want her dead."

Alan and Duke sucked in a breath but didn't protest. Emotion radiated from them and my body tightened in response.

"I get the blood in return for what you want?" he asked, leaning back in his chair.

It was a dangerous move, but I was out of options. The four of us had failed to bring her down. I wouldn't be able to stop her. If my mom feared him, he was my best chance.

I shrugged noncommittally in acknowledgment.

"I'll need to train you how to get it."

Figures. He was a next-level Soulless, like Not-Isaac, a type I hadn't seen before, whatever was higher than a Level One. I could make my mother bleed, I already had, but I doubted I'd survive long enough to bring it back again. Her Companion... Wait, if she was a Soulless since my conception, she didn't have a Companion anymore. Her friend was worse.

His gaze slid to Alan and Duke, and then to me. "Get your business resolved. I'll be here in the morning to pick you up."

"We gonna set up camp?"

"My compound is safer. She can't track you there even without my intervention."

I let that roll around a bit. I was the fucking mouse again. But he had a point. And I was out of better options.

"What about Oliver?" I asked around a lump in my throat.

"She's not fancy with her poisons, but she likes them to fester," Nicolai said.

I should have been shocked he knew Oliver was poisoned and by what, but that ship had sailed. It was easier to accept that he knew and move on than to stew and press the subject. Like I did about them, or me, being born a Vessel. It's not like he'd tell me the full truth, anyway, or that I really wanted to know.

He pulled a piece of paper from his pocket and handed it to me. I scanned the document and nodded. I recognized the ingredients from our kitchen growing up. I just hadn't known she used them for things other than cleaning up blood.

He inclined his head toward it. "Make that, give him a week. It seems the poison didn't work on you."

I stared down at my body, forcing itself to heal. He didn't need to know the poison had slowed my body down.

My eyes traveled to my wrists. They didn't have scrolls, but then, he'd have to have scrolls until Oliver healed, since I was apparently a Vessel, too. He must have realized it, too, as I saw his gaze flick to my wrists. He frowned.

"She can't go alone to your compound," Alan said and grabbed my hand. He squeezed it.

"I'll be there," Nicolai assured him.

"Not reassuring," Alan said.

"We'll come too," Duke said, his normal smile gone, a steely expression carved in its place.

Alan's eyes full-on glowed orange.

I sighed and rolled my eyes. There wasn't a point to protest. They'd figure out a way anyway, and to be honest, I loved that they wanted to support me. Still, lead hardened in my stomach at the idea of them getting hurt. But they could protect themselves.

Nicolai shrugged. "Is the boy coming too, then?"

"I'm going where she's going," Oliver said. He hunched against the wall, a grimace tugging on his lips as sweat beaded on his brow. His body trembled but he kept his gaze steady.

Big brother bullshit, again. But then if Duke and Alan were coming, it'd be easier to make sure he healed.

Nicolai smiled. "Understood."

BY MORNING, he didn't mean a sane hour like nine or ten, or even a semi-sane time like eight. No, he showed up at five a.m. I'd been asleep for about two hours when the pounding started. A loud, confident knock that assumed it'd bring fear and doom to the person on the other side. I rolled my eyes and growled.

I threw off my covers and winced as I stood. My wounds were healing much better since making the antidote, the skin pulling closed with ridged lines forming. My shoulders were scabbing and itchy and my stomach only bled a bit. Scar tissue was already forming. I'd normally complain about the slow process, but Oliver was still struggling to breathe.

Duke's sleepy voice cursed as he answered the door.

I pulled my bedroom door open to find Alan in the hall still in his pajamas, which meant boxers. I'd never seen him shirtless before, but it was a sight. He was built like a swimmer, lean and muscular.

Duke's grumbling grew louder as he neared, and I saw he wore matching pajamas. His broader chest was like a linebacker. His green eyes narrowed in on me. He ran a hand through his curly blond locks and blinked, sleep still pulling on his face. "What the fuck is he doing here so early?"

I shrugged and suppressed my smile by pretending to yawn.

"We'll just shower there," Alan said and ran a hand over his face. "It's too damn early."

"I'll be ready in five," I said and closed my door. I was already packed with the shirts and jeans Alan and Duke had provided. I pulled on a pair of jeans with the T-shirt I was wearing and grabbed my duffle bag.

Alan and Duke were talking in their room, so I knocked on Oliver's door. When he didn't respond, I knocked louder.

"Just come in," Oliver called back in annoyance.

I slowly pushed the door open and peeked around the door. I ogled Oliver as he sat on the bed, gathering the energy to stand up. He wore briefs and nothing else. I bit my lip and took in the full view.

"Dessa?" he asked, his voice tinged with alarm.

Color stained my cheeks as I realized I'd been caught creeping.

"Need help?" I choked out.

"I thought you were Duke or Alan. Aren't you injured, too?" he said and flinched when his attempt to stand failed.

I rushed over to offer support.

"You're looking a bit better," I said.

"Your dad was right about the cure." He shrugged.

At least he honored his end.

I sat next to him and put his arm around my shoulder and wrapped my arm around his torso. Hot curls radiated through my body and tightened in my core. My breath hitched at the contact, and I swallowed.

"At the count of three," I said, strained.

"What are you doing?" Nicolai's voice sounded like a rifle going off.

I whipped my head up, guilty of something. I'd only ogled him, which wasn't that bad.

"I'm only helping him," I said, feeling like a childish fool.

"I can see that, but why? You're injured," he said and took a few steps in.

I narrowed my eyes at him. His concern had to be a ploy. Unless he was afraid I wouldn't be able to help him, but he'd never cared about the damage I'd sustained before. I gave him the "fuck off" look and patted Oliver's torso in attempt to focus us. It didn't work; it distracted me when his muscles rippled beneath my fingers.

"Get up," Nicolai said and extended a hand to help me.

I stared at it and then his face. My jaw clenched. This whole caring thing was new and unwelcomed. And likely came with strings.

"I'm okay," Oliver said and turned to face me. We were sitting close, and his face was now in my zone. I stared at him with my body frozen, looking at his hazel eyes. I didn't like this new behavior of mine. I preferred the time before we kissed, before we'd talked. Back when Tones was alive, I had a silent crush, and Oliver only teased me. I understood that relationship. This one left me tingly and confused.

Nicolai cursed and brought my attention back to the room.

Without asking, Nicolai bent over and lifted me up. I was shocked by the sudden movement but not enough to freeze. My face reddened and I swatted his hands and went to kick him.

He was swift and put me down before turning to Oliver. "Here," he said and offered him a hand.

Oliver accepted it with a weak, apologetic smile toward me.

"Oh," Duke's voice cut across the room.

"We ready?" Nicolai asked, annoyed, and looked at each of us. "Let's move."

"This'll be fun," Duke said as we filed out of the room.

He wasn't joking when he said compound. I'd expected a creepy old mansion. The ones that are about the size of a modern house but have twisting staircases, closed-off rooms, not enough light, the tall, narrow gothic look, with dark colors and transparent figures in the windows.

The compound was set in a forest dozens of miles from the city on a large, flat acreage that had a clear several-mile radius view. The twenty acres surrounding the property were fenced in with ten-foot fences. I was surprised to not see barbed wire spiraling around. Instead, the top had black wires running the length. It was likely an electric fence.

The area inside the fence held several buildings and parts that were sectioned off. There were courts for different sports, a swimming pool, and a track that ran around the perimeter.

One of the buildings appeared to be a garage, based on the doors, but they were oversized, so I figured industrial transportation might reside within.

He drove us up to the main house. It was stunning and modern. It had hard geometric shapes with long walls made entirely of glass. I sat in the passenger side front seat for the ride while the other three sat in the back.

"What the hell do you do?" Duke asked.

"This and that," he responded.

"Uh-huh," Duke pressed, but I shook my head at him. He gave me a questioning look.

I closed my eyes and shook my head again. I didn't want to know what he did. I wanted to live in ignorance. Ignorance of his profession and ignorance of his and my trueborn nature.

Duke frowned but let it go.

I hopped out of the car and surveyed the area. I was surprised my mom would have left this house, but she'd never focused on amassing physical wealth. Just money. She liked comforts like good sheets and good food, but I got my more sparse housekeeping from her.

"Is this where you and Mom lived?" I asked, looking at Nicolai over the roof of the SUV.

He shook his head.

"Ok, great talk," I said.

Entering the house felt like walking into another world. Everything was sleek lines and clean but eccentric. Abstract art covered the walls in splashes of greens and blues. There were vases and sculpture things around the house, all tasteful and out of a magazine. Nothing felt lived in or used. I felt like I'd entered a showroom.

"This is where you live?"

"This is the receiving room." He nodded to a staircase that led to a galley-type walkway that ran over the middle of the room. The rails were thin iron, providing an almost unobstructed view.

I followed him up. The left side had bedroom doors along the hall and opened into a large, shared space that was made of window-lined walls.

To the right was another zone. The doors were shut. I got the do-not-enter vibe and couldn't wait to visit once we were alone.

"What's down there?" I asked.

"My private office and bedroom." He gave me a knowing look. He inclined his head to the left. "Guest bedrooms are over here."

There were four guest bedrooms, two on each side. Between the pairs were two en suites.

"I'll see you in an hour," Nicolai said to me, and then addressed the others. "Be good guests."

So, the threats had begun.

The other three just looked at him.

Yeah, this was going to be fun.

Other Worldly Magic Excerpt

Practitioner — Humans, beings born without magic, who can conjure magic with spells.

Vessel Practitioner — A Vessel who can use their natural magic and conjure through spells. A rare combination that requires years of study and training. They are likely Soulless.

CHAPTER 26

SOMEHOW NICOLAI MADE Mom's training look like a walk in the park. I flopped on my bed, full of sweat, blood, and whatever else drips from the face.

"Go away," I shouted at whoever was knocking on my door.

"I have pizza," Alan's voice called back.

"Come in," I grunted back and pushed myself up.

The door opened and Alan stifled a sound. He grimaced when I turned around.

"You look like shit."

"Feel it, too," I said. "How'd you get pizza?"

"Duke found it in the freezer."

At least they were making themselves at home. I grabbed a slice. After swallowing a bite, I said, "You two didn't have to come."

Alan patted my hand and smiled at me.

"I'm not a child. I don't need a chaperone."

Alan snorted a laugh.

"I'm not," I whined.

"Oh sweets," he said. "We love you. We want to help."

"I do appreciate your care, but you have your own lives."

"We do, and we want to make sure you have one, too."

I blew out a sigh. My life was something. It was familiar and bloody.

"You always feel like you deserve…" Alan paused and rolled his eyes upwards staring at the ceiling for answers. "Like you deserve the hardest path, to be a punching bag."

"I'm not a punching bag," I said and glared at him, but I wasn't sure what I deserved.

"You are literally a punching bag. Soulless punch, kick, and stab you."

"I do it to them, too." I grimaced. Fuck, I was like them. Was one of them. Fine, if I was like them, or was one of them, then I was doing what I should be doing. I'd keep rounding them up and they could keep trying to stop me. In the end, Soulless would be off the streets, even if it was me. I knew what I rounded up. I knew what they did. I knew what I did.

Alan sighed, the long-suffering parental type of sigh. "You accept less."

I shrugged. "What more do I need?"

He frowned and shook his head. "You accept that your mom used you to provide the income since you were six. You accept that your dad shows up after your mom kills you and wants a favor and you agree. You live minimally so you don't have to suffer losing anything. You don't let people love you because you're afraid they're playing the long con."

"I let you love me," I said defensively. His truths were too spot on. It was the Finder's life. Love was a liability. Our lives were short and deaths often brutal. It was just easier not to go the alone route.

"With much resistance and arguing."

I smiled and nudged his shoulder with mine. "I love you and Duke."

"We know," Alan said. "But that's not what I'm talking about."

"What are you talking about? Wait, wait, wait, I don't want to know," I said, rethinking my declaration, and grabbed another slice of pizza. I didn't need more truths.

"You accept mine and Duke's love because we're platonic. We're not a threat to you."

"Love is a threat to me?"

"No, letting yourself be vulnerable is."

"I don't like where this conversation is going."

"Sweets, you lived a life of half-ways before your mom killed you. You got a second chance. Is that how you want to live this one?"

***

I DIDN'T LIKE my conversation with Alan. I wasn't a retrospective person. I lived to survive the moment. He wanted me to think about more than that, and I wasn't ready or likely able to. Beyond the personal stuff he was referring to, I had to think about my existence, and neither sounded fun to do.

I found my way to the shared space. Oliver sat on the sofa, eating chips and watching TV.

I plopped down and grabbed the bag.

"Yes, Dessa, I'd love to share. Here, why don't you have some?" Oliver said, staring at the show.

"Now I'm not giving it back," I said.

"You weren't going to, anyway." He pulled an unopened bag from the side of the sofa.

"Holding out?"

"No, planning ahead. I remember nights in Mom's office with you."

"You were very bossy." I gave him a disapproving look and crunched a chip loudly.

"Me? You were constantly trying shit. I was supposed to make sure you were safe, but you had a death wish," he said, and then murmured, "Still do."

I sucked on my teeth to stop my retort. I didn't want to fight with

Oliver. He was injured, and he usually did large arm gestures when arguing.

After a few beats, I asked, "Do you want a lift to a hospital or back to the bar?"

"What?" he asked.

"Let's cut the crap. Being around me is likely going to get you pissed off. You need rest. I already have Alan and Duke playing big brother."

"I'm not playing brother," he said, his voice dangerously low.

"No? Then what are you playing?"

He turned his face from the TV to stare at me. His expression was dark and his eyes unblinking. His lips were a tight line and his jaw muscle twitched.

"I'm not playing," he said, over pronouncing each word.

"Then what are you doing?"

His eyes traveled over my face before returning to my gaze.

The moment passed and he shook his head and turned back to the TV.

———

SLEEPING in the new room was unsurprisingly hard. I was cautious by nature, so I had my blade. I tossed and turned but my mind wouldn't shut off.

I finally shoved the covers off and quietly opened my door. I scanned the hallway and slipped out. The house was dark except for the light coming in from outside. Ground lights swirled around the yard in an elaborate design. The space behind the house had been designed for outdoor living and led to the pool. Lights dotted the path, creating a warm glow and magical ambiance.

I walked to the skywalk above the living space and looked down. Even without light, I could still see with my night vision. It was then I realized that the shadows didn't move. There were no noises or motion. I walked along the walkway to the private quarters. A light shone under the door. A beacon cutting into the dark. I stood at the threshold of the wing that Nicolai said was his sleeping quarters. There was definitely a do-not-enter vibe.

I figured he had traps set or had it rigged to tell him if anyone entered. Or even a camera. I'd have to find a way to get in with him. Being caught by him or on video would only complicate matters.

I walked back to my room and jumped when I noticed a shadow swirl. The hiss was weak but familiar.

I wanted to talk to it, ask what was going on with the main room, with the private quarters, but it didn't feel safe. I wasn't sure if this shadow was on my side or not.

———

THE NEXT MORNING, I got my first chance to get a peek at the rooms. Nicolai had gone to shower after our practice. I needed to, also, but decided to stalk him first.

I waited ten minutes after his water turned off and meandered back to our section of the second floor to linger. When he emerged from his bedroom and headed to his office, I called out.

"Are you a Shadowtalker?" I asked as he crossed into the office.

He startled and swung his gaze to me, brows furrowed.

I walked across the skywalk and stood by him in the doorway. I repeated, "Are you a Shadowtalker?"

He stared at me. His brown eyes searched my face.

I stared at him and then the floor and traced a circle with my eyes large until I locked gazes with him again.

"Why?" he finally asked.

"Mom said she wasn't, but I think she lied."

His face scrunched in confusion. "She wasn't a Shadowtalker."

"You sure?" I asked. Even though I kept eye contact, I used blinks and head shifts to get glances of his office. It looked like a legal office, with rows of large tomes along all the walls.

"Why?"

"Afraid to give me info?"

He narrowed his eyes.

I narrowed mine back at him mockingly.

He sighed. "What has your mother told you about her? Or you?"

I pulled back slightly at that question. I thought I'd known the basics, but they all appeared to be lies. I'd thought two born Vessels couldn't procreate. I thought I was born to a Practitioner mother and Vessel father. A mother who taught me how to hunt the Soulless as she herself hunted her kind, and I followed in her footsteps.

"Come in and sit down," he said.

Sweet, an open invitation to the room.

"What do you know?" he asked again, sitting in a wing-backed chair. He gestured to its match across a small coffee table. A book, *Otherworldly Magic*, lay on it.

"What I know seems to be lies."

"Let's start with it."

"I'm a Finder. I can track and retrieve Soulless. Mom taught me the skills. She implied she'd been a Finder at one time, and even introduced me to John at my first Agency. Her powers lie in persuasion," I said, focusing on the parts that I had believed and still appeared truthful.

"Persuasion is a cute word for it." Nicolai's face pinched in disgust.

"What do you call it?"

He growled.

I'm guessing I didn't want to know.

"I was under the impression she became a Choicer."

"Why?" Genuine curiosity lighted his expression.

I blinked at the question. "Her target sheet said so, and I didn't believe she was a Vessel before then."

"You can't sense your own kin and often anyone you were raised around."

"What?"

"You were immersed in her scent from birth. Her smell became invisible to you. It happens with blood folk and when you spend time with the same Vessels."

"Is that why I can't sense you? Our blood?"

He stared at me, his face blank.

Guess I was right. How had they gotten married? They were both arrogant and self-serving. How had they not only not killed each other, but been together long enough to conceive a child? Which brought around another question.

"So, if you were both Vessels, how was I born?" I blurted out, staring him in the eye.

His eyes darkened while his face remained emotionless.

"I'm sure you already know."

That was bait.

I shrugged. "So, if you've been Soulless since it happened, how come you don't have a target sheet out on you?"

His mouth twisted into a grin.

"You have a broad and oversimplified understanding of how the system works."

"What?" Add on to the lies I believed.

"Can you sense the Soulless from the Vessels?" he said, templing his fingers and leaning his elbows on the desk.

He already knew the answer, so I shrugged.

"Didn't it occur to you that others couldn't sense the Soulless, that it was an ability? That the death arts remnants aren't noticeable to others? Didn't your perfect record seem suspicious?"

Yep, that was a direct shot at me. I fisted my hands so I didn't flip him off. He also knew about my success rate, which should have been shocking, but wasn't.

"So, if you and Mom have been Soulless from my conception, what does that make me?" I asked. I waited for the lie. For the chuckle. For something.

His eyes opened in surprise, and his shoulders tightened before he regained his relaxed composure. Then an entertained smile flittered across his lips. "Are you concerned you're a Soulless? That you're hunting your own?"

What concerned me was that I hadn't known. That I missed a vital part of myself. I couldn't change who I was. It wouldn't stop me from bringing in the Soulless. It made me more resolute. Someone would come for me again one day if my parents didn't kill me. Either a target would be issued on me or it would be retribution. I knew their crimes and they would know mine. Until the day I was caught, I'd continue to do my best.

"No," I said. "How would I know if I have a target on me?"

"Someone would show up to take you in," Nicolai said.

"Is that why you have oversized fences and a compound? So a Finder can't collect you?" It obviously wasn't. Mom didn't have the same fixtures. He was keeping something else out. Be it Mom, her Companion, or something else yet.

"Why do you think there is a target out on me? What have I done?" Nicolai asked.

Shit. I realized it was because I believed my mom. Double shit. But if he resurrected me with the death arts, one was warranted.

His eyes lit up in mirth when my gaze met his, and I knew the comment was meant to distract me. He was fucking playing around with me.

"How would I really know if I have an Agency target on me?" I asked again. Mom had a personal one out on me, but that was different than a target sheet from an Agency, and more dangerous.

He stared at me for a bit, and then leaned back and let out a long breath through his nose. Finally, he said, "You're correct on some of it, oversimplified on some, and ignorant on the rest."

I snorted. As unreassuring as it was, I had to agree. The more I learned since dying, the more I realized how little I knew.

"You've seen the target sheets. The Soulless are brought in for using the death arts to harm others. However, not all those who harm others are given target sheets."

"Why not?" I interjected.

He smiled. I hated it.

"The Soulless are those who broke the Vessels' rules."

"The Vessels' rules?" I echoed.

He glared at my interruption but continued. "Vessels use magic. You know it as part of the Finders' code, but the death arts aren't to be used. It is punishable. To say what falls into the death arts is subjective. Being labeled Soulless means you were caught and pissed off someone who had the power to put a target out. All Soulless are considered dangerous. They've used the death arts in sacrifice or ritual, and so long as it can be proven the person is Soulless, a reward is issued."

I bit my tongue to not say anything. I knew what Soulless smelled like. He could say it was subjective, but sacrifice had an odor. There was a difference.

He waited a beat, and then said, "You're one of the few who can detect a Soulless without a target sheet. They have blood on their hands. The stain of the death arts taints them. You can smell it. That is very rare."

"So, all Soulless should have targets but those without didn't piss off the wrong person enough, yet?" I'd always thought it was hard proof that they were Soulless to get a target sheet, not pissing someone powerful off. It was a fucking game and I'd been playing along. John and Mom played me for Level Twos, and the system was another game about exploitation, power, and money.

"Close enough," he said. "We must oversee our own kind. That's why they created the laws we follow."

"The Finders' Trust is well established. They collect the Soulless from the Agencies."

"For the targets they issue," Nicolai injected.

My veins ran cold. Colors flashed in my brain, as I couldn't focus on words or thoughts.

I knew the Finder's code. I knew about the governing body, the structure, and how the process worked. I knew it from a technical and application standpoint, but staring at him, and knowing both my father and my mother should be Soulless with target sheets, I still wasn't ready for this reality.

Nicolai settled back in his chair. With a blink, all emotion erased from his face. "Targets are usually identified when a Soulless is rounded up and snitches on others for leniency or when a do-good Vessel reports them through an Agency. You obviously know the Trust collects the Soulless, pays out to Agencies, disposes of Level One targets immediately with decapitation and cremation to halt any death arts, Level Twos often follow the same consequences but not always, and others are fined, rehabbed, or both depending on their crimes. This is all clearly labeled in the Handbook."

He was correct, but there was definitely a "but" coming and although I didn't want to hear it, I needed to. "So what about the targets they don't issue?"

A grin curved his lips. "Now that's a different story. Vessels and humans aren't all that different. Even if we obey most of their civil laws, we have more, determined by Vessels. Humans have cops."

Nothing he was saying was new.

"Like humans, we have our own secret societies. Your mom purposely kept you in the dark, especially as she was in one."

My vision blurred but I didn't interrupt. Just add this to the list of fucks my mom had done without me knowing, like her being a Vessel. Sure, I knew Soulless could group together to try to target Finders, but what was she a part of?

"It's like our version of the mob, but much deadlier and more powerful."

"Mob?" I choked. Now he was going to Hollywood on me?

His eyes narrowed and darkness skittered behind them.

I rolled my hand for him to continue.

"They make deals with Agencies. Issue their own targets so the Trust doesn't know."

Oh fuck. Was this why she kept me at John's? So, I wouldn't know? I didn't associate with other Finders except Oliver, who used John, too, and until John cut me loose, I'd only been to him. Seen his way. Learned it all from him. And didn't know what he kept hidden. Finally, I managed, "Why do they issue their own targets?"

"Couple reasons." He paused.

I sighed. I was already deep. Whatever he said could be a lie, but it could also not be.

"One, someone they dislike, who went against them."

When he went silent, I prompted, "Or?"

"The best ritual blood is another Soulless's. Their use of the death arts amplifies the magic. They issue the targets based on what they want to do."

Oh fuck. Oh fuck. Oh fuck.

"Who's they?" I asked, a knot forming in my stomach. I'd lived my life knowing my truths. They were simple. And yet, it clearly wasn't. There was a layer my mother had kept me from. Even if he was embellishing, I could dig for more info. I'd brought targets in for years, assuming they were issued by the Trust, because why the fuck wouldn't they be? That was the process.

He smiled at me, turning my stomach. It was so bright and cheerful, it likely meant the answer would crush me.

"Who runs the Coving version of the 'Soulless mob'?" Regardless of not wanting to know, I had an obligation to not move forward blindly. I'd ignorantly followed what my mom had taught me. Now was the hard part of unlearning ingrained beliefs. To make sure I believed in what I was doing.

"The main one goes by the name Isaiah."

OTHER WORLDLY MAGIC EXCERPT

The Finders' Agency was created in 1886 to monitor Vessels, a naturally magical being. A group of Vessels created specific parameters on the type of magic that could be used. They labeled the Death Arts illegal due to the base element of the magic. Overtime, the Agency's intent has grown to a bounty-style system. The original founders turned into a systematic reporting system. Little is known outside of the Agency about who investigates claims. It is funded by the investments of the original founding Vessels who all provided seed money to encourage the reporting of Soulless.

CHAPTER 27

I SAT IN THE POOL. The warm water lapped at my body, relaxing my muscles. I'd taken ice baths, had healing ointments applied, and the wounds had finally closed.

The sun was setting, painting the sky watercolor swirls of blue, red, and orange.

I'd left Nicolai's office after he'd mentioned Not-Isaac. Apparently, Not-Isaac was more important than I realized. He was likely the boss of my boss. And my mom was connected to Not-Isaac. It wasn't a hard leap to see my dad was likely the same thing in whatever city he was in before now.

I stared at my hands, seeing the phantom speckles of blood. I knew the ones I brought in. I knew what they'd done. They preyed on their own kind just like I'd done in different ways and would continue to do. Vessels had to regulate Vessels; they were stronger than humans. But Not-Isaac could be connected.

I leaned back and groaned. I didn't want to deal with the moral ramifications of what I'd just learned. My life had been bloody but simple. Full of chaos and violence, but it was cut and dried. Now I had to deal with Not-Isaac along with my mom. Too many thoughts swirled in my mind, mostly about me being a Vessel.

I needed a distraction.

Duke and Alan were on the courts, playing basketball. They both cheated and it turned more physical than an actual game.

Oliver was propped up in a lawn chair for the fresh air. I watched him, looking for signs of Not-Isaac and Isaac in him. He hadn't reminded me of his father growing up. Isaac was a loud, joyous man. He had a ready smile for everyone. His mischievous eyes twinkled right before mocking you or doing something that'd get Tones to swat him.

He'd been a big man, but not as tall as Oliver. His death had taken a toll on all of us. Oliver had been put into the position of man-of-the-house by his own declaration. Tones constantly tried to get him to be a kid, but he felt the burden of being the eldest of all the boys. A burden he'd made for himself. He always had the big brother issue.

The younger boys had grieved but didn't have the relationship Oliver had. I'd forgotten all the memories, just blips of a life that wasn't mine. I'd been the outsider kid eating at their backroom table. While the boys did homework, I practiced on the punching bag.

I couldn't recall seeing Not-Isaac much, but I'd learned early to ignore faces. I was only a liability if I could remember seeing someone with my mom or at the bar. If I remembered them, I could be used as a witness or source of information. Now I could only wonder who they really had been.

I pulled myself from the pool, dripping water on the pavement. I felt eyes watch me as I walked back to the house. I itched for my blade. Even being with my friends and dad, I still felt naked without the protection.

The house was empty as expected, but it still pulsed. I glanced at his private chambers and back to my room. I ascended the steps, silent but steady.

Our rooms were dark as we'd left them. I wouldn't doubt if he had rooted in our stuff or had the shadows do it. I may be his child, but I was still a stranger and I brought three unknowns with me. Well, they should be unknowns, but knowing him he had a full dossier on them.

I went to my room and pulled my swimsuit off and flung it into the shower. I pulled on underwear and a bra, cargo pants, and a baggy t-shirt. As I exited the room, I stared at his private study. I was going to be stupid.

I crept down the hall. A thin ray of light lined the study's door. I knocked on the door, but he didn't respond. I knocked again and twisted the handle. The door inched open, spilling light into the hall.

"Nicolai? Are you in there?" I called for appearances. I pressed the door a bit more and scanned the room. Able to take in the room in greater detail than with Nicolai staring at me, I took in the books lining the walls in wrinkled leather bindings, some flaking, while others were in pristine condition with shiny gold lettering.

His desk was scattered with papers and more books. Around the room were various articles of magic. Most of the books had swirling designs on the covers, marking them as death art books. They confirmed he was a Vessel who practiced. It was an odd combination. Vessels usually didn't try conjuring. But Mom had conjured, too, when I was younger. But being Practitioner Soulless is likely how two Vessels procreated.

I growled and rolled my eyes. His words were playing with my mind. This was why I never reflected on life. Why I just focused on survival. I didn't have the answers. I didn't know anyone who could tell me. It'd only flood me with doubt and distort my focus.

I closed the door and stepped back. My neck hairs raised, but it wasn't like when a Soulless was nearby. I didn't feel ready for the strike, the kill.

I grasped my blade and turned to face whoever lurked.

Only shadowless darkness filled the space.

I glanced back at the door. I didn't think I let something out.

I crossed the skywalk and hesitated. I kept my guard up and my back to the wall as I descended the steps. I ducked outside and surveyed my surroundings. Nothing but bushes and trees dotted the house. No other being was there.

That's when I heard it.

"Dessa, what the fuck is wrong with you?"

"Tones?" I croaked.

"What are you doing here?"

"Me? What about you?"

Her shadow form pulled from the cement wall and materialized in a translucent shimmer, the edges raw and hazy.

"Oh, Dessa," she said, her voice soft and soothing. I sighed and my heart felt heavy. I missed her so much.

"I'm sorry about Oliver," I said, rolling my lips between my teeth. I blinked to keep my emotions in.

"He made his choices," she said, her tone firm.

"He's being overprotective. This isn't his fight."

Tones laughed and I rolled my eyes.

"You see so much, can flush out any Soulless, but you're so narrowly focused in your life."

"He's no match for her."

"Neither are you."

"She's my fault."

Tones sighed. "I didn't come here for your self-loathing. Your mother is an adult. She's your mother. You're not hers."

"Tones, my parents are Vessels and not Choicers."

"Yes," she said.

"You knew?" I scolded.

"Yes," she whispered—or she was fading. "I told you."

"Tones, that means... that means..."

"It means what it means. You were born to your parents by their will, but you make your path. You decide what your life will mean."

"I don't understand why my mom would train me to be a Finder. She trained me to hunt her?"

"You don't?" she laughed.

I stared forward at the wall.

"You don't," she said flatly. "Dessa, your mom is a shrewd person. You were her weapon."

"How was I a weapon?" I'd been a Finder. She trained me, but it was the job.

Tones chuckled. "Since you were six, she's used you to hunt out her opposition. You've eliminated her competition."

"What?" I sputtered. I rounded up hundreds over the years. Target or not. How had the targets been decided? How had they been assigned to me? John and my mom had history. It wasn't hard to believe he'd do whatever she wanted, but had he always known she was a Soulless since my conception? The Trust came to his location, so at least some of his targets were legitimate. But what about the rest? What about the Soulless I brought in without a target? Fuck.

"You took out bad people, but many were also jockeying for the same spots your mom was. Some Soulless snitch on who they were told to snitch on. You paved the way for her to move up Isaiah's ranks."

Well fuck. I had been a weapon or tool.

"You know about Isaiah?"

"Of course, so did Isaac. It's why Isaiah killed Isaac and then fled to the coast to strengthen before returning."

Age-old family drama. Brother kills brother.

"But my dad…"

"He wants you for the same thing," Tones said. "They both always did. They created you to be a hunter, a Finder."

"Then why did they break up?"

"I don't think they really did at first, but time severed them, and your mother's alliances shifted to just herself."

"Why didn't my dad come sooner?"

"You were right where he needed you. You were taking out Soulless. Even if you hated her, you were loyal to your mom."

"How? When I thought Mom turned to a Choicer, I hunted her."

"That's when your father stepped in. Claudine and Isaiah made a play against you and *him*."

"So, most of my targets are just enemies of Not-Isaac and Mom and those like them who issue their own targets at corrupt Agencies or snitch to the Trust?"

Tones sighed. I didn't like it. It likely meant I was right.

My entire life had been a game, one I didn't know I was playing, and I was used as a token. John used me for Level Twos and skimmed the wages. Mom used me to take out her competition. My dad was now using me to get to Isaiah. I'd ignorantly let them control me.

"So, I've been a pawn."

"Do you bring in dangerous people?"

"Yes."

"Then focus on that."

"Why didn't you tell me before?" I whispered.

Tones made a clucking sound. "Dessa, we aren't perfect. Had I said anything when you were a child, your mother would have moved you away. You'd have had only her in your life. I loved you too much to sacrifice you to her, even if it meant hiding some truths. As you grew, you were ferocious and determined. Your moral compass isn't due north, but you are a natural protector. Despite everything your mom did and tried to instill in you, you weren't her. You've always been Dessa. I thought I had more time to tell you. Time isn't something to be wasted."

"Tones, what do I do?"

"You didn't listen to me before."

"I know, I just wanted my mom to pay for all she took."

"You've made your choice. You're going to have to see this through."

"To her death?"

"You'll need to decide what the end is."

"That's vague and cryptic."

Tones chuckled. "You don't do well being told what to do. So, decide what you want to do, and you'll do it. You can't hide now."

Something my mom said tickled in the back of my brain. "Tones, my mom said something… about Isaac." Each word was acid on my tongue to bring up Tones' late husband, but my mom would use it against me and Oliver if it helped her. I needed the truth to not fall for her bait.

Tones image flickered. "Yes, Isaac created the neutral spots with magic."

Oh fuck, my mom hadn't lied. "He was a Soulless?"

She sighed. "No. Isaac's Vessel powers could mask the scents of others. Two of his brothers have it to some degree and have neutral spots in other cities. I use my spells to amplify and maintain what he created. Isaac always believed someone deserved another chance. He saw his powers as a way to help. Isaiah saw a different opportunity. He saw it as a way to operate without Finder Law interference. Isaac wouldn't let his brother into Mason's or help him."

Her frame flickered again. Red and blue pulsed through it. "Isaiah killed Isaac in the ritual to get control of his powers. He created the other spots using Isaac's blood. It's why I never shared the other locations. Your mom didn't because she used them, but I knew you weren't protected there. With Isaiah focused back on Coving, he rarely leaves one of the sites or safehouse. The three of them can sense each other, they are so powerful, but the sites offer them protection from each other finding them."

"Tones..." I had no idea what I wanted to say. So many thoughts slammed together in my brain.

"We all have sins and secrets in our past and whatever futures we have. Oliver and his brothers never knew."

And they'd never hear it from me.

"Tones, I miss you. Oliver misses you."

"I miss you both. You both had to grow up in unfortunate ways. Draw strength from each other."

OTHER WORLDLY MAGIC EXCERPT

The Finders' Agency was created in 1886 to monitor Vessels, a naturally magical being. A group of Vessels created specific parameters on the type of magic that could be used. They labeled the Death Arts illegal due to the base element of the magic. Overtime, the Agency's intent has grown to a bounty-style system. The original founders turned into a systematic reporting system. Little is known outside of the Agency about who investigates claims. It is funded by the investments of the original founding Vessels who, all provided seed money to encourage the reporting of Soulless.

CHAPTER 28

THE NEXT DAY, I shoved Nicolai as he lunged at me, catching him in the chest and ramming him backward. His hands clawed at me, digging into my muscles and leaving long bruises up my arms. He anchored on the floor and I felt the buildup of momentum before he unleashed and I crouched. As he sprang at me, I dug my blade deep into his gut.

A visceral smile cut across my face and a spike of adrenaline flooded me.

He stuttered, mouth open, and moved a hand to the wound.

I yanked my blade out and took a defensive stance.

His hand touched his side, and he turned it over, marveling at the blood. He looked back at me with pride lighting his face. "Nice move."

So apparently gutting my father made him proud. He and Mom may have been a pair.

He slackened his stance and, smiling, pulled his shirt off and wiped up his blood. I ran the blade over the towel he provided to clean it. I had a feeling a sneak attack was coming.

"So does Not-Isaac bleed or not?" I asked. That'd be a new option, but with a Soulless of his level I wouldn't be shocked if he defied laws of nature.

"Isaiah bleeds," Nicolai said.

"Then can I just stab him?" My stomach eased at the knowledge he had at least one normal trait.

"How do you plan on collecting and bringing back the blood?"

"Could I just decapitate him and drag him here?"

His smile fell and he stared at me with a mixture of admiration and concern.

"Would that not work?" It worked well with banshee type and poison spitters.

"She really didn't teach you subtlety?"

"Is there a reason I can't?" I pressed. "Do you need to control his behavior? You want to see him suffer?"

"Him alive is preferable."

"Preferable but not necessary? Like a target?"

He frowned at me and shook his head.

"What? You know how I operate." For as much as he knew about me, this couldn't have come as a shock.

"She raised you to be a butcher."

My stomach turned as my mouth dried. I didn't like the term. Butcher meant someone who sold meat. I didn't sell meat. It was used as a term for serial killers, and I wasn't one of those either. Wait.

"Why did you say butcher?" I asked, holding his gaze. My breath caught, waiting for his response.

"You were only a weapon to her," he said with inflection, but it seemed forced.

This was a fucking mind game. I didn't have time for more of their games.

"And how would you have raised me? I'm sure you'd send me after targets. Our own kind, too."

His eyes narrowed, and his features darkened. I wouldn't have been shocked if snakes or black smoke rolled out of him.

"I really want to know," I lied. "How would you have raised me differently?"

He licked his lips and moved them like he was going to speak but kept stopping himself. He searched my face, but I kept it blank. Mom said he loved others' fear and sadness, and I suspected she'd been right.

"Session's over," he said, grabbing his water bottle and breaking my gaze.

"Hm, that afraid to answer the question or is it the follow-up questions you fear?"

His eyes shot up, full of rage. He tried to control it, but a snarl rippled across his face.

"I don't fear."

Nor did he have a conscience.

"Good to know," I said and walked out of the training room.

AFTER WATCHING from our shared room until he went into his office, I ambushed Nicolai in his office a few hours later. I ignored Duke and Alan arguing over a chess game, their request for me to play the winner, and Oliver mocking me for something.

I decided to press my brazenness after giving him fifteen minutes to settle. With a notebook, pen, and water bottle, I stormed into his office.

He didn't jump or yell at me. He looked more curious than surprised by my sudden appearance.

My nerves itched to look around the room, but I didn't want to show my cards. I pulled a chair that faced out the window over to his desk and plopped down.

"What are you doing?" he asked.

"Sitting in here with you."

"Why?"

"Well, Not-Isaac needs to give me his blood. You've made it clear you don't want me to use my methods with a difficult Soulless. I'm sure you'll teach me all the physical stabby things I need to do, but he also wields magic."

He templed his fingers and stared at me with a brow raised. He looked amused.

"What about his magic?" he said.

"I go after Soulless. I've yet to see them conjure, but I saw Not-Isaac kill Harvey without touching him and deform his body."

His look turned more sinister. "Did he do that?"

"Yes. If you want his blood returned, you'll need to teach me ways to survive his attacks."

"What makes you think you haven't gone against magic already?"

I decided to play along. I may have, but if I did go against magic, it wasn't strong. "Would any be as strong as Not-Isaac's?"

Nicolai rubbed his chin as he considered. "It's a fair point if you don't think you have the physical skill to bring him in."

Nice zing. He'd paid me a compliment and slam in one sentence.

"You want the blood. I'll go for it and bring his head in. If you want an intact body and all the organs still working, I need to be able to thwart his attacks without him touching me."

Nicolai smiled and pulled out a thick grimoire.

My stomach curled and I swallowed. The symbol on the cover was the same symbol my mom had tattooed over her heart.

***

I refused to draw the symbol on the book. Symbols held powers, especially for Practitioners, and seeing a shared symbol of my parents had me wondering about Tones' words. They'd been a team, even after my mom left. Even if my mom had moved on and focused on her usual self-preservation stuff. I didn't blame her for that; I lived by the same motto. But seeing a symbol that they both showed respect for—Mom on her body, and Nicolai on a sacred book—I had to question who the real pawns were and if Not-Isaac wasn't just a tool.

But if Mom was by his side each day, she could have brought the blood in any day if they were still partners. Or she could have used it for herself. He'd tried to use my blood, but said it failed.

Both my parents saw me as a weapon. A tool in their arsenal for the game they played.

I could consider both sides and try to find out what each was motivated by and what they wanted. I could then weigh all the options to see if I liked one philosophy and goal better. Or I could ignore all their motives and retrieve the blood. None had a side I wanted to be on, so their motives and goals meant nothing.

Not-Isaac was nothing to me. He'd killed Isaac. That alone was worth death. He also used death powers.

Mom clearly needed to be brought down. She killed me, Tones, and made attempts on Oliver, Duke, and Alan. She had nothing to redeem.

Dad brought me back. He had an ulterior motive. Tones clearly didn't trust him. The shadows feared him. He let Mom raise and use me. I hadn't yet seen him kill, but I had no doubts he did. Of the three, though, he'd been the one to use me the least, so far. It wasn't saying much, since the entire time I'd known him, he'd used me. There was no out for me.

Not only was I in the lion's den, but Duke, Alan, and Oliver had followed me there. I wondered what it would take to convince them to leave.

I didn't have to wait long to come up with an idea.

Duke popped in my room, freshly showered, and grinning. "We're doing a supply run, want to come?"

"Supplies?"

"Food. Beer. Video games. You know, the essentials."

"Nicolai approved?"

"Alan's talking to him now. Oliver is itching to move around."

NICOLAI DROVE US. It was like a parent chaperoning a double date. He white knuckled the steering wheel as Alan and Duke bickered about something.

Oliver sat quietly in the back. He stared out the window, wearing a pensive expression. Every once in a while, he'd glance at Nicolai's head and frown and then return his gaze out the window.

Our happy little kumbaya group exited the vehicle at a superstore in Coving. Nicolai wanted the least number of stops and picked a behemoth of a store and told us to get out. The river snaked behind it, twisting into the horizon.

"Are we going to hold hands and skip through the store?" Alan asked, his face remaining blasé and his tone monotone.

Nicolai sighed.

"It's not like we are prisoners. Neither is Dessa," Oliver said and leaned against the SUV. His eyes were dark and his mouth was pinched into a tight line.

Nicolai passed him a glance and rolled his eyes.

"It's five. Do what you need, meet back here at nine."

"Four hours? Do you plan on us getting lost in the store?" I asked.

"I have errands. Meet back at nine."

The four of us started toward the store, but Nicolai raised a finger, pointed at me, and did the universal "come hither" sign.

I did an exaggerated "me" gesture, pulling back in feigned surprise, and pointing to myself and looked at the other three.

"Yes, smartass," Nicolai said.

"He knows you," Oliver said and grinned when I slapped the air toward him.

The other three gave us space but hovered in earshot.

"She's looking for you," he said.

"Okay," I said with a shoulder shrug. How was this new?

"She's mad. Be careful."

I lifted an eyebrow and grimaced.

I considered that, and all I knew about my mom. She always had a chip on her shoulder. She felt entitled to more than she had and resented those who had it. She was the type to steal it from them and then tout it as her own. But I couldn't say I'd seen her angry until the club.

I nodded and glanced back at the other three. "Got it. See you in four."

He could warn me all he wanted, but hiding wasn't my forte. As my short stint proved. I was more of a throw punches and stab type of girl.

He tossed me a burner phone. "If you need me sooner."

———

I'M NOT A SHOPPER. I'd eat whatever was provided. I shrugged off Duke and Alan's invitation to stroll the river with them.

"How about you guys meet back here at eight?" I asked.

"That'll only give you an hour," Duke said.

"If it takes me longer than fifteen, I've done something wrong."

"You know they sell clothes here," Duke said.

"Okay." I turned to head downtown.

"Where you going?" Alan asked. "We can tag along."

I smiled. "It's okay, you two do your thing."

"I think she's tired of us," Duke said, smiling.

"I'll see you at eight." I waved them off.

I wasn't alone. Oliver trailed me.

I turned down a corner and ducked into an alley. A scuttle of rats scurried by. Food, decay, and the back-of-your-throat burn of unknown ick pinched my throat. I didn't have to wait long. Oliver sauntered by, scanning the streets, his brow pinched in concern. I waited until he passed and crept up behind him. When we passed another alley, I grabbed him and flung him into the passage.

He was still recovering, and close to healed with the stuff Nicolai was using, but he was still fast and strong. He pulled my arm with him and dragged me further into the alley like I was one of his Soulless targets.

I kicked off the wall, and grabbing him flipped him over the air, sending him to his back and I landed next to him in the superhero fall pose.

"What the fuck, Dessa?" he gasped.

"Why are you following me?" I asked and offered him a hand up.

He shrugged away my hand and gingerly stood up. He brushed the dirt off him and rubbed a hand over his face.

"You shouldn't be alone." The fucking big brother act.

"You're injured."

"You saying I'm a liability?" His tone turned dark.

"I caught you."

"You're Dessa the Destroyer, you should catch me. Just because you're better than me doesn't mean you should be alone or that I can't help."

I frowned at his flattery and his correctness that I shouldn't be alone if Nicolai had already warned me, but I didn't need to get him hurt or worse. My eyes flicked back the way we came. I didn't want him to go back alone, and I didn't want to go back before I had to. Acceptance settled on me like a spiderweb.

"Where are you going?" he asked, changing the subject.

I shrugged and looked back at the street. I didn't really know. It just felt good to be back in my world. I couldn't explain the longing I had for the streets, for the hunt, for the chaos. Even with my new knowledge.

"Feeling like a caged tiger?" he asked, raising an eyebrow.

I rolled my eyes.

"Come on." He wrapped an arm around my shoulders.

I let him lead me and asked, "Where are we going?"

"A good, familiar place."

He took us to his bar. The colors spilling out were like a welcome lighthouse beacon on troubled seas.

"She could be here," I said, not liking the new twisting feeling.

"She won't be, but let's go in the back, anyway," he said and steered us to the family entrance.

It had only been a few days, but it felt like finding land. I drank in the aroma, the familiar comfort, and the nostalgia.

Food remnants littered the kitchenette along with textbooks. The smell of tomatoes and pasta whirled on the air.

Oliver rolled his eyes and said, "My brothers. Matteo graduates in a few months. Leo came back from the dorm to help since I was going to be away."

We slipped in by the bar. As the ever-present sentinel, Benny stood guard behind the bar, frowning at his patrons and pouring drinks.

"Is Claudine here?" Oliver asked as I stood to the side.

Benny whipped around in surprise and stared at us. A rare small smile tugged on his lips as he took us in. Oliver still had his arm around my shoulder and somewhere along the way I'd wrapped my arm around his waist to balance us out and find a steadier pace.

"Naw, she knows better," he said and nodded toward me. "Haven't seen you since the night you sat at a table."

"You saw me?" I asked.

"You had the whole place stirring. Yeah, I noticed."

"You didn't tell me?" Oliver asked and passed a dark look to Benny.

"Didn't realize I was her babysitter or her whereabouts needed to be reported. Noted for the future, though," Benny said and pulled two glasses and filled them with cola. He slid them our way and nodded at our usual stools.

"So, they knew I was here," I asked, questioning if I'd lost my touch to slink by Soulless. "Shit. I thought they couldn't tell."

Benny grinned. He actually fucking grinned.

I stared between Oliver and Benny, trying to understand the change and if I was having a stroke or hallucinating.

Oliver didn't react to the change in his demeanor, so I asked, "What's so funny?"

"She doesn't get it." Oliver shook his head.

Benny leaned on the counter and turned his smile to me. It was like the night I creeped outside and saw him smiling at Oliver. I stared cautiously at him. I tried to see if he was a shifter in disguise, but his scent and vibe was all Benny.

"You eat something funny?" I asked, still scanning his persona.

"You okay with her checking me out?" Benny asked, still smiling. He nodded once to Oliver.

"What is wrong with you?" Oliver asked.

"Me?" I asked, this time genuinely surprised. "He's the one smiling."

Both Benny and Oliver laughed this time.

"He has emotions," Oliver said.

"Yeah, anger, annoyance, and indifference." I sipped my cola.

"They didn't know you were Dessa the Destroyer," Oliver said with a smile.

"Then why did I have the place stirring?"

"They wanted to get to know you." Benny winked and leaned against the counter to take in the patrons. "They have no idea what you do."

"Any word on Claudine?" Oliver asked, his eyes narrowing in on Benny.

Benny's smile dropped and his eyes shuttered. "No, she's hiding out."

"Hiding?" I asked.

"I guess it's more that no word has been circulating."

"I wonder if we did wound her," I said and sipped my cola.

Benny raised his eyebrow in my direction. "You hurt Claudine?"

I nodded. "I stabbed her a few times and Oliver put six bullets in her."

"Right on," Benny said, his smile returning, and raised a hand to each of us for a high-five.

I snorted a laugh at the absurdity of it, but high-fived him back.

"Ok, Benny, I know why I hate her, but why do you?" I asked.

"She's an evil bitch."

"Yes. Did she do something specific to you?" Questions of my youth burned in my mind. A lover's spat? Mom courted his significant other? She had some secret on him? Or maybe he knew all along she was a Soulless?

"Does she have to? Can't I just watch what she does and hate her?"

"Good point." I raised my glass in salute to him. "So why do you let her in?"

Benny rolled his eyes and looked away.

I turned to Oliver.

"Mom always let her."

"Why? She knew what she was and who she operated with."

Oliver and Benny passed me a confused look.

I didn't want to mention I'd talked to Tones again, and said, "She had to have known. She's known my mom for decades."

"I think she always hoped she could change her," Benny said.

"She's Soulless, you can't change that," I countered.

Benny chuckled and shook his head.

"What?"

"You're too black and white." Benny met my gaze. His brown eyes were warm and inviting. "It's not about being Soulless."

I opened my mouth to recite Finder Law and some code but shut it again. How did I apply to it? How had anything I learned recently apply to it?

"Take me, for example," he said.

I pulled back slightly in hesitation of what he was about to say. I didn't bother to ask what he meant. He didn't ignite my Finder senses.

"I was born to a Soulless and a human," Benny said.

"That's not uncommon," I said, waiting for the big enlightening tidbit. "Lots of people have a Vessel parent."

He smiled at me, that *shut up and listen* patronizing smile. "Do you know what happens when you have a Soulless and human parent?"

"If it's a Choicer, you're human. If it's a Vessel and you didn't get magic, you're human."

"I said Soulless."

I stared at him. This was part of the gray abyss I was trying to grapple with, except mine were two Soulless parents.

"See, your hesitation right there," he said, causing me to bristle, knowing I'd been called out on my hypocrisy, "is the problem with the Finders' Law."

"Then what are the children of a Soulless and a human? Or even two Soulless?" I asked before thinking better of that. Wanting to hear someone else's truths.

"We don't know," he said and smiled sadly at me.

"Yes, we do." Oliver placed his glass down while staring at the shiny bar top reflecting the neon bar lights. His legs shifted to face me.

"We do?" I choked. For some reason his opinion had me tasting fear.

"Yes," he said and looked up at me, then Benny, and then back to me. His knees pressed into mine. His warmth inviting but undeserving. "It means you're not human."

I stared, waiting for more. For the incrimination. The final straw. The cuffs on my wrist as he hauled me in for the fee.

"And?" I asked, not wanting to live in limbo.

"And nothing, that's it. You're born to people who aren't human," he said, staring at me like it was obvious. "You aren't guilty of your parents' crimes."

"What if you're a product of them?" My mouth dried and he blurred in my vision.

Oliver's eyes narrowed. "You aren't guilty of your parents' crimes."

"How can it be that simple?" I blinked.

Benny and Oliver chuckled.

"What?" I barked.

Oliver shrugged, seemingly unfazed. "We can't control other people. Your responsibility is you and your choices."

"You're too concerned about the label," Benny said, wiping the countertop, pulling me from my thoughts.

"That label has defined my boundaries my whole life. It put food on my table." It was how I categorized people. It was how I decided good and bad on people. And here I was, a product of it.

"I'm not saying what you did was wrong," Benny said. "You brought down some shitty people."

"But?" I poked stupidly.

"But nothing. You're not wrong, you brought in people who purposefully harmed people and you were paid for it. Others tried, and many died or failed. You were good at it. Good people don't lurk in shadows waiting for people to prey on."

I nodded. I wasn't a good person. I did exactly that. "You're right," I said and stood up.

"Dessa," Benny said. His voice hard as iron.

"Yea," I said without looking up.

"You don't prey on prey. You prey on predators."

Finders' Handbook

Tonguer – A Soulless who uses the arts to gain extreme taste and the ability to use their tongue as a weapon. Their tongues become elongated with poisonous pus and can be used as an extra appendage. Some say they have lizard eyes.

CHAPTER 29

OLIVER FOLLOWED me out of the bar. The streets were clear of clutter and freshly hosed down. I wasn't big on pity, for myself or others. I believed in revenge and vengeance, the angry side of coping, but not pity.

I called over my shoulder, "You can stay. You're healed up. You can return to your normal life."

He didn't respond, and my neck hairs raised. I heard the scrape of his shoe and turned around with my blade drawn. Oliver was silent. It was part of the job, otherwise it was a death sentence.

A banshee type Soulless held Oliver pressed to her, a gun to his head. Her auburn tresses fell in waves around her shoulders. She was stunningly beautiful, like a badass *Little Mermaid*.

"I'll trade," she said, smiling and licking her lips.

"You want to go on a romp with me?" I asked and extended my arm and hands out in the universal "come at me bro" gesture.

Her smile tilted up on the right and she shook her head. "Drop your weapon, and hands on the building."

I swallowed. I'd be exposed. It was Oliver. Despite what he said about not being good enough, I'd put money on him.

My eyes cut to him. Sweat beaded his brow, and his color had drained. He tried to shake his head no as his eyes bored into me. He should be able to break free easily. He was a brawny hunter and although she looked tough, he was built and trained to take down much stronger opponents in hand-to-hand. Then I noticed her hand. Brass knuckles raced over her fingers and pressed over his healing but present wound.

"Ok." I nodded as I placed my blade down. I could take her down without my blade.

Oliver made a shrill noise.

"I already told you to shh, loverboy," she said. "Don't make me get loud."

"No need for that," I said and backed up to the wall.

"I said hands on the building facing it." All mirth drained from her face. Her eyes darted around me and she licked her lips.

I realized then she was afraid of me. A twist of excitement twirled in my stomach but I schooled my face before a smile ticked up. Anticipation warmed my veins.

"Quick question," I blurted out before she could respond. "Is she sending red cards around again for me?"

She gulped and fear skittered across her face before she hardened it again and stiffened her grip.

"Does it still say 'alive'?" My lip curled up momentarily.

"Either is fine."

"Good to know." Liar. Mom wouldn't want anyone to get her chance at making me suffer after hunting her and the hall scene. "You hurt him." I lifted a chin to Oliver. "While I'm facing this wall—"

"You'll kill me?" she drawled.

"Nope." I shook my head. My fingers curled at my side. "I'll let you take me in."

Confusion pinched her face.

"And when we get to her, I'll crunch the fake tooth in my mouth.

It'll kill me instantly." I didn't have a poison tooth. I ate too many hard foods to even consider it.

She stared at me, trying to see if I was bluffing. The thing was, I wasn't certain I was bluffing. I may not have a cyanide tooth, but I knew how to kill. Even if I was the target.

"Do as I say and your boyfriend goes free," she grunted, and holding the gun to his head, took a good faith step backward. Idiot.

I turned around.

Fabric rustled and they grunted as she wrestled with Oliver.

I snuck a peek over my shoulder to see how he was faring. She'd knocked his head with the knuckles and a gash ran down his face. He stumbled but punched her in the gut and broke her arm holding the gun.

I pushed off the wall, picked up my blade, and put my hands on my hips, waiting.

She fell like a sack of potatoes, cradling her arm.

"I'll carry her," I said and reached for the zip ties always in my cargo pants.

"It's my catch," Oliver argued.

I considered it. "All right, the gun was to your head. You disarmed her."

"She disarmed you." He smirked.

"No, nope, nuh-uh, I put my blade down."

"On her command," he said and stepped back from me and my fists.

"To give you the space needed to save your stupid self."

"'Cause you like me," he said and jumped when I went to punch him.

OLIVER STILL WORKED FOR JOHN, so we went to his office. My dad's words flicked around in my mind. What would happen to this Soulless? Would John hand her over to the Trust or my mom? But he issued my mom's target, so were they still on speaking terms? I hadn't told Oliver yet, not certain I wanted to share what could be lies or horrific truths.

He called a Driver. The half faded yellow, half white SUV pulled up in front of us. The Driver wore a baseball cap over his beady eyes and fleshy nose. Stringy yellow hair curled around his collar.

He flicked a confused gaze my way, but didn't question when we both jumped in.

I'd knocked the Soulless unconscious when she started to wail and carried her over my shoulder out of the car. I dropped her at the stoop and checked my phone. It was 5:43. Too early for John to be there.

John's office looked the same but felt wrong. My veins tingled and I wondered what he had stored in the back room. I itched my neck and forced myself not to fidget on the stoop.

"You can stay outside," Oliver said, taking in my agitated appearance.

I shook my head and looked around to the shadows.

"He won't be here for hours," I said and scanned the alley. My fingers wrapped around my blade and I backed up to the wall. I looked to the shadows, but they were silent.

"I called him. We have to be back before he opens," Oliver said and pushed the door open.

The stale chill of AC swirled in the air laced with coffee and death.

"What the fuck you doing here?" John's voice barked.

I didn't respond but picked up the Soulless and dragged her inside.

"You ain't got business here," he said, his big form stepping in front of me. His dark eyes narrowed and he snarled.

I saluted him and clicked my heels.

"You are a bitch, just like her," he said. The problem was, he was right. I was like her. I preyed on my own kind. Good reasons or not, I did.

"Enough," Oliver said.

Both John and I turned skeptical gazes to Oliver. He never spoke out of turn to John and never in a reprimanding way.

"What the fuck you say?" John said, crowding Oliver, shoving him with a hand.

Oliver stood his ground despite the shoulder lurch. Had John put muscle into it, he'd be on the floor in pieces.

Oliver's hazel eyes met John's, and he said slowly, "I said, enough."

John's eyes blazed and red splotched his face.

"John, what the fuck you doing?" I said, drawing his ire my way.

"I ain't putting up with this disrespect."

"Oliver here brought you a banshee bitch, and you're gonna go all ego on him?"

"He ain't brought her. He's not good enough. He's taking your scraps."

That was an insult to both of us. The Oliver insult was obvious, but he was implying I couldn't sell my Soulless and needed Oliver's help to get in with John.

"Whatcha going to do with those scraps? Hm?"

Both Oliver and John stared at me. Oliver in confusion and John in stunned curiosity.

"Who you gonna hand her off to?"

"What?" Oliver mouthed.

I ignored him.

John's fist curled around his arm rests. The white knobs reflected the screen's blue light.

"Will the Trust be here or someone else?"

Something skittered behind his eyes, fear or anger. "I work for the Trust."

"Sure you do." I might be taking the banshee with us. Isaiah or Mom or even Nicolai didn't get to have her.

Oliver stepped closer to me, his gaze now locked on John.

"I ain't lying," he growled.

"Like the Level Twos I hauled in regularly?"

His eyes darkened and he stood straighter. "Walk away while you can."

Oh shit, already getting dangerous. A thought occurred to me, and I ran with it before thinking too much, as usual. "You let me in, John. You knew damn well I was outside."

His face hardened and he folded his arms over his chest. "Dessa."

Well fuck, he'd already gone to my name. Tonight was going to be short.

"Already threatening me?" I said and postured toward him. "I'm that big of a threat to you? Worried I called the Trust about your double dealings? Or is it the red cards that have you concerned?"

He slowly blinked at me, reining in his temper.

"The bitch wants me alive," I said. "Or are you not afraid of her?"

"I ain't afraid of no one." He stepped toward me.

Fuck. I could either call his bluff or run.

I decided to call his bluff. "Then why the fuck you fire me?"

"You died," he said flatly.

"It was my first miss."

"Past your prime."

"And I'd have brought her in, and you know it."

"Maybe you should just cut your losses," he said softly.

"Gonna start caring now?" I said. "Cause it doesn't suit you."

"Dessa, you fucking bitch, I've always cared," he roared.

The show of emotion was disorienting only because he seemed sincere, like he actually cared about me.

"Sure, John, sure. Firing me shows you care."

"Getting you out of her line of sight is the most I could do."

He ran a hand through his hair. His gaze shifted away.

I looked to Oliver to see if he understood the tension shift.

He shrugged at me.

Lights reflected off the faded once-yellow curtains. A roll of sage and lemon dosed the facility. John had called the Trust already. Either for what was already in his backroom or because Oliver called, but either way, the Trust was taking the banshee.

He nodded toward the parking lot. His lips pressed into a line.

"Dessa, I got some free advice for you."

"Sure, just stop calling me Dessa."

"It's your fucking name," he said, but continued. "You're running out of time to have a choice."

I didn't bother telling him that time had passed.

"Back the fuck off, and don't look back," he said.

We both knew that wasn't going to happen. But he could at least feel good about warning me.

———

WE MADE it back to the store with fifteen minutes to spare.

There hadn't been a ton of blood, but we were dirty.

"And what were you two doing?" Alan asked when he caught sight of us.

"Oh, please tell me it was fun in the dirt." Duke pulled up with a cart stacked full of groceries.

"It was fun." I nodded in agreement.

Oliver choked a laugh.

"Where are your groceries?" Duke looked behind me, his brow pinching.

"I gotta grab them."

"You have twelve minutes," he said, disbelieving.

I was done in ten minutes. My cart was filled with my favorite insta-craps, prepackaged cupboard treats, and cola.

Duke stared at my cart and then back at me. "Everything you have has no nutritional value and has a shelf-life longer than a person."

"Okay," I said and tossed in a package of chips. "What's in your cart?"

"What most people consider real food."

"I have real food."

"For a college bachelor."

As we pulled into the checkout line, Alan tossed in two new shirts.

"What are those for?" I asked, reaching to hand them back. "I already got three new flannels." I'd used three of my ten minutes to pick them out since I grabbed three of the same print.

"You want your dad seeing you two like that?"

I looked back at Oliver and then down at my clothes. I saw his point. Unless we wanted to own up to chasing a Soulless my mom had sent after us, it looked like we went for a romp in the park. Not that I would be ashamed to do it, but I wasn't sure how Nicolai would take it. He'd already assumed it seeing Oliver in my apartment, but I didn't want to risk anything while under his roof. I didn't know what it'd mean for Oliver.

Nicolai stood by the SUV as promised. He scanned us over and squinted. "Were you wearing that when I dropped you off?"

I shrugged and said, "Sure."

<hr>

I SAT in Nicolai's library. He'd taken a call and stepped out. Unable to remain sitting, I stood up and walked around. I hovered over his books, looking at the titles, but not touching anything. It was another of my mom's rules. Rule Six: Don't touch.

It wasn't the rule you tell children so they don't break an item or teach them manners about respecting other's property. No, it was a rule born of the simplest of necessities. An item could be brushed with poison, have a sensor, or moving it could release something. In retrospect, I think it was one of the reasons why I had so few knick-knacks. I didn't want the lure of them. Who knew if one would randomly be placed with my dust collectors? Having nothing meant anything would stand out.

Hovering though was acceptable, and I learned to gauge and assess objects with a cursory glance and to read upside down and recall facts without touching it.

I peeked at the door and listened for Nicolai. The rumble of his voice carried from his bedroom, which meant he was distracted. I walked to his desk and stared at the books lining the shelves behind him. Those would be the ones he'd want easily accessible. After stealing another glance toward the door, I allowed my eyes to look down at his desk and his personal effects.

I didn't expect to see a smoking gun, and I didn't, but I still learned about him. He had spreadsheets sprawled across his desk, which meant nothing to me. What did stand out were some business cards stacked in a corner. There were generic ones for household needs, which may be covers for other things, but one was a red card.

My vision tunneled and I stared at it, trying to understand why he'd have her card. Why'd he trust touching one? But then I'd come across them too. If he ran his own version of a Soulless mob and issued targets, perhaps he'd come into contact with those carrying the cards.

His voice drew closer but I didn't scurry for my chair. If he'd left me, he wasn't afraid of what I'd find.

He came in and nodded at me and placed his phone on the desk. I caught his eye and then turned my attention to the card. He followed my gaze to the card and made a "hm" sound.

"Just hm?" I asked.

"What do you want to know?"

That was a loaded question.

"How'd you come across her card?"

"I found it."

"Mhm," I said, placing my hands on my hips.

"She's looking for you. You need to be careful."

"Does she know where you live?" I asked.

He hesitated too long for me to trust him. "No."

He was keeping us apart as long as I was helpful to him.

"When will my training be done?" I asked.

"When you can make me bleed and escape."

I raised my eyes to him.

"Not-Isaac's on your level?" I asked, phrasing it carefully. There was no doubt Isaiah and Nicolai were higher than Level One. They likely issued targets for and immolated Level Ones like candy.

Nicolai smiled in understanding. "If you can make me bleed and escape, you can make him bleed and escape him."

Finders' Handbook

Flying Soulless - A Soulless who can do suspended leaps that appear like they are flying. Maintaining the powers requires frequent sacrifices. Some say they have silver eyes.

CHAPTER 30

I STARED at the rundown bar. The neon sign outside had missing sections, and two windows had plyboard nailed over the panel. Wrappers and yuck piled up along the crumbling brick foundation. Old urine stains dribbled down the brown peeling paint. He'd decided on a non-neutral zone to test my training.

"I'm going to get a drink at the bar." He nodded at the front door with a painted black window.

"Why are you telling me what you're doing?"

"Because I still don't think it'll help you best me," Nicolai said and walked into the bar.

I counted on my watch for three minutes. I said I'd give him five, but fuck him for telling me where he was going.

I figured it was a misdirect, but he sat at the bar as he said he would. He'd chosen a spot next to a light casting a little halo around his head.

He chatted with the bartender and flirted with several women at the bar.

Walking up would be easy, but he was an apex predator. He was expecting everything.

So instead, I grabbed a tabletop and ordered a beverage. I watched him as he flirted, and then as he glanced around, trying to figure out where I was.

Instead of ducking down in an obvious attempt to avoid his gaze, I pretended to drink my beverage. My hairs raised and I felt the welcoming pulse of adrenaline kick through my veins as a Soulless man slid into the seat across from me. Short, dark curls framed his face. His eyes were a piercing blue on a pale ivory skin. His too-tight polo shirt highlighted his pronounced muscles. Even if he wasn't a Soulless, he wouldn't normally turn my head.

I'm sure he took my lip licking as a come on, when it was all I could do not to spring up and restrain him and haul him in.

He raised an eyebrow and winked at me.

My skin crawled and my lips trembled into a grimace.

"Can I buy you the next?"

Manners. So odd. I shrugged. He'd be waiting a long time as I'd yet to drink any of my current cola. And colas were free at bars.

In the end, it didn't matter.

A drunken fool crashed into our table, spilling my beverage and upending our table. I'd cleared the mess, but the guy took a swing at the Soulless trying to buy me a drink, and then leered at me, his dark brown eyes glossy and unfocused.

He wasn't a Vessel, just a drunk idiot.

"Hey, sweetass," he slurred.

I thought about stabbing him, but figured the witnesses would be upset, and I couldn't haul him off to Mandy's for a fee.

"Do you know him?" I asked the Soulless who wiped blood from his nose and stood up on shaky legs.

"Yeah," he sighed and shot the drunk a dirty look.

"We had a bet, and he's too close to winning," the drunk said.

"Bet?" I asked.

"Who'd tap that ass," the drunk said, nodding at me and making a lewd gesture.

It'd be his last. Two large hands grabbed the drunk human and yanked him off the table and away from us.

I cast a glance back at the Soulless who a few moments before had me ready for a chase, and all I felt was pity for him. I was turning weak, a heaviness settling in my veins and stomach, but I didn't have time to dwell on it.

I tailed Nicolai out of the bar and caught up to him in the alley. Much like the front, it'd been probably a decade or two since someone cared enough to clean the trash up. Rodents scurried away from my footsteps. Fresh blood tinged the air. The metallic smell unlike the inky mustiness of Soulless blood. Ice raced through my veins.

"What the fuck?" I asked, seeing the remains of the drunk behind Nicolai. My stomach twisted and I looked around for witnesses. He'd at least made it quick by breaking his neck.

"What?" he asked, confused.

"You fucking killed a human?" I sputtered. I took a step back from him and the scene.

"He was inappropriate."

"He was fucking drunk and I had control of the situation!" I turned on my heel, but he trailed behind me.

"You're mad at me?" he shot, his eyes bulged in indignation.

I BEAT the shit out of the punching bag in the workout room. Each punch landed with a thwack and clang of the metal hook.

I paused to catch my breath, sweat running in my eyes, nose and mouth. I swiped at it with an equally sweaty arm and only managed to smear it.

I shook my body and readied for another onslaught as an image of the drunk popped into my mind. Death wasn't new. Blood didn't bother me. I didn't know why this one bothered me so much.

"Try some water," I heard Oliver call out.

"Leave me alone," I spat and went after the bag again.

"What happened?"

I punched the bag harder. A slit cut across the fabric and I punched it again, sending the purple bead innards spilling onto the floor.

"You don't look like you feel better," Oliver said and put a water bottle in my hand.

I chucked it across the room. It hit the brick wall and burst, spraying water everywhere.

Oliver pursed his lips and gave me a side-glance. A lock of dark hair swept across his face. He hadn't shaved in a few days, and an enticing stubble covered his jaw. My stomach twisted as heat flooded my core.

My eyes fluttered shut and I sighed. Even when pissed, my body found a way to get turned on by Oliver.

"Come with me, please." He held out his hand.

I glowered at him and refused his hand. It was a bad idea—I should practice or considering hauling Nicolai in—but finally I nodded. He led me up to our bedrooms and opened his door.

"Come on," he said as if coaxing a puppy.

I bit back a sarcastic laugh.

"What do you want?" I asked, standing a few feet from his entrance.

He reached out and tugged me forward.

"Go shower," he said and pointed at his bathroom.

"I have my own bathroom," I said, folding my arms.

"Yes, but now you can peek on my secret life and find out the shampoo I use."

"People do that?"

"Normal ones do," he said, nodding and crowding me toward the bathroom.

"Fine," I rolled my eyes and headed for the shower.

"Wait," he called.

I turned around and was smacked in the face with a t-shirt and sport shorts.

"Don't put dirty clothes back on."

He knew me too well.

I wouldn't admit it to him, but the shower eased my muscles and I did enjoy spying on his personal effects.

Exiting the bathroom, I found him lying on his bed.

"Feel better?"

"No," I said, trying not to smile.

"Come here."

I stared at him. Heat curled in my stomach and my body hummed. What had I expected to happen?

He scooted over and patted the spot next to him.

"Why?" I choked. My neck itched and my mouth dried.

He sat up and smiled. He stood and tugged my arms toward the bed. I lurched forward, unsure what was happening.

He didn't pull me onto the bed but leaned back to his spot. Again, he patted the area by him but didn't wait for me to join him before saying, "Remember when we were kids, and your mom was late?"

I sat on the bed, trying to not focus on our proximity and location.

"You'd get so mad. You were never scared, just pissed."

I laughed at the reminder. I wasn't worried about my mom's well-being; I was just pissed that she'd forgotten me. An odd twist of numbing comfort settled on me.

He reached out and held my hand, rubbing a thumb over my hand. "You'd start plotting how to get back at her."

I chuckled and nestled into the spot he'd made for me.

"My favorite is when you poured out all the two-liter soda bottle flavors of the same color and mixed them up. So when she thought she was getting one flavor it'd be another."

"That burned me when I forgot what they were."

He laughed.

"Yeah, but she was mad and that made you happy."

"I had a fucked-up childhood."

"Yeah, you did."

"Thanks for always being there for me," I said and felt my cheeks heat up.

His hazel eyes cut to me, searching my face. Then he murmured, "I'm still here."

I WOKE from my nap with Oliver refreshed.

My stirring woke him up and he tightened his hold.

"I have to go to train," I whispered, prying myself away from him.

He blinked, and looked at me with his sleepy gaze, still not aware, still mostly asleep. His hand cupped my face, and he ran a thumb over my lip and cheek.

I ran my tongue over my lip and nibbled on it.

"You're so amazing," he said, his eyes searching me and then he shifted up, his lips soft as he kissed me.

I sat there frozen, until my body took over and returned the gentle embrace.

Oliver murmured again, and I pulled the covers up for him. He wouldn't remember this moment, just a flash in a dream, and yet I'd now fixate on it. A smile cut across my face. It was a better memory to fixate on than the drunk one.

Exiting his room, I ran into Alan.

His eyes lit up when he looked from me to the door.

"Shut up," I hissed and pointed a finger at him.

A smile spread across his handsome face and he reached out and embraced me.

"Nothing happened," I said, and for some reason fear gripped my stomach.

"Sure, if you say so."

"Not a word."

Alan stood, nodding, but I doubted he meant anything other than he was waiting for me to go downstairs so he could tell Duke.

My feet froze as I entered the training room. Nicolai was already there, moving through warmups. Seeing him, my veins flared with anger and the desire to maim overtook my system. He'd killed a human as if it were nothing. He broke more than human laws.

"Over your temper tantrum?" he called when he noticed me.

I paused, putting my bag down, and my eyes lasered in on him.

"Nope, I see you're still angry," he said, shaking his head with disappointment.

I steeled my jaw to not retort. Without looking at him, I pulled my hair back, wrapped my fists, and started warmups.

"So, the silent treatment?" He sauntered toward me.

"I didn't realize we're having a conversation," I said, blasé.

He stood next to me, arms folded over his chest, head tilted, giving a parental look. Something inside of me snapped.

It was childish, but I lashed out with my leg. My foot connected to his knee and sent him tumbling. He caught himself from face planting by bracing his arms in front of him.

His face reddened and expression darkened as he pushed himself up.

His reaction was fast and fierce. He had my leg in his grip and ripped me from my feet, slamming me backward against the ground. My head bounced, and stars popped in front of my eyes.

On instinct, I threw my arms over my face to protect it from his attack, but he'd anticipated it, and I took a shot to the ribs.

I probably should have called "uncle" or raised the symbolic white flag. Instead, a visceral rage rippled through my body. I pulsed with fire and the desire for blood.

I took a cheap shot with a knee to the groin, and as I expected he'd anticipated it and moved to protect himself. But this was my move. I brought my fist crashing down on his neck. He lurched forward. Instead of the groin shot that would've trapped my leg, I was able to roll away. I scrambled to my feet, keeping my body ready in pouncing mode.

He twisted to right himself and I drove into his rib cage, sending him sprawling against the floor and coughing. I took an elbow shot to the ribs as he went down, gasping for air.

Grabbing my blade strapped to my arm, I slashed him as he retracted his arm, spraying blood everywhere.

Nicolai paused too long in his shock, and I darted for the corner, leaving him exposed and alive. I fled the room and ran through the house and outside. His feet pounded behind me. Blind instinct took my feet. I climbed on top of his SUV, holding my blade, panting heavily. Adrenaline coursed through, ready for the escalation of the attack.

My heart pounded in my chest, matching my breath. A wicked smile cut across my face.

I sat on the roof and watched the house as Nicolai came running out with Duke, Alan, and Oliver shortly behind him.

"What the fuck is going on?" Duke bellowed. The air charged and crackled with electricity.

Nicolai tore across the ground quicker than I had, his hand clasped over the slash, but blood left dots behind him.

"You'll pay," he seethed.

I raised my blade while staring him down. "I have your fucking blood. I got away. I win."

His expression changed, hardened, and he looked at me like I was new, a mystery. There was pride, respect, and fear behind his eyes.

He looked at his arm and turned to see his blood darkening the cement in a trail from his defeat. His eyes flickered to my blade and me, covered in his blood. Bruises he'd inflicted raced up my arm while his blood dripped off my blade down my hand.

"I guess you're ready."

OTHER WORLDLY MAGIC EXCERPT

There are many types of magic used to control the environment and other creatures. To have permanent control over another person, their blood must be used.

CHAPTER 31

HE TOOK my blade and cleaned it. I guess he didn't want me to have his blood. I meandered to my room, my mind spinning about what had happened. Fear had finally found me as I closed my doors, and my knees gave out. I crumpled to the floor, sobbing.

I touched the tears, unsure what they were at first. There hadn't been anything to cry about.

The shadows shifted, and the only one brave enough to make contact at his house pulled from the corner and materialized into the familiar form.

"Dessa, get up," Tones urged, her voice frantic.

Pinpricks raced down my arms.

I got up. "What's wrong?"

"Hurry, get to the bathroom."

It was Tones, so I listened.

"What's wrong?" I asked again, anxiety curling in my stomach. A blood-dampened spot on my flannel stuck to my skin.

"Grab the pill container from your bathroom travel kit."

"Why?" I asked, grabbing it. "It's empty."

"Carefully get as much of his blood into it as you can."

I stared at the container in my hand; the clear plastic kind that came in standard airport-approved travel kits. It had been included in the toiletries Duke and Alan bought us when they cared for Oliver and me.

With fast hands, I scraped it against my arms, hands, and face, collecting every drop I could. It amounted to little more than a teaspoon.

"Why am I doing this?" I asked.

"Get your flannel off," she said.

Her panic made me flinch and my hands trembled as I took off my flannel.

"I get I reek, but I didn't realize shadows could smell," I said and balled it up.

"Stop it," she hissed.

"Stop what?" I spat back, ready to pitch the flannel in the hamper.

"Hide the flannel, don't wash it," she said and shifted away, the movement coiling through the air.

I followed her movement and found her hovering by the door.

"Tones, what the fuck is going on?"

"Get your other flannel, slice your hand and rub it on it."

"No, this is ridiculous."

"I don't have time to argue. He'll figure out I'm here. Do it."

Fuck. Nicolai. He still didn't know. Tones was risking everything… again.

Without arguing, I pulled out one of the flannel's triplet sisters. After I sliced my hand, I rubbed it on the fabric.

"Put the other flannel back in the bag. Keep it hidden."

"Tones, what is with the blood?"

"Keep it hidden. When the time comes, take it with you."

"What time?"

"When you're ready to end it all."

I should have been shocked, but after Tones' frantic display, I shrugged and handed my flannel to Nicolai when he came to wash it. He offered some lame excuse about bloodstains.

He peeked in my shower and scrutinized my towel to see if any blood remained. Doubt darkened his face and turned his lips down. His fingers twitched at his side as the rest of him forced a relaxed stance.

He nodded at me and said, "Good job today."

It didn't have the same ring as my mom calling me baby, but something of pride still warmed my veins. "You liked getting blindsided?"

"Don't get too cocky. It won't happen again."

I shrugged.

He stared at me for a while, stepping closer as he searched me, but I ignored it. His posture was meant to be menacing, standing tall over me, slightly arched forward like a tower. It was typical chauvinistic crap.

I faked a yawn, rubbed a hand through my hair, and walked out of my room.

He took more than a few seconds to follow me, so I assumed he was searching my room for traces of blood or my possible trickery. Even though he wouldn't find anything, I itched to turn around and see what he was doing. I forced my feet forward.

His unhurried steps thundered down the stairs and headed in my direction.

"Do you have a grill?" I called out without looking back at him.

"What?" He sputtered at the distraction.

"A grill, you know, a thing that cooks food with fire?"

Nicolai stuttered a bit, trying to make sense of my question, and finally said, "You want to grill food?"

I turned to him with a "you dumbshit" expression and rolled my eyes.

"Yeah," he said, regaining his composure. "You got steaks?"

"Me? Naw, that shit's too expensive. Duke and Alan grabbed some hamburgers. It's a nice night out," I said and took a quick glance out to make sure I was correct. It was overcast but didn't look like rain, so I'd go with it.

Apparently talking about food brought the others out of the woodwork, and Duke and Alan appeared on the floor.

"Are we talking about food?" Duke asked and rubbed his stomach.

I smiled.

Nicolai frowned and studied Duke. "What are you? A Veiner?" he asked, almost embarrassed. He'd obviously checked them out before they arrived, and had he felt them a threat, I doubt he'd let them have come inside. He likely wanted to learn about them or use them. My guess was to use them.

Duke cracked a half-grin and straightened up. He winked at Nicolai and said, "Alan's husband. So, are we doing burgers or hotdogs?"

"I vote burgers." I went to the kitchen to pull out chips and the other salty treats I had.

Nicolai stared at us, and then fixed on Alan. "Aren't you a half demon?"

Alan mocked offense, even laying a hand over his chest, and scoffed. "I'm half nothing," he said. His eyes flashed orange and charges snaked over his nose and temples.

I smirked. They never triggered my predator response, but I knew they weren't human.

"Are you making food?" Oliver said, appearing in the kitchen.

I stole a glance at him, and noticed he only looked at me. As I averted my gaze back to the cupboard, heat clawed at my cheeks, and I stuck my head deep in the shelves.

"You aren't fooling us," Alan whispered behind me and poked my side.

"Fuck off," I seethed.

He laughed.

I chucked a can of something at him. It hit him squarely in the arm. Duke chuckled and Alan scowled at me. I'd pay for it later, but that'd be okay.

I ATE three burgers and a bag of chips. I leaned back, enjoying the feel of the food in my stomach and not the bloated feeling after eating my normal.

Duke and Alan cuddled on the outdoor loveseat. Oliver lounged in an overstuffed chair, and Nicolai sat with us, brittle and stiff as he watched us.

Oliver pulled out his phone and turned on a playlist. "Janie's Got a Gun" blasted out, causing Alan and Duke to hoot.

"You know—" Alan shifted to meet Nicolai's eyes. "Dessa has a gun."

"Meaning?" Nicolai drawled.

"Don't go near the tracks," Duke said.

I cracked a grin.

The playlist cycled to Lily Allen.

Nicolai rolled his eyes. "Gee, that's subtle."

Alan and Duke burst out laughing. Tears rimmed Duke's eyes and he doubled over.

Oliver shrugged and leaned back to enjoy the song.

"So," Nicolai said, breaking the moment.

We all sobered, and though we didn't look at him, he had our attention and knew it.

"You two are married," he said, nodding at Alan and Duke.

"Yep, about two months," Duke said.

"How long have you been together?"

I furrowed my brow. It was a simple enough question, hinted at politeness, and yet, it felt like it was a trap.

They looked at each other and shrugged. "We dated about three years before getting married," Alan said.

"You've known each other three years?" he said, looking between the two.

"We've known each other about ten." Duke's jovial expression evaporated, and his look shuttered into annoyed indifference.

"So, the first seven years were?" Nicolai asked and gestured for them to continue. "Friends?"

"No, the first few years I wanted to kill him," Duke said, gesturing to Alan.

"You hunted him?" Nicolai pressed, leaning forward.

"No, not like that," Duke said, flicking a glance my way.

I shrugged. I didn't know the end game either.

"But you hated him?"

"I worked for his family," Duke said measuredly. "I had to watch his back, and he made piss-poor decisions."

Alan frowned at him and mocked his stance.

Nicolai raised a curious eyebrow to Alan.

"We all have our reckless period," Alan said, blasé.

"But not everyone gets horns from it," Oliver snorted.

That caused Duke and me to burst out laughing while Alan sulked.

"Hm," Nicolai said.

Ah, it was coming. That 'hm' was the quintessential threshold to an about-face of questioning, the ambush sprung.

"How long have *you* two known each other?" Nicolai asked, turning his attention to Oliver and me.

Was he seriously going to pull the concerned parent routine?

With a quick look to Oliver, I shrugged. "My whole life."

"You two are like siblings then?" Nicolai asked.

"No," Oliver and I said in unison. He may always do the big brother bullshit, but not now or ever did I consider him a sibling.

Nicolai took protracted looks at each of us before continuing. "Oliver, you're Tones and Isaac's oldest, correct?"

"You already know I am," he said.

"Oliver, you are a young man with your parents' charisma. I'd assume you have several girlfriends." Nicolai gave him a pointed look. His fingers drummed on his jeans, but I saw his eyes cut momentarily back to catch my reaction.

The gathering went silent. I held my breath to not react. I was not dumb or innocent. I knew Oliver had girlfriends, some more temporary than others.

"I do not have several girlfriends," Oliver's measured response came back.

I felt eyes watching me, but I kept my focus on Nicolai. I didn't want to react to Oliver or the overly thoughtful Alan and Duke.

"Dessa, and you—" Nicolai started.

"You gonna pretend to give a shit?" I asked.

He smirked at my offense, but it didn't deter him. "Father or not, as a curious bystander, I've made observations," he said.

"No one gives a shit about your romantic observations."

"Then as a father, I want to catch up."

"As a daughter I don't give a flying fuck."

"Why are you so defensive about it?"

Fuck it. I'd walked into his emotional trap, and it sprung. He was like Mom, but I'd gotten too lax.

"Do you have a specific question?" I challenged.

"Do you have a boyfriend?" he said, turning a sharpened glance toward me.

I snorted. "Do you know what I do for a living?"

His face scrunched in confusion. "What does that have to do with it?"

"Ask Oliver. Relationships are a liability. It puts a target on the other's back for those trying to retaliate. We also don't know nightly if we're coming back, and it's not like most dangerous lines of work. They may never know, and if they do find our remains, they may wish they never did."

"Seems overdramatic," Nicolai said, his expression turning amused.

"Like killing a drunk?"

His face slackened and his eyes darkened.

I felt the others' confusion but appreciated their silence.

A piercing screech broke our moment. It was a familiar one, and I cursed.

We all turned to the gate and crawling over the barrier were three banshee type Soulless, their pink eyes glowing in the dark.

"What the fuck," a bunch of us said in unison as we bolted up.

"That's brazen," Oliver said and looked to Nicolai. "Can your fence electrocute them?"

Nicolai gave Oliver an approving smile. "I may have underestimated you."

I didn't think that was a compliment.

"It's a message," Nicolai said and looked at me. "She's found you."

A familiar numbness snaked through my veins. As with everything, my mom always infiltrated. Like the roach she trained me to be, she kept coming back. I was taking too long to hunt her, and made a show of it.

"I thought you said she couldn't find us here."

"It delayed her, but she's motivated."

"Duke and Alan, go inside," I said and nodded to the house. "Take Oliver."

"We can help," Alan said.

"I know you can, but they aren't here for you." I pulled my blade out and unholstered my gun.

"You came to dinner armed?" Nicolai asked.

"You didn't?"

"Maybe she did do a few things right," he said and drew his own Glock.

I flinched at the compliment. I noticed the looks of disgust from the others.

"Go," Nicolai said to the guys.

"No."

I didn't wait for their pissing war and sprinted at the fence. The banshees wailed in my direction. I flew back a few paces, my head ringing and my vision blurred.

I licked my lips and locked eyes with one of them. My lip curled into a half-smile as I felt my skin ripple and the hunt kick in. I bit my lip in anticipation.

I raised my gun and let go two rounds at the one on the left. At least one hit as it howled and fell to the ground. The smell of blood tanged in the air, exciting the hunt.

My eyes flicked to the next one. It stared between its fallen comrade and me.

"Run, little piggy," I taunted.

I was an awful person. Even if I was one of them, I still enjoyed the hunt. Still enjoyed the win.

I raised my gun, but before I got the shot out, a bullet tore through the middle one and the one on the right. What the fuck? I looked at my gun but knew I hadn't pulled it.

"Do you always play with them?" Nicolai scolded as he sidled next to me.

Oliver joined us. Both of them had their guns out.

Robbed of the kill, disappointment flooded my veins and pooled as acid in my stomach. I walked toward the Soulless writhing on the ground, the silver bullet poisoning their blood. I should have felt remorse, despair, something other than disappointment and relief.

Their wails were tempered by pain, losing their power, but it sounded like nails on a chalkboard.

I climbed the fence, avoiding the jagged points at the top, and flung myself over. I bit the landing, but a few new bruises wouldn't be much.

"What the fuck are you doing?" Nicolai called and hurried to the gate.

I plunged my dagger into one, silencing its pain. That's when I noticed them. The ground and air swarmed with shadows. Their screeches were deafening and I stumbled back toward the fence. I could see some distinguishable faces, but I couldn't keep up with the shapes flashing before my eyes.

They clawed at me, their translucent forms dissolving when they touched me, but they left my skin burning ice cold. I clutched at my arms, trying to remove the taint, the sting.

Their words blurred together in a shriek. I grabbed my head to silence them, but voices started to pull out. Each pleaded their own case, some in languages I didn't know, but I could still feel their pain.

"Hold on, baby girl," Nicolai said.

He must have picked me up, because he carried me onto the compound through the gate and into the house.

The instantaneous silence was maddening. My ears rang, trying to right themselves. Closing the door didn't deter the hazy feeling of the vacuum in my head.

I gasped, sucking in air. Nicolai laid me on a sofa, the cool leather soothing my skin.

"Drink," he ordered and handed me a water bottle.

I drank.

His hands rubbed my head and neck and shoulders. "It'll be okay," he murmured.

My eyes found focus, and my ears stopped straining to hear their cries. I pushed myself up, my head going light, and I swayed.

"Take it easy," he said and rubbed my back.

I swatted him away. "What are you doing?" I barked.

"Watching your back," he said and leaned back in the chair watching me.

I swallowed and subconsciously looked out the windows, past the fence into the void. I'd noticed the shadows didn't enter his house, but Tones had. The shadows not only feared him in my apartment, but also literally shied from his house.

I stared at my hands, and slowly tracked up to looking at him. His eyes were shuttered as he regarded me.

"Why aren't there shadows in your house?"

"What are you talking about? There are shadows," he said pointing to the shadows of objects.

"They don't talk."

"Shadows shouldn't talk," he said darkly.

"And those that do?" My vision swam as his words surrounded me.

He narrowed his eyes at me and smiled humorlessly. "Those need to be eradicated."

"How do you do that?" I whispered, not wanting an answer or to be so close to him.

He leaned against the sofa, extending his arm to encompass most of the sofa's back, including behind me. His other arm hung in the air, with his elbow resting on the armrest, and cradled his temple.

"Why'd you climb the fence?" he asked, changing the subject.

I let him change it. I didn't want the conversation, anyway, but I was determined to find the shadows. He was forcing them out for a reason. Tones had risked a lot coming to me. He may not physically be afraid of them, but he was anxious of their possibility.

"I wanted to end the banshee's screaming," I said honestly.

"Their pain should be music to your ears," he said.

What a creep.

"You're a Finder, you bring them in all the time."

"I make the end quick," I said, more to myself than to him. Even if they did evil, I didn't make them suffer long.

"And the live ones?"

I cut my eyes to him. "What about them?"

He smiled at me, and I wanted to vomit. The Trust had their protocols, but how many of the Soulless I brought in went to the Trust? How many ended up in some tortuous sacrifice or to the benefit of Isaiah or Nicolai or another like them? I'd blindly done so much without thought of the next step. I'd accepted I'd removed a threat, which I had, but I accepted all of it at face value and it was a house of cards.

I moved my gaze away.

"Your mother allowed you to be weak," he said, shaking his head.

I blinked but didn't respond. I was something, but I didn't think weak was the right word. I was a monster. I was a failure. I was guilty, but weak didn't fit. I'd been strong in all my convictions and never backed down from what I believed in, but I didn't know what I believed anymore.

Finders' Handbook

Guideline - Avoid friendships or long-term relationships. Most civilians are too weak to understand the reality of a Finder's life and dedication to the Finders' Law.

CHAPTER 32

MY PHONE CHIRPED. There were three people who would text me, and all were staying in the house. I didn't want any of their support. I didn't deserve it and I didn't want them to try to convince me I did.

My phone chirped again, and I put it on mute and tossed it across the room. It bounced off the wall with an odd cracking sound and fell into my pile of clothes.

I turned on my bed, nestling deep into my pillow. I stared ahead unseeing as moonlight arched across the room.

A soft knock echoed through my room and I rolled my eyes.

I lay there, not moving, hoping they'd get the message.

Another knock. Then another.

Finally, I whispered, "Go away."

The door opened, spilling the dull glow of the overhead light into a thin blade across my bed.

"I said go away," I growled, grabbing my pillow, ready to toss it.

"Oh, I heard come in," Oliver said and stepped into the room, closing the door behind him.

"You did not."

"You're right, but I couldn't understand the words. Duke and Alan are light sleepers, so if I keep knocking, they'll come to investigate."

"Go back to bed."

He sat down at the foot of my bed instead.

"What happened in the field?" he asked.

I didn't answer.

"Dessa, it was like you were in a war with invisible attackers. Your screams—" He choked and cleared his throat. "Your screams were worse than banshees'."

"Did you see them?" I sat up.

"No, I didn't see anything, but you did."

"There were so many," I said, emotion building in my chest.

"So many what?" He rested his hands next to my leg.

"The shadows."

His brow furrowed. "There are shadows everywhere," he said and looked around the room.

I shook my head. "It's not the same. The shadows I talk to aren't the inanimate shadows," I said, casting random hand gestures toward the chair, desk, dresser, and other items.

"What are they, then?" he asked.

I looked at him, and my eyes unfocused. "I don't know. I think they're souls. Or something from the rituals."

"Do they belong to the Soulless?" he asked.

I think he meant it as a joke to maybe ease the mood, but we looked at each other, the uncertainty sitting heavy between us.

He scooted closer, resting a hand on my ankle, rubbing small circles. "You'll figure it out."

"Will I?"

"Do you want to?" he asked.

"I think so," I said, the idea forming as we spoke.

"Then you will. You're Dessa the Destroyer."

WE ENDED up sneaking downstairs and eating ice cream. We sat silently together in the expansive kitchen, overlooking the other side of the property from the field. The moon made its slow progression across the sky, consuming stars and bringing the sun along.

I must have fallen asleep on the sofa because I startled awake when Duke and Alan's hurried steps thundered down the stairs and sunlight flooded the room, casting away the night and burning away the remnants of shadows.

They walked into the room, didn't give us a double take, and pulled items from the fridge and pantry.

"Pancakes or waffles?" Duke asked and pointed a spatula at us.

"Pancakes," I said and held a finger to Oliver, warning him not to argue. "I'll make bacon."

"And what will you do?" Alan asked Oliver as he pulled hash browns from the fridge.

"Guess I have egg duty," Oliver said and pulled a carton out.

"Oh, but Dessa likes the gross over-hard eggs," Duke said, making a face.

Oliver shrugged. "Well, I can only make scrambled."

"That'll work." Alan pulled ingredients from the walnut cabinets.

"Where's Nicolai?" I finally asked.

"He left before sunup." Alan placed the hash on the griddle pan. The sizzle charged the air and my stomach rumbled.

I frowned. I was a light sleeper, but he hadn't woken me up.

Alan and Duke shared a look, each frowning hard at the other and widening their eyes.

"What do you want to ask? Is it about last night?"

They nodded.

I didn't know if the house was bugged, but I'd been pretty candid in my room and Tones had risked coming into it. It shouldn't be different here. My room was more likely to be bugged than the space Nicolai spent time in, but something about the openness of the room held my tongue.

Alan met my gaze, seeming to read my mind. "There're cameras, but they just don't seem to work in any area I am in," he said with a forced confused look. Then added, "And for some reason, whatever floor I am on, they go wonky."

I chuckled, then sobered, and said, "There aren't shadows here."

"I noticed," he said.

"There are so many beyond the fence."

His eyes darted to the perimeter and back to me. "Really?"

"I hadn't noticed until I crossed the fence."

"Hm," he said but it seemed more to himself, and he scratched the base of his skull.

"So, you're saying, from here, you can't see them out there." Duke waved toward the outdoors.

"Exactly, it's like a dead zone in here, but it's an ocean just beyond."

"Ok," Duke said and nodded to Alan.

"Ok?"

"Ok," Duke said and nodded at me. "You get to your training and we'll figure it out."

"But..." I started to protest.

"Nope, sweets, you get to being the best you and we'll figure out the creepy barrier."

"You're not alone, sweets," Alan said and threw an arm around me.

NICOLAI DIDN'T COME BACK the rest of the day, or into early evening, skipping our practice session.

Finally, around ten, I dug out the burner phone he'd given me when we went shopping. I plugged it into a charger and waited for the death symbol of the empty battery to tick up to red before booting it up and planned on dialing the one number in it.

But as it cycled through, a notification flashed for a missed call. My heart skipped a beat, realizing the call was from today. There was no voicemail or text message.

I pressed *call back* and waited as the electronic beeps sounded out.

"Get here, now," Nicolai said. It wasn't a bark or yell, but there was no denying the annoyance in his voice and I wasn't going to deny the request.

"Where's here?" I asked, staring at my bedroom wall and the generic art.

"John's," he said, and the call ended.

I didn't race out. I wasn't sure what was going on. It could be a test of loyalty, my stupidity, or training. I wasn't welcome at John's, but I doubted Nicolai was, either. I swallowed my reservations down and grabbed my blade and gun.

As I shut my door, I considered rousting the others from their rooms, but I decided against it. I grabbed a set of keys on the hook by the garage door and beeped the lock button to figure out which vehicle they went with.

Now in all honesty, I didn't have a driver's license. My life was focused within a square mile around the apartments I lived in. I went to places I could walk. But I could drive, even stick.

I was unfamiliar with Nicolai's area, but GPS got me to a part of town I recognized. The vehicle would be a hindrance here, just a target. I pulled into a restaurant well out of my price range and hopped out. The valet gave me a disapproving look until I flashed a fifty. They pulled it away to their secured lot, and I pocketed the retrieval ticket.

My pulse ticked up a beat as I ran to John's. The days of being at Nicolai's rolled off my back as my feet pounded on the terrain. The shadows shifted in their welcome. Their buzz of excitement rippled as I crossed the distance. A temporary wave of relief washed over me having them back.

My senses went off, deprived of so much. I was in overdrive. I could smell, hear, and sense their presence. I wasn't in danger, but I could feel the Soulless as I trudged along. I could have my pick. I licked my lips in anticipation but forced myself forward. Maybe afterwards, I'd bring one in.

The hiss of the shadows drew my attention and I slowed.

"Careful," they hissed.

"What's going on?" I stole a glance in their direction. They formed into one bulge, but individual shadows slithered in the mass, contrary to the group.

"He's there," they said, fear stilling their motions.

I stopped subconsciously and shifted my focus to their stalled dance.

"Why are you afraid of him?" My voice echoed off the walls, sounding distant.

They faltered and their dance turned agitated.

"You must hurry," they said and darted around.

I rolled my eyes at their fear but crossed into the alley by John's. It was void of the shadows, and my shoulders hunched as I scanned the area. The hairs on my neck raised.

There were no Soulless nearby, which wasn't odd, but normally John's office hummed with a vibe of them. Their scent lingered, tickling my thirst.

I pulled my blade and walked to the door. It wasn't a Soulless, but blood hung in the air, the metallic odor fresh.

I pushed the door open and regretted it immediately.

John lay gasping on the ground, his large form cradled in a fetal position. Someone had carved pieces out of him but left him to suffer.

My stomach tightened and I willed down my food.

"What the fuck?" I whispered as I backed up to the wall to take in the scene.

"No," John croaked, and he made a whimper sound.

"John." I knelt by him, still watching around me. Anger from his Level Two betrayal and the possibility of him selling Soulless outside of the Trust balled into a tight kernel as I watched him gasping for breath. Despite all the bullshit, he had worked with me. Always gave me targets, even if he skimmed from them.

"Go," he wheezed, and fell into a coughing fit with blood splattering his lips.

"Who?" I whispered as I went into methodically looking at his wounds. My brain fell into autopilot, focusing on the injuries and forgetting my ire about the Level Twos.

"What the fuck did you do?" a voice roared. A very familiar voice.

My blood pounded in my ears and my heart leaped in my throat.

I jumped over John toward the door, whipping my gun out and pointing it at my mom.

John made a sound.

"Shh, John, I'm here," I said. With her here, it'd delay treatment he needed. I licked my lips.

"You fucking tried to kill John?" my mom said. Her eyes bulged. Her face flamed red and her whole frame heaved.

I saw red, my vision tunneling on her. My anger hung heavy around me.

"Don't blame me for your shit!" I leveled my gun at her chest. I'd learned one thing from Nicolai: silver alone wasn't enough. All my bullets had been repacked with an additive.

John's arm wrapped around my ankle, stopping my motion.

"What the fuck?" I said as I stumbled, cursing myself for falling for the trap.

"All because he wouldn't give you jobs?" she said and rushed at me.

He yanked me behind him with his hand and John's fist stopped her. He let out a guttural roar, his body oozing from the effort. He collapsed, releasing a wheezy cough that meant death was close.

Mom lurched back, swaying and clearing her head. I took the advantage and shoved my blade into her torso.

She collapsed forward, and I pulled my blade out while kicking her backward.

I emptied my gun into her and grabbed John.

He was a massive man; at least three times my weight, but I'd carried countless Soulless. I dead-man lifted him over my shoulder and hauled him out of the office.

She stirred behind me. The bitch was still immune to bullets, but the additive kept her sluggish. Ignoring her, my heart in my throat and my mind spinning, I crossed onto the street, back into the shadows. They swarmed around me, pushing me forward and bearing some of John's weight.

It doesn't matter what life brings you. When in distress, you revert back to your most basic survival skills. We all have different ones. Stress hones them and they become old friends. Mine kicked in and I started to run for my old apartment. I guess it still seemed like home even after John, my mom, and Nicolai had defiled it.

Unable to get in, I realized my mistake and that my other apartment was out of the target zone. But I was close to the bar, and headed there, the shadows aiding.

Like before, I opened the employee entrance and slipped inside. I dropped John off in the office and slumped against the wall, sinking to the floor. All my adrenaline fled, leaving me tired and confused. John's blood pooled out, darkening the floor.

"What the fuck, John?" I said though he was unconscious.

He groaned and blood bubbled in his mouth.

"Shit," I breathed and forced myself up. I found the stockpile of medical supplies under the kitchenette. Oliver and I had used the office for more than a few dozen emergency procedures.

"Dessa?" Benny's voice was like a sledgehammer to my brain.

I jumped and whirled around.

"Holy shit, I startled you," he said, awed and confused. Then his eyes darted to John. "You fucking bringing them here now?"

"No," I yelled, "I didn't do this."

"Sure," he said, his awe turning to disappointment.

"Fuck it, Benny, I didn't. I found him. I don't think I can help him. Help me," I said, my voice shrill as I fought to rein in my emotions.

"Ok, ok, ok." Benny pumped his hands at me, his voice soothing and void of the previous incrimination. "Who is this?"

"John."

"Dessa, you gotta get out of here, now," Benny said, his eyes and voice filled with fear.

"Ok," I conceded, annoyed I'd asked for help and been shunned. I went to lift John.

"No, Dessa, I got him. You gotta get out of here and hide."

I stared at him.

"She was looking for John. He's been missing for a day." He crowded me toward the door.

"She was there. She did this," I said, dread clawing at my nerves. Red pulsed behind my eyes.

"No, she was trying to protect him."

"What?" I sputtered.

"Dessa, she used him to get you. She forced him to make her a target and give it to you to get you to come for her. It was the only way she could get close to you alone."

My vision tunneled and my brain just flashed warning.

"But... then who did this?" I asked, the answer flashing in my brain.

I didn't wait for Benny's answer or plea to leave.

OTHER WORLDLY MAGIC EXCERPT

Few understand how magic truly works. There is a belief it can be categorized and lumped together in neat order, but all magic is interconnected. It bleeds together, erasing edges and distinction. Magic is magic. All magic can be used to harm or help. It is the intent that truly matters.

CHAPTER 33

I STORMED INTO THE HOUSE, throwing the keys toward the hook without looking to see if they made it.

"Where the fuck are you?" I bellowed into the house. My voice echoed loudly, filling the space, but it still didn't match the ferocity inside of me. Not breaking stride, I ran toward his office, taking the steps three at a time in my sprint.

In my peripheral, Alan, Duke, and Oliver hurried to my aid. I waved them off and kicked open Nicolai's door.

He sat behind his desk, readers on his face, looking at spreadsheets. He smiled at me; a tight one you'd give a defiant child to make them pause. It just pissed me off.

I launched across the desk to grab at him, but he stood and blocked my attempt.

He scowled at me, his eyes like mine, narrowed and annoyed.

"Dessa?" I heard one of them say, but I was too focused on Nicolai to know who.

"What is wrong with you?" Nicolai said as I lunged at him again and managed to slice his arm with my blade.

A presence sidled up next to me and it took me a moment to realize the three had joined us and were standing with me.

Nicolai's eyes darted between us.

"Why are you mad?" he asked.

"Why? You fucking maimed John!" I roared.

I felt the shift of the other three but didn't take my eyes off Nicolai.

"That made you mad?" He shook his head in disappointment. "That was a gift."

Red blurred my vision and I lunged at him again, but two of them restrained me. I yanked to pull free, but they just dug into my muscle.

"Why?" Oliver asked, moving in front of me. It meant Duke and Alan were holding me back and they'd pay for it. He asked again, his voice even, but I knew the dangerous tone. "Why'd you go after John?"

Nicolai's betrayed gaze tracked to Oliver and morphed into comradery, like he was willing Oliver to be on his side. "He sold Dessa out."

"What does that mean?" Oliver asked.

"Claudine made John assign you to her," Nicolai said.

"Why?" I asked, seeing if his reasoning matched with Benny's. At the mention of my mom, a familiar burning numbness crawled in my veins, settling the brewing rage that would destroy those around me. Nicolai was distracting me, knowing my mom's name was like a dog whistle to me, but as much as I hated it, it worked. It seemed I missed a lot of rumors being away from Coving, but even if I was there, it seemed most everything with my mom and John went on under my awareness.

"She couldn't get you alone. She had him assign it, knowing you'd go after her. She wanted my blood and used you, but it didn't work."

"John knowingly sent you to your death," Oliver filled in, his eyes dark as he processed the information.

Duke and Alan completely let go of me and I shrugged my arms in agitation.

Uncertainty twisted in my stomach. My mom was a manipulative bitch. Yes, John had not paid me for Level Twos and lied about their levels, but it was likely her doing... I sucked in a breath. Could John have done it on his own? Years with him sped through my mind, including him warning me away and defending me from her attack and finally her target sheet. "Wait, John gave the target to Oliver though when I died and wouldn't let me go back after her. He refused to reassign it to me."

Nicolai gave Oliver an amused look. "John probably regretted it, wanted her to pay, but not as much as he does tonight. He betrayed you and needed to pay for it."

Pay for it? With his life? Was this how parents helped? Create more debt for me to have to pay him back?

"You wanted me to find him butchered so I could thank you?"

"You don't have to thank me," Nicolai said, emphasizing the words like I really should, "but you shouldn't be angry with me. He'll never betray you again."

SITTING OUTSIDE ON THE PATIO, I contemplated leaving the compound. I didn't know what to think. I wasn't shocked Mom had used John to get at me. I wasn't even shocked John had done it. He'd always sided with my mom. But I'd been surprised when he continued my employment after I left my mom. Giving me my mom's target had made him so upset, but I'd thought it'd been her betrayal, not his, that had spurred the emotion.

And I wouldn't be shocked if Mom was somehow related to him selling Soulless under the table, either.

I didn't have Stockholm Syndrome or anything that justified John's behavior, but it wasn't for Nicolai to resolve. I was disappointed in myself that I wasn't certain what I would've done to John. I felt more numb toward the revelation than anger. It actually made sense in the stream of events.

Oliver joined me, pulling a chair over and sitting down wordlessly.

"What would you have done to John?" I asked.

His eyes shifted to me, bright with curiosity, and he watched me for a bit. "If I found out what he did to you or if he did it to me?"

"If it was you?"

He sighed and shrugged, then shrugged again. "I'm nobody."

"He gave you the same target."

Oliver snorted.

"What?" I asked.

"He didn't think I could bring her in, and he's right. She almost killed me."

"Then why'd he give it to you? He doesn't joke with targets."

Oliver shot a guilty glance my way and then looked away.

"Tell me," I demanded.

"I made him," Oliver finally relented.

"Made him?" I scoffed.

He pulled in his lip with his teeth as he chose his words. He muttered something.

"In a volume I can hear."

"I didn't make him."

"Then how'd you get it?"

"I took it."

"What?"

"I hauled in a Soulless, saw it on his desk, your blood splattered on it, and when he took the Soulless, I took the target."

"What?" I asked incredulously. "Didn't he come at you?"

"He didn't know it was me until..." His voice dropped.

"Shit, Oliver, I'm so sorry." I grabbed his hand. John had to have found out when Tones died and Oliver was almost killed. John wouldn't have shown sympathy or care.

"But you were bragging about it," I said.

"I hadn't taken it yet."

"What? But you said..."

"I wanted you to get out. I wanted you to escape her."

My mouth dried. He helped me and paid the ultimate price.

"But you lost everything," I said, pulling my hand back in an attempt to cleanse him of me.

He held onto my hand and tugged it back slightly. "No, I didn't lose everything. I miss my mom. I lost her, but so much remains."

"So, what would you have done to John?" I asked my original question again.

"He wouldn't have done it to me. I'm a nobody." He shook his head when I started to protest. "I'm a nobody Finder. I bring in the hulks, but I don't bring in the truly dangerous ones like you did."

"I hunt my own kind," I whispered, the words bitter on my tongue.

He cut his eyes to me and raised an eyebrow.

"Both my parents were born Vessels," I muttered out loud and braced for his reaction. My breath stilled and my muscles tightened as I stared forward.

He shrugged. "I kind of figured that out. Claudine had said your dad was one and after meeting him, I don't doubt it. Thinking about your life, it's not hard to believe it."

"They're both Soulless. What does that make me?" I pointed to myself, too repulsed to touch my chest.

Oliver's face scrunched, and his mouth hooked up in a small sad smile. "That night at the bar makes more sense now. It makes you Dessa."

"But I hunt my own kind." I leaned my head back to stare at the sky and not see his eyes.

"You hunt Soulless."

"But..." I sat forward, unseeing. That didn't change what I was.

Oliver shook his head. "Dessa, humans use human laws to govern humans. Vessels have their own laws to govern Vessels. Every target sacrificed another soul to gain power or benefited from someone else sacrificing a soul. You are not a Soulless."

"I was created from sacrifice."

He blew a breath out. His head tilted back and his eyes searched the stars.

"Dessa, I'll pull a human line…"

"You are human," I snorted.

His eyes cut to me.

I waved for him to continue.

"You aren't responsible for the sins of your parents."

"But I'm a product of them," I whispered, patting my chest.

"No one asks to be born."

I shrugged. His words made sense, but I wasn't ready for them.

"Okay," I said to change the subject back. "What would have happened if you found out John set me up?"

"Bullet to the brain," Oliver said so matter-of-factly that I stared open-mouthed at him.

I made an odd sound instead of words, which drew his attention.

"You fight your own battles. But sometimes, your battles are our battles. He got you killed. He gave you the map to your murder. I can't forgive him."

I still didn't know if I blamed him. Mom was a manipulative bitch that used John.

"You're used to people fucking with you. Your mom made you into a weapon and target at the age of six, and made you fight for your breath and dinner. You believe John gave you a choice, that you could've turned down the target. But he knew you. I know you. You'd never turn down a target, and with how much you hate your mom, it was easy. He used your anger against you and twisted it into demented, hopeful happiness."

"I did make the choice. He warned me off afterwards. He tried to take it back. Told me I wasn't ready." He snorted in disagreement. "Oliver, she came at me in his office. He used all he had to defend me."

Oliver didn't look like he bought it.

"I thought for a moment it was a trap when he pulled me back, that I'd been lured into a snare."

"In his death moment, he regretted what he did. He knew it was wrong, but him defending you doesn't make it okay."

"He watched out for me, gave me targets."

"Dessa," Oliver said, turning and moving his feet to the ground. He clasped both my hands and waited until I met his eyes. "John never watched out for you. He used you for all you are. He profited off of you and did what was necessary to keep you an asset. Nicolai made an extreme choice. Torture is not the answer. A bullet to the brain would have been better."

"He was like a father to me," I said, realizing the reality of it.

"Yeah, with your mom as a role model, I can see how you'd think he was a father figure."

Fuck. He was right.

OTHER WORLDLY MAGIC EXCERPT

A person's will can be stronger than a magical spell.

CHAPTER 34

NICOLAI WAS CALLED AWAY on business, or so he claimed. The four of us spent the night in a blanket fort in the great room with popcorn, candy, cola, and a movie marathon.

I woke up with a crick in my neck and breath of the dead. The smell of bacon lured me into a sitting position, and I found my way to the kitchen.

Duke and Alan had whipped up breakfast. I stuffed my face, letting my stomach bloat with the greasy goodness.

"When's Nicolai coming back?" Duke asked.

"He said a day or two," I said and shrugged.

"We could marathon again," Oliver said and tilted his head toward our nest.

We replenished our snacks with chips and set up a series to binge.

We'd made it to the fourth episode when I felt the first flicker of craving.

"What's wrong?" Oliver asked, turning to me but keeping his eyes forward, distracted by the show.

The welcoming curl of excitement for a hunt twisted in my stomach. My body tensed, and I grabbed my blade.

That got all their attention.

"Is it Nicolai?" Alan asked, shifting in repulsion.

I shook my head and lifted a finger to my lips in the universal "shut up" sign.

I didn't know how it got past all the security, unless Nicolai sent it as a test, but a silver-eyed Soulless flew at me. Yeah, I mean flew. They jump and can stay suspended in the air, giving the illusion of flight, but in the space, they were flying about.

He came for me, directing his attack at my face. I didn't duck but shifted and punched him in the throat. The crunch of cartilage was music to my ears. I licked my lips as they curled into a smile.

"Dessa," Oliver yelled.

Duke or Alan wrestled him back, my focus on the Soulless.

He reared back, clawing at his throat, gasping for air. I sprang at him, grabbing his waist and slamming him into the ground. He coughed and gurgled.

The unmistaken metallic clip of Virginia sounded behind me, but I wouldn't be able to give Duke a clean shot as I crowded his frame for the next attack.

The Soulless hissed, spraying fiery spittle across my face. I wiped the abrasive fluid from my face to avoid the welts and burnt flesh. He took the opportunity to latch on to my arm holding him down, sinking his teeth into my muscle. Then he ran his tongue, with poisonous spit, across my skin.

I pulled back and punched him in the face, and as he clawed for my face to send another projectile to it, I dug my blade deep into him.

He arched, gargled, and screeched as his life drained.

"Well." Nicolai's voice cut across the room.

My eyes turned to him.

"What the fuck," Duke and Oliver growled at Nicolai.

The air heated as orange zipped around Alan. "What was that?"

He looked partially amused and annoyed by the mess. His eyes met mine, ignoring the others. A shiver stole through me and the urgency to release my muscles in a punch or attack pounded in my veins.

"I think it's time," he said, nodding at the Soulless and then me.

"Time?" Oliver parroted. "Time for what?"

"You sent him?" I asked, already knowing he had, or it wouldn't have gotten into the house. I itched for something to dig my fingers into. To release the tension and ease the ache. My eyes narrowed in on Nicolai.

He smirked. "You need to set up a meeting with her."

Her… Numbness burned over my muscles, sizzling out the raw, uncontrolled sensation. Her mention grounded me into reality.

"I don't do appointments," I said as my body and breath calmed.

"Tell her you want to discuss John," he said and gave me a knowing look. He handed me a folded sheet of paper with ten digits sprawled across it.

The familiar numbers blurred in my vision. They were for John's personal cell.

"You're going to meet Claudine?" Oliver asked, crowding toward us.

Duke and Alan shared a look.

"She blames me," I said and stopped. The fucker had been plotting all along. He was priming her for the attack, making her distracted and disoriented as she did to me.

"Tell her I did it, and you want help."

I laughed. It started as a snort, but I couldn't contain it and it came out in rolling waves, rocking my frame.

"You're kidding right? I wouldn't ever ask her for help."

"You can't be serious," Oliver said.

Duke placed a hand on his shoulder and cleared his throat. Something passed between them. Oliver's face darkened in rage, but he kept silent.

Nicolai's eyes flicked to them before back to me. "What're you going to tell her, then?"

"I want to slice her face."

"She won't meet you for that."

"Oh, she will."

I CALLED JOHN'S CELL. I guess she took it to continue his business. Like when I was younger and called our home number from a burner, I let it ring six times and hung up. Then I called back and let it ring five times and hung up. She didn't answer and the voicemail had been disconnected, but she'd know it was me.

I paced in my room, unsure of everything. I felt a presence and watched as Tones' shadow emerged from the room's shadows and hovered slightly from me. She wasn't in her normal humanesque form, but I knew it was her.

"Tones, it's time," I said, but I suspected she already knew.

"Don't trust any of them," she said, her form wavering and the edges blurring out.

"What do I do?"

"Take the blood."

"And do what with it?" I asked, even though I had added the drops from my blade when I went after him for John.

"It'll be your ace."

I nodded even though I didn't understand how it would be. I knew it was best to have all the cards.

I LAY awake watching the clock. The minutes ticked by and I watched the hours flip over. I'd never been a big planner, and the night was a reason why. The mind game, the overanalyzing, double guessing, plotting moves, not knowing the other's moves.

I was a gut person, a heat-of-the-moment type. I went on instinct and survival. Thinking beyond that fucked with my head and set me up for flubbing and failing.

I had accepted I was likely going to die. How would I not? I was a pawn in a big war. I'd gotten Nicolai's blood, and would likely get

Not-Isaac's, but that left my mom and Nicolai, and they'd likely make sure I didn't leave.

I didn't regret coming back. In the end, when faced with everything, I'd leave Not-Isaac for Nicolai and I'd take out my mom. I'd make her pay for killing Tones, destroying her family, and for robbing me of the only person who loved me. But that wasn't right, I realized, lying in bed. Three others had followed me, uninvited, into this peril so they could offer help and support.

Alan and Duke were my best friends. There was no score, no owing. I'd extinguished the Soulless hunting Duke. They'd pretty much adopted me after that.

Oliver was here for Tones. She'd want him to help. My gaze shifted to the shadows, and I knew it was a lie. Tones didn't want either of us here, and she wouldn't encourage Oliver to follow my foolishness or rescue me from it. I'd made the choice. She would have helped, she always had, but she had told me what mistakes I'd made along the way.

I wasn't really certain why Oliver was there. Why he'd risk so much for me. I'd never considered him a brother. He'd been protective, but that was who he was to those he loved. I stilled and my pulse quickened in a different way.

I threw back the covers. I had less than twenty-four hours and I wasn't going to go out a coward or with unspoken truths. I owed it to myself to be honest and lay it out. I could be embarrassed, but there was nothing wrong with my feelings even if they were one way.

Maybe telling him would help explain my behavior that usually left him in the lurch or kicked out. Let him have closure before I died whether he needed it or not. I tossed my tank top off and pulled on a t-shirt over my boy shorts.

I looked around, feeling ridiculous that I was being shy. I knocked. No response. I closed my eyes and took a steadying breath. I'd knock once more. If he didn't answer, then I'd just go back to bed and write him a letter. Yeah, no. I'd just knock louder.

I knocked again, and whispered, "Oliver?"

The covers shifted like I'd startled him awake.

"Dessa?" he asked, moving around.

"Yes," I said, anxiety making my feet jittery. I rubbed my thumb over and around my fingers. Opening the door uninvited, I asked as I entered, "Can I come in?"

"Are you okay?" He moved to get up.

I raised my hand in a "stay" gesture. "No, I have to tell you something."

"No? What's wrong?" He reached a hand toward me as I crowded him so he'd stay in bed.

His hazel eyes were heavy with sleep, but concern burned its way through. Words were hard to form looking down at him.

"Um, I am likely going to die tomorrow," I said and flinched in regret seeing his face darken.

He growled and set his jaw.

"But that's not what I wanted to tell you," I said, trying to force my voice to be calm.

"Okay." He pulled out each letter, looking at me quizzically.

"I don't want to die being a chicken."

He lifted an eyebrow and settled back a bit, regarding me, causing me to lean forward as he continued to hold my hands. "I'd never describe you as a chicken."

The dark covered the heat that crept up my cheeks. I closed my eyes, rolled my lips between my teeth, and inhaled deeply through my nose. I pried my eyes open. I wasn't going to chicken out at the last second, and I wanted to see his shunning so when I died, I wouldn't have any lingering questions or regrets.

My voice soft, but strong as I said, "I had, well, I have... a crush on you."

His posture eased, which made my pulse tick up. His eyes softened as his gaze lowered to my lips and back to my eyes. A slow grin spread on his face as he said, "Good, I have one on you too. If you don't die tomorrow, we can go on a date without calling it a fake date."

His thumbs rubbed over my hands, sending warm gooey feelings through my body, and I melted. Melting from his heat, my heat, and the cracking of my heart as I absorbed his words. I didn't want to die.

I didn't want to miss out. I wanted to enjoy my life. Before I could stop myself, I said, "It's a date."

He smiled at me. It was so genuine and sincere I lost myself and returned it. His eyes darkened, and once again skimmed to my lips and lower before returning to my gaze. His eyes were now a liquid pool and I wanted to swim.

Shifting closer, I closed the gap. I leaned forward and he leaned in, his one hand letting mine go to cradle my head as our lips met.

I climbed on his bed, arching a leg over him to straddle him. His hands found my hips, and his thumb slipped beneath my underwear, rubbing circles.

I moaned into his mouth and he responded back by grinding into me. I gasped and pressed back in return. He sat up, brought a hand back to my cheek.

My hands roamed everywhere on him. They fisted his hair, cradled his jaw, rubbed his chest, and pushed the sheet aside. To my delight I discovered he slept in the buff.

"Oliver," I moaned his name, and he slipped his tongue into my mouth.

I pushed him back slightly and tore my T-shirt off, exposing myself. He sucked in a breath.

My fingers dug into his shoulder as I ground into him. No longer wanting my underwear on, I tore them from my body and tossed them aside. He chuckled against me, sending tingles deep into my belly.

His erection thumped against my exposed core. I eased the sheet back more and centered him.

His breath hitched, and I smiled.

His mouth found mine in hot need.

I pulled back, gasping as I rubbed on his tip. I said, "If you tell me to stop, I will."

"That'd be stupid," he said, grinning. He moved his hand to the dresser, fumbling with the drawer.

He tried to shift to see inside, but I held his face steady with my hand as I kissed him. I rubbed against him, and he groaned.

"Hold on," he murmured, and pulled out a box from the drawer. He held a box of condoms. "Gift from Duke and Alan."

With a chuckle, I took the square foil package and tore it open. I slipped the sheath over him, and then he entered me.

WE SLEPT a few minutes between rounds. He took top next, and I took top again the third go. We tried different poses from the Kama Sutra and went a round in the shower. My body relaxed and excited all at the same time. Once again, he was a distraction, but this time in the best way possible. Instead of overanalyzing my attack on my mom, or what Nicolai or Not-Isaac's plans were, I focused on his body and mine and all that we enjoyed.

Our physical excursion caught up to us in the early morning, and we'd fallen asleep in our bliss.

It was short lived.

Duke and Alan barged in without knocking while cheering as they entered with cake. Yes, cake. It was chocolate with chocolate frosting and sprinkles. Written in white frosting was the word "Congratulations."

When the fuck had they baked a cake?

"This deserves celebration," Duke beamed, sitting his large frame on the end of the bed while Alan shut the door and then joined him. Alan wrapped an arm around Duke's shoulders and Duke wove his free hand around Alan's waist.

"It's about time, we were getting ready to lock you two in a room," Alan said.

"I'm glad our presents got some use," Duke said and nodded at the dresser.

Sleep tugged at my brain, dulling my care, and my body was too comfortable to protest their presence. Then I noticed I had a leg draped over Oliver with my thigh resting on his pelvis. His hand rested on me while rubbing slight circles against my flesh. A delightful shiver stole through me and I nestled closer; my chest pressed against his and his other arm snuggled me closer to him.

When Alan asked, "Big or little piece?" while holding up the cake, Oliver pulled me closer and rubbed his cheek against my head. It was at that point I realized we were both naked and uncovered.

"I'll take a big piece," I said while shifting the sheet up but not leaving Oliver's warm embrace.

"You two are so loud. I'm so proud," Duke said and gave us a thumbs up.

I looked at Oliver to see if he was embarrassed and braced myself for the disappointment. He smiled at me, and leaning in, gave me a featherlight kiss. It wasn't enough and I wrapped my hand around his neck, staying him and drawing him closer. He acquiesced, and then ran his tongue over my lips.

"Hey, cake first, then more lovemaking," Duke said, swatting the bed and our legs. Alan took the cake with paper plates tucked beneath. They both smiled as they cut the cake. Oliver's arm tightened around me, holding me closer as he accepted a piece of cake with the other.

My stomach clenched. In a matter of hours, all this would be over. I'd be marching off to my death. For the first time, I cared if I came back. I didn't want to let go. I didn't want to die.

***

SEVERAL HOURS LATER, I finally rolled out of Oliver's bed. My hair was a tangled mess and my body hummed.

"Dessa," Oliver whispered.

I turned to face him. He lay sprawled on the bed, unclothed and uncovered. I forced my eyes to his face.

His hazel eyes watched me, warm but guarded. "I need to apologize."

"For?" my voice hitched. He wasn't going to do the whole "I regret having sex" crap, was he?

My face must have shown my thoughts because he shook his head and reached his hand for mine. "It's not bad. At least, I don't think it is."

"Okay," I measured out.

"For so long, since we were kids, I wanted to prove I was good enough."

"What?" I stammered.

He ran his other hand through his hair as his eyes searched the bedspread for answers.

"My first memories include you showing up at the bar and creating chaos with my brothers. I mean, in kindergarten when that kid took your lunch, I tried to intervene, but before I could get a word out you had him on his knees, offering you money to let him go."

The memory flickered through my mind, another of his big brother bullshit attempts, but my focus remained on Oliver and his unspoken words.

Silence hung between us. He licked his lips and his fingers tightened around mine.

"You never needed anything."

I stilled, my breath in my throat. Uncertainty slid as acid in my stomach. Where was he going with this?

"But that's not right."

He lifted his gaze to mine. Emotion shone in his eyes.

"You didn't need what I thought you needed. I kept trying to protect you. I became a Finder because you were one. I'm not like you and will never be as good. It's not just your natural skill, whatever that means, it's you. You have a drive to rid this place of Soulless."

He was being too kind. Too flattering. Ignoring the rest that lay beneath and in my veins.

He lifted his hands to me, palms facing me, once again seeming to read my thoughts. "I'm not giving you false accolades. You are one of the best. Your record speaks to that. Mandy's enthusiasm and admission of the levels you have brought in for years backs it up. Gah, I'm sucking at saying this."

He ran his hand through his hair again, leaving long spikes. I itched to run my hands through his hair again. Maybe trail them lower… He spoke again, pulling my attention back to him.

"Based on your world, your mom, and I guess your dad, I thought you needed protecting. But you don't. Because I… care about you, I wanted to give you everything even though I didn't understand what you needed and kept trying to shove it at you. I'm sorry. It almost got me killed twice, and shockingly it was Nicolai's remedy that fixed it the last time."

"Oliver…" Words failed me.

He shook his head. "I'm sorry, Dessa. I've only wanted to be your friend, help you, but I never could see past me to see what you needed. But I see now that you don't need someone trying to shield you from danger. You don't need someone to fall back on, either. You may not *need* anyone to survive, but I hope you *want* someone to be there to share your life with."

OTHER WORLDLY MAGIC EXCERPT

Not all death is final.

CHAPTER 35

I FOLLOWED TONES' advice. I'd gone back to my room, Oliver's words spinning in my brain, and noticed a missed call. A voicemail in my mom's muffled voice said, "John's at ten."

I stared at it and willed myself to keep moving. I had less than twelve hours to live.

After I sluggishly got dressed, my body on autopilot as I considered everything at stake, I slipped the pillbox of Nicolai's blood into my cargo pants. I tied my flannel around my waist, covering his blood spots.

It didn't matter what I wanted. If I didn't finish this, my mom and likely dad would destroy everything in my world to make me pay, to make me their weapon against each other. The only way I stood a chance at a life was to take my mom and her companion down tonight.

My weapons were stashed and ready to go, but I wasn't ready.

I'd been planning to just end it, sacrifice myself to make my final kill, but now I wanted more. That was the double-edged sword. Now I wanted to live for something after I'd already accepted my death.

Rubbing a hand over my face, I tried to feel regret over my time with Oliver. I looked in the mirror to scold myself and chuckled when I saw the subconscious smile dominating my face. It was the worst possible timing, but I didn't care.

I walked down to the training room, slipping silently down to avoid Oliver, Duke, and Alan. I didn't want the distraction or for my doubts to rear up more.

"You ready?" Nicolai asked as he paced through warmups.

I shrugged. "Sure."

He frowned and stood. "No, you need to be confident that you'll succeed."

I mimicked his serious tone. "I am confident I'll get you the blood."

He eased back and examined my face. "Then what's different about you?"

My eyes bulged, and I shrugged as I quickly turned away in case my face gave away the sordid details of the morning.

"They can't come," Nicolai said, directing his chin to the house.

"Wasn't planning on inviting them."

"Don't let them follow."

"Should I shoot their legs?"

"If you have to," he said with a shrug.

"You're acting like you're going," I said as I watched him strapping up.

"Of course I'm going."

"Afraid I won't succeed?" I queried.

He turned his gaze to me but said nothing as he stared at me and finished gearing up.

"Won't she sense you?" I asked as I followed him to the garage.

"We'll need to hit a portal."

"You know about them too?" I asked.

He snorted. "Of course."

"I'm supposed to meet her at John's."

"She's calling the shots now?"

"Aren't you trying to right now?" I shot back.

"I'm trying to guarantee success."

"Mine or yours?"

"It's the same."

But it wasn't.

JOHN'S PLACE WAS DARK, as expected. I watched for the shadows, but they recessed when Nicolai joined me. I'd be alone.

Yet again, the place had a barren vibe, and this time I didn't even sense John there.

"It's probably a trap," Nicolai said and took position at my back, searching the perimeter and rooftops.

"Of course it is," I said. Mom wouldn't play fair.

"Where do you think she really is?"

"She thinks I hurt John."

"No, she's aware I did it."

That didn't help. She was already pissed I was in contact with him, and now he was doing something to "help" me.

I crept up to the building, staying to the shadows despite the knowledge she had night vision. Even if my stealth was an illusion, it was a comfort. I leaned against the brick building, it didn't talk to me or offer any support, but I tried to see the place from a different perspective.

I slid down the wall, searching around, and that's when I noticed the red card, discarded in a rock pile.

I stood up and cautiously stepped forward. I used my boot and kicked it free from the rubble. It was her card all right, and on the back her writing had been scratched out that read "I want her alive." In its place was "I'm coming for you, Claudine."

I stared at the writing. It wasn't Mom's neat writing, which I had to rule out as I suspected she would pretend she had a threat on herself as a distraction. No, the sharp words were irregular and jagged, and very much the small scrawl I'd seen on Nicolai's notes.

She'd sent us a sign.

"She wants you," I said, gesturing toward the card.

"She always has," he said with a cocky grin that turned my stomach. He may be a stranger, but I still didn't want to hear about my parents' exploits.

"She left me a voicemail for this location, I'm guessing I have a message too," I said.

As if on cue, my phone rang.

Nicolai scowled at me and said, "Why isn't it on vibrate?"

"No one calls," I said. I'd received more calls and texts this week than I had the entire rest of my adult life.

Still, I answered it.

"Dessa," Benny's voice cracked from the other side.

My vision tunneled and I braced myself against the wall.

"Is she there?"

"Don't come," he whispered and then he screamed. His line cut off and a sob lodged in my throat.

"Where?" Nicolai asked as he guided me toward the car.

He opened the door and he started boosting me in like a toddler.

I came to reality and pushed away. After jumping from the car, I tore down my familiar paths to the bar. I'd get there faster than a vehicle.

The phone rang again, and I thought about chucking it to not hear I'd failed.

On the third ring I answered, "What?"

She laughed.

"You fucking bitch," I seethed, my voice bouncing off the walls and startling the rats and those hidden in the shadows.

"You're so focused on people who've let you down, you haven't thought about that lovesick boy at your daddy's."

"What did you do?" My voice was all shades of wild.

"Me?" She laughed, the sound sweet and melodical and completely uncalled for. "Your daddy took down his protections. Little Ollie was easy pickins. Can you get here before my Driver can?"

I stared at the street signs.

"Your daddy's house may have been impregnable, but it seems he either got sloppy or hopeful. He never did like others meddling in his life or his property."

The fucking asshole. If she was to be believed, he left my friends at his house and took all his guards down for the creepy crawlies that had been trying to get in. And she took Oliver.

"What have you done to Oliver?"

"Nothing yet," she teased. "He should be here in two minutes. How about you?"

I screamed. Tears burning my eyes, I forced my feet to move faster. The shadows swirled and gave me speed as I raced toward my mom. I was at least five minutes out.

I called Duke and Alan.

I almost let out a cry when the line clicked and Duke said, "What's up, sweets?"

"Where the fuck is Oliver?"

"He's in his room."

"Go check," I yelled. I knew he wasn't. She'd been too sure, or she wouldn't have taunted me.

I heard curses through the line. I'd kill that bitch with my bare hands.

"What's going on?" Alan said, taking the phone.

"She has him," I said. "You guys gotta get out of the house. NOW! He took his protections down. He set you up. To stop you from coming."

Alan moved the phone from his mouth as he told Duke to help him check.

"Ok, we're coming," he said. Duke's muffled voice responded.

"NO!" I yelled and couldn't think. She'd just kill them too. "No, no, no. She'll hurt you too. Just go to the portal and stay there. Stay safe. Please." The last few words caught in my throat and came out garbled.

"Sweets, where are you going?" Alan said, his voice deathly calm.

I didn't respond.

"Where?"

When I didn't respond to his question and went to click the phone off, I felt a string in my body lurch, causing me to stumble and I hit the pavement. I left skin on the pavement and blood and dirt streaked my cheeks and hands. I scrambled back to my feet, ignoring the searing pain in my side as I continued on.

"You won't get up again. Where are you running to?" Alan asked. He was moving based on the changes in his tone.

"I have to help him."

"It's too late if you aren't there yet."

My heart lurched and the wind ripped from my lungs. I wailed, my body shaking.

"I can make it," I sniffed.

"No, she'll kill you. You're too emotional."

"Fuck you!"

Glass shattered on the other side of the call, from the verbosity, likely one of the big picture windows. The Soulless were coming for them.

"Fuck," Duke barked. "They're going to get in."

"Give me Virginia," Alan said, his voice distant as he spoke away from the phone. "Get the Porsche here now."

More glass shattered and garbled screeches sounded. Six rounds sounded, followed by horrific screeching and blathering.

Alan's voice returned, calm and serene as ever. "Sweets, I'm thrilled you love Oliver. Don't waste the breath denying it, but she's doing this on purpose." A car door slammed on his end of the line and the whirl of Duke's Porsche filled the air. "She's banking on you being stupid. Where are you going, or the next tug will remove organs?"

"Did you fucking tether me?" I yelled, anger edging out the sadness and fear. "You fucking tethered me!" I roared as my chest tightened.

"Of course I did."

The bar came into view, and an odd wobbling breath came out of me.

"The bar," I whispered, hoarse from crying.

The front was its normal inferno of color, the hues splashing across the recently wet pavement. Patrons moved around behind the glass, but I stopped.

They weren't drinking. They were talking and watching. They were waiting for me.

My phone rang.

I answered but didn't speak.

"Don't want to go in, huh?"

My eyes darted around, trying to find her.

"You're too late."

I blinked slowly; I knew I was too late.

"I'm not completely heartless," she said and chuckled at her own joke.

I didn't take the bait.

"Maybe I am," she said, and then continued, "but I will give you goodbye."

"Dessa," Oliver's voice cracked.

It was like a sucker punch to my heart. I was breathless. "Oliver?" I managed.

"Don't come," he rushed and made a groaning noise like he'd been hit.

I heard my mom say from behind him, "That's not what you're to say."

"Oliver, where are you?"

"He's in a car," my mom's voice blasted through. Her voice muffled as she said, "As we practiced."

"Dessa," Oliver whispered, his voice like a soft caress.

This was going to be the last time I ever heard from him, and my emotions ran from my eyes and lodged in my throat.

"Oliver, I love you," I said, taking my last seconds to leave no regrets as I ended it all. "I'll find you."

"No, Dessa," Oliver pleaded. "Run, I love—"

The phone was ripped from his grasp. I'd rip her head off and parade it around on a stick.

"You're too good for him," my mom's voice scolded.

I hung the phone up without another word. I'd made a decision.

OTHER WORLDLY MAGIC EXCERPT

Regardless of magical ability, decapitation kills all.

CHAPTER 36

DUKE'S PORSCHE BURST through the air and landed with a skid next to me.

Duke and Alan jumped out of the car.

"How many came for you?"

Duke and Alan shared a look.

"They were to distract us, but let's focus on Oliver and your mom," Alan said.

"We're too late," I said, my voice like sandpaper.

"Did she kill him?" Duke asked and Alan shot him a disapproving look.

"Not yet," I said and looked toward the bar.

"What's your plan?"

"I'm going to fuck up some Soulless," I said. I didn't care if they were my kind. I didn't care if I was a hypocrite. All I cared about was that they supported her.

"Will that help?" Duke asked.

"They're waiting for me. I shouldn't disappoint them."

Duke holstered Virginia and nodded at me. "Let's do this."

An unearthly wail sliced the air, and the ground rumbled, setting us off-kilter.

"What the fuck?" I said.

A car engine revved, and I noticed Nicolai's SUV speeding toward us, his lights blasting us in the face. Instead of slowing down, he sped up.

Realizing his intent, I ran to Duke and Alan and tried to push them out of the way. Duke realized a moment later and aimed Virginia at the SUV. Alan glowed orange and lightning shot from him, arching over the car, but it dissipated on the vehicle.

Nicolai floored his vehicle, ramming us and sending us flying.

My head rang and I couldn't focus. My body felt shattered. My bones protested as I pushed myself up. I was covered in blood and my vision blurred.

I struggled to stand, but Nicolai hauled Duke and Alan into his vehicle. He turned toward me and said, "Collateral. No running. No suicide mission. Get me the fucking blood or know they died for you."

He got in his vehicle and drove away.

I fell back to the pavement.

"Get up," the shadows hissed.

My head spun and my body lay broken. I lifted my head up and vomited.

"They'll find you," their urgent voices pleaded.

I knew who they referred to, the ones waiting for me inside.

"Dessa, love." Tones' voice tore through the hissing and wrapped around my heart.

"Tones," I choked.

Her ethereal presence sat by me, and although she had no temporal, concrete form she made the gesture of petting my hair and rubbing my back. Even if my body couldn't feel her, my soul could.

"Oliver, Duke, Alan." I cried my failures out.

"Stop it, there is no time for pity," she scolded, but her voice was soft.

"I can't," I said, blood spitting from my mouth.

"You are Dessa the Destroyer." Her voice sounded so sure. I could almost believe it.

"I lost."

"It's not over, love," she said and shifted to an upward position. "You a quitter?"

"No," I spat. She knew those were fighting words, and as manipulative as it was, it helped.

"You going to let them take the people you love? Use them as pawns to control you because they can't win their own war?"

I growled and then choked.

"Thatta girl. They can't beat each other, but you can. That's why they want you."

"How can I beat them?" I asked, my mind grasping to form a plan. The shadows stirred by me, and I felt them canvassing my body, entering my wounds. It was incredibly creepy, but I couldn't stop them and whatever they were doing numbed the pain.

"Blood."

"Blood?"

"Did you bring what I told you to?"

"Yes."

"They want to control each other, all the Soulless."

"How?" I asked, finally able to push myself off the ground. Grossness dripped from me, but the more I hovered up, the more the shadows seemed to clean my wounds.

"They're master levels," Tones said. "They can control each other if they have the other's blood. Use each other's powers."

"Not-Isaac and Nicolai?"

She laughed humorously. "Don't forget your mom."

"But…" I said, my voice tapering off with the new revelation.

"Your mom and dad were strong, not nearly as strong then as they are now. They separated when you were a baby. He went to Detroit. Your mom stayed here. They both built their own following. Isaiah was forming his own on the coast. When he came back to Coving, your mom joined him, combining their forces. They're building an empire together. One that could shift the power of the Soulless in Coving and beyond."

"She turned on Dad?"

"I don't know if she turned. I think they are all about their own wants and goals, to rule all the Soulless at this point."

"How'd they get strong enough then?" I asked, fear curling in my stomach.

Tones sighed.

"Did the targets help?" I choked out.

"Yes."

"Why didn't you stop them?" I asked, unable to stop myself. I wasn't angry with her; I knew they killed her husband and she had children.

"If I'd known when I was alive, I would have. I had no idea your mom was as powerful as she is. Nicolai only came back when they went after you. They were trying to harness his powers using your blood. I learned most of this snooping around Nicolai."

"How'd he not find you?"

A proud chuckle rumbled from her throat. "Alan tethered me to you. Nicolai can't see past Alan's magic. It's one reason Duke and Alan followed, to keep it intact."

They were the best of friends.

"But Dessa, your parents are strong now, and all three of them want the same thing and need you to do it. They can't get to each other. You've seen Nicolai's fortress. His magic is different, but effective. Isaiah uses his powers he stole from Isaac to hide himself and your mom from Nicolai in his safehouse outside of town. You can bring them all down."

"Why me?"

"They bore and raised you to be their weapon."

"What happened then?" I asked, looking up to her, watching her shadow flicker in the dim streetlamp.

"You are a weapon, but you decide for whom, including yourself."

OTHER WORLDLY MAGIC EXCERPT

In recent decades Soulless have started to infiltrate the Finders' Agencies. The Trust's well-established processes and systematic removal of dangerous Soulless led to many Soulless' attempts to combat the Finders. A small group of Soulless started making deals with certain Agents to create targets outside of the Trust and purchase Soulless without an established target sheet. In the process, they used the Soulless they collected for powerful death arts and to surpass the skill associated with a Level One target. They are often referred to as a "Master" Soulless.

CHAPTER 37

BOTH MY PARENTS had kidnapped people I loved to control me. I guessed my mom would keep Oliver alive long enough for me to find her so she could watch me as she killed him. She got sick delights, and my pain was a top favorite.

Nicolai, although I couldn't read him, I didn't think he'd kill Duke and Alan as long as I got him the blood.

This was always the drawback of friends and was a reason Finders rarely had family. Loved ones were liabilities. When I'd left just two months ago, I'd been able to walk away. Tones was alive, Oliver had a future that I was certain he didn't want to share with me, and Duke and Alan had recently been married and were starting life together. I figured Tones, Duke, and Alan would miss me, but they'd move on. They had rich lives. When Oliver hadn't called during that month, I'd figured I had been like a piece of furniture he donated.

Now I couldn't see my future without them. I could see why people would turn their backs on love and embrace the pain and numbness of loneliness. You could avoid all extremes and just exist.

I couldn't remain in limbo anymore. After leaving the bar, my feet had carried me to my apartment. I stared at the building, having no yearning to go into my easy existence. The brick building void of character and life was no longer home.

I walked on and found myself at Mandy's. I hadn't expected to go there. Although I was wandering, I usually ended up at the same points. I'd thought I'd go to John's or the river, but I found myself at Mandy's stoop.

I entered and stood in the dimly lit office.

"No bloody corpse?" she asked from behind her desk.

"What do you do with the targets?" I asked.

"Why do you want to know?" she asked, sitting back in her chair, spine straight and her arms resting in her lap.

"Who do you sell them to?"

She narrowed her eyes; her mouth formed a thin line.

"Do you sell outside the Trust?"

"These are dangerous questions," she cautioned.

"I've been a tool to just about every person who claimed to be looking out for me or should have been."

"I never claimed to be looking out for you. I'm pretty sure I said I was the winner in this arrangement."

"Yep, and that's why I'm here asking you."

She regarded me from behind her too-big glasses. She pursed her lips; nodding softly, and finally said, "Sit down."

I sat in the proffered chair, my hand hovering on my blade.

"There's a bank of targets."

"How do you select them?"

"We all have access to them."

"So you can have the same target as John did at a given time?"

"Yes," she said with a wry smile. "Why do you think I knew you so well? You never missed."

I blinked instead of rolling my eyes.

"Who issues them?"

Mandy tapped her finger on the desk as she regarded me.

Deciding to try a new strategy, I name dropped until I got a reaction. Her eyes widened with each name. "Whom do you report to—Isaiah, Claudine, or Nicolai?"

"Those are not names to be thrown around."

"Two of them are my parents," I said and watched the color drain from her face.

"I knew Claudine..." she said, her eyes darting around the table, trying to find answers.

"John sold to the Trust and Soulless on the side."

"No he didn't," she shook her head.

I waited. My muscles coiled ready for her deceit. Ready for her to pull a gun or knife or hell even some blood out.

"There are Agents who sell to Soulless." She licked her lips and her eyes flickered around the corners of the room. "John did not. The Soulless who put the targets out outside of the Trust are rare. Very rare. Evolution works for Vessels and Soulless too. The arts have grown and evolved into something more powerful than the original target levels, but the targets changed over time from three to five. This small group doesn't want to increase their numbers but their power. They are powerful. And rich."

Without taking my eyes off of her, I knew she had blood-soaked carpet, chipped paint on the exterior, and a plywood bathroom door.

"You don't get into being an Agent for the wealth of it. Sure, it comes with the job if you can hook the right Finders and move up the Trust's list for the target bank for higher levels, but trouble increases as you do. This place is warded to the hilt. I sleep with guns and knives. I barely leave this place. You don't enter unless I let you."

"Then why do it?"

"One, it's a family business. My family has been in the business since the Trust was built. Second, I believe in the cause. We remove dangerous parasites."

"Have any of the Soulless asked you for side deals?"

She licked her teeth. Her dark eyes assessed me behind her too-big glasses. "Yes."

"So, let's start over. Who do you report to?"

AFTER MANDY HELPED BANDAGE my bleeding wounds, I clutched my phone as I stared at the river. Its black swollen form snaked beneath, purging the shores after the recent rains.

I held the scrap of paper, Mom's number jotted down on it.

I dialed the numbers and listened as the electronic rings sounded.

She answered after four rings.

I could hear the smile in her voice, but I snarled when she said, "Baby girl?"

"Let's meet."

"Of course, baby, meet me at—"

I cut her off blurting out, "Stakeout, thirty minutes."

Next, I dialed Nicolai.

"Where?" he said when the phone connected.

"Stakeout, twenty minutes."

He hung up.

I tightened the phone in my fist, listening as the plastic case cracked, and then I dropped and crushed it beneath my boot. There was no turning back.

I made it to Stakeout in ten minutes. I didn't doubt they'd show early, so I didn't enter. I hung back in the shadows a few blocks down, watching the entrance.

"Tones," I whispered, but she didn't respond.

The shadows thickened around me, rippling in fear. It didn't help my focus, and so I asked, "Why are you afraid of him?"

They hissed but didn't say anything.

"Are you..." I stopped and pulled courage from my gut. Now was the time for answers. "Are you Vessels we have killed?"

The shadows whipped around me, and I pulled back from their funnel.

"It's not so simple," they said and hovered before me.

"Are you the innocent ones?"

"No one is innocent," they said back.

"How does he cast you away?"

"We stay away. He absorbs us for power."

"Aren't you afraid I will, too?" I thought, but when they responded, I figured I'd spoken it out loud.

"No, we don't fear you."

That was either humbling or demeaning, but as they'd witnessed all I did, it gave me a glimmer of hope. "Why?" I asked before thinking better of it.

"You fight all they are."

That was something. I wasn't sure it was accurate, but it bolstered me as I readied my mind.

My body was bandaged, by the shadows and then more completely by Mandy. In my arsenal, I'd added more bullets and an additional blade, but I didn't see the point. I had no misconceptions of escape. I just needed to stay alive long enough to end it all.

Revenge wasn't ever going to work. I'd been narrowly focused on my mom and had missed everything else going on. She'd cut deeper than even I knew. She was her own master, like she'd raised me to be.

But she was one of three.

Revenge would only be a battle of retaliation from the other two. None of us would win; we'd just be one-upping the others for the rest of time. I needed to go for the head. The kill shot. I needed to end it all. It's like with the green-blooded creatures, it's best just to shoot them in the head and be done. I'd sided with Nicolai and got played. I didn't plan to become a fourth player. I decided to end the game.

"Are they here yet?" I asked, scanning the street again, seeing nothing.

"No," the shadows answered.

I ENTERED THE BAR. The music thumped, and the lights displayed cool tones casting long shadows around the room, providing intimate pockets for the patrons.

I walked up to the bar, noticing the same bartender. Like most Soulless, I'd forgotten his name.

His eyes bulged when he saw me and he stumbled a step.

"You alone?" he asked, raising a brow, and quickly masked his surprise with a mischievous gleam. But fear skittered behind it.

I pulled my gun out and aimed it at his face.

His color drained and he raised his hands. He tried for a mocking grin and opened his mouth to say something but shut it when I cocked the trigger.

"What do you want?"

"I should kill you; you gave me up."

He searched my face, confusion darkening his eyes.

"You're not going to?" he asked.

"No, not unless you give me cause."

"I haven't yet?"

"She's a bitch, and you owe allegiance."

He stared skeptically at me.

"Make sure you do it again."

He swallowed.

"I'll be in the office," I said, gesturing to the room my mom had thrown a Soulless through.

"Okay," he said, pulling the word out and staring at the bar top.

If she couldn't sense me in the building, I wanted to make sure to speed this along.

I walked into the room and turned the lights off. All the players had night vision, and the lights would only provide a show for the patrons. I just wanted a soundproof room.

The room appeared to be an office-supply stock room more than anything else. Claustrophobia tightened my throat and I had to force the lump down.

I wasn't much for patience. I opened the door and leaned on the frame, welcoming my guests to my game.

Nicolai was the first to arrive, as I'd given them a separate time window to avoid early bloodshed and to improve the chances one of my friends would survive.

He sauntered down the hall, comfortable with his surroundings and headed straight for me as if he had been here before.

He came alone and I frowned, staring at him.

Nicolai smiled brightly at me, the mirth shining in his eyes. He enjoyed the game like I enjoyed the hunt. I understood the want to not share characteristics with our parents, but hating them completely forced us to hate ourselves. I had his intensity for my passions, but my passion wasn't his. I'd had to reconcile this difference early in life when I saw myself as a mirror of my mother. Not having her physical attributes had been a big help, but her words and manners dominated me. It'd taken me years to appreciate that I'd selected the ones that served me. I was her daughter, raised by her, but I was my own person. I made my own choices, even if at times they mimicked her.

"Interesting location choice," he said, raising his brows at me.

"Where are Duke and Alan?" I asked, keeping my voice level despite the hatred bubbling inside.

He chuckled. "Safe, for now," he added, giving me a pointed look.

"I want a guarantee they'll be released."

He smiled at me like a loving parent tickled by their child's antics, and probably would have ruffled my hair had I not been holding my blade. "There are no guarantees."

"Hm," I said, picking some gravel off my shirt from him running into me. "If they're already dead, then I guess we're done," I said, pushing off the frame and walking away from the room.

"Leave and they do die," his voice dangerous.

"I already assume they are," I said without turning around.

I don't know what battle warred behind me, but after I'd taken five steps, he barked, "Fine."

I paused and turned to stare at Nicolai. I knew one of the rules was to never turn your back, but I was acutely aware of his actions. He also was just as lethal when I faced him, if not more when he could read my emotions.

He snapped his fingers like a loon, and I heard rough shuffling and violent grunts as the bartender dragged Duke and Alan around the corner. They were bound in chains, zip ties, and what appeared to be magical shackles.

"Overkill, much?" I deadpanned, starting to lose the battle to keep my voice calm.

"Possibly not enough," Nicolai countered.

"They stay in the room," I said, making a rapid decision.

"That's not our agreement."

"We don't trust each other," I said. "This proof of life could just be a final viewing."

He made an annoyed grunt, and then the bartender started dragging them toward us.

Alan caught my eye, his eyes orange as they bored into me. He shook his head, and mouthed, "RUN!"

I smiled sadly at him.

Duke wasn't as subtle and yelled, "Get the fuck out, Dessa."

"Enough," Nicolai said, and magical binders wrapped around their mouths.

I bit my cheek but didn't show my hand yet. I needed one more in my view before I could finish this shit show.

The bartender escorted them into the room, shoving them into a corner. I had to avert my eyes to keep calm. Having them in the room would be a reminder to keep me on track. This wasn't about me, my revenge. This was about everyone.

I resumed my position at the door, waiting for Mom.

She came at the assigned time. She had Oliver hauled over her shoulder. His limp body draped unceremoniously around her. He wasn't rigid, so I assumed he was drugged. Not-Isaac sidled up next to her.

"Baby," she drawled. "So glad you had time for your mama."

I rolled my eyes.

"You ready to bargain?" she asked and strode into the room, coming to an abrupt halt. Her gaze swung to me. Her fake merriment dissolved, and in its place was hardened hatred.

"Yep," I said and gestured into the room.

"Claudine," Not-Isaac said, and guided her further into the room with her elbow. His fingers tightened around her arm when his gaze fell on Nicolai. With a tick of his jaw, his gaze moved between Mom and Nicolai, betrayal burning right in his eyes.

"Nicolai," Not-Isaac gritted out.

I closed the door behind me, sealing our cage.

They'd each entered, each taking their own corner.

Mom and Nicolai stared at each other, years of history warring on their faces. Mom swallowed and looked away. It was the closest I'd ever seen her come to showing regret.

"Love," Nicolai said, his voice soft and gentle.

I cringed.

Not-Isaac's gaze swept between them, a look of understanding passing over his eyes. He nodded to himself and stepped away from Mom.

Mom eased in relief as he went to his own corner.

Nicolai and Not-Isaac eyed each other like boxers before the match, but that was it. They didn't engage in any bickering or threats.

Mom's eyes swept over Nicolai again. She licked her lips and moved away from both of them, taking her own corner.

They were three beings all playing the same game. All on their own side. Waiting for two to go at it to get the upper hand. Unless one of them showed a weakness, if they went after one, the other would attack.

Then they turned and stared expectantly at me. Each one looking victorious, like they'd already won. And I realized they had. They each had the audience of the one they had wanted, one they had not been able to get, and I stood there able to deliver the unattainable to them. I'd played my part.

But I wasn't done.

Not-Isaac's gaze shifted back to Mom, a look of regret passed briefly, and he looked to me with hope. His eyes darkened and my stomach flipped. It was a common look, one of possession and domination.

He smiled at me; his sights now set.

Mom noticed the look too. She didn't look offended or put out, just full of acceptance.

They'd used each other and were both done.

Her gaze shifted to Nicolai. There was real pain when she focused on him. Something I hadn't thought her capable of.

Nicolai watched me. None of them trusted me, but the difference was Nicolai thought I had loyalty to him. He still thought I just wanted revenge, his pride blinding him from reality.

"Dessa," my mom's voice cut into the room. "I thought you wanted to bargain."

"*You've* yet to tell me what you want," I said, knowing what she wanted. "Based on your previous actions you wanted my blood. You put a hit out for me, but alive. If my blood wasn't good enough for you before, what could you possibly want?"

"Don't be cute."

"Dessa," Not-Isaac said, causing my attention to shift to him. "Your parents are playing a lovers' spat game. They only want to hurt each other. Let them."

That was bullshit. "And what are you playing?"

"I'm not playing anything," he said, his voice velvety. "I have a goal to rid this world of the filth, and you've been helping so much. I have a proposition for you."

I blinked at him. Acid threatened my throat.

"What proposition is that?" Mom barked.

Not-Isaac ignored her, and said to me, "Join me. I'll give you all the power you need to cleanse the world of the Soulless. You'll be my queen."

Yuck.

"What are you offering my daughter?" Nicolai spat. His fists balled, and charges ricocheted in the room.

"Claudine has only had eyes for you, and it stilted her powers."

Mom made an uncharming sound that likely meant Not-Isaac was going to get hurt.

"I'm offering Dessa my hand to be all she could be."

"This isn't the army," Nicolai spat. "She's too smart to join you."

"Your parents used you in their lovers' game to one-up each other. I offer you the power to control all the Soulless."

He was full of it and creepy.

"And what do you want for this offer?" I asked, gagging on the words.

"I just need Nicolai's blood."

I shot a glance at Nicolai. His expression was unreadable as he regarded me.

"I'm going to decline," I said, causing Nicolai to chuckle.

"So, Nicolai wants Not-Isaac's blood, Not-Isaac wants Nicolai's blood, but Mom, what do you want?" I asked, turning toward her. "You've had the chance to get both of their blood."

"You've always underestimated your mom." Nicolai gave her a loving look.

"I'm reminded of it daily."

Nicolai smiled at her. It was creepy how much he loved and respected her all while also seeming to hate her. "If she took my blood with her, she'd only have powered Isaiah. If she took Isaiah's, she'd have to face me alone. She wants to ensure her own victory."

"How's she doing that?"

"Playing you," he said, sending me a dark look.

I looked around and realized he was fucking right. She'd done it again. We were locked in a room. Her two biggest competitors before her, my friend-family bound around me, all tools to use me.

"Don't fret, baby," she said, smiling at me. "You've done good."

"You fucking bitch," I roared.

"Uh-uh," she said. "I think you owe Nicolai something."

"And what about him," I said waving to Nicolai. "How do you plan on doing that?"

"Oh, I'm sure you'll figure it out."

I stared at her. She'd outplayed me again.

"Tick tock, Dessa," she said, her eyes moving to Oliver. "I can become motivating."

It didn't matter what I did, she was going to kill them. She didn't plan on any of us leaving this room alive. She'd be the sole survivor. I had no idea what her plan was, but Nicolai was right. I always underestimated her. In my attempt to trap her, she'd trapped me again.

No matter what I chose, I didn't like the outcome.

"What does it matter?" I said. "I can see you won."

She smiled.

"You'll kill them anyway," I said, gesturing to Oliver, Duke, and Alan.

"I could make them suffer first," she said, like it was a valid option.

"Death is death," I said. "Once I'm dead, you'll lose interest in them."

"Saying that to make yourself feel better, or do you really believe it?"

"What joy would you have? Why waste your time? You couldn't enjoy my pain witnessing it."

Her eyes darted to the side for the moment, but she turned back to me, smiling. "You're probably right about that."

Oh fuck, another trap.

"But," she said and pulled something from her pocket.

"Bribing me with jewelry?"

"This," she said, "is Tones' blood. I drained it from her when she died."

"She's already dead," I said, but uncertainty clawed at me and warred with the anger building in my core.

"I will damn her to hell. Torture her soul," Mom said.

"Tones was your friend," I said lamely. I wasn't sure she could control Tones in the beyond, but Not-Isaac and Nicolai looked amused by the declaration.

"So? That's your weakness: you owe no one but think you do."

I looked around the room helplessly. I didn't want to give her the power. She was always a step ahead. She always knew my weakness. She could predict my moves.

I had to be brash. Bold. I had to act like her. I had to draw on every piece of training she provided me.

She wanted me to give Nicolai Isaiah's blood, and then Nicolai's blood to her so she could have both of their powers. But I needed to deprive her of all the power. Destroy it before she could absorb it.

A few shadows shifted around the door, drawing my attention up.

Nicolai frowned at the door.

Gulping, I rested my hands on my hips as I regarded her. My hand landed on a dry patch on the flannel I'd worn when I attacked Nicolai and his blood had splattered back. My hands fisted and felt a lump in my cargo pants. I ran a finger over the vial I'd gotten for my father. Tones had told me to bring it, I then understood why.

A new idea came to me.

"Tones." I whispered her name, centering myself. I'd always trusted her. She'd always protected me. Even in death she did.

The three's attention drew to me, and their surprised expressions were unusual on their faces as Tones flickered into existence. She formed more solid than usual; I could even make out the shape of individual curls.

Her form stood beside me. The three actually drew back a bit.

"Oliver and Dessa, I love you." Tones' voice filled the room.

Oliver stirred, his mom's voice ringing through to him.

"Mom?" he murmured.

"My boy, I'm so proud of you," she whispered.

My throat was thick watching the love between them.

"I love you, Mom." He reached for her.

"I know." She hovered by him.

She turned to face the room, standing in front of him, a final protection for her son.

"Dessa, you can end this," Tones said, nodding at me.

"Shut up," Mom hissed. "Quit meddling with my kid."

"She's not yours," Tones said.

"I birthed her!"

"Blood doesn't make family. It's just used to control it."

I then knew what Tones had tried to tell me. Had led me to. She'd shown me all the keys I needed.

I laughed, drawing the others' attention.

I withdrew the vial from my pocket, feeling its weight in my hand. Only a few drops were inside, but it was his blood. It was bled from battle. I'd taken it, earned it.

Twirling it in my hand, I held it in front of my face between my thumb and pointer, showing the room the contents.

My gaze jumped to Not-Isaac who was curiously watching me. I smiled at him and said, "See this?"

"I'm not blind."

I looked to my mom and back at him. "You might be."

"You want his blood?" I said to Not-Isaac and gestured toward my father.

He smiled wickedly, showing his answer.

I flicked my gaze to Nicolai, betrayal and amusement on his face.

"Remember how you told me I couldn't get your blood?"

"I cleaned your blade," Nicolai said, his facade cracking, showing his concern as he searched my face.

"I scraped my skin to collect this."

The color drained from his face. Nicolai licked his lips and looked at the vial, and a smile tugged on his lips. "That's not enough blood."

"What about this?" I said and took off the flannel I wore. I lifted the heavily bloodstained shirt and shook the vial, recognition dawning on his face.

"I took that," he said, trying to make sense of what happened.

"You took a flannel."

Mom snorted. "Her fucking fashion sense finally paid off, wearing the same shitty clothes every day."

I lifted the shirt and vial toward Isaiah. The keys to shift the power in his favor. Give him an edge over the other two. "This much of his blood. Dried from injury and collected. All his blood. As I've been told, all blood works, dry or wet, it's still blood."

"We can rule the Soulless together." He smiled.

"Yuck, no," I said, shaking the image. "It's yours if you release them." I gestured toward Oliver, Duke, and Alan.

"Done," Not-Isaac said, and the binds disintegrated.

"You little bitch," Nicolai roared as Duke and Alan stirred.

I smiled at Nicolai and flinched my eyes in the "listen, idiot" gesture.

His gaze narrowed, realizing the message I was sending.

"You'll get what's yours," I said with a wink.

His eyes flickered to Not-Isaac, intent on the promised delivery. Smokey tendrils twirled around his fingers, snaking out for the bloodied gifts.

Before his magic could reach me, I tossed the flannel, the material catching and dragging in the air as it arched toward him.

Not-Isaac's eyes flickered to the flannel, his attention split between us and the blood.

I used his distraction, his breaking of Rule Five, to my advantage. I chucked my blade at him.

The heavy metal beat the flannel to him, slicing his arm. His blood, though only momentarily dripping, covered the dagger's blade as it landed with a thud on the ground.

Nicolai had prepared for my double crossing and lunged for the blade, and for the blood I promised and delivered. The offering to too much to pass up on.

"I owe you nothing else," I said to his back.

Nicolai and Not-Isaac's rage was lost with each other as they clawed at the few drops of blood given. A dark mist spiraled from the ground, twisting around them. The air crackled with heat and I stepped back.

The shadows hovering at the door howled out.

Nicolai snarled at them, reaching for them, to absorb them and steal their power, but they slithered away from him and toward me.

Nicolai's face contorted in rage, and his murderous eyes turned to me, his humanness fading away into the darkened mass of muscle and leathery skin.

His attention focused solely on me as he wiped Not-Isaac's blade into his hand. His body pulsed with a red aurora and forms clawed through it.

As he neared me, the shadows dove for me, blocking me. It wouldn't last long, but it didn't need to. Not-Isaac, despite his powers waning, drew from the flannel and shattered vial, and flung himself at Nicolai.

The shadows descended from all the corners of the room, under the door, and materialized around the rest of us, blocking us from the blowback of the death match, surprising us all. They'd risked my father consuming them to protect us.

My mom, true to form, observed the change in the game and adjusted instantaneously.

"My baby," she babbled, a sob wrenching through her. "You saved us from their control. I'm so proud of you."

She ran to me, her arms outstretched, so I'd embrace her. Save her.

"Fuck you," I spat and drew my second blade. I had one more target to deal with.

She stopped mid-run, her expression returning to her normal snarl.

"Fine, you want it that way," she said. She didn't draw a weapon on me. Instead, she twirled the vial in her hand, the one with Tones' blood.

My face didn't obey, and my eyes darted to the vial as I let out a low, desperate note.

"I will trade," my mother said, edging away from her destroyed lovers. Her hand was outstretched, but her fingers guarded the vial. "Tones' life for mine. Let me go, and you can bring her back."

I would have taken the trade, brought Tones back, and offered my mother escape. In all my desire to get revenge, Tones was worth so much more than trumping my mom.

I would have, but Tones wouldn't. She shot forward from the shadows, engulfing my mother and her shrieks. The vial crashed to the floor, leaking onto the ground.

Tones dove for her blood as my mom tripped back. Her blood floated in a swirl around her as she absorbed it. Tones' form was the most solid I'd seen.

She wasn't fully Tones, more a transparent version of herself, separate from the shadows. Her dark curly hair hung around her as her eyes sparkled in her skin.

"I love you kids," Tones called as her body radiated and pulsed. The empty vial clanked around the ground.

Mom lunged forward. Her shirt crept up, her tattoo visible. The ink swirled and flickered, the red lines like glowing veins.

A scream echoed in the chamber. Mom held Tones' form in a suspended state. Her fingers gnarled together.

"You fucking bitch, I said leave my kid alone." As Mom's body heaved, her eyes shuttered white and her flesh grayed. Red veins laced her body, growing and pulsing as she tightened her hands. Tones gasped against the magic, her form starting to dissolve.

"Leave her alone!" I roared and rushed at my mom. Before I could drive my blade into her side, she whirled around. Red magic slashed from her, searing my flesh.

Burning fire raced through my veins. My step stumbled. A ragged breath heaved my chest.

"You dumb bitch," she seethed. Her attention now focused on me. "You aren't strong enough to defeat me."

Years flashed through my mind. Her lies echoing in my brain. She'd used me for so long. No more. They had borne me to be a weapon. And a weapon I would be.

As if they could read my mind, the shadows lunged toward her in unison with me. Instead of the easy gut shot, I drove my knife through her neck. Blood splattered on my hands. She reached for me, her fingers going for purchase, but the shadows held her at bay for a few moments. With strength I didn't know I had, I drove my blade cleanly through her.

Everything stood still. Her blue eyes shifted to me. Hateful pride shone back as she registered what was happening. Then they went cold and rolled back. She slid from me, gravity finishing my work as her body hit the floor.

I fell to my knees. A sob lodged in my throat.

She was dead.

My mom was dead.

And I killed her.

The room chilled as the magic fizzled out. Around me the shadows swam in the air, more than I'd seen before in any place.

Instead of hisses, their frenzy babbled in excited tones.

Nicolai and Not-Isaac had vaporized into an ashy mess that bubbled and contorted as the shadows consumed it.

In the wake of my mom and Tones' showdown, only the shattered glass vial remained.

"Dessa?" I heard Oliver whisper.

My heart ached. I'd taken his mom, again. This time though, I was here for him to show me hatred. Despise me, as I deserved. I wouldn't hide again. I'd face the repercussions.

He stood and wobbled forward in my direction, in slow steps to find me in the dark.

I stood and looked to Oliver, to apologize and offer any help I could, but when he reached me, he just embraced me, smothering my head against his chest.

"I'm so sorry," I mumbled against his torso and wrapped my arms around him.

"No," he said, placing lingering kisses on my head and temple. "You aren't your mom. You didn't do this."

I pulled away, still with my arms around his body. Despite the lack of light, I could see the tears smeared on his face.

"I was so worried about you," he said, pulling me back.

"Same here."

"You didn't listen," he chuckled, the ripple vibrating through him.

"Did you think I would?"

"No, but I hoped. She was going to kill you."

"Yeah, I wasn't useful anymore."

"Are they gone-gone?" he asked.

"I think so."

A light blinked on, flooding the room in a neon glow, the aftermath even more disturbing in the light. The room was covered in goo, and the shadows frantically teemed around it. Blood and ash covered the floor.

Alan stood by the light switch, his face swollen and grimy from his ordeal, but he smiled at me.

Duke, though weak, stood and joined Alan, wrapping his arm around him and pulling him into a hug. Alan reciprocated.

Oliver and I separated our embrace, but he never released his hold on me. He turned so his arm draped over my shoulder.

"You two don't listen," I said pointing at them.

Duke waved me off.

"What did he do to you?" I asked.

"He drugged us in the car. I didn't come to until the bartender was dragging us."

"What did he want with us?" Alan asked.

"Collateral so I would still get him the blood."

"So Dessa ran into multiple situations, knowing they were traps," Alan said, his head tilted down as he smirked at me. "Yet somehow turned them around. We ran into one, knowing Nicolai was trying to delay us, and almost got killed."

"We should agree, no more running into known traps," Duke said. "I want to live to see our children grow up."

"You don't have children," I said.

"Not yet, so I need to live extra long."

"I agree," Oliver said. "I'd like to live to see our children grow up."

He stiffened, realizing what he said, and heat raced up my face.

Alan and Duke burst out laughing.

"Hey, our kids could date," Duke said and gestured between Alan and him and Oliver and me.

"Sure," I drawled.

Oliver pressed me close and rubbed his hand in massaging circles on my upper arm.

"You should really continue working on them," Duke said and winked.

"We know how we'll be celebrating tonight," Alan said, and then nodded at us. "I'm sure you'll do your version of it too."

Duke choked a laugh and held Alan closer.

Oliver laughed and nudged me with his shoulder. Leaning over, he asked, "Whatdaya say, we celebrating tonight?"

I rolled my eyes, smiling like a fool looking forward to the evening. I'd gotten a chance at a future. I planned to live it and not just survive it.

"Well," Duke asked, running a hand through his hair and surveying the room. "What now? What do we do about all of this?"

"I'd guess a new master will come forth," I said, realizing a new head would grow. "There's an entire network built by these fools to hunt our kind and take power."

"They'll see you as a threat, as you took down three," Oliver said.

"I didn't," I said, shaking my head. "Nicolai and Not-Isaac took each other down."

"Sure, because that's how I'm going to tell it," Duke monotoned. "Sheesh, take credit."

"We agree," the shadows hissed, again talking to me.

The other four turned and stared at them.

"See, even the creepies agree." Duke nodded toward the swarming masses.

"You can hear them now?" I asked Oliver.

He nodded, his eyes growing large.

"There's a ton of magic in the room." Alan frowned as his eyes flashed orange.

"We'll have Soulless running amok to gain the fallen places and upend the system," Oliver said.

"I guess there's more work to do," I muttered.

"Yes, our Queen," the shadows hissed. "And we're here to help."

"Me too," Tones said, her faint outline flickering in the shadows.

ACKNOWLEDGMENTS

As my debut, my acknowledgements here are going to be long. There are many people who helped me along the way, if they know it or not. Since I don't know a better way, I'm going to start from length of knowing a person...

Mom – you are the foundation of my creativity. You've supported every hobby I've had, even standing by booths at conventions so I wouldn't miss one. You never let me settle for less and always pushed for more. You are the voice inside my head, even when I cover my ears.

Beth – we spent our childhood building worlds and stories. Reading your books in high school brought back my love of reading. WSB was written before you unexpectantly passed away, but you didn't get a chance to read it. Your influence will forever inspire me. I miss you so much, sis.

Adam – you never read so I can say many nice things and you'll never know! We've been together decades. You call me stubborn and that when I decide on something, I'm all in no matter how wild. Thank you for your support over the many years. You selflessly played video games for hundreds of hours so I could write.

Bethany – you slid into my DMs and one day asked if I'd do this thing called "fast drafting" with you. You've been a friend, teacher, and a swift kick in the ass. You're the June to my May Gemini. I love you. Remember, a spreadsheet will fix just about everything.

Madelyn – who I met because of Bethany – you've read almost everything I've written. You're also why this book is finally in physical form and no longer just in my computer. You've championed Dessa and my other works. You yelled and bullied me when I wanted to give up. You brought the freaking receipts. You've been a support through every step, even when we argued. To anyone looking for writing help, she now offers her services to other, check her out at MadHope Editorial.

Shannon – who I met because of Madelyn – omg I would not have survived this without you. You've been a constant support. Your enthusiasm for WSB helped me through one of the toughest revisions. Thank you for everything! Also, YES, I READ THE LAST PAGES FIRST. And to anyone reading the acknowledgements, go buy Shannon R. Lir's amazing books in her Soulland Series. Just make sure to have number two ready to go after number one. She destroyed me with the finale.

Megan – who I also met because of Bethany – you've been a rock for me these past months. Thanks for your love and encouragement.

Staircase Scream Queens – assembled by the fabulous CARO who I met because of Bethany – you're the best group ever! Thank you for the support. Thank you for not putting up with my crap. And thank you for looking at countless covers.

My BETA readers – Lili and Emilie – thank you for your feedback and encouragement. Lili – I hope you like the ending.

My editors – Carly and Jessica (Book Light Editorial), and Tory (Tory Hunter Books), thank you for your enthusiasm for WSB and help to make it even better.

And lastly, my four-legged kiddos who have supported my writing for decades. You made sure I sat and wrote all the time, laying on me so I could not move, but also, knowing when I needed a break, insisted you need to go potty, go for a walk, needed a treat, or simply annoyed me to get me up and see what was in your mouth to break a bad session. You all have been my heroes. I wouldn't be here without you.

Amelia J. Rivers is a bitter cinnamon roll who lives in the Midwest with her husband, a legion of demonic cats, and a pampered dog who she suspects is a reincarnation of a medieval princess. She is an emerging author of paranormal fantasies. This is Amelia's first book.

https://www.ameliarivers.com/
    https://linktr.ee/ameliarivers